Sue Gedge is a retired drama teacher with a passion for the gothic. She enjoys writing in a secluded corner of the basement of the London Library where the dim light and spooky noises from the overhead pipes have proved inspirational. Her short stories have appeared in various publications, including *Loves Me, Loves Me Not, The Mechanics' Institute Review, His Red Eyes Again, Supernatural Tales* and *All Hallows*. Her first novel, *The Practical Woman's Guide to Living with the Undead*, published in July 2022, is available on Amazon.

Mandragora By Moonlight

The Apprenticeship of a Novice Witch

Sue Gedge

Grosvenor House
Publishing Limited

This book is published by
Grosvenor House Publishing Ltd
Link House
140 The Broadway, Tolworth, Surrey, KT6 7HT.
www.grosvenorhousepublishing.co.uk

A CIP record for this book
is available from the British Library

ISBN 978-1-80381-266-3

Hemlock in the morning,
Aconite in the afternoon,
Mandragora by moonlight,
A potion for a lover and a fool.

From the Spell Book of Maudie Herrick,
hedge-witch. (1895-1971)

Part One

The Witch Stone

Prologue

March 1967

"Face the Witch Stone, Jeanie."

My father's voice cut through the roar of the wind as it blew over the scrubby ground, whipping thistles against the back of my bare legs. I stood there, shivering in my thin gingham frock, utterly bewildered. I had no idea why I'd been brought to this place. The journey had taken us over three hours, the wheels of the Morris Traveller juddering over muddy pot-holes for the final queasy, lurching, twenty minutes, and my father had been silent for the entire time. We'd left without breakfast and now my stomach was achingly empty, but I knew better than to complain. As the daughter of Angus Gowdie, I was accustomed to having my bodily needs ignored and on this day, my thirteenth birthday, as I was soon to learn, he was far more concerned with my soul.

"*Do as I say*." He uttered the instruction like a curse.

I gazed at the stone in front of me, seven feet of ancient, jagged granite crusted with yellow lichen. Then, without thinking, I stretched out my fingers towards it.

"Do not touch the heathen thing!"

I flinched as he jerked my hand away. A bird shrieked above my head. The blood sang in my ears. I looked down at the ground, anxious to avoid my father's gaze and saw a beetle scuttling towards my foot, its blue-black carapace a jewel-flash against the wet moss. Was this a sign? I was a firm believer in omens.

"Do you know why this is called the Witch Stone?" My father lowered his voice but I could sense his barely-contained rage. "I daresay not. Then allow me to inform you. They call this the Witch Stone because this is where they gathered centuries ago, the ungodly, sinning women. Here they communed with evil spirits and practised their unholy rites. But this, too, is where they were righteously punished, cleansed in the purifying flames. And now you must stand before the stone and pray. Pray to be spared the fires of hell. Pray that you will never sin as your mother did."

I didn't understand. What sins had my mother committed? I had no memory of her. She'd disappeared when I was two.

"*Put your hands together and pray!*"

It seemed I had no choice other than to submit. I clasped my hands and closed my eyes, blanking out the moor and the woodlouse-grey sky. And then I remembered Nana Herrick's words. '*Your father's beliefs have as much worth as a blast of gas from a cow's backside.*'

I was so flooded with relief that I almost laughed out loud. My father could do nothing here. Nana would always protect me. Nana believed in me.

I counted to a hundred before opening my eyes. My father stared at me, apparently searching my face for signs of dissent. The silence seemed interminable. At last, he spoke.

"Now we can go."

He sounded satisfied. It seemed he didn't know how deeply I'd defied him in my heart. He couldn't know that instead of praying, I'd made a very different vow. And he would never know that, quite unwittingly, he'd made me all the more determined to fulfil my destiny.

One

December 1971

"Take my hand, Jeanie," said Nana Herrick. "Help me down on to the beach."

She stood at the top of the breakwater, a slight, white-haired figure in a green anorak and black ski-trousers. As she reached out to me, I was filled with dismay. How had her once-deft fingers, so clever at patching my clothes and making little rag dolls, become these sea-bird talons, the joints swollen, the nails thickened, the skin so stretched and shiny? It seemed so wrong that she should need my help at all. Barely a year ago, she would have jumped down without difficulty and leapt across the huddled rocks with nimble abandon. Now her body had betrayed her, a stumble here, a plate slipping from her grasp there, signs of ageing that had taken us both by surprise.

"Thank you Jeanie." She stepped on to the shingle. "I'm not afraid of falling, but I don't want to fall just yet. Let's go over there." She pointed to the smooth, wet sand by the shore-line. "We'll sit for a while."

Here in Newbiggin-by-the-Sea the waves had destroyed the old graveyard, mingling the powder of human bones with the chalk of the cliffs. Above the promontory, the spire of St Bartholomew's Church nailed the sky to the land; below, the beach glimmered in the anaemic winter sun. This was our special place where we gathered seaweed and driftwood, and where Nana told me stories about the seal-people, how sometimes they swam this far south to gather chosen souls and take them back with them to the summer-lands. But today, she didn't seem to be in the mood for folk tales. She sat in silence for a long time, her hands folded in her lap, her face tilted up towards the sky.

"In a few more months, you'll be eighteen," she said at last. "Have you thought of leaving?"

"Leave my father, you mean?" My spirits rose at the prospect of escape. I hated living at the Knox Hill Guest House, an establishment my father ran as though it was a place of penance. "I've thought of nothing else. I want to live here, with you. That will be all right, won't it, Nana?" I turned towards her, anxious for her agreement.

"I'm afraid not. I'm sorry to have to tell you," she spoke softly, "But I'm soon to die."

"But you *can't* ..." I swallowed, the words of protest sticking in my throat. I could hardly believe it. How could she be so calm about this terrible thing? And how was I going to exist without Nana, the only person who really cared for me?

"There's a doctor wants me to go to the hospital." She squeezed my hand. "But I'll not go there. I won't spend my last days languishing in that place, where I'll be prodded and examined, and given pointless treatment and with no good outcome at the end."

"Oh, *Nana*." For her sake, I tried to keep back my tears.

"Hush! Don't fret about me. But this has come sooner than I might have hoped." She sighed. "I had so much more to teach you in the ways of magic, although I'm only a simple hedge-witch, Jeanie. I know cures and charms but little of deeper sorcery. You have the capacity to journey so much further than I have ever done. So here is what you must do. As soon as you finish your schooling, you must go to London."

"To London?" This was a daunting suggestion.

"Yes. You will meet others of our kind there, practitioners of magic, adepts and witches, sorcerers and shape-shifters. They will teach you to hone your skills."

"But how will I find these people, Nana?"

"Oh, fate will lead you to them although they may not reveal themselves to you easily. There will be hints and signs and you must be careful not to trust them all without question. There are some who use their skills to gain power over others, adepts known as spell-charmers who seduce women with the old trick known as Glamour. Never give your heart to a spell-charmer or you will be lost for ever."

"I don't ever intend to give my heart to anyone."

"But one day you might. I've looked into my scrying-vessel and seen your future as a great sorceress, standing with a powerful magus by your side, the two of you crowned with lights. You were born to the Craft, Jeanie, always remember that." She traced a strange hieroglyph in the wet sand with the tip of her index finger. "And now I must tell you where to find your apprentice tools and give you the gift of your true name."

"What does that mean, my true name?"

"Your true name is the one you will adopt at your Coming of Age ceremony when you are twenty one, the age of majority for our kind. You must not repeat it to a living soul until then. Come closer, so that I can whisper it. Even those birds in the sky could be spies."

*

A week after that day on the beach, Nana filled her pockets with stones and walked down the shore and into the waves. A man who was walking his Airedale terrier along the promenade saw her go under and raised the alarm, but by the time help arrived, she was gone. According to the note she left under the china frog on her mantelpiece, she knew her time had come, and so she had gone to join the seal people who would help her pass into the summer-lands without pain.

Mrs Wallace, our cleaner at Knox Hill, said Nana Herrick had always been round the twist and my father snorted in agreement. I knew they were mistaken. Nana had known about the tides and the phases of the moon and she grew herbs and sang to the plants in her garden to help them grow, and if she said the seal-people had taken her, then so they had.

I went back to her cottage alone and let myself in with the key that was kept under the loose stone on the pathway. I knew this was my last visit. In a few days, the place would be reclaimed by the landlord, Mr Braithwaite of Braithwaite's Bakeries for whom Nana had worked all her adult life.

The house seemed so still and silent without her. Her red felt slippers were still on the mat by her bed, and there were dried hops and sprigs of lavender lying on her pillow. I opened the old oak wardrobe, brought a chair and reached up to the top shelf. Here it was, just where she'd told me I'd find it, a hexagonal tin that had once held sweets and toffees. It was very old; there was a dent in the side and the picture on the lid of a woman in a Regency bonnet with purple ribbons was faded and chipped. I prised open the lid and gazed down at the contents. To an inhabitant of the ordinary world these objects would have looked like nothing at all, just an old butter knife with a cracked bone-handle, a rounded white stone, a candle stub, and a metal dish, the kind you might use for baking a small pie. But these were my apprentice tools, and I noticed the scratches on the blade of the knife, and I knew they were runes and that soon I would learn to read them.

I left the house, locked the door and dropped the key down the drain. All the signs were propitious. There was a stormy petrel flying across the beach and a white rose blooming on the bush by the gate, even though it was late December. Hope filled my heart and I had no premonition whatsoever of the disaster that was about to descend upon me, blighting the next two years of my life.

Two

October 1974

The London square was dense with drizzle and the pavements were plastered with liquefying brown leaves, a slip-hazard for the unwary, but I felt sure-footed and confident. I was twenty, soon to come of age, and autumn, with Hallowe'en fast approaching, was my favourite season of the year. And now, despite having taken several wrong turnings, I'd reached my destination at last. The brass plaque on the wall confirmed it: *The Antioch Corey Memorial Library. Established 1905.*

It seemed strange that I'd never seen this building before. I'd been living in London for several months now and I usually spent my solitary weekends exploring the city, wandering down side streets, discovering old churches and quiet courtyards and yet this imposing edifice, built from stone that must have been blackening for decades, had eluded me. And what an architectural extravagance it was, such amazing pillars, carved in the style of a Native American totem pole; grotesque birds, reptiles and sea-monsters all piled on top of each other in a profusion of teeth, claws and snarls. I stared at the bas-relief above the entrance; it depicted a blindfolded, naked man kneeling before a masked figure holding a raised sword. Was it an execution or an initiation ceremony of some kind? I couldn't tell, but I was certain of one thing. The Antioch Corey Memorial Library was no ordinary place.

I'd chosen my outfit for this interview with care, hoping to give an impression of maturity and efficiency. Black court shoes, tan tights, a straight knee-length grey skirt, a high-necked white blouse, all neat and proper under my belted mac. I'd tied my unruly fudge-coloured hair back from my face with a black velvet ribbon, and put on just a hint of lipstick. I was desperate to get this job. I couldn't bear the thought of another day in the insurance office where I checked forms in a grey-walled booth with the fluorescent lighting hurting my eyes and Derek Finsworthy always finding an excuse to lean over me, his breath heavy with Fisherman's Friends and his chin a triumph of razor rash.

I glanced at my watch. Six twenty three. I'd arrived with only a few minutes to spare. Making an effort to steady my nerves, I walked up the steps and went in through the the revolving doors. *Oh*! I uttered an involuntary gasp of astonishment.

The grim exterior of the building hadn't prepared me for such palatial beauty. I'd found myself in a circular entrance hall ringed with marble pillars; at the far end, a wide, curved stone staircase swept up to three tiers of book-lined galleries. There was a shimmering blue glass dome set high in the ceiling; it was partially open, giving a glimpse of the night sky. The air was suffused with incense; the lighting was dim and mysterious. I felt a sense of awe as I gazed at my surroundings. It was as though I'd entered a temple dedicated to some arcane, ancient deity.

An ebony plinth stood in the centre of the tiled floor, half-lit by a flame encased within an ornate gold brazier. At first, I mistook the object displayed on the plinth for a sculpture of a head but then, as I stepped forward to examine it, I saw, with a shudder of recognition, that it was a death mask. I bent down to read the inscription on the brass plaque at the foot of the plinth:

Antioch Corey 1799-1901. The flame of his scholarship burns for eternity.

I looked up again at the death mask. The sight gave me an uneasy feeling. I'd heard it said that the faces of the deceased display a calm absence, suggesting that the soul has moved on to a higher dimension, but this rigid grey mould with its shuttered eyes and grimly set mouth conveyed the opposite impression, that of a spirit trapped in anguished, earth-bound permanence. I was half-afraid that at any moment the stiff eyelids would open, the lips would move and a sepulchral voice would speak.

"I see you have met our founder."

To my embarrassment, I realised I'd jumped visibly.

"Gee, I hope I didn't startle you." There was no hint of apology in that deceptively soft American voice.

"No, not at all." I tried to sound casual as I turned to face the person who'd approached me so silently from behind; a woman dressed in denim jeans, a checked shirt and sneakers. Her long, auburn hair was held back in an Alice band and her skin looked as if it had been regularly scrubbed with carbolic. The backwoods, pioneer look, with just a hint of puritanism. I knew, instinctively, that here was a person who would never be my friend.

"Clemency Nantucket." She spoke her name as if summoning herself to take pride of place at a school prize-giving. "I am the Senior Archivist."

"I'm Jeanie Gowdie." I held out my hand, but she ignored my gesture. I couldn't decide whether she simply hadn't noticed or whether, in some obscure way that I didn't understand, she considered I'd committed a social gaffe.

"Is Antioch Corey buried here, under this plinth?" I uttered the first thought that came into my mind, in an attempt to cover my awkwardness. I regretted it immediately, seeing Clemency Nantucket's scornful expression.

"Of course not!" she snapped. "This is a private library, not a mausoleum. It would hardly be hygienic to place a body under the floor."

"I was thinking of ashes, or..."

"Or what?"

"Nothing." I glanced away, focusing on the empty benches at the foot of the stairs where I might have expected to see other people waiting to be interviewed.

"Are there many other candidates?" I asked.

"Candidates?" She frowned at me.

"I thought perhaps..."

"You are the only person with an appointment tonight."

My flagging spirits soared. *The only person with an appointment.* That must mean I had a very good chance of getting this job.

"Come this way." There was a degree of impatience in her tone. "The Custodian is expecting you."

I followed her towards the stairs, uncomfortably aware of the clatter of my heels on the tiled floor in contrast to her silent, sneaker-clad tread.

"I often think visitors should be issued with felt over-shoes." Clemency glanced at me over her shoulder. "These floors need preserving."

Another reproof, and yet I saw her point. If I did come to work here, I'd buy a pair of black canvas slippers to wear indoors, the Chinese ones with the single strap that I'd seen in the market. But I mustn't get ahead of myself; that would be unlucky.

"*The Obeah man, he come, he come and take you away...*"

The crooning voice floated down from the first floor gallery. Looking up, I saw a dark-skinned woman in a vividly-coloured kaftan. She was mopping the floor as if in a trance, spooling slicks of soapy water out of her tin bucket, apparently oblivious of the flood she was creating, too absorbed in her reverie of singing to notice.

"He come, he come and take you away....You see him soon....the Obeah man."

"Good evening, Psyche," Clemency paused at the top of the stairs. "This is a visitor, Miss Jeanie Gowdie."

The woman turned towards me, hooking the pole of her mop into the crook of her arm.

Her figure was short and tub-like and her features were sharp, more Asian than African, although her accent had seemed Caribbean. I caught the pungent scent of patchouli. She stared at my face, scanning my features as if memorising them for future reference. Her eyes had a milky, half-blind appearance.

"You come then," she said. "You come at last. Two years late, but you come." Then she spat into the palm of her right hand and held it up.

I didn't know how to respond. Was I expected to spit on my hand too? I glanced at Clemency; her expression was passive and unhelpful.

"I don't want to interrupt your work, Psyche," she said. "But you must have the other floors to do. Shouldn't you be moving on now?"

A flash of irritation crossed Psyche's face, but then she reverted to her former dreamy expression and, with a nod, picked up her bucket and walked away, trailing her mop behind her. Her singing, accompanied by the slip-slop of her backless sandals, became fainter as she retreated. "*The Obeah man, he come, he come and take you away...*"

"I suggest you pay no attention to her gibberish," Clemency remarked in a low voice. "Psyche has been here for many years and she has her ways. Follow me." She led me along the gallery in the opposite direction to the route Psyche had taken.

"Here we are, then." She stopped at an oak-panelled door. The word *Custodian* was inscribed on it in gold. "This is Mr Llewellyn's room. He's waiting for you. Go in." She opened the door and propelled me into a gloom so intense that I could barely see the figure behind the desk.

"Good evening, Miss Gowdie." The man's voice was teasingly ambiguous, somehow menacing and seductive in equal measure. "Do you believe in fate?"

The door slammed behind me. Clemency had gone and I was alone in the dark with this enigmatic stranger.

Three

"Well, Miss Gowdie? Do you have an answer to my question?"

My mind was racing. *Fate. Destiny. Providence.* These were things Nana had talked about on many long winter evenings. Of course I believed in fate. But his question was too soon, too sudden, and replying might lead me into dangerous, uncharted territory with a man whose face I couldn't see and who I had no idea whether to trust.

"Forgive me," Mr Llewellyn continued. "I should have asked you to take a seat. And perhaps you'd like to take off your coat. Is there anything you'd like to ask me before I begin?"

"Yes." I fumbled with the buttons of my mac. "Can you please turn on the light?"

"The light?" He repeated the word as if I had mentioned something exotic and strange.

"Yes. I can't see a thing." I felt, unsuccessfully, for the chair that I assumed must be in front of his desk.

"So it seems." He sounded puzzled. "And yet I can see *you* quite clearly."

"Is that a joke?" I was afraid I might have sounded abrupt, even rude, but I was considerably unnerved by this situation.

"No. I'm not very good at jokes. I've been told it's one of my many failings. There." I heard the sound of a match being struck and a moment later, there was a yellow glow in the room coming from the oil lamp on his desk. "Can you see me now?"

My stomach flipped over. I could indeed see him, and his appearance had startled me. He was younger than I'd expected, no more than thirty five at the most, and he was devastatingly handsome. Handsome, that was, in an old-fashioned way, rather like one of the Edwardian matinee idols that I'd seen in Nana's collection of sepia postcards. She kept them in the top drawer of her dressing table, souvenirs from her girlhood, and I'd often admired those elegant men with their chiselled features, penetrating eyes, and luxuriant dark hair. And now Mr Llewellyn was staring at me with such intensity that I had to look down for a moment to cover my excitement.

"Let's try some other questions," he said. "Yes, do sit down, and take off your coat. Now, tell me, how did you come to apply for this job?"

"I saw the advert in the paper." I remembered what I'd been told about interviews; *sit straight, knees together, don't cross your legs.*

"Which newspaper was it?"

"I...that is...I..."

This was awful. I knew I couldn't be making a good impression, but I didn't know how to explain without sounding unprofessional. The truth was I'd been sitting in a steamy little café, Mustafa's Kwik Bites, where I often had breakfast, when I'd found a ragged piece of newspaper sticking to the bottom of my saucer. It was damp with spilled coffee and only partly decipherable but it had felt like a message intended just for me. The fragment was in my handbag at that moment, but I'd read it and re-read it so often that I knew the wording off by heart:

A vacancy for the post of... (The next word was obliterated) *has arisen at the Antioch Corey Memorial Library. The Library houses a unique and esoteric collection of literature and artefacts relating to North American folklore, philology, belle-lettres and literature. This is a specialist job and is only suitable for a person who is prepared to...* (There was a hole in the paper here) *It is not a requirement for the applicant to be a qualified librarian but he or she must have a passion for books and erudition. Apply by letter, in handwriting, to the Custodian. Closing date, Sept. 29th...* (another tear in the paper here, followed by the address.)

"And why, I wonder," Mr Llewellyn laid his hands palms down on his desk, "do you, such a young person, want to work in an antiquated place such as this? There's very little of the modern world here. No telephones and as you can see, parts of the building don't even have electric light."

"That doesn't worry me." I noticed the heavy gold ring he wore on the little finger of his right hand. I could see the insignia clearly; the plumed head of a dragon with a deep-red jewel for an eye. "I don't like the modern world very much. I prefer the past. I haven't even got a television."

"Then we have much in common." Once again, he looked at me with such a penetrating expression that I felt my insides twisting up. I was too overwhelmed to return his gaze. Instead, I focused on the tall, glass-fronted cabinet behind him. The shelves were crowded with dusty pieces of taxidermy, pottery, wooden carvings, and other curious objects. I caught a glimpse of something pallid and bulbous floating in a jar, and a huge claw that seemed far too large to be from any known, living bird.

"So, your letter." He took it out of his desk drawer. "You write fluently, six whole pages and you've expressed so much enthusiasm for books. And you've certainly been imaginative with your choice of ink."

My cheeks warmed with pleasure at the compliment and then my spirits sank as it occurred to me that he was being ironic.

"Oh." I bit my lip. "I shouldn't have done it, should I? Used that green ink and underlined my main points in purple?"

"Perhaps it's a style that wouldn't have gone down well if you'd been applying to join the Civil Service." There was no hint of reproof in his tone. "But this is the Antioch Corey Library. The rules of the ordinary world don't apply here. But something does puzzle me."

"Oh?"

"Yes. You say you left school when you were eighteen, and I can see you had excellent 'A' level results. And you've been working in an insurance office for the past two months. But there's nothing about what you did in between. There's a mysterious two year gap in your account of your career, Miss Gowdie."

My mouth felt dry and my stomach was churning. How stupid of me to think that he wouldn't notice, that he wouldn't ask. All I wanted was to wipe away my past, pretend it had been nothing but a bad dream. But it hadn't been a dream; it was my shame. They knew at the insurance office, of course. Derek Finsworthy never tired of reminding me: *'A girl with your background can't be too choosy, you know.'*

"I..."

"Perhaps you were abroad?"

For a wild moment, I thought that, in all honesty, I could say I'd been abroad. Crowsmuir Hall with its grey-green institutional walls, the clatter of breakfast trolleys in the morning and the sound of endless games of ping-pong being played at night, while others screamed in solitary confinement, had felt foreign enough. I'd been like a traveller who'd taken the wrong train and had their passport impounded. But Crowsmuir Hall hadn't been abroad and I'd crossed fire, not water to get there. I opened my mouth to speak, but felt as though I'd been struck dumb.

"You weren't incarcerated in the Bastille, were you?" Mr Llewellyn asked. "Or perhaps you were marooned in Alcatraz?"

Alcatraz. A prison on a rock in the middle of freezing, rough water; bars and shackles and warders and no chance of escape. *Oh!*

"Or even locked up in the Chateau d'If?"

To my surprise, I saw he was smiling, only very faintly, just an amused twitch at the corners of his mouth, but smiling nonetheless. Oh! What a relief. He hadn't suspected the awful truth. He was teasing me. The Bastille had been stormed centuries ago, Alcatraz had only been for men, and as for the Chateau d'If... With that last reference, he'd thrown me a life-line, transporting me to a place of safety, to the books that had always been my comfort through the more troubled times of my life.

"Like the Count of Monte Cristo, you mean?" I said. "Of course, in Dumas's novel, Edmond Dantes escaped from the Chateau d'If and had his revenge on all those who'd wronged him."

"And what about you, Miss Gowdie? Did someone wrong you, and will you have your revenge?"

"I..."

"You needn't answer that. Just tell me something about those two years. Anything you think that might be a suitable qualification."

"I....I looked after a library."

"A library?"

"Yes." I was telling the truth, wasn't I? It might have been only one room, full of grubby paperbacks and old encyclopaedias, but it *had* been a library all the same.

"And what did you do in this library?"

"I read all the time. I improved my general knowledge."

"Then let me test that knowledge. Can you get with child a mandrake root? Do you think Paracelsus was a charlatan? Do you believe that sasquatch-hide can cure croup? What is your opinion of succubae and incubi? Have you read Ovid's *Metamorphoses*? Where can one buy catnip? Have you remembered all my questions and can you answer them in order?"

"I think so." I'd rather enjoyed the playful way he'd fired those questions at me, delivering them with the dazzling speed of fireworks in the night sky. "First, you quoted John Donne. '*Get with child a mandrake root*'. It's a reference to the Renaissance belief that the mandrake plant, otherwise known as mandragora, has roots that resemble the human form. Paracelsus was a medieval alchemist and physician; I don't think he was a charlatan. It's highly possible that sasquatch-hide would cure many complaints, if applied correctly under a full moon with the right incantations, but no-one has proved the existence of the sasquatch or, as it is more commonly called, the American Big-Foot."

"Indeed." Mr Llewellyn agreed. "Although Antioch Corey believed that he had. The section of hide he bought from an Iroquois medicine man is there." He pointed to the cabinet behind him. "Do go on."

"Incubi and succubae are demons. Lilith, the mythical first wife of Adam, has been described as a succubus. Typically, a succubus appears in a man's bedroom at night and..." I faltered, suddenly embarrassed.

"I'll spare you the need to describe the habits of the succubae." He held up his hand. "And what about Ovid's *Metamorphoses*?"

"I've read it, some of it in translation. It was the text I studied for my Latin 'A' level."

"And do you have a favourite passage?"

"Oh, yes. The story of Ceyx and Alcyone."

"The two lovers who escape death when the gods turn them into birds so that they can fly together." He nodded. "And do you think such things are possible?" He twisted his dragon ring round his finger. "Do you believe in spells and magic and the possibility of shape-shifting?

My suspicions had been growing and now I felt certain. Mr Llewellyn, with his dragon ring and his teasing, esoteric talk must be one of the people Nana told me I'd meet in London. *Fate will lead you to them*. He was an adept. He must be!

"Yes." I met his gaze as coolly and steadily as I could. "I do believe in those things. My grandmother taught me about them. She was a wise-woman."

I was disappointed by his response. His expression was completely blank, showing no sign that he'd understood, picking up on the hyphen, *wise-woman*, that made all the difference to my meaning. Instead, he was suddenly brisk and business-like, thrusting my letter into his desk drawer and closing it with a bang.

"Well," he announced. "I have no doubt that someone with your knowledge and enthusiasm would be a positive asset here."

"Thank you." My heart was thumping very fast.

"There's just one problem. When you sent in your application, you missed the closing date."

"I don't understand." I did my best to conceal my dismay. "Surely you received my letter by the twenty ninth of September?"

"I did. That is, I received it by the twenty ninth of September of this year. But the advertisement stipulated the twenty ninth of September, 1972. Two years ago, when the successful candidate, Mr Brunswicker, was appointed. I'm afraid there isn't a vacancy. I'm truly sorry, Miss Gowdie."

Four

I stared at him, too poleaxed with shock to speak for a moment. Then, as he gazed back at me with a maddeningly inscrutable expression, my dismay gave way to anger. Just what kind of trick was this? I remembered Nana's warning about spell-charmers, those practitioners of magic who lured women using an old trick known as Glamour. Was Mr Llewellyn a spell-charmer? Had he been trying to lure me with Glamour? Well, if that was the case, I was a match for him. I was Maudie Herrick's grand-daughter and I could look after myself!

"I see." I leapt to my feet, pushing my chair back sharply. "In that case, I'll leave."

"There's no need to do that." His tone suggested a hint of amusement.

"Why should I stay?" I spun round from the door to face him. "What other humiliations have you got in store for me? How could you do this? Invite me here, get me to talk about my life, about my feelings, raising my hopes and...." I knew my voice was getting louder, but I saw no reason to control my feelings. "If there isn't a job, why bother to interview me at all? It would have been better if you'd just thrown my letter in the bin!"

"After reading it, that was the last thing I wanted to do. And now my suspicions have been confirmed."

"Suspicions?" I didn't like the sound of this.

"Miss Gowdie, won't you sit down again and hear what I have to say?"

"No, I want to leave." I could feel my lower lip trembling.

"You sound as though you don't trust me." As he held up his hand, the red eye on his dragon ring glinted in the lamp-light. "I'm sorry about that. But you see, while it's true that there isn't a vacancy at the library, I believe I could still find a place for you here. And that's what I'm offering to do."

"Oh." My legs felt so weak I was forced to collapse back on to the chair. "Oh. Oh, I see. I'm sorry, I didn't understand. I thought...but when you said..."

"I apologise. I should have expressed myself more clearly. And perhaps you don't want to come and work here after all."

"I do. I want that very much."

"Good." He picked up a pen, turning it round in his fingers. "How soon can you leave your present job?"

"I'm not sure. I'll have to ask them. I think it might be a month's notice." I felt faintly dizzy at the speed with which this situation was progressing.

"Then let's hope they'll let you go without too much difficulty," Mr Llewellyn said. "But don't say anything to your employer just yet, or mention this to anyone here at the library. I have to speak to Mr Corey first."

"Mr Corey?" An alarming image of the death-mask in the entrance hall flashed into my mind.

"I'm referring to Jabez Corey, the senior Trustee." He pointed to a photograph on the wall of a white-haired man in an academic gown. "He's the great-nephew of Antioch Corey. It may take a while; he lives in a very quiet, rural area of New England and I'd prefer to talk to him in person. But I'm due to pay him a visit and...So, what do you say?"

"That will be wonderful but...wait!" A sick sensation hit the pit of my stomach. "There's something I've got to tell you. I haven't been honest with you...when you asked...I didn't explain about those two years."

"You don't have to do that now."

"But I do." I took a deep breath, and then began speaking rapidly as the confession spilled out of me. "I told you I was in charge of a library. But that library, it was just one room, full of tatty paperbacks and sets of old encyclopaedias and cheap editions of the classics. And there's something else, something far, far worse. This library, it was in an institution and I didn't choose to go there, I was sent there. I was ..."

I bit my lip.

"An inmate?" he suggested. His eyes were soft, gazing at me with such sympathy that all my fears seemed to dissipate.

"Yes." I nodded. "This place, it was for girls who were considered better out of the way, dangerous even. When I was eighteen, something very bad happened and they thought I'd done something awful, but I hadn't, it wasn't my fault, but no-one believed me. If my Nana had still been alive, she'd have known the truth, but there was no-one to speak for me and..." I broke off, gasping for air.

"I believe you, Jeanie."

I felt a lump gathering in my throat. One more kind look from him and I might burst into tears of relief. No-one had ever believed me when I tried to tell the truth. Instead, I'd been shut away from the world, excluded, treated as an offender. And now, at last, here was someone who wasn't going to treat me as a misfit, here was someone who was prepared to trust me.

"But you don't know what I was supposed to have done," I said.

"That's irrelevant, Jeanie. I know you're innocent because I've read your aura."

My aura? What did that mean? I wanted to ask, but somehow didn't dare.

"Just one more thing." He leaned back in his chair. "I'm curious to know how you came to make that mistake about the closing date."

"I didn't make a mistake," I assured him. "That part of the newspaper was missing."

"Missing?"

"Yes. It was just a fragment, sticking to my saucer."

"Sticking to your *saucer*?" His eyes widened.

"Yes. I was in a café. That's where I found the advert for the job. Well, part of it, anyway. Just a fragment, as I said, but with enough information for me to write my letter."

"So it *was* fate, then. You were summoned through the old magic of London."

"And when you say, 'magic'..." I faltered. "Do you mean...?"

"Oh, I think we understand each other, Jeanie." He gazed at me with a knowing expression. "Remember when I asked if you believed sasquatch-hide could cure croup and you said if it was genuine, it would cure many complaints if applied correctly under a full moon with the right incantations? You said that with conviction and you didn't seem surprised by the question. Your answer told me everything I needed to know about you."

And the fact that you asked such a question tells me everything I need to know about you.

I didn't have the courage to speak the thought out loud. Nevertheless, our eyes locked and we gazed at each other in what seemed to me to be mutual recognition, a moment freighted with significance.

"There's one other thing," he said. "I must ask you to be careful. Please don't tell anyone just yet that you might be coming here. I must speak to Mr Corey first. But I promise you, I'll do my utmost to keep you safe."

"Safe? But what possible danger could I be in?"

"None, I hope." He stood up, and held out his hand. "It's been a pleasure to meet you, Jeanie. I look forward to seeing you again."

It seemed to me that he clasped my hand for far longer than was strictly necessary and the way he was looking at me made me feel excited although a little apprehensive. I still wasn't entirely sure whether to trust him, but if he really was an adept, then he could help me arrange my Coming of Age Ceremony. And if he wasn't, then he was still the most beautiful man I'd ever met, the only beautiful man, in fact. His eyes were green, as green as the Emerald City of Oz, and here I was, about to step on to the yellow brick road of my future.

I stepped into the corridor, brimming with excitement, only to be stopped short as I was confronted by Clemency Nantucket. Had she been there all the time? I was dismayed to think that she might have been standing right outside the door, eavesdropping on my interview.

"Oh!" I exclaimed. "I wasn't expecting...that is..."

"I was instructed to give you a tour of the library," she interrupted. "I don't have time to show you everything; I have more urgent things to do. But I could take you to the reading room for a brief glance."

"Thank you." I tried to sound grateful, despite the veiled snub. "That's very kind."

"This way then." There was no graciousness at all in the way she said that.

Psyche had obviously been at work on this upper gallery; the floor was awash with rivulets of soapy water and ox-bow lakes of foam. I had to take care not to slip, clattering along in my heels behind Clemency as she walked briskly ahead. We passed high shelves lined with leather-bound volumes; there was an enticing scent of old paper and vellum.

"So many beautiful books," I remarked.

"There often are a lot of books in libraries." Clemency spoke in such a flat tone that I couldn't be sure if her apparent sarcasm was intentional. "Of course," she continued. "We don't keep any of the really valuable material on these open shelves. These are bound editions of Congress reports, legal papers, and other collections of official material, but an essential part of the Corey Collection, nonetheless. The rarest books are kept in the archive room."

"I'd love to see them."

"Out of the question. Only employees of the library and life members are allowed to...Stop!" She stretched out her left arm. "You'd better stand to one side."

I was aware of a flapping, frenzied confusion as a shape hurtled towards us; a person in a long mac wheeling a heavy, ancient bicycle.

"Coming through! Coming through!" The man's head was bent over the handlebars. He was tall and skeletal, with thinning, grey hair sticking up on either side of his balding head like a disintegrating lavatory brush. "Good-night, good-night, good-night." He glared at us through his thick-rimmed glasses, clutching the handlebars with fingers so elongated they appeared deformed. "I'm taking the stairs, can't use the lift, good-night." He fled past us, leaving a strong whiff of moth-balls behind him.

"Have a nice evening," Clemency called after him, an incongruous remark, I thought, as it was difficult to imagine that anguished apparition enjoying anything of the kind.

"Who was that?" I turned to her.

"That was Ernest Brunswicker."

"And is he…" I hesitated, hardly knowing how to phrase the question. "Is he *all right*?"

"Depends what you mean by 'all right'." She shrugged. "He'll survive as long as he has his bicycle. He'll wheel it all the way home to Southwark now."

"Wheel it? Why doesn't he ride it?"

"Who knows? I'm afraid Mr Brunswicker is a messed-up kind of guy. He can't go anywhere without that bike. He has to hold on to it most of the time. But never mind him, there's something I want to ask you. How *did* you get an appointment? I wasn't aware that anyone had died."

"Died?"

"When people join this library, they take out a Life Membership, and the list has been full for some time," Clemency explained. "Vacancies only arise if a member passes away, and the last time that happened was four years ago. And besides, I hope you don't mind my saying this, but you look very young to be a senior academic. Well, here we are at the reading room."

She opened a set of double doors and led me into a labyrinth of dark mahogany book cases and alcoves set with little tables and green-shaded lamps.

"How lovely," I looked around me, genuinely appreciative of the calm and seclusion.

I walked over to a section marked 'American Literature' and glanced at the shelves. I could see books by writers I knew, but the titles were completely unfamiliar, not to say strange: *My Secret Diary including an Account of*

My Mysterious Death by Edgar Allan Poe, *A Connecticut Yankee in the Stews of New Orleans* by Mark Twain, *Bartleby's Evil Twin* by Herman Melville. I took the Mark Twain off the shelf, flipped to the title page and read the words '*As told to Ethan Crowley Jnr, medium and necromancer, in the year 1915*'.

"How absolutely amazing," I exclaimed. "Didn't Mark Twain die in 1910? So, this Ethan Crowley contacted his spirit and..." Before I could say any more, Clemency snatched the book out of my hands.

"Scholars donate books to the library from all over the world." She thrust the book back on the shelf. "And I'm afraid that while some volumes are rare, there's also some blasphemous nonsense."

"Blasphemous?" I flinched; that had been one of my father's favourite words.

"Yes, blasphemous. Do you really think the Almighty would allow the dead to dictate works of fiction to the living?"

"It depends who you mean by the Almighty," I said. "I don't think there's a man in the sky with a long white beard. I think the pantheists were right to see something divine in all living things."

"I see." Her lips tightened.

"Anyway," I added hastily, "These books look fascinating."

"You reckon?" She breathed in deeply through her nose. "All I can say is, sometimes, people come here with very strange ideas. Encouraged by Mr Llewellyn, I might add. Between you and me, I don't think he's the kind of Custodian this place needs right now. But I guess he's been using his charms on you."

"His charms?" I repeated. "So you mean he really *is* a ..." I stopped abruptly, realising I had said too much.

"He's a what?" Her eyes narrowed. "What exactly are you implying?"

"Nothing. I…" Abashed, I looked down at my feet, at my over-noisy court shoes.

"It's quite clear you meant something," she persisted.

"No, I didn't mean anything." Anxious to change the subject, I moved towards the window. "There must be a wonderful view over London from up here," I said.

The moment I looked out, I realised my mistake. There was nothing to see from where I was standing, only an inner well of brown-grey brick splattered with bird droppings and a drainage grid surrounded by mildewed paving stones.

"But perhaps not from this particular window," I added.

"People come here to study," Clemency said. "A view would be distracting."

A pigeon landed on the sill, a very distinctive pigeon with far darker plumage than the usual London stock dove. I'd never seen one quite like it. It looked oddly sentient; there was something about its raffish appearance that suggested a somewhat disreputable man about town. Perhaps it was a cross-breed, with a large dollop of crow or jackdaw in its DNA. Whatever it was, it was definitely looking at me, cocking its head over to one side, as though sympathising with my discomfort.

"*Scram!*" I was startled by Clemency's coarse tone as she banged on the window. The bird didn't move. I had to admire its defiance. "It's closing time." She turned back to me. "I'd better show you out. We'll take the lift down."

"Thank you," I said.

Clemency pushed back the concertina-style gate and ushered me into the lift. "Be careful of this piece of ancient machinery." She stepped in after me, closed the gates and pushed a button. The lift began to descend with an ominous clanking sound.

"Dreadful noise, huh?" Clemency said. "Still, the ropes have held for over eighty years. Right! We're at the bottom of the building now. Here we are." There was a resounding clang as she opened the lift-gate. To my surprise, I saw that we'd arrived in a dingy basement area, not the entrance hall where I'd come in.

"This way." Clemency led me towards a door marked 'Fire Exit'. "You can go out through here." She released the door by pushing the metal bar. "Good night." She grasped my hand and, with an adroit movement, turned what should have been a hand-shake into a dismissive jerk, propelling me outside. A moment later, the fire-door clanged shut and I found myself in a dank, unlit space below street level. There was an overpowering smell of rotting refuse and drains. All I could see around me were high brick walls topped with spiked railings and there was no sign of an exit. I appeared to be trapped. Clemency had succeeded in wrong-footing me once again.

I stared up at the back of the building, hoping I might see someone at a window to whom I could signal for help, but all the lights were out. Clemency might still be in earshot, of course, but I doubted if she'd respond if I shouted or banged on the fire doors. In any case, I had no wish to give her the satisfaction of knowing she'd got the better of me. No, I must find my own way out.

There was a huddle of industrial-sized bins in the left hand corner of the yard; could I use them to get up to street level, I wondered? No, almost certainly not. It would be a slippery, if not impossible ascent and even if I could reach the top of the wall, I'd still have to clamber over those fearsome spikes. I'd have to think of something else.

I edged along the perimeter of the courtyard, searching for a gate or a door. It was deathly quiet, no sound of traffic and that was odd in itself, as I must hardly be any distance from Kingsway or the Strand. I stumbled over a loose paving stone, grazing my hand on the wall as I reached out to save myself from falling. Then I heard the fluttering of wings and a pigeon landed in front of me. Not just any pigeon; it was the same bird that had looked in at me from the reading room window. There was no mistaking those raffish dark feathers and intelligent, beady gaze.

"Hello, again," I said.

Some people, I suppose, aren't in the habit of speaking to birds, but Nana taught me the importance of saying 'good morning' to magpies and although this wasn't a magpie and therefore not a potential bird of ill-omen requiring extra respect, (*one for sorrow*), there was every chance it was a messenger.

"Is there something you want to tell me?" I asked it.

Apparently in reply, the bird lifted its wings, flew across the yard and landed near the wall. It stood there for a moment, head on one side, fixing me with its intelligent eyes. Then it pecked at the ground, uttering a series of throaty *coos*, before taking off again to roost at the top of one of the bins.

I went over to examine the place where it had landed. I found a circular metal disc, rather like a manhole cover, set into the paving stones, with numbers, letters and hieroglyphics engraved around the rim and a bronze arrow in the centre. Could it be that this was a combination lock that would open a secret door, provided I could work out the code? I knelt down and turned the arrow in an anti-clockwise direction, widdershins as Nana Herrick would have said. It was very stiff; it took all my strength to move it. Laboriously, I tried spelling out the word 'exit', pausing for seven seconds at each letter. Nothing happened, which was disappointing, as seven is usually a significant number. I tried other words, 'Help' and 'Way Out', but again, without result.

I looked round for the pigeon, but it had disappeared. Latin, I thought, the universal occult language, why not try that? I called out the words as clearly as I could. "*Dimitte me, ostende mihi faciam portae.*" Release me and show me the gate.

A moment later, a scrap of paper fluttered down towards me. As I tried to catch it, it swirled upwards again, skittering away as if on a sudden breeze and then coming closer before eluding my grasp a second time and then a third.

"Is anyone there?" I looked up at the dark building. I thought I detected a movement up on the roof, but I couldn't be sure. Perhaps it was a coincidence or perhaps I really had successfully summoned assistance; either way, the paper fluttered down again and this time it fell at my feet. I picked it up. There were a number of symbols inscribed on it in black ink; I could just make them out in the dim light and realised they corresponded to the marks on the circular disc I'd found. So many of them; I counted them, forty nine in all. Of course! *Seven times seven.* A combination spell; I was going to have to concentrate if I was going to get it right.

Once again, I seized hold of the arrow and set to work. At last, as I marked the last hieroglyph, I heard a clanking sound as the section of the wall above me began to slide to one side, except, as I now recognised, it wasn't solid brick at all but a *trompe l'oeil* painted on wood and behind it, there was a set of stone steps leading up to street level. Thanks to the mysterious agencies at work at the Antioch Corey Memorial Library, I was soon back in the familiar London streets and walking briskly to Temple Station to take the tube home.

Five

As soon as I'd learned to read, Nana Herrick gave me the books my mother had owned as a child; *The Wizard of Oz, Peter Pan, Alice in Wonderland, The Lion, the Witch and The Wardrobe,* stories of magical transportation that made a deep impression on me. I kept them hidden under the floorboards of my attic room, away from my father's prying eyes; he disapproved of fairy tales. Once, I'd won a school prize, a bright picture book resplendent with images of castles, tangled forests and talking animals. I carried it home, hugging it to my chest with pride, but as soon as I came into our dingy hall, my father snatched the book from me and hurled it into the cellar.

"Reading such pap won't help you *gi-rrr-l,* this will turn your brain to mush, filling your head with unholy fantasies!" There was a little fleck of spittle on the corner of his mouth, and his eyebrows seemed to jut out even more than usual. Later, I asked Nana what unholy meant and she said it was a word used by those too tight-arsed to open their cheeks to fart. It was only when she spoke of my father Nana resorted to such coarseness.

She must have known, when she gave me those books, how much I longed to escape from Knox Hill. If only I could fall down the rabbit-hole into Wonderland like Alice, or walk through the wardrobe into Narnia like Lucy, or be whirled away in a hurricane to the Emerald City. *Whoosh!*

Here we go! Second star on the right and straight on until morning, follow the yellow brick road and off to see the wizard! When they locked me up in Crowsmuir Hall, I clung to the comfort of my childhood dreams and now, living in London, I still indulged in them. I liked to imagine as I travelled on the tube, hurtling through those tunnels, that I was about to discover a portal to another dimension. And then, indeed, I did…but I am getting ahead of myself and that part of my story must come later.

I loved the underground; each line had its character. I liked the Victoria Line because it was clean and fast, and the Circle had great appeal, but the District Line was my absolute favourite, punctuated as it was with such evocatively named stations, Kew Gardens and Turnham Green, West Brompton and Baron's Court, Ravenscourt Park and Ealing Common. It snaked so elegantly and inclusively in all directions, west, north, south and east, and was such a pleasing mixture of underground and over-ground. That night, coming home from my interview, I felt deeply reassured as the train emerged from the subterranean depths, revealing the grey-brown panorama of London brick and tiled roofs in the district I now thought of as home, a place of sanctuary where nothing evil, as I thought, would ever find me.

As I emerged from the station, a fox darted out from behind a dustbin and crossed the road in front of me. These fearless animals were getting increasingly common around here, having colonised the wilder parts of the nearby old cemetery, and I was never sure whether to view them as friends or foes. They had a predatory look and I was certain they were responsible for the remains of slaughtered birds I sometimes found on the pavements.

I'd been too apprehensive about my interview to eat lunch and now my thoughts were turning to supper. Perhaps I'd call in at Kosminky's deli and buy some cheese, olives and French bread. The shop stayed open late on most evenings. I turned the corner, about to head in its direction, when I was distracted by an unexpected sight. Light was streaming out across the pavement from the window of the old junk shop. I was sure the place had been boarded up when I passed it this morning; it had been like that for weeks, ever since old Mr Rogers was found dead amongst his jumble of threadbare chairs, moth-eaten taxidermy and stacks of tatty copies of *Picture Post.* But now, it seemed, the shop had re-opened and there was a new plate-glass window inscribed with curly gold-lettering:

Pyewacket's Curios

Proprietor: Dorian Pyewacket

I stared at the neatly arranged window display, so different from the dusty clutter of Mr Rogers' time. In front of a varnished screen plastered with Victorian images of flowers, cherubs and birds of paradise, a number of interesting objects had been artfully arranged; a blue porcelain umbrella stand containing walking sticks and parasols, a Chinese rug, three striped hat boxes, some pieces of antique, leather luggage and a lead crystal brandy glass standing on a small rose-wood table. I'd never been tempted to go into the shop before, although I had occasionally peered in through the door. Old Mr Rogers had a fearsome reputation, lurking in the darkest recesses of the shop like a funnel-web spider, ready to attack anyone who dared to show an interest in buying anything, even for the asking price. But perhaps the new management would be more sympathetic.

I gazed at the brandy glass, captivated by its perfection and the way it reflected the light. If I owned a glass like that, I'd have the perfect excuse to buy a bottle of brandy.

My father always warned me about the evils of drink. He refused to install a bar at the Knox Hill Guest House, and if any guest came in late after a trip to the pub, stumbling over the mat and swaying slightly, they were treated to an excoriating dose of condemnation. *"I object to one thing and one thing only, and that is in-eeeeee-breeeee-ation."* That was the word he used, 'inebriation'. Not drunkenness or getting sloshed, plastered, wasted, one over the eight or several sheets in the wind. No, he had to say *'in-eeeeee-breeeee-ation'*, placing self-righteous emphasis on each elongated syllable. And all the time, his own consolation, a bottle of scotch, was tucked away in the kitchen cupboard behind the Quaker Oats and the Camp coffee. There was always one rule for him and another for the rest of the world.

Nana Herrick, on the other hand, taught me how to pour libations. She always kept a 'nip' of something in her kitchen cupboard for special occasions. As well as her home-made elderflower wine, she used to brew a strong concoction from crab apples and herbs. She'd make this particular bottle last the whole year after opening it on New Year's Eve: *'You must always savour a strong drink,'* she told me, *'Never gulp it back as though it's medicine. Take your time with it. And always use a special glass.'* The brandy glass in the window of Pyewacket's Curios did, indeed, look special. It was almost as if it had been placed there deliberately to lure me in.

"Hi." A young man with bleach-blond hair appeared in the doorway. He was wearing striped green and red trousers and there was a long, feathered earring hanging from his left earlobe. He was as different from Mr Rogers with his hacking cough and rumpled corduroy trousers as it was possible to be. "Do come in and feel free to browse."

I hesitated for only a moment before stepping over the threshold.

"Thank you."

The interior of the shop had changed out of all recognition. The filthy coconut matting had gone and the floor boards had been scrubbed and varnished. There were bright spotlights on the walls, and various items such as period lamps and statuettes were displayed on a variety of little antique tables that had been polished and restored to perfection. Sandalwood joss-sticks were burning and there were real flowers in the Chinese vases. I felt over-awed by this chic opulence and felt sure that whatever the young man wanted for the brandy glass, I wouldn't be able to afford it.

"You've done wonders in here." I turned to the young man. "Are you Dorian Pyewacket?"

"Indeed I am. But perhaps I should explain that it's my stage name." Dorian treated me to an insouciant smile. "I chose Dorian because of Dorian Gray, although I don't have a portrait of myself mouldering in the attic, you'll be relieved to hear."

"And what about Pyewacket?"

"No particular reason." He shrugged. "I just liked the sound of it."

"So you don't know where it comes from?"

"No. It just dropped into my head."

"Oh, well, I know all about Pyewacket."

"Do tell!"

"It's from a seventeenth century witch trial," I explained. "There was a man, Matthew Hopkins, he called himself the Witch-finder General and he tortured a woman until she told him the names of her familiar spirits: *Holt, Jamara, Vinegar Tom, Sacke and Sugar and Newes, Elemanzar, Pyewacket, Peck in the Crowne and Grizzel Greedigut*. Most of them appeared in the form of strange animals but Pyewacket was an imp."

"Goodness!" Dorian lifted his eyebrows. "In that case, I'm glad I chose it! Who wouldn't want to be an imp? So," he flicked his feathered earring. "Is there anything here that's caught your eye?"

It seemed better not to mention the brandy glass immediately. I walked over to a green leather Chesterfield.

"I love this," I said. "But I don't think it would fit into my small flat. You do have some gorgeous things though." I turned to look at a mahogany writing table with a galleried back.

"If your space is limited, how about a mirror?" Dorian suggested. "They can make a room seem twice as big. This is a particularly fine piece." He wheeled forward a tall mirror in an elaborately-carved frame. "A cheval mirror, in the Victorian Gothic revival style. See the pointed arches carved here?" He pointed to the top of the frame. "And look at these trefoils and crests, not to mention the flying buttress feet. I'm afraid the glass itself is somewhat spotted, but in my opinion, that adds to its character. A patina of use. But they do say, don't they, that you have to be careful with old mirrors? They can be portals to other places and sometimes, the souls of the dead are trapped in them forever."

"That sounds terrifying."

"It's just a spooky superstition." Dorian laughed. "Don't take me too seriously. Sixty years ago, this one stood in a Bond Street store. Think of all the exquisitely dressed ladies who must have paraded in front of it, adjusting their hats. Take a look at yourself."

I gazed with dismay at my reflection. How staid and conventional I looked. My sensible mac was like an item of school uniform and my other clothes were more suitable for a woman twice my age. Those tan tights! What an awful colour; the manufacturers called the shade Tinker's Gold but it was more like Egyptian mud. And there was nothing flattering about my sensible, knee-length skirt. My plain blouse, so severely buttoned up to my neck, might have belonged to a Victorian governess and as for my court shoes, they were of a style favoured by elderly members of the Royal Family.

"Anything wrong?" Dorian gave me a sideways glance.

"It's just that I don't feel like one of those exquisitely dressed ladies you mentioned," I said.

"Then perhaps you should try wearing period clothes." He plucked a black velvet cloak off a bentwood stand and held it out, revealing the purple silk lining. "This is hand-embroidered." He pointed to the frogging across the front. "And it's genuine. You'll see a lot of so-called Victorian clothes in the Portobello Road or in Camden Market but most of the garments will be reproductions, made by theatrical costumiers. But this isn't a fake. You can tell by the fabric and the stitching. This is real velvet, not polyester. And look at this label inside: *Avery's Tailoring, Mayfair.* I happen to know that firm closed before the First World War. Do you want to try it on?"

I hesitated. The cloak was in perfect condition. It must surely be a collector's piece and quite out of my price range.

"Don't worry, there are no fleas!" Dorian assured me.

"Oh, I wasn't worrying about that! Yes, I'd like to try it on."

I took off my mac, threw it over a chair and took the cloak from him. The moment I touched the soft, seductive fabric, I felt a shiver of excitement. And then, as I slipped the cloak over my shoulders, the folds of the material draped themselves round me like a caress. It was such a beautiful garment, made for romance, for eloping in a horse-drawn carriage at midnight, or for engaging in an intrigue in a royal court. I felt transformed.

"I can hardly believe this is almost a century old," I said. "It's in such good condition."

"It certainly suits you." Dorian looked at me approvingly. "It would look even better if you let your hair down."

When I was a child, my father had always insisted my hair should be tied back and secured with grips; I could still hear his voice echoing in my head: '*Women who adorn their faces with paint and wear their hair loose are no better than the kine of Bashan whom the prophet Amos smote!*' At Crowsmuir Hall, too, there'd been strict rules about hair, but no-one was going to lecture me in the manner of Angus Gowdie now. I undid my hair ribbon.

"That's better," Dorian said. "With your hair loose like that, you look like a real stunner."

"A stunner?"

"That's what the Pre-Raphaelite artists called their models. Lizzie Siddall, Jane Burden and the others. You must have seen those painting of women with masses of luxuriant red hair."

"Yes, I have. Only my hair isn't red."

"You could always use a little henna."

"Yes." I took hold of a strand of my hair and gazed at it. "So I could." *And be free of my dreary natural colour forever.*

"This cloak," I said. "Where did you find it?"

"Interesting question," Dorian said. "I can show you if you like. You'll need to come out into the store room. Would you like to see?"

"Yes. I would."

"Then allow me to take the cloak from you and hang it up again. It's a bit messy out there."

There was a smell of damp in the back room and a general air of chaos; stacks of musty old books teetering against the walls and random items, chair-legs, table tops, a door of an oak cabinet, piled up all over the place.

"I still need to sort out the rubbish old Rogers left behind." Dorian picked up a cracked floral chamber pot and placed it on a shelf. "But one thing I've learned in this trade is not to throw anything away until you've had a really good look. I need to sort through the records, and that means sifting through at least forty box-files. Rogers wasn't the most organized person."

"Did you know him?"

"No. I bought this place at auction. He only had one heir, a great-niece in Canada, who just wanted to get shot of everything. Anyway, here's where I found the cloak." He pulled back a curtain, revealing an old-fashioned wooden trunk with curved metal slats. "Quite a nice piece in itself, I'd say, with this domed lid and the decorative clasps at the front. A lady's travelling trunk, late-nineteenth century. But as you'll see," he lifted the lid, "the satin lining's quite stained. Why not sift through the stuff in there, see if there's anything that takes your fancy."

"Thank you, I will."

I bent over to look. The contents didn't appear to be very promising at first glance, just a heap of unprepossessing, yellowing linen undergarments long past their best. I knelt down, placing my left hand on the rim of the trunk to steady myself and then, quite suddenly, I was gripped by a queasy sensation, as if I was on a ship that was being tossed around on a stormy ocean. Then I heard a voice, shrill and commanding: '*How dare you let sea-water seep into the luggage! Didn't I tell you to take better care?*' I leant back, closing my eyes, fighting the rising nausea.

"Are you all right?" Dorian sounded concerned.

"I'm fine." I took a deep breath. I wasn't going to tell him what I'd just experienced, but I was convinced I'd been given a glimpse into the past, a scene connected with the woman who'd once owned this trunk. She had obviously been a formidable person, used to getting her own way, and she must have been powerful too, otherwise her imprint wouldn't be still here, after so many years. I felt a surge of excitement; what if I could make a connection with her? I leant forward again, and began rummaging in the trunk, taking things out one at a time. It was a disappointing haul: more yellowed undergarments, a chemise, a tattered black lace veil, several kid gloves with buttons, none of them matching, a tangled heap of silk stockings. But what about this little pocket in the trunk's lining? Perhaps there was something special in there, a piece of jewellery, perhaps or...I felt inside and pulled out a square of gilt-edged card. I held it up to the light. There was an address written on it; I could just about decipher the spiky and faded script: *23 Coleton Street, West London, Great Britain.*

"What have you found?" Dorian asked.

"This." I showed him the card.

"Goodness!" He raised his eyebrows. "Clever you, I had no idea *that* was in there. You can keep that. Maybe even look for that address. You might fancy doing some detective work."

"Thank you, I might just do that." I slipped the card into my bag. "Did you really find that cloak in this trunk?" I asked. "It seems odd when it's in such beautiful condition and all these other things are really manky."

"They'd have been of the very best quality when they were new," Dorian said. "And some of them have hardly been worn. You need to dig deeper." He reached over my shoulder and unearthed a pair of black, lace-up Victorian boots. "These, for example. Your size, do you think?"

"Yes, I think they are." I gazed at them admiringly. "And they'd look perfect with the cloak. And what's this?" I picked up a little black velvet drawstring bag. "There's something inside. I wonder what…oh, how lovely! I just have to have this!" In my excitement, I'd forgotten all about keeping up a show of indifference. "You see, it's…" *No! I mustn't tell him that!*

I turned the object over in my hand. It was a silver powder compact, exquisitely fashioned, the only flaw being a long scratch on the back, but on the front there was a monogram, embossed in gothic script, and representing a letter that had special significance for me. Nana's voice echoed in my mind. *Come closer, so that I can whisper it. Even those birds in the sky could be spies. You true name is M.....*"

No, I mustn't! Until the day of my Coming of Age ceremony, it was bad luck even to think about my true name when I was in the presence of others. I mustn't share it with anyone, I mustn't write it down, I certainly mustn't speak it out loud. But now, knowing that the woman who'd owned these things had a name that began with the same letter as my true name felt like a sign. I undid the clasp of the compact and flipped it open.

"The mirror's in perfect condition," I said. "But the powder receptacle's empty.

"Oh, I don't think that ever did contain face powder," Dorian said. "It's a double mirror, but the glass on one side must have been broken at some time. These things were popular in the eighteen-nineties. They used to call them spirit glasses."

"Spirit glasses? What did that mean?"

"No idea." Dorian shrugged. "Well, what do you think? Would you like the cloak and the boots and that little mirror?"

"I would but..." I hesitated. "I really don't have a lot of money to spend."

"Oh, don't worry." He flicked his feathered earring. "I can let you have anything you want relatively cheaply, including the cloak. The thing is, I'm planning to concentrate on furniture and *objets d'art* and I need to make space for new acquisitions. Besides, it's sad to think these things have been neglected for decades. It will be lovely to pass them on to someone who will cherish them and use them well. In fact, it's almost as though they've been here all this time just waiting for you. Their next true owner."

"Me?"

"Yes. When I sell things to people and they call it a lucky find, I always say, 'No, you haven't found those things. They've found *you*."

A few minutes later, I was walking home through the West London night, happily swinging a glossy *Pyewacket* carrier bag by its twisted silk handles. I wasn't worried that I'd just written a cheque for the amount of my money I'd been keeping back to pay my electricity bill, not now that I'd taken possession of the cloak, the boots and the mirror in its little velvet bag. Dorian's idea of a reasonable price hadn't quite coincided with mine, but he'd proved to be a very persuasive salesman. And it really did feel as though the things that had once belonged to the mysterious 'M' had been waiting for me to discover them.

An old woman was pushing a supermarket trolley along the gutter ahead of me, hunched over the handlebar, her rear end sticking up. She was wearing bedroom slippers and a flimsy nylon frock that was rucked up at the back, revealing her bare, mottled thighs. The trolley was brimming over with rubbish; plastic bags filled with crumpled balls of newspaper and crushed cans. She was mumbling to herself: '*Fuck the government, fuck the welfare, go away old man, I'll get you for this...she never done it...I'll get you, I'll get you!*'

On a sudden impulse, I took off my mac.

"Would you like this?" I held it out to her. "It'll keep you dry."

She squinted at me; her eyes were like squashed currants. She pursed her mouth as if she was about to spit and for a moment, I half-expected to be treated to a tirade of expletives but then she simply snatched the mac out of my hands and flung it into her trolley. Then, with a grunt, she shuffled off. No gratitude then, but at least she'd accepted my gift.

I took the cloak out of the carrier bag and put it on. I felt like a new person. Prudent Jean Gowdie, who had always been prepared for rain, was going to ignore such practical considerations from now on. She was going to wear a velvet cloak and show herself to the world as she really was at last.

Six

The moment I turned the corner by the old cemetery, the storm broke. A flash of lightning illuminated the roof of an old sepulchre half-hidden amongst the dark yews, a clap of thunder sent rooks chattering up into the sky, and then came the deluge, water spilling on to the pavement as if the clouds had been rent with a knife. I ducked into a doorway and whipped off the cloak, thrusting it back into the *Pyewacket* bag, anxious to preserve the antique velvet from the dirty London rain. Perhaps I'd been too hasty in jettisoning my mac but only a minute ago, it hadn't looked like rain at all.

Another flash of lightning, more thunder. I wanted to shelter, but I knew I couldn't stay here in a stranger's porch. I'd have to make a break for it and run. Freak weather, I thought, as I clattered down the road heading for home.

It was only much later that I understood what had happened, and just who it was that I'd offended.

No. 179 was a narrow, three-storey house in a nineteenth-century terrace. I rented the basement flat; it was little more than a bed-sit, with the front door opening straight into the main room. There was a tiny bathroom at the back, but no kitchen, although I did have a kettle and an electric ring that was kept behind a curtained alcove. That suited me; I had no interest in cooking and lived mainly on cold food from the deli. I had everything I needed; my books, a window sill for my pots of herbs, a mantelpiece for my joss sticks and candles and a few pieces of furniture I'd bought second hand. There was a couch that doubled up as a bed, a gate-legged table, a chair, a patterned Eastern rug that I'd found in a skip outside a big house in Baron's Court and an oak bookcase from Portobello Road market that had turned out to be infested with woodworm. (One of Nana's simple spells had soon dealt with *that*.)

I was pleased that the rest of the house was unoccupied; after my experiences in the hostel in Upminster where they'd sent me when I first came to London, I needed my privacy.

At Crowsmuir Hall, the other girls had left me alone at first and then, after a while, I'd begun to enjoy a certain status as the library monitor, in charge of those tattered paperbacks and reference books. Plenty of bored inmates relied on me to dole out the comforts of historical romance, ghost stories and thrillers and I'd even started teaching one or two of them to read. The hostel in Upminster had been different; there, I was a nobody, just an awkward girl with frizzy hair the colour of stale-fudge who knew nothing about fashion or popular culture. I'd never heard of Roxy Music, or any popular TV shows, and I wore the wrong kind of shoes. Before long, I became a target for derision.

Laughter and cheerful chat stopped the moment I came into the shared kitchen, there were whisperings behind my back and there was a callous disregard for my personal belongings. A girl called Claudine used my face flannel to clean the bath: *('Oh, sorry, Jeanie, was that your flannel, thought it was an old rag'.)* As if she hadn't seen me caring for that flannel, boiling it regularly in a pan on the stove to keep it clean! I received criticism disguised as well-meaning advice: ('*Jeanie, have you ever thought of doing something about your hair? I could lend you my smoothing cream.'*) And then, quite accidentally, I played into their hands.

It was a special evening, Lammastide, a festival I'd always celebrated with Nana, when we'd go out into the fields and give thanks for the harvest. There didn't seem to be any fields near the hostel, but I'd decided to mark the time in my own way, quietly and discreetly. I placed some leaves and a corn dolly on the top of my chest of drawers, filled my scrying vessel with oil and water and lit a candle. Then I knelt down and began:

"Blessed Lugh, god of the good things of the harvest..."

The door crashed open and Claudine burst in. We each had our own room, mine was the box-room over the garage, and I'd put a notice reading PRIVATE on the door, but that was of no consequence to Claudine when she was planning to filch a pair of tights or a lipstick from a house-mate. I don't know what she was hoping to get from me, possibly something as mundane as a safety pin but the sight of my make-shift altar quickly deflected her from her purpose. She stood there, gawping at me, her mouth hanging open, her eyes startled and hostile. Then she backed away, one hand on the hideous floral wall-paper, her expression suffused with as much revulsion as if she'd seen a poisonous snake rearing up from the toilet bowl.

Later, I overheard them in the kitchen, talking in low voices: *"She came from some loony bin, or was it a prison? Didn't you know? They had to lock her up. Crazy....thinks she's some kind of bloody witch...putting the evil eye on us. Creepy!"*

I packed my case, left a week's rent on the kitchen table and slipped out of the house at three in the morning. For a week, I had to sit up all night in a twenty four hour transport café, nursing a cup of cold tea, until I found a temporary room in a tatty B. and B. in Becontree. And then I began my search for a flat I could afford. It had taken a while, but at last I'd found this place, somewhere quiet and private where no-one would trouble me. And here I was, perfectly settled and content, safe, as I thought, from all the threats of the outside world.

My clothes were soaked, so I stripped down to my underwear, dried myself and rubbed my hair vigorously with a towel, then slipped on the kaftan that I wore in the evenings. Then I took the cloak out of the bag, found a hanger and hung it up on the picture rail. I heard a dull *thunk* as the bottom of the garment touched the wall. I felt the place; it seemed there was something solid concealed in the hem. I found my nail scissors and began cutting carefully through the stitching. And then the hidden object seemed to jump out into my hand.

I held it up against the light, a small gold key with an upper section in the shape of the pentacle and with an embossed *'M'* in the centre. The letter was in a gothic style that exactly matched the one on the mirror, an exciting discovery but also one that made me feel somewhat apprehensive. I knew that curses reside in certain objects; mirrors, native carvings, bones, necklaces, amulets, dried animal paws and jewels that might even be the green eyes of little yellow gods. Keys are especially troublesome, unlocking entrances to places where it's better not to go, especially if you haven't been invited. And then there's another consideration; if you acquire something from a curio shop without the proprietor's knowledge, there can be all kinds of evil consequences. I knew I must go back to

Pyewacket's and tell Dorian about this find; it would be unlucky to do anything else. In the meantime, I'd keep it safe.

I placed the key on the mantelpiece between two black candles, made myself a mug of camomile tea and sank down on my couch, leaning back against the cushions, sipping my drink, and reflecting on the events of this momentous evening. I couldn't stop thinking about Mr Llewellyn and his enigmatic, contradictory behaviour. There had been many times in my lonely, bookish life when I'd fantasised about falling in love with a man with all the qualities of Mr. Rochester, Maxim de Winter and Heathcliff, but until now, I'd never met anyone in the real world who was possessed of such mysterious volatility. Ordinary men, I'd concluded, were not like that; romantic heroes were just in books. But Mr. Llewellyn was not an ordinary man; he was an adept, possibly even a spell charmer, and he was uniquely placed to help me fulfil my destiny. And that was why I must guard against anything as self-indulgent as falling in love with him. It would be an unnecessary distraction from my purpose and I must guard against it at all costs.

How heavy my eyelids felt, almost as if I'd been drugged. I put my mug down on the floor and pulled my eiderdown over me. Before long, I'd fallen into a deep sleep.

Lace curtains blazing against a dark window; sirens wailing, the charred remains of a leather settee propped against the laurel bush, a framed text under cracked glass, *Prepare to Meet thy God*, lying on the path. Hose-pipes, a man in a mask coming out of the house carrying something heavy over his shoulder, pools of water. And there was Bushy standing by the police van, a blanket over his shoulders, his bare legs stick-like and absurd, his eyes like poached eggs, bulging with dope and triumph.

"Gowdie! I did it! I did it! Aren't you proud of me! I raised a fire demon, did you see it?" He attempted to wave at me but someone held his arms behind his back.

"You fool, you utter fool." I ran up the path and headed around the house towards the back door.

"Come back, you can't go in there!" A neighbour shouted.

"*But I must! Let me go! I have to go back. No!"*

Now I was in the house, stumbling around, choking in the smoke, searching desperately for the thing I had to save, and now I was in the flames, and the pain was unbearable and I knew I'd lost it, the most precious thing I owned. I'd lost it forever. I opened my mouth to scream, but no sound emerged, and then I was falling through a dark space and finally, just as I realised this wasn't real, just a memory, I opened my eyes and found I was awake.

Seven

For a moment, I didn't realise this was the present. I thought I was back in Crowsmuir Hall, the place where I'd been roused from nightmares so often, sitting up in bed, screaming and clutching my arm, feeling the scars, remembering the pain and being told by the member of staff on duty to be quiet at once and stop disturbing the others in the dormitory. Then my eyes focused and I saw the glow of the urban street-lights leaking through the curtains and the shape of my black candles ranged along the mantelpiece. So I wasn't at Crowsmuir, I wasn't at Knox Hill, I wasn't in the hostel in Upminster, I wasn't in any of the places where I'd spent unhappy times. I was in my rented flat in West London. I was safe.

Despite my relief, I still felt shaken. Why should that fatal night at Knox Hill have come back to me now, just as my life had begun to move on, and I'd been given the chance to put my past behind me? And in the form of such a vivid dream too. It had been full of authentic detail. Bushy, that was just how he'd looked, those were the actual things he'd said... and now I was seized with an irrational fear. What if it really was gone? What if someone had got into my flat while I was out? What if...?

I leapt out of bed, throwing the duvet aside, then fell on my knees and began scrabbling under the couch. Yes, of course, here it was! How could it be anywhere else, this battered brown leather case? Hadn't I saved it from Knox Hill, that awful night, and hadn't they given it back to me the day I left Crowsmuir Hall?

I snapped open the clasps and gazed with relief at the contents, my school certificates, the little rag dolls Nana made me, the tin containing my apprentice tools, my mother's copy of *The Wizard of Oz.* I flipped the book open; there was her inscription written on the flyleaf: *Elspeth Herrick is my name, England is my nation, Cliff Cottage is my dwelling place, I'll make my own salvation.* The handwriting was firm and round, and made me think that she'd been assertive and strong, that she'd known her own mind from a very early age. But then she'd married my father, something that made no sense, and Nana would never tell me what became of her, other than to wrap it all up in a fable, the tale of the mortal man and the seal-girl.

"The seal people live best in their own element." Nana always began her story that way. "It's better if they never stray on to the land. But sometimes, the new moon beckons them, and they are washed up on the sands, where they lie marvelling at the stars and listening to the sound of the waves. And once there was a young seal girl, her name was Elspeth, and she came ashore, and left her pelt, her shining, wet skin, on the rocks, so that she could transform herself into the shape of a human woman, but she was far more beautiful than any woman you would ever see in the humdrum world and particularly not on the sanctimonious streets of Aberdeen. So there she was, Elspeth, the sleekest and most cunning seal girl of them all, dancing in the moonlight, alone, away from all her people and the dark headland where she had been spawned, when he came along. He was a mortal man and he didn't have an ounce of poetry in his soul. But he saw Elspeth, and he wanted her, wanted her so badly that his mouth dropped open like a fish about to be hooked and his breeches bulged with lust. Elspeth saw him, and she was an innocent, she knew nothing of the evils of men, and she went with him willingly enough. He threw his gabardine over her to hide her beauty from the world, and he picked up her pelt and thrust it inside his coat, and when he had got her back to his house, he locked the pelt in a trunk, so that he could have the keeping of her. But he didn't succeed. She was too wily for him and planned to get away even if it meant her death. Then he grieved, but he only grieved for himself. So whist to that man, I say!"

And that was always the end of Nana's story, however much I begged her to tell me what had become of Elspeth in the end. Perhaps that was her way of telling me my mother would never return. Perhaps she didn't even know the end of the story herself.

Nana's home, Cliff Cottage, was my haven. It suited my father to send me there during the school holidays, and I was only too pleased to go. When I stepped out of the kitchen door, I faced a steep chalky hill into which two terraces had been cut, one for the herbs, the other for vegetables. There I'd play for hours, heaving up rocks to find the woodlice and centipedes that fled in panic, and capturing slugs that I dropped into Nana's beery jam jar traps for the sake of the cabbages. There was the smell of the sea and the screeching of gulls, and if I was alone for too long, I'd feel overwhelmed with fear, imagining how the land might slip, sweeping away everything that I loved, the whitewashed cottage with its blue window frames, the dark yew tree by the ramshackle shed, Nana's cosy, old-fashioned kitchen. When I had thoughts like that, I'd press my finger-tips against my eyelids and tell myself that nothing would change, even though I sensed, deep in my soul, that one day it must.

I'd always dreaded going back to Hexham when the school term was about to begin. I couldn't think of the Knox Hill Guest House as home, it was so cheerless and dominated by my father's peculiarities. Mrs Wallace, who did the cleaning and the laundry, was the only person who took a charitable view of his character. A heavily-built woman who wore a knitted bonnet resembling a tea-cosy, she was, like him, an exile from Scotland, adrift in Hexham without a haggis, as Nana Herrick used to say with a wicked twinkle in her eye.

It was Mrs Wallace's contention that the loss of my mother had embittered my father. I remained unconvinced. How could my mysteriously-absent mother be responsible for his behaviour? Was it her fault that he'd turned Knox Hill into such an unwelcoming place? Was she to blame for the single tea bag he put in the bedrooms alongside a rusting kettle with a broken plug, or for the solitary, thin slice of toast he offered at breakfast? The rooms were cold, the dark brown wallpaper was gloomy and the bed-sheets were left unchanged if a guest only stayed for one night. Very few visitors came to the Knox Hill Guest House a second time and when I was two, my mother left it forever. I never blamed her for that, even though she'd failed to take me with her.

I put the case back under the couch. I was wide awake now. Perhaps if I made myself another herbal tea, I might be able to get back to sleep. I filled the kettle, turned off the main light and lit the two black candles on my mantelpiece. As the light glimmered on the little gold key, I found myself wondering, once again, about the woman whose name began with the same letter as my true name. There must be some way I could uncover her story. I was convinced she must have been someone significant. *Perhaps even a sorceress.* I felt a tingle of excitement at the thought. I *must* find her. Who knew, that might even be what she wanted.

Eight

Llewellyn

He had come, as he often did at this time in the evening, to seek the peace and solitude of the roof top. The spiral staircase that led up to the place was concealed behind a bookcase on the uppermost floor of the library; very few people knew of its existence, which was as well, since it was a perilous vantage point. The narrow walkway around the top of the blue glass dome was little more than a ledge and the parapet in front of it just a foot high. There was no protection against a missed footing or even a sudden, violent gust of wind but the thought of a physical risk to his person never entered his mind. Here he stood, gazing at the London sky-line and observing the passage of birds as they returned to their roosts in the ancient brickwork and stone.

Most of the birds he saw these days were of the common variety, pigeons and sparrows, starlings and crows, but sometimes, with his keen adept's vision, he saw others, distinguishable by their unusual plumage and patterns of flight. These were the familiars, the guides and emissaries, flying between this world and the nether regions of the dead. Once, long ago, he'd seen a raven with three gold tail feathers circling the dome of St Pauls, but such sights were rare in these secular times.

"Master?" A man with a ravaged face emerged from the trap door and stepped out beside him, a dark-fledged pigeon perched on his wrist. "May I join you?"

"Of course." Llewellyn smiled at his old companion. "But how many times must I remind you that you don't have to address me in that way? Konrad, you're not my servant anymore."

"Old habits die hard." Konrad leaned against the edge of the blue dome. He looked like a gargoyle that had come to life; the long birth-mark on his left cheek livid in the half-light. "I am dubious about the benefits of social leavening. That might be all right for *their* world," he pointed downwards. "But too much parity will destroy ours."

"You think so?"

"It is simply my view." He stroked the head of the pigeon with his forefinger. "You appear troubled, Master."

"What makes you think that?"

"You can't conceal it from me." Konrad continued to stroke the bird. "And I think I can guess what has disturbed you. I saw that girl although she did not see me. I sent her on her way."

"You did?"

"Yes. She was down there, locked in the rear courtyard. A trick of the Nantucket woman, I suspect. But," he spoke in a regretful tone, "I have to concede that the girl is certainly resourceful. She can ask significant questions and communicate with the right spirits. But I beg you, don't allow her to return."

"I have already invited her."

"I wish you had not."

"I have no choice. She needs our protection. It's what the Magus would wish."

"Then why not send her to the Magus?" Konrad frowned at him. "Why allow her to come here? I have a dark premonition about this situation. I believe she will bring destruction raining down on all our heads."

"I'll do my best to prevent that."

"And you think that will be easy? That girl looks innocent enough but she has a certain quality, I sensed it... I hoped that you would be more careful of your own safety than this, Master." The reproach was spoken with quiet force. "I've watched over you since you were a boy. You owe me something for that, surely?"

"I owe you my life."

"Then, I beg of you, don't put that life in danger again."

Far below their feet, everyday London went about its business; a world of red buses, taxi cabs, neon lights, shops and pubs, crowds of people scurrying towards the tube station in complete ignorance of the followers of the occult path with whom they shared their capital.

"That girl...no, that young woman, has been sent to us for a reason." Llewellyn turned towards Konrad. "She is... special, in a way that she herself doesn't recognise. I feel a duty of care. And this place will be her sanctuary. I have to do this, whatever the consequences."

"You must, of course, do as you think best." Konrad lifted his wrist, prompting the bird into flight. The two men watched as it soared upwards into the night sky and disappeared into the clouds. Then the silence between them was absolute.

Nine

I lay awake for hours after that nightmare about Knox Hill, dozing at last in a few fitful snatches. At half past six I woke again with a muzzy head and a throat that felt as if I'd just been gargling with razor blades; I could only assume that the soaking I'd received on my way home last night had taken its toll. I knew I'd just have to let this feverish cold run its course. Nana Herrick taught me everything she knew about herbal remedies and simple spells but she'd also told me that no practitioner of magic, whether plain hedge-witch or advanced adept, can cure themselves, not even of the most basic ills. At least I had the perfect excuse to stay away from my dreaded work-place, even if that did mean going out into the bucketing rain in order to phone the office.

As I pushed open the door of Mustafa's Kwik Bites, I was met by an overpowering smell of fried bacon, for me, a nauseating gust of greasiness that was far too reminiscent of the Knox Hill Guest House for comfort. I remembered how every Sunday evening my father used to grill fifty rashers of cheap streaky bacon from the cash and carry. This batch would then be re-heated to tooth-breaking crispness by Mrs Wallace as required throughout the week. Breakfast was not a pleasure at Knox Hill, except, perhaps for my father, who enjoyed telling visitors that they would not be getting the food of their choice since they'd failed to give him twenty hours' notice of their requirements by filling in a breakfast card, or as he called it, *'a breakfast caaaaa—rrrrd'*. Any guest who attempted to point out that he'd concealed these cards under the table lamp in the hall without drawing anyone's attention to his system got short shrift, of course. Angus Gowdie, as always, was impervious to reason.

All the tables in Mustafa's were empty; perhaps the rain had kept people away. I looked around me; how strange that this should be the place where I'd found the fragment of newspaper that had led me to the Antioch Corey Library. Fate must have had a hand in it, as Mr Llewellyn said, and yet Mustafa's was an ordinary greasy spoon café, mundane rather than magical, with its Formica tables, custard-yellow walls, and lino the colour of tomato ketchup. The only newspapers to be found lying around the tables were of the tabloid type, splashed over with pictures of models and headlines about footballers and TV stars; they were hardly the kind of publications to print adverts for staff in an academic library. *Summoned through the old magic of London...*How wonderful to think I'd been called.

"You look well rough." Nasir, the owner's nephew, looked up from loading bread into the toaster as I closed the door behind me.

"I think I've caught a chill." I shivered as I pulled my old cardigan around me. It was a poor substitute for my mac and the wind had blown my umbrella inside out three times on my way here; I hated feeling so bedraggled.

"You should be in bed." Nasir flung a dirty dish cloth over his shoulder.

"I *am* planning to go back to bed," I told him. "But I need to call in sick at the office. I wonder if you'd be kind enough to let me use your phone?"

"Yours out of order?"

"I don't have one," I admitted.

"Ain't that a fucking nuisance?" Nasir took off the white cap he wore for cooking and scratched his shaven, blue-tinted scalp.

The first time I met Nasir, I'd asked him whether he'd dyed his head blue because he was a Druid and whether he'd used woad which, I believed, you could still gather along the further reaches of the Thames. He looked at me as though I was faintly mad, and then explained it was all to do with a gang he'd been in, and that the blue was the same ink used in tattooing. After that, I'd avoided mentioning anything strange or random to him and I'd restricted our conversations to the weather and football, although I knew nothing about sport.

"It's never been a problem before," I said. "Not having a phone. This is the first time I've needed to make a call."

"Still think you ought to have one though," Nasir persisted. "What if yer flat caught fire or you tripped and broke yer leg? Or worse still, you saw a stalker out the window?"

"A stalker?"

"Men what like to prey on lone women." He grinned. "If you saw one of them, you'd need to call 999, right? You can't be too careful."

"Oh, I live in a very quiet street. And no-one's ever bothered me."

This was true enough. A nervous, rabbity-looking girl called Doris at the hostel had warned me that the streets, cinemas and underground system of London were teeming with dangerous men but so far, I hadn't encountered any of them. No man had placed his hand on my knee on the bus or on the tube, or put his hand up my skirt on the escalator or even attempted to 'flash' at me from behind bushes or railings. I'd never been followed, not even on the darkest of nights. Apart from the behaviour of Finsworthy, my life had been unaffected by predatory males and I knew exactly what to do about them in any case. A pin, judiciously placed in a clay model of the offender will always be a good deterrent. Nana taught me that.

"Oh well." Nasir shrugged. "Sounds like you've been lucky. Anyway, help yourself." He pointed to the phone at the end of the counter. "No need to pay, compliments of the house."

"Thanks." I dialled the office number. After only three rings, a voice answered.

"Martyn, Hegarty and Martyn?"

Damn! It was Finsworthy. There was no mistaking those pinched, oleaginous tones.

"This is Jeanie," I spoke huskily into the receiver. "I'm afraid I won't be able to come into work for a few days, I'm developing a really heavy cold. In fact, it might even be 'flu."

"That's a pity." Finsworthy sounded distinctly miffed. "I was planning to go over some procedures with you today. I also want to do a thorough appraisal of your work. Are you quite sure you can't struggle in?"

"Quite sure," I croaked.

"Then please be aware, if you stay away for more than three days, you must bring in a signed certificate from your doctor."

"But I'm not registered with a doctor. I'm never ill. Not ill enough for a doctor, I mean. Actually, I don't even *like* doctors. I *have* got a bad chill now, of course, and..." I broke into a fit of coughing. "Sorry. Excuse me..." I continued to cough, my eyes streaming. I reached into my bag and pulled out a tissue, spilling half the contents on to the counter.

"A signed certificate." Finsworthy insisted. "After three days." There was a click at the other end of the line. Good-bye and good riddance!

"Well, they certainly can't accuse you of skiving." Nasir was looking at me with a sympathetic expression. "So, what can I get you?"

"Just a coffee please." I began to sweep up the things I'd dropped, three pens, my season ticket, a packet of extra-strong mints, my home-made charm against woodworm and a jumble of notes and papers.

"Don't forget this." Nasir held out a piece of card, the one I'd found the previous evening in the trunk at Pyewackets.

"Oh thanks!" I stared again at the address. *23 Coleton Street, West London*. "Just wondering," I tried to sound casual. "Do you know Coleton Street? I think it might be around here."

"Coleton Street?" Nasir frowned. "No. But there's Collyaton Road and Coleton House. I know them all right. Council flats. My auntie lived in one."

"Does she still live there?"

"No. She moved out in the end and went down to Southampton. She never really liked Coleton House. She thought it was too close to the cemetery. She said that must have been the reason the flats were haunted."

"Haunted?" Now this *was* intriguing.

"So she said, but my auntie was superstitious. She was always saying a cup had moved from where she'd left it, or a door had opened all by itself, or that she'd felt a 'cold spot'. And then she got talking to this old bloke in the pub on the corner and that really set her off. Apparently he was always telling her stories about all the weird stuff in London, Jack the Ripper, the haunted theatres, Spring-Heeled Jack, the ghost in the Bloody Tower. And then she told him where she lived and he said....Here's your coffee." He slapped a mug down in front of me.

"Thanks. Do go on."

"Well, the old man said that where they built the council flats, there used to be some really old houses, two hundred years old, and that some of them had deep cellars. The houses got demolished after the war, but he reckoned some of the cellars were still there, bricked up under the flats. And then he talked about two people. Arthur Lewin and Mandy. Bad people, he said. They were supposed to have lived in one of those houses when Queen Victoria was alive. And according to him, they were still around in spirit. What he actually said was, 'They still walk'."

"Still walk? You mean they were haunting the place?"

"Got it in one! My auntie told me that, one night when I was staying over at her flat. I was only seven. I felt like pissing in my pants!"

"I'm not surprised!"

"Yeh! I was convinced this Arthur Lewin and Mandy were going to appear in my bedroom. And then, late at night, when I was all on my own in there, I started hearing stuff."

"What kind of stuff?"

"Voices, talking in a language I didn't understand. And there were other noises too. Someone beating a gong. And then there was chanting. And a smell, like perfume, only so strong it made you feel dizzy. And after that, I refused to sleep at my auntie's ever again."

"You're not making this up, are you?"

"Straight up, it's true. Mind you, I don't believe in ghosts these days. I can understand it now. Kids imagine things, they wake up, they hear the tele, they think it's ghosts or they dream that there's a monster in the wardrobe and think it really happened. I heard those voices, all right but that doesn't mean they were anything spooky."

"Hmm." I wrapped my hands around my mug, reflecting on his story. "Where is it exactly?" I asked. "Coleton House?"

"It's on the other side of the cemetery from here. You go across the main road, down past the bookies. But the other thing is, that pub on the corner, it was..." Nasir broke off, as three workmen in donkey jackets and big boots came in through the door. "Anyway, I wouldn't go looking for trouble if I were you. Coleton House is best avoided and you should definitely avoid the cemetery at night."

"Really? But you just said you didn't believe in ghosts."

"I wasn't thinking of *real* ghosts. I just meant you might scare yourself looking for them. Sorry. Got to get on. Yes, gents, what can I get you?"

I picked up my coffee and went over to my usual table. I'd have to question Nasir further about his story on a later occasion, but in the meantime, I'd start my own investigations. *'M'. 'Mandy'. Coleton House*. Just a coincidence or a connection? If 'Mandy' was the same woman who'd owned the mirror, the key and the cloak, then.....what if her spirit really wasn't at rest? *Arthur Lewin and Mandy. Bad people.* A pattern seemed to be emerging. Perhaps Nasir knew more than he was admitting. And how ironic that he should have warned me about the old cemetery because now, of course, I felt eager to go in there and explore. And it would take more than a few ghosts to frighten me away, I was sure of that.

Ten

Llewellyn

This was new to him, travelling to America by air, and he was finding it an unhappy experience. The quiet hum in the grey cabin, the confinement, the ocean so far below him, half-obscured by cloud, was yet another reminder of how alienating he found the modern world. It was all so different from his first journey across the Atlantic all those years ago. He could still conjure up the smell and the taste of that sea trip. He'd thrilled to the exuberant sprays of salt water and the relentless swell and toss of the ocean, and he'd remained on the deck while others retreated, stricken and pale. He remembered how he'd stood there, gripping the rail and laughing into the face of the wind, exhilarated to discover he had the stomach to withstand the turbulence, feeling invincible. Since then, he'd been punished for his youthful arrogance many times over. Now, as he stepped from the plane with a headache nagging away behind his strained eyes, he felt nothing like a hero and rather more like a gate-crasher at a party from which he now wanted to escape.

There was a long and inexplicable delay in baggage reclaim and that, he feared, meant that he'd almost certainly missed the upstate bus that would have got him to the Corey Mansion before nightfall. He stood in the echoing hall, drawing on his reserves of patience as other passengers flapped and fretted, children ran about, toddlers screamed and unintelligible announcements blasted out from a speaker above his head. As time passed, he became abstracted, lost in thought, turning the disturbing question of Jeanie Gowdie over and over in his mind, but coming no nearer to a resolution. Konrad was right; it might have been sensible to send her on her way. But how could he have rejected such wide-eyed eagerness, such an appeal for his sympathy? And, most importantly, there was her innocence. It hardly seemed possible, but she was evidently in complete ignorance of her unique identity and yet he'd recognised her for what she was the moment he'd seen her. The shock of that moment had shattered the peace and quietude of his reclusive life and now he was appalled by the feelings that were stirring within him, feelings that he'd hoped never to experience again. They filled him with guilt; he had no right, no right at all, to think of that young woman in that way, and yet...

"Say, Mister, is that your valise?" A burly man in a checked shirt and dungarees had appeared beside him. "It's done three circuits. You in some kind of trance or what?"

Valise? For a moment, as he emerged from his reverie, he didn't understand the question. "Thank you." He turned to face the man. "Yes, that's mine."

"Thought so!" The man reached out, grabbed hold of the leather case and handed it to him. "After all, you're the only passenger left standing here. And I reckon I know just who you are. You want the Corey Mansion, right?"

"Yes, that's exactly where I'm going. But how did you...?"

"Happen to be here, on the wrong side of security?" The man beamed at him. "Let's just say I have an ability to get snuck in to all kinds of places where I maybe shouldn't be.

And in the case of this airport, I work here, part-time. Just finishing my shift. So I can take you just where you want to go."

"That's very kind, but I really can't impose."

"No imposition. It's for your own safety. There are people around here who'd be only too happy to send you off in the wrong direction. Don't go with any of them; if you see anyone holding up your name on a card at the barrier, go straight past. But you can trust me. I'm Cal Conway. Pleased to meet you, Mister. You go through passport control and I'll meet you on the other side, by the parking lot. You'll recognise my truck; it's forty years old. Now, best to git going!"

Half an hour later, he was sitting at the back of the truck, sharing the space with two collie dogs and a crate of pumpkins. Cal Conway drove in a manner that would have upset a person of nervous disposition or anyone prone to motion sickness. He took the bends like a racing driver, speeding over pot-holes and pumping the gas, as if determined to test the vehicle's suspension to the limit. Everything rattled and shook; the landscape flew past in a dizzying diorama of decimated autumn beauty, just a few splashes of russet, yellow and gold amongst the bare trees.

"So you're the cousin from Birmingham, huh?" Conway said, in a conversational tone. "Understand you're keen to do some fishing. Hate to tell you, but it's not the best season. Still, the old guy will be pleased to see you after all these years."

A cousin from Birmingham? Fishing? It sounded as though Jabez had given Cal Conway a cover story and it seemed best not to challenge it.

"So you work for him, for Jabez Corey?" Llewellyn raised his voice above the roar of the engine.

"In a manner of speaking. Just a few odd jobs. Jabez is a great old guy, often run errands for him. Those two women are a different sack of beans though. Salutation and Providence, what kind of names are those in this day and age, I ask you? Neither of them friends of mine and Jabez won't know no peace now that they've moved back in on him. Vultures!" He spat on the floor. "'Scuse me. That had to happen."

As the truck began to ascend the low hills ahead, Cal slowed down at last. There was a change in the landscape, the trees thinning out and the ground taking on a stark and burnt appearance, as if it had been subjected to a blast of demonic breath. It was getting dark and an unhealthy-smelling mist was rising; it caught in his throat, making him cough. The drive had made his headache worse and even though he was unafraid of the phantoms that might be lurking in the Corey Mansion, he was beginning to wish that he'd stayed overnight at a comfortable hotel and left this visit until tomorrow morning.

"I'm dropping you here." Cal Conway pulled up outside a pair of wrought iron gates. "I don't much relish the prospect of meeting either of those two harpies. You OK to make your own way?"

"Of course. Thank you." He stepped out of the truck, hoping that the walk up the long drive would clear his head.

The tall, asymmetrical house with its cedar-shingle tiles, pitched roof, mock-medieval chimneys and gothic gables, loomed up at him, its appearance as welcoming as that of a nineteenth century mad-house. He went up the steps into the cobweb-festooned porch and reached for the bell-pull, but before he could touch it, the door opened. It seemed that he'd been observed approaching the house; he'd certainly had a strong sense of being watched and by a distinctly hostile presence at that.

"What do you want?" The woman standing on the threshold croaked out the question like a corncrake guarding its nest. She was dressed in a long skirt and a linen blouse, her hair dragged back into a wispy bun. Her face resembled an apple that had been left out on the grass to rot. He knew at once who she was, even though he'd only ever seen her in a photograph. This was Miss Salutation Corey, one of the last of the puritan section of the family, the older sister of Providence Corey. Both of them staunch enemies of magic.

"I'm here to see Jabez Corey. He sent for me."

"But what are you thinking, arriving here at such a late hour?" Salutation Corey demanded. "What gives you the right to disturb Mr. Corey? He is in the last months of his life!"

"I didn't know...I had no idea..."

He felt the grief like a punch in his solar plexus. Of course, he should have known, he should have guessed. That letter he'd received, the wavering hand-writing, the urgency of the message, *Come soon, my old friend, as soon as you can. Tempus fugit...*

"I'm so sorry to hear this," he said.

"Sorry? What use do you think mealy-mouthed British expressions are at a time like this?"

"I meant to offer my sympathy. And I'm here to help in any way I can."

"It's his time, that's all. Everyone dies in the end. Even you, Mr L.A. Llewellyn. Oh yes, I know who you are! Your reputation precedes you. But I do wonder how you managed to get here; there are no buses until Tuesday."

"Mr Conway was kind enough to bring me here."

"That useless bum! And now he's deposited you here like an unwanted package. I cannot understand why Mr. Corey should want to see *you*, when he should be speaking to his own people. Well, you had better come in. Wipe your feet on the mat. You can sleep in the Iroquois room and see Mr. Corey in the morning. Then you must leave."

The chill of the Corey mansion seemed to sink into his very being the moment he stepped over the threshold. He found himself in a narrow entrance hall dimly lit by oil lamps. Stuffed animal heads, moose and caribou, bear and native foxes, gazed at him with fixed glass eyes.

"This way." Salutation moved towards the stairs. "Don't lean on the banisters unless you relish the idea of breaking your neck."

He followed her up the creaking stairs, passing the portraits of many stern Corey ancestors in their gilt frames on the wall. The smell of damp was pervasive and as they reached the upper corridor, he noticed the cracks in the wall, and the sections of bare plaster.

"Here." She unlocked a door on the upper corridor and ushered him into a small chamber containing a four poster bed, a wash stand, and a threadbare winged armchair. He noticed that the lattice window overlooking the lake was thick with grime. Clearly, there was little comfort to be had here.

"You should have everything you need." Salutation picked up a box of matches and lit the lamp. "A water closet through that door on your left. Hooks on the wall there for your clothes. Please don't touch the chest or the wardrobe. If you wish for anything else, speak now."

"I'm so sorry to inconvenience you, Miss Corey. There is just one thing; it's some time since I've eaten. Just some tea and toast would be fine. I could get it myself, of course, if you could just tell me where to find the…"

"Kitchen? I don't think so." Her voice dripped with disapproval. "The rooms on the lower floor are locked up for the night. I'm sure you can wait until morning. There's a road house on the way back to the airport; perhaps you could stop off there if you insist on sustenance. And now I must bid you goodnight." And with these inhospitable words, she turned on her heel and left him to his own devices.

It must be possible to extract some humour from this situation, he thought, but the prospect of spending such an unpleasant night filled him with gloom. He knew he should care less about his own comfort, it was self-indulgent even to be thinking of it when he'd just received such sad news about his old friend. He massaged his aching forehead and went over to examine the bed, quickly coming to the conclusion that unless he wanted to contract pneumonia from the damp sheets or get bitten by the bed-bugs that were almost certainly lurking in the mattress, it would be better to sleep in the chair by the window. He picked up the lamp and explored the room. A closer examination of the paintings on the wall revealed their perverse subjects; a naked man cutting the throat of an ox while others crouched underneath drinking the blood, figures in horned masks dancing barefoot on burning coals, a woman in a white robe with a rope about her neck being forced to crawl on all-fours by a dog-headed man armed with a whip. At one time, he might have regarded these images as interesting curiosities but now he felt repelled by such savagery.

He put down the lamp and did his best to get comfortable on the chair, using his coat as a bedcover. It was some time before he fell into an uneasy doze and then, less than an hour later, he woke, aware of a crick in his neck and an acute, gnawing pain in his stomach, a sensation of hunger that was as sharp as if someone had placed a famine curse upon him. And perhaps someone had. It was going to be impossible to sleep.

He got up and left the room, making his way along the upper corridor in the vain hope of finding something edible, perhaps a bowl of fruit placed conveniently on a table somewhere, but there was nothing. A fruitless search, in the literal sense of the word, he thought grimly. A door creaked open ahead of him. He froze, hoping he was not about to be confronted by Salutation Corey or her even more formidable sister. Then he heard a familiar voice calling his name.

"My dear old friend." The voice was faint. "You're here. Enter, please. And close the door behind you."

Llewellyn stood on the threshold, hardly able to contain his dismay. Until this moment, he'd been entertaining the possibility that Jabez's condition wasn't quite as serious as Salutation Corey had said, but now, the evidence was in front of him, he could see it was true. The Magus was dying.

The chamber, lit by a single oil lamp, was cluttered with the paraphernalia of a sick room, bottles and potions, a commode, a jar of leeches, an oxygen mask attached by a rubber tube to an antiquated wooden case. A person more attuned to the modern world would have thought these items resembled exhibits in a medical museum, but Llewellyn knew little about such things and, in any case, his attention was focused on the man in the four-poster bed. Frail and looking so much older than when they'd last met, Jabez Corey was propped up on a pile of pillows stacked against the elaborately carved mahogany headboard, struggling to breath. And yet, despite his stricken state, his eyes were bright and there was a faint smile on his face as if he was viewing his imminent passing with wry detachment.

"My dear old friend," Jabez spoke in a whisper. "Don't look so gloomy. This comes to us all. My passion for Turkish cigarettes has proved my undoing at last."

"Magus..." Llewellyn approached the bed. "Magus, I'm sorry I didn't come sooner. If I'd realised..." He was unable to say any more, choked by emotion.

"No sentiment, please." Jabez held up his hand. "But allow me to say how much it cheers me to see you. And no need for an apology. You are here in good time, as it so happens."

"Are you comfortable? Is there anything I can fetch for you?"

"I have all I need." Jabez's thin hand twitched towards the oxygen mask and then drew away from it. "Please...sit by me. Fetch a chair, that one over by the window. That's right. Good. So—when did you arrive?"

"A few hours ago. Your cousin told me I mustn't disturb you until morning."

"Ah!" Jabez nodded. "And no doubt she greeted you warmly, offering you all the New England hospitality for which this house is famous. Did she treat you to an excellent repast before taking you to the luxury guest suite?" He chuckled faintly. "No? I thought not. I must remedy that."

"I'm all right, please don't trouble yourself."

"My dear friend, I cannot have them neglecting you. You have a pale and famished look, if you don't mind me mentioning it." He reached for the speaking tube hanging above his head. "Ezra? Are you there? I am sorry to disturb you at this late hour. A plate of cold chicken, and a glass of bourbon for my visitor, if you would be so kind. No, nothing for me…perhaps, just another carafe of fresh spring water… yes, send it all up in the dumb waiter. And then, can you place fresh sheets and towels in the Guest room? Thank you." He replaced the mouth-piece.

"It's good of you to think of me at such a time, Magus."

"Nonsense," Jabez shook his head. "You are my guest. I must have been asleep when you arrived. I hadn't intended to be. Now, we have much to discuss. There is the question of ..." He gasped and reached for the oxygen mask, placing it over his mouth and nose this time and taking several deep, rattling breaths before dropping it back on to the patchwork counterpane. "There is the question of my successor. The person who is to succeed me as Magus. As far as I'm concerned, there is only one possible candidate. Do you grasp my meaning?"

"I'm not sure that I do. As I understand it, there are no other descendants of the Corey family apart from..."

"My delightful cousins, Salutation and Providence? Quite so. You may be wondering why I have allowed them into this house at such a time; suffice it to say, I have little defence against the forces of righteousness in my weakened state. Salutation is intent on saving my soul, while Providence believes I am beyond redemption. Personally, I have no interest in the matter; and what neither of them realise is that they are inadvertently guarding this house from far darker forces than even they could recognise. And there's the rub; I'm only too aware of the chasm that will open up in our world when I am gone. The forces of opposition will feel empowered and there could be an orgy of persecutions. And that is why I have sent for you. Put simply and succinctly, I wish you to become Magus in my stead when I pass into the Summer lands.

"Magus." Llewellyn had neither wanted nor expected this, and now he was painfully aware of just how unthinkable it was to counter a dying man's wishes. "I'm honoured, of course, but I can't help feeling that there must be a worthier candidate."

"Find me that person and I will consider him. Or *her*." Jabez smiled. "We live in changing times after all. But I know of no-one else with your experience and knowledge. Oh, I can think I can guess your objections, but let me assure you, this is no time for modesty."

"Magus, you must surely know the reason for my hesitation."

"Oh, indeed I do." Jabez's hand fluttered towards the oxygen mask again. "But soon it may no longer be in your choice to abstain from using your powers. It will take a powerful adept to counter the machinations of our enemies. And that can only mean one person. You."

"The Magus should be an adept who has never used his powers unwisely," Llewellyn protested. "The Magus should be a pure soul, without a stain on his character. The Magus should be irreproachable, whereas I..."

"Baloney!" Jabez's voice lifted a creaky octave. "The Magus should be one who has passed through the fire and survived."

"And yet that is the thing I regret most in my life."

"Then you shouldn't. The important thing is that you are neither lazy nor a coward, and the fact that some of your choices in life have led to suffering and regret have made you all the stronger. When I placed you as Custodian at the Library, I was hiding you in plain sight. It was always my intention that when I passed, you would take my place. Surely you guessed my plans?"

"No. I had no idea."

"I see. Well, I'm afraid I must order you to accept, even though I fear I'm offering you a poisoned chalice."

"I'm not afraid of the danger, Magus."

"Then there's no more to be said. Now, let us turn to other matters. I received your message, telling me that you had something important to impart to me. I'm getting tired. You must tell me about it now."

"Of course. You see, there's a girl..."

"A girl?" Jabez's eyes brightened. "Are you coming out of your long seclusion at last?"

"Certainly not." He realised he sounded prudish and defensive. "I wouldn't dream of...perhaps I shouldn't have said a girl, she's a young woman, twenty years old. She came out of nowhere, she sent a letter, a long, rambling letter....there was something about it... so I summoned her and she came and as she entered the room I saw she had an aura of shimmering, white energy that lit up the darkness around her."

"Something that only an advanced adept such as yourself could have seen."

"Exactly." He nodded. "And so, you see, I have a reason to believe she's a heritant."

"A heritant." Jabez repeated the word thoughtfully. "A carrier of the blood-line of the adherents of the Old Religion. It has long been believed that last true heritant died in Prague in 1941, at an advanced age, leaving no issue. And this young woman..?." He broke off, coughing. "Excuse me. So, this young woman. Her name?"

"Gowdie. Jeanie Gowdie."

"Gowdie! Ah!" The old man's eyes lit up in recognition. "And tell me, does she know? That she is a carrier of the bloodline, that is?"

"It would seem she does not. But she is a believer in magic. She appears to know about charms and spells and she described her grandmother as a wise-woman."

"Then it is better she remain in ignorance. Of course, she must be sheltered by us. As to her general character, would you describe her as clever or naïve?"

"She is an engaging mixture of both."

"Engaging! Ah! I see." The old man smiled. "So you are falling in love with her already."

"If I was, I'd do my utmost to resist it."

"And why would that be?"

"Such a thing would be unthinkable. She's young. Young even for her age and I am..."

"One who would be healed and strengthened by such a union. Think of the greater good. Think of what the two of you could achieve together. The last heritant and a curs...." Jabez broke into another paroxysm of coughing before he could complete the word.

"Save your strength, Magus. You need to rest. We can talk again in the morning."

"In the morning, my delightful cousin will attempt to eject you although I will not allow it. We need to make many plans. And I have something else I must ask you to do. Something you must...ah!" He held up his hand. "Do you hear that ominous clanking? Don't be alarmed, it's only your supper arriving courtesy of the dumb waiter. Eat, while I close my eyes and rest for a while. Then we can talk further. I have one more task for you, something of the utmost importance to preserve my uncle's legacy and it seems to me that this young woman, this Miss Gowdie could be of great assistance and...." His eyes closed.

At two in the morning, having sat up with Jabez all that time, Llewellyn bent over to examine the old man and found to his relief he was only sleeping, although his breathing was shallow, almost imperceptible. He lowered the lamp and walked over to the window. Outside, the darkness was impenetrable. He was conscious that a great burden had been placed on him but if the Magus truly believed he should succeed him, then so he must. But as for the other suggestion, the old man must have been rambling and confused. Jeanie Gowdie might be the last heritant but she was also an innocent young woman. She deserved the love of someone better than a jaded and damaged man such as himself.

Eleven

I couldn't understand it: I was never ill and yet here I was, confined to my flat for three days. I felt hot and cold by turns, my head ached and anxious thoughts kept me from sleeping. I placed some hops and dried valerian flowers under my pillow in an attempt to ward off any more disturbing dreams and comforted myself by re-reading *The Wizard of Oz* but I still grew increasingly anxious as the time passed. No letter had arrived for me from the library and now I was beginning to doubt that I was going to be offered that job after all.

On the fourth day, I felt so much better that I had no excuse to stay away from the insurance office any longer. I'd been hoping to return in triumph, my letter of resignation in my hand, but all I could do was slink back into my strip-lit booth as unobtrusively as possible. I managed to fend off Derek Finsworthy by coughing noisily into my hanky and waving him away with a croaky cry of '*Careful, you don't want to catch my germs!*', but apart from the grim pleasure I got from this, my working day was even more tedious and trying than usual.

There were several envelopes lying on the mat when I got home, but it was a disappointing haul; my electricity bill (a final demand, printed in accusatory red), a flier for a new Indian restaurant with a coupon offering a 5% reduction on a takeaway provided you collected it between 6.00 p.m and 6.30 p.m, a catalogue of bath-aids, walking frames and stair-lifts, and what appeared to be a very early Christmas card addressed to one of the previous tenants. It was the same the following night and for the rest of the week; bills, junk mail or nothing at all, but ten days after my interview, I came home to find a long black cardboard tube sticking out from behind a row of empty milk bottles on the area steps. And squatting next to it was a very large and exceptionally warty toad.

Now this *was* encouraging. I knew that Guardians often manifest themselves in humble form and this creature had every appearance of one. As I bent down to pick up the tube, the toad leapt to one side, landing in a heap of fallen leaves with a decisive *flump.* It paused for a moment, blinked at me, and then, moving in the sedate but lumbering manner of a gouty old gentleman, made its way across the paving stones and disappeared into a hole in the wall with a croak.

"Thank you," I said, remembering how important it is to treat emissaries with respect.

I went into my flat where I examined the package. The handwritten label clearly indicated it was for me, although given the vague way it had been addressed to *Miss Jean Gowdie, West Brompton, England,* it was more than a little surprising it had been delivered. Not only that, but above the label there was a profuse stickering of American stamps that couldn't possibly constitute legal postage since, as I happened to know from having seen Bushy's stamp album, those images of Jefferson and Lincoln dated back to the First World War.

I opened the tube carefully, using nail scissors to cut through the piece of hessian secured with sealing wax that had been placed at one end. I slipped my fingers inside and drew out a roll of parchment that I laid flat on the table, weighing it down at the corners with some herb pots. It smelled of mushrooms, damp earth and cinnamon and bore a letter written in a spidery, wavering script:

Dear Miss Gowdie,

Circumstances preclude me from meeting you in person but I have put my trust in the judgment of my colleague, Mr. L.A. Llewellyn. He has told me much about you and how fate brought you to us. On his recommendation, I am both gratified and delighted to appoint you to the post of Reading Room assistant at the Antioch Corey Memorial Library with immediate effect. Please send word to Mr. E. Brunswicker, our Librarian, advising him of the date of your arrival. I wish you a long and happy association with us. I enclose some tokens of my confidence in you; use them well.

I remain your humble servant, Jabez Corey

Surprised to learn that the black tube contained more than just the parchment, I upended it and shook it out over the table. A handful of dried beetles and pumpkin seeds showered out, along with a small square of yellow vellum on which the words *Cavete ira mortuis* had been written in red ink. Turning it over, I found a collage on the back, consisting of a pentacle created from pasted-on hemlock seeds and with a single black feather in the centre. This didn't puzzle me in the slightest. I was Maudie Herrick's grand-daughter and I knew a Talisman of Protection when I saw one.

"Good grief!" Derek Finsworthy stared at Jabez Corey's letter. "Are you *quite* sure this is a serious offer of employment?"

"Oh yes." I was struggling to keep a straight face. Perhaps it hadn't been necessary to show it to him, but it was worth it just to see his consternation. "It's genuine all right."

"You think so?" He frowned. "Then why haven't they sent you a contract to sign?"

"Oh, I don't think that's necessary. I've been told that the Antioch Corey Library doesn't operate by conventional rules."

"Is that a fact? Well, I find that little short of disgusting!" He was staring at my blouse, as though hoping to see right through it. "This private library sounds very dubious to me. I've never even heard of the place. And why do you want to leave here? I thought you appreciated the prospects we can offer. I was looking forward to supervising your annual appraisal. I would have given you a good report. Provided," he took a Fisherman's Friend from his pocket and popped it into his mouth, "you had met the necessary targets."

"Targets?" I repeated the word with just a touch of irony in my tone but he didn't seem to notice.

"Yes, targets! We all need targets, and under my guidance you might even have met them."

He was speaking loudly, playing to the audience. He must have been aware that everyone in the office was listening to our conversation. People were hovering around the photocopier and the water fountain while casting intrigued glances in our direction and one young typist was actually standing on a chair and peering over the top of her partition.

"How soon can I leave?" I, too, raised my voice.

"There is a statutory month's notice." He sucked his lozenge noisily, shunting it against his teeth.

"But what about my holiday entitlement?" I asked. "Can't I just take that in lieu?"

"I'm afraid not."

I paused. Then, "What would happen if I just walked out?" I asked.

"I wouldn't advise you to do that. An employee who left without warning would be laying themselves open to suspicion. Head Office would investigate their record and if any financial irregularities were to be discovered or there was even a hint that they'd helped themselves to items of stationery, even so much as a paper clip....I'm sure you take my point."

"But I haven't done anything wrong."

"Perhaps not, but I do think you should consider your position carefully, Miss Gowdie. And what about this new job? You seem to have no details about it, no conditions of employment, salary, or pension scheme and there's no contract!"

"I'm not worried about that."

"Aren't you? You should be! Haven't you been sent *anything* apart from this peculiar letter?"

"Now that you mention it, there *was* one thing." I reached into my bag, took out the Talisman and placed it on the desk in front of him. "Here it is."

Finsworthy glanced down at the card.

"What on earth is this piece of rubbish?" he demanded to know.

"Are you sure it's rubbish?" I placed my hands behind my back and made the necessary signs with my fingers. The awakened conscience spell. I'd never tried it before, but it might just work. "Look at the words on the back," I said. "*Cavete ira mortuis.* That roughly translates as *Beware the anger of the dead.* Is there, perhaps, a person you've treated badly in the past? One who might now be dead?"

He swallowed. The boozy bloom leeched from his face. He turned a shade of mildewed grey-green. His eyes bulged like a bullfrog perplexed by a sudden loss of the ability to croak. He clapped his hand to his mouth. He gulped and emitted a ghastly, gurgling sound.

"Aaagh...uuuurgh!"

"Oh dear," I tried to sound solicitous. "Have you swallowed your Fisherman's Friend? You're only supposed to suck them, I believe."

"I...uuuurghhhh!" His shoulders heaved and he lowered his head, resting his forehead on the edge of his desk. "I..."

"Shall I call for First Aid?" I suggested.

"No...I....*urgh*!" With what seemed to be a supreme effort, he hawked violently and spat out the lozenge. Then he looked up at me, his eyes watering profusely. "I hope you'll be very happy in your new job, Jeanie," he gasped. "You can leave today and take an extra month's wages as a bonus. I'll arrange for the money to be delivered to you in cash by the end of the morning. After that, you're free to... *urgh*... go!"

"Thank you." I slipped the Talisman back into my bag. As I walked back to my desk, I kept my eyes down, avoiding the gaze of anyone who might have been watching. I didn't want to draw too much attention to myself.

I spent my bonus money on new clothes. I'd never had any interest in the latest fashion, so I didn't bother with the West End stores but trawled the street markets instead for ethnic garments in non-synthetic fabrics, in cotton, satin, silk and velvet. I bought long, beautifully patterned Indian skirts with tasselled belts, I bought wide-sleeved, scoop necked, embroidered cheesecloth blouses, I bought brocade waistcoats, a velvet dress and the pair of soft-soled canvas Chinese slippers that I'd promised myself. I dyed my hair with henna and bought myself a bagful of mascara, eye-shadow and blusher. Then I hurled all my sensible office clothes, the neat blouses that buttoned up to my chin, the gruesome tan tights, the old-fashioned court shoes, and the straight, knee-length skirts, into a black plastic sack and took them to the Salvation Army. I need never conceal my identity behind the staid façade of Miss Gowdie from the insurance office again. Now I was *really* ready to begin my new life.

Twelve

I knocked on the door marked ‘Custodian’ and waited, my insides fluttering with excitement. I’d been up since six o’clock, washing my hair, splashing on perfume, (a musky, enticing scent with a patchouli base), applying mascara and eye-shadow and choosing what to wear, and now here I was in a full length purple dress, my velvet cloak and my soft-soled Chinese shoes, ready for my first day at the Antioch Corey Library. But where, oh where, was Mr Llewellyn? I thought he’d be here to greet me and I’d been looking forward to meeting him again.

I knocked again but there was no response. I tried the handle; the door was locked. This was very disappointing and now, here was Ernest Brunswicker heading towards me, rattling along the gallery at an alarming speed, hunched over the handlebars of his ancient bike.

“Good morning, good morning,” he panted. “Delighted to have you on board. Come on up. I’ll show you the ropes. Follow me, follow me. Lots to explain.”

“Yes, of course,” I said. “Only...I thought I should report to Mr Llewellyn first.”

“Not here! Not here!” Mr Brunswicker shook his head. “Been away for days.”

“Oh.” I tried not to show my disappointment. “Do you happen to know when he’ll be back?”

"No idea. Don't even know where he's gone. Mystery tours! Mystery tours. Right! Let's go up to the Reading Room. Take the lift if you like. I've got to use the stairs!"

"I'll use the stairs too," I said.

"Follow me, then. Now, first thing I have to tell you, forget the Dewey system, assuming you ever knew it."

"The Dewey System?" I struggled to keep up as Mr Brunswicker hurtled ahead. "Isn't that how books are catalogued in all libraries? Oh, do you need any help with your...?"

"Bicycle? I can manage!" He began hoicking it up the stairs. I followed him, ready to assist if necessary, but he seemed to prefer an unaided struggle, a procedure that involved a lot of grunting and getting his untied shoe-laces entangled in the pedals.

"You have to understand," Mr Brunswicker heaved his bike up the final stair on to the top gallery with a stifled groan. "That everything we do here is in accordance with the instructions and systems that Antioch Corey laid down at the turn of the century. It was his wish that there should be no major changes. We still use the card indexes and the ledgers that were in use in his time, and have simply added to them. It's what our members expect. They hate anything new-fangled. Here we are then." He took a bunch of keys from his pocket and unlocked the door of the reading room. "Go and take a look. See if you can understand the classifications."

I walked along the shelves, reading the handwritten labels that had been placed inside small metal casings: *Language and Literature, Psychopathology, Philosophy, Teratology, Follies and Freaks in Philadelphia, Carnivals of the Mid-West, Native American Folklore, Neo-Platonist Survival in Nebraska.*

"Got it?" Leaning on his bicycle, Mr Brunswicker looked at me with an inquisitorial expression.

"Hardly anything appears to be in alphabetical order," I observed cautiously, unwilling to reveal my bafflement just yet.

"I should hope not!" he exclaimed. "The organization of the shelves isn't intended to be obvious. Antioch Corey devised a system of cross-referencing. Abstruse cross-referencing. You might say obfuscation. Yes, that's it, obfuscation!" Mr Brunswicker propped his bicycle against his desk and flexed his fingers, cracking the joints.

"Obfuscation?"

"I'm speaking of a necessary complexity. It can take weeks to find certain books. But, on the other hand, the way these volumes are arranged enables anyone browsing to make their own discoveries. Antioch Corey believed that a library should be like life, with all its strange, inter-connectedness. Random and surprising. And that's what stimulates good scholarship." He clenched his fists and rubbed his fingernails together, making a rather unpleasant sound. I did my best not to flinch.

"Yes," I agreed. "I suppose so."

"It takes years to learn anything worth knowing." He nodded his head vigorously. "Years! Agree?"

"Yes. I think I do."

"Good! Right then, let's get down to brass tacks. You'll be based in the parcels room. This way, this way."

I followed him to the far end of the reading room and through a door set in a partition resembling a gothic choir screen.

"As you can see," Mr Brunswicker indicated the partition's small glass windows. "You have a clear view of the reading room from here. Great advantage. Best to keep an eye on some of the visiting scholars. You can trust the regular readers implicitly, but sometimes certain people come here and break the rules. Just because a person is the top academic in their field it doesn't follow they're a paragon of virtue. Libraries are vulnerable places; the odd page snipped out with scissors, even an entire book slipped into a briefcase. Vigilance on our part is vital. Look around. Take stock."

He pulled out a chair, knocking over a stack of box files and disturbing a huge black moth. The creature, ragged-winged and of a species I'd never seen before, fluttered up to the ceiling and began to dance a fandango on the cracked plaster. I wasn't sure whether it was agitated or joyful.

I looked around my new work space. The sight of all these shelves, crowded with ancient ledgers and stacks of papers, filled me with joy. It was delightful, quite Dickensian in fact, and what fantastic old furniture too, that big desk with the ball and claw feet, the spoon-backed chairs, and the mahogany cabinets with the inlaid marquetry doors.

"What do you think?" Mr Brunswicker asked.

"I love it," I said.

"Good." He pulled at his finger-joints. "Now, let me explain the basics. Many of our members either live too far away or are too elderly (or both!) to visit the library in person, so we send books out to them. We allow a generous loan period, but academics can be forgetful. There's a Professor in Budapest, for example, who's had a volume on the Concord Transcendentalists out for fifteen years. It can be a problem getting books back, which we must do if another reader sends in a request for them. You'll have a lot of chasing-up letters to write!"

"I see." I nodded.

"Now, your main role will be to send out and check in the postal loans. Here's what you'll do. First, open the post. If you get a request for a postal loan, check that the person who sent the letter *is* a member; you'll find the directory of members over there." He pointed to the ledgers on the shelf. "Then find the book, and check its condition. Make a record of any hand-written notes you find, any torn pages or omissions. Then, of course, when, eventually, the book is returned, you have to do a counter-check. Make a record of any buffing of the bindings or marks that hadn't been there when it was sent out and look at every page. Any *new* pencilled notes in the margins can remain if they add to intellectual debate."

"How will I be able to judge if that's the case?" I asked.

"Simple enough. Comments such as 'piffle', 'nonsense' or 'imbecile' are cheap rhetoric, whereas a comment such as '*Professor Trilling has disproved this assertion in his footnote to....when he observes that....*' etcetera. I'm sure you can imagine the kind of thing I mean."

"Opinion backed up by evidence?" I suggested.

"Exactly!" He nodded vigorously. "Now, there are four main locations where books are kept. Here, in the reading room, obviously, on the shelves in the open galleries, no doubt you've noticed those, in the stacks and in the archives. It's very rare for anyone to want one of the books that are kept in the galleries; they're mainly legal documents and very few of our members take an interest in such things. If a book is on the reading room shelves, you can send it out straight away but you need the custodian's authority for any books in the archives. If the book's in the stacks, prepare for a long search and take a packed lunch with you!"

"What are the stacks?" I asked.

"Three floors of unclassified books at the back of the building. You'll need courage to venture up there. I never go there myself. Any questions?"

"So with these postal loans, where do I take them to be posted? Is there a post room or...?"

"You'll need to go to the post office in person. It's three streets away in Lincoln Terrace. Go in the mornings, between ten and eleven, before the queues build up. You can get money from the petty cash box, key in my desk. Help yourself, but, of course, keep an account of your spending and any receipts. We also have a cheque book for larger payments, collect it from me when you need it. I hope you like to be active, Miss Gowdie! You'll be moving around a lot."

"I shall enjoy that. I sat at a desk for hours on end in my last job. We weren't even allowed out of our cubicles except at set times."

"No such constraints here. Feel free to explore the building, take your lunch break when you choose, any time after twelve. And you can rearrange this room as much as you like, but don't throw anything out, unless, of course, it's an old apple core or a toffee wrapper. Have a read of the ledgers! Get to know the records. I expect you'll want to clear up that desk first. All those books shouldn't be piled up there, they need re-shelving. Glad to have you here! I'll let you get on. Yes, delighted!" He nodded vigorously and then charged out of the room backwards, returning, I supposed, to the comfort of his bicycle.

I sat down at the desk. It looked as though I was going to have to undertake a considerable amount of re-organising and tidying and, as Ernest Brunswicker had said, this was the logical place to start. Best get to work then.

I began clearing the teetering pile of books, sorting them as best I could into categories and placing them on the shelf behind me. I'd just managed to diminish the pile by half when I noticed an earthenware pot containing a small rosemary plant standing on the window sill. There was a tiny envelope sticking out of the soil, marked with my name. I tore it open and read the note that had been placed inside:

Welcome to the Antioch Corey Memorial Library, Jeanie.

I hope you will be happy here.

The message had been typed, but there was a squiggle at the bottom, handwritten in black ink. I couldn't quite make it out, but I was fairly sure it was 'L'. Ah, that must be 'L' for Llewellyn! How thoughtful of him to leave me a welcome gift. It seemed a little odd that he'd used a type-writer with several of the keys out of alignment and a worn-out ribbon; the letter he'd sent inviting me to my interview had been written in longhand. I sniffed the plant appreciatively; I loved all herbs, but rosemary was quite possibly my favourite, and this specimen, unseasonably enough, was still flowering. Rosemary. That signified remembrance. What was he trying to tell me? That he knew all about Nana, and the practical charms she'd taught me, using ingredients from the natural world? Or perhaps there was no message at all, it was simply ...My train of thought was interrupted by the door crashing open and a woman entering like a human tornado.

"*Vilkommen*!" The exuberance of the greeting was startling. I was about to meet a very loyal ally, and although I didn't know it yet, I was going to need all the support I could get.

The elderly woman had an ink stain on her blouse, her hair looked as if it had been in a wind-tunnel and the hem of dirndl skirt was hanging down. There was something rather endearing about so much dishevelment.

"I bring you home-made *apfel-strudel*." She bounded across the room and deposited a large plastic box on my desk. "So," she whipped off the lid with a flourish. "Every veek, I bring real Austrian pastries for my friends in the reading room and a few days ago, Ernest tells me ve have a new member of staff arriving today. So I make this especially for you."

"Thank you." I gazed down at the sugar-dusted confection with genuine pleasure. "That looks delicious. It's really kind of you."

"Enjoy!" She beamed. "But I am forgetting to introduce myself." She held out her hand. "I am Professor Gerda Goldfarb, Emeritus Professor, in fact, but let's not vorry about such details. Please call me Gerda."

"Lovely to meet you, Gerda." I shook her hand. "I'm Jeanie."

"Hello, Jeanie. Ve vill be seeing much of each other, since you are in charge of the parcels room and I am in the reading room every day. I come to research my book. I am vorking on it for five years now." She smiled, revealing two gold teeth on the upper left side of her mouth. "But I have yet to start the writing. I am still deep in the research."

"What's your subject?"

"My vorking title is *The Golem of Yonkers*. You are familiar with the Golem?"

"I've heard the legend, yes. A rabbi in Prague made a huge clay figure and brought it to life to protect the Jews."

"That is indeed the most famous account of a Golem," Gerda agreed. "But there are many other stories concerning such creations. In Africa, for example, straw men made by vitch-doctors have been known to dance. And some of these stories are not legends, in my opinion, but accounts of actual events. My book vill demonstrate that there was a Golem in

Yonkers, in the United States, at the time of Prohibition. Some vill, I expect, greet my book with scepticism, but it happened and I vill prove it!"

"It sounds really intriguing."

"I am certainly hoping to stir things up a bit in the vorld of folklore. Although the Yonkers Golem is the motif of my book, I vill also describe how many supernatural ideas came to America as a result of immigration. The people who arrived at Ellis Island from Eastern Europe did not leave their ghosts, their vampires, poltergeist, golems and demons behind, far from it! They brought them vith them, and so ve have American gothic. But I must not rattle on about my thesis, or ve vill be here all day. So, Ernest has been helping you settle in, I hope?"

"Yes. He's been very helpful. He seems a nice man."

"I am glad to hear you say that. And you are not vorried about the bicycle?"

"No...not at all...although it does seem a little.." I glanced back into the reading room where Ernest Brunswicker was bent over his desk. "Unusual," I added, in a whisper.

"Ah! You are vondering vy he is so attached to it." She, too, lowered her voice. "I tell you. He vouldn't mind you knowing." She closed the door behind her. "It began ven he vas fourteen. He saw God—or rather vat he conceived to be God—as he vas valking across Clapham Common. The terror of that moment, of that sensation of vastness and omnipotence, has never left him."

"How awful."

"Yes, awful in the true sense of the vord; he *vas* filled with awe. The bicycle is the only thing that stands between him and the shock of infinity. So now you know."

"Can't anything be done?"

"Vy should anything be done?" Gerda shrugged. "He had a mystical experience. I do not think he vould vant it any other way. So, do you like the library so far?"

"Yes, very much."

"Good. Ve are a happy group here, although I must varn you about one person. Be careful of Miss Plymouth Rock. I expect you know who I mean?" She gave me a knowing look.

"I've heard of Plymouth Rock," I said. "It's where the Pilgrim Fathers are said to have landed when they first came to America."

"Indeed. Their ship came aground on a cold, hard place. They vere fleeing persecution, but before long, they found their own means of oppression. No doubt you have heard of the vitchcraft trials that took place in Salem, Massachusetts in 1692, all those accusations, all that hysteria, all those people condemned to death? Even an ancestor of Antioch Corey vas a victim, Giles Corey, an old man pressed to death under rocks. That is vat they did. *The Puritans.* Puritans are dangerous people. So, ven I speak of Miss Plymouth Rock," she tapped the side of her nose. "Just look out for the Puritan."

Clemency Nantucket, I thought, that was who she meant. Clemency, with her well-scrubbed face and preoccupation with hygiene and blasphemy, her veiled hostility towards me and her disapproval of Mr Llewellyn.

"Are you referring to..." I chose my words carefully. "The person in charge of the archive room?"

"Indeed I am," Gerda said. "And that is not good. Yesterday, for example, she informs me that a particular book that I vant to consult has been lost, one that contained an account of a young voman in Pennsylvania possessed by a *dybbuk,* by a lost soul or demon, such a seminal piece of

Jewish folklore. I do not believe the book is lost. I believe Miss Plymouth Rock has disposed of the book herself."

"Why would she do that?"

"Vy? Because there are things of vich she does not approve. Magic, mythology, folk-lore, anything that does not conform to her narrow moral compass! And she harbours resentment. She vas here in the library long before Mr. Llewellyn came, and she thinks that she is senior to him. But she is not. Mr. Llewellyn is the person that Jabez Corey chose, and thank goodness for that. I did not care for his predecessor, a man alvays stupefied by drink."

"So how long has Mr Llewellyn been here?"

"It has been seven years now. I like the man. He is alvays so pleasant ven our paths cross, and yet, in all this time, I have learnt nothing about his personal circumstances. I believe that he is alone in the vorld."

"Why do you think that?"

"There is a certain sadness about him, the sadness of a man who has lost much, one who has been solitary for too long. He interests you, yes?"

"No! Not at all, that is..." I could feel my cheeks getting warm.

"Vould it be surprising if he did? Mr. Llewellyn is a handsome man. But I have gossiped enough. I must let you get on with your vork. You vill be thinking you have had enough of this tiresome woman who talks so much and knows everyone's business."

"I'm not thinking that at all. I'm interested in what you have to say. And I'm really grateful for the lovely strudel."

"*Bitte,* don't mention it. Enjoy your first day. If you need my help at any time, do not hesitate to ask. And remember," she winked at me. "Be careful of Miss Plymouth Rock!"

Thirteen

I'd enjoyed my morning's work. After tidying my desk, I'd opened the post, and made a start on the postal loan requests. I made slow progress, unfamiliar as I was with the shelving system, but by twelve o'clock I'd managed to locate three of the requested books; *The Myths and Legends of the Hopi Indians,* wanted by Mr N. Pardreson of Great Tarpots, Essex, *The Life and Death of Paul Bunyan*, for Professor Coldstream who lived in Victor Harbor, Australia, and *The Posthumous Poetry of Walt Whitman as dictated to Ethan Crowley Jnr,* requested by Dr Adam Furbridge of Nuneaton, a subscriber who clearly had a more open mind than Clemency when it came to mediums. After writing out a few address labels, I ventured back into the reading room.

"Mr Brunswicker, sorry to disturb you but..."

"What?" He looked up from his crossword with an impatient expression.

"I was wondering about stationery. I've looked in the cupboard and I couldn't find any sellotape or any packaging apart from brown paper, string and sealing wax."

"Why would you want anything else? It's what our subscribers expect! Tradition, the old ways! Sellotape is a cursed modern invention. Antioch Corey would never have touched the stuff. Have you any skill with string?"

"Oh, yes," I told him. "I'm a dab hand at knots. When I was at school, I had a friend who'd been a boy scout." Poor

Bushy; he'd unwittingly caused me a lot of unhappiness, but at least I could be grateful to him for that.

"Good." Mr Brunswicker cracked his knuckles. "Then use plenty of string and make sure you wrap the books in several layers of old newspaper first, putting extra padding around the spine. Don't omit the sealing wax; you'll find the library stamp in your desk drawer. Do you want to take your lunch break now?"

"Yes, thank you."

"Good. Suggest you go down to Psyche's place. Small café, for staff and scholars. Take the lift to the basement, turn sharp left. It's at the end. You can't miss it."

The low, curved ceiling in Psyche's place suggested this had once been a cellar of some kind, perhaps for storing wine. The room contained several tables, with seating for six people at each; there was a serving area with a small kitchen at the back. Clemency Nantucket, dressed in her jeans, sneakers and checked shirt, and with her hair covered by a brown scarf, was the only person there. She had a slice of fruit cake on her plate but she wasn't eating it, just pushing it around with her forefinger.

"Oh, it's you." She looked up at me as I entered. "I didn't know you were starting today. No-one told me."

"Yes, here I am." I did my best to sound bright and friendly.

"Psyche has popped out but help yourself to whatever you want," she said. "The honesty box is over there, by the cutlery."

"Thanks." I went over to the counter. There was a soup tureen standing on a hot-plate, and a selection of cakes, sandwiches and rolls. I picked up a cheese and tomato sandwich, found the right change and dropped it into the box. Now I faced a dilemma; should I sit with Clemency or at another table? I didn't want to appear unfriendly, but I also doubted if she'd welcome my company. It occurred to me that whatever I chose to do would be wrong in her eyes.

"It's very quiet in here," I said.

"It usually is at this time of day. That's why I chose to come in now. I'm not fond of socialising when I'm eating." She picked a sultana out of her cake and laid it on the side of her plate with the same expression of distaste she might have shown if she'd found a dead fly.

"I won't disturb you, I hope." I sat down at an adjacent table.

"Well, you're here now." Clemency spoke in a flat, unenthusiastic tone. "To tell the truth, I was very surprised to hear of your appointment. A year ago, I approached the trustees to ask if I could have an assistant in the archives and I was informed that there was no money to pay for extra staff. Still, Ernest Brunswicker will be glad of your help. He'll be able to stay at his desk all day, instead of clanking around the building all the time with his bicycle. Did you know he even takes it to the Gents with him?"

"Well, that's really his business, isn't it?"

"Gee!" She opened her eyes wide. "I hope you don't think I'm criticising the poor guy!"

"Oh, no, I didn't think that at all," I assured her.

"Mind you," she picked out a currant. "It's not exactly restful having him around. At least he rarely comes in here and never when soup's on the menu. He has a phobia about spoons."

"Spoons?" I hadn't intended to be drawn into gossip but now my curiosity was aroused. "Why spoons?"

"I have no idea." She rubbed a cake crumb between her fingers. "Is he still encouraging all those hangers-on?"

"Hangers-on?"

"I daresay Ernest would call them the reading room regulars, but I call them hangers-on. You'll see a lot of them about, especially in the winter. I strongly suspect that some of them aren't engaged in any serious scholarship at all. There's a filthy old man who sits by the window and does nothing except encourage the pigeons. Have you seen him yet?"

"No." I took a bite of my sandwich, wishing I was somewhere else. I wouldn't eat in Psyche's place at this time of day again, I told myself.

"And then there's the woman who calls herself a Professor," Clemency continued. "Her name's Gerda Goldfarb. Maybe she was really a Professor once, in some obscure European hole, but I doubt it."

"I've met Gerda. She seems nice."

"You reckon? Well, whatever you do, don't eat any of her pastries. I suspect she bakes them in the cockroach-infested kitchen of some dirty little flat off the Balls Pond Road." She held another sultana up to the light.

"What on earth makes you think that?" I'd intended not to rise to her bait, but now I felt stung into defending my new friend.

"No reason." She shrugged. "Although you will find that hygiene is a low priority for many academics. Tell me, have Salutation and Providence taken you on to the permanent staff or are you on a short term contract?"

"Salutation and Providence?" I was surprised to hear such archaic names. "I'm afraid I don't know who they are."

"Miss Salutation Corey and Miss Providence Corey are two long serving trustees of the library. They sent me here to England fifteen years ago to take charge of the archives. It's rather remiss of Mr. Llewellyn not to mention them to you."

"But I understood that Mr. Jabez Corey was the senior trustee," I said. "He was the person who offered me this job. And yes, it is permanent."

"I *see.*" The second word emerged as a hiss. "In that case there is no point discussing the matter. Well," she stood up, pushing back her chair with a violent scrape. "I've got a lot of work to do. I think I'll finish my lunch at my desk." She turned, seized a banana from the counter and, leaving the remnants of her demolished cake where it was, stalked out without another word. I stared at the scattering of crumbs and dried fruit. It seemed Gerda was right. I *would* have to be wary of Miss Plymouth Rock.

At half past five, Ernest Brunswicker appeared in the doorway of the parcels room and informed me, in an abrupt bark, that I was free to pack up for the day.

"So soon?" I looked up from the *Directory of Life Members* in which I'd been engrossed. "I didn't realise the library closed this early."

"It doesn't." He clenched his hands and rubbed his fingernails together, jerking his body around on the spot. "Different closing times each night. Seven o'clock on Tuesdays and Thursdays. Eight o'clock on Mondays, Wednesdays and Fridays, closed Saturday afternoons, open alternate Saturday mornings, closed on Sunday, closed on Bank Holidays, and on the fourth of July and during Christmas, Easter and Whitsun. Got that?"

"I think so," I said, my mind reeling. "Although," I added, "It would help if I could have all that written down."

"I can do that. And I'll work out a rota. Some nights, I'll leave early, others, you will. The last hour or so in the reading room is always quiet, doesn't need two of us to be here. We'll share the responsibility. Will that suit you?"

"Yes. That will be fine."

"You'll need keys, of course." He ran his fingers through his toilet brush hair. "Completely forgot to order you keys! I'll get on to Jim about it."

"Jim?"

"Jim is the caretaker."

"Oh, I see. I haven't met him yet."

"You won't meet him. I've never met him."

"Not met him?" I was surprised.

"Of course I haven't met him! He's not on duty in the daytime."

"Oh?"

"He works here at night, night watchman as well as caretaker. He clocks in when the library closes. But if you need anything done, like a cupboard door put back on its hinges, or a light bulb changed, write Jim a note and pop it into the box outside his room. That's in the basement, at the opposite end to Psyche's place, near the fire doors. Got that? Good." He glanced at the *Directory of Life Members* lying open on the desk in front of me. "Ah, I see you're acquainting yourself with the records. Excellent."

"Yes, they make fascinating reading," I said. "All these details about the people who've used the library, their dates of birth, and the books they borrowed. And there are so many famous people listed here as subscribers, Bertrand Russell, Sir Arthur Conan Doyle, William Butler Yates, Dion Fortune, and even Aleister Crowley."

"The notorious, self-styled Satanist!" Ernest exclaimed. "Indeed he was a member at one time although I think you'll find Crowley was expelled from the library in 1934 for an attempted theft."

"Oh, that explains the big black cross against his name," I said.

"Quite."

"I'm just wondering...." I hesitated. "Are all these records complete?"

"As far as I know. Why do you ask?"

"Well," I turned over the stiff pages of the ledger. "I've noticed that most of the early entries end with the word 'Deceased' and the date of death, but there are quite a few with only a date of birth. There's one here for example, Professor Clarence Galsworthy, born 1855."

"What of it?" Mr Brunswicker pulled at his knuckles. "Perhaps some of these elderly scholars outlived their next of kin and there was no-one around to inform the library of their demise."

"I thought of that," I said. "But Professor Galsworthy last borrowed a book in 1968, when he'd have been..."

"A hundred and thirteen," Mr Brunswicker nodded.

"But that's extraordinary."

"Some people are blessed with unusual longevity, you know."

"But not very many, surely? You see, Professor Galsworthy isn't the only member who seems to have survived well beyond his hundredth year. There are about thirty or forty of them. Blavatsky Cummings." I peered at the list I'd scribbled down on a scrap of paper. "Annie Kensington, Maximilian Stanhope...I couldn't quite make this one out, it looked like Hardy Sackeandsugar, but surely no-one could have a name like that?"

"No point in speculating." Ernest Brunswicker dismissed my interest with a warning look. "Well, as I said, you're free to go home now. Oh, and don't expect the Antioch Corey Library to yield up all its secrets at once. That really wouldn't do at all. Please be patient, Miss Gowdie."

Fourteen

I sat down on a bench in the entrance hall, removed my soft-soled Chinese slippers and took my boots out of a draw-string canvas bag that Dorian had given me when I first bought them. As I put them on and began to lace them up, I marvelled once again at how well they fitted me. And the leather was so soft, that too was remarkable.

There was an eerie stillness all around me in this solemn space; blue flames flickered from the brazier, casting shadows on Antioch Corey's death mask, thin ribbons of smoke spiralled up from the incense burners. If you dropped a coin here, the sound would echo throughout the building. I was about to get up to leave for home when rain began pattering down on the glass dome high above. Perhaps it was only a shower. I might wait here until it stopped.

I leant back against the wall; how drowsy I was, suddenly, but I was tired in a pleasant way after a day well spent and one that had included two gifts to welcome me, Gerda's home-made strudel and the pot of rosemary, a sharp contrast to my first day at the insurance office where no-one even showed me where to find the tea urn. I was sure I was going to be happy here.

So the Antioch Corey Library wasn't going to yield up all its secrets at once, eh? It did seem there were several mysteries to solve; a caretaker that no-one ever saw, books that were shelved in disorder, a plethora of centenarians amongst the subscribers. And then there was peculiar hostility of Clemency Nantucket. Well, I was determined I'd get to grips with all of this. I liked a challenge.

"The Obeah man, he come, he come and take you away." Psyche's voice drifted down from the first floor gallery. I looked up and caught a glimpse of her carrying her mop and bucket but she seemed oblivious of my presence *"You see him soon, the Obeah man..."*

My eyes closed, but a moment later, I was roused by the sound of the revolving doors as a man with a long black coat over his shoulders entered the building, a Gladstone bag in his left hand and his right arm bent across his chest. He was walking so slowly and wearily that for a moment, I didn't realise who it was. Then I saw that it was *him.*

"Mr Llewellyn?"

"Good grief!" He stopped in his tracks, standing stock still and staring at me as if deeply shocked.

"What's wrong?" I leapt to my feet.

"Forgive me." He put down his bag. "I wasn't expecting... At first, I thought you were...seeing you there, your hair, so different, that cloak, the boots..." He rubbed his forehead with the fingertips of his left hand. "I'm sorry. Pay no attention to my ramblings. I'm over-tired and ..." His coat slipped from his shoulders, and now it was my turn to be shocked.

"Oh!" I moved towards him, gazing in consternation at the blood-stained cloth that was roughly knotted around his right hand. "Mr Llewellyn, you're hurt!"

"It's nothing."

"But it's very far from nothing!" I exclaimed. "There's blood on your shirt too, on the collar and... Please let me see, I want to help."

"Jeanie, *no.* Please lower your voice." He looked up towards the gallery. "Not here...no-one must...anyone could overhear..."

"There's no-one here, only Psyche and she's up there and surely she wouldn't... "

"Even so, we can't talk about it now. Please sit down again. I'll join you and we'll pretend to be having an ordinary conversation about something trivial."

"But..."

"*Please.*" He picked up his bag and coat.

"All right." I felt very reluctant about complying with his request. Suppose he'd sustained a really serious injury? He certainly looked very pale.

"So, Jeanie," he sat down on the bench. "I hope you've had a good first day. I'm sorry I wasn't here to greet you, but my flight was delayed."

"Oh, that's all right. I got your note."

"My note?" He sounded puzzled. "I'm afraid I didn't leave you a note. Now I really do feel remiss."

"So you didn't you give me this?" I pointed to the pot of rosemary that was sticking out of the carrier bag I'd found in a cupboard in the parcels room.

"No." He smiled. "If I was going to give a lady some vegetation, I would have chosen something more exotic, something with crimson petals and scented blooms."

"Oh, but I like herbs," I said. "And this is rosemary for remembrance."

"Except that I forgot." He smiled ruefully.

"It's my mistake." I tried not to show my disappointment. "But if you didn't give this to me, then who did?"

"The Obeah man, he come and take you away..." The crooning voice was getting fainter.

"Perhaps it was Psyche." He glanced upwards. "She can be very taciturn, but she has other ways of communicating and she has a good heart. You've met her, I assume?"

"Yes, when I came for my interview. It was...a little strange. It was as though she'd been expecting me. I'd never seen her before in my life."

"Interesting." He looked down at his hand. I could see that some blood was seeping through the makeshift bandage. Why on earth were we sitting here, having this conversation, when I could be administering the first aid he quite obviously needed?

"I suppose you've just come back from America," I said.

"Yes, and I'm sorry to say that I found Jabez Corey in much poorer health than I anticipated. He's reached an advanced age, of course, but the Coreys are a hardy family. I wasn't expecting to find him so frail. It's possible he won't last long into the New Year."

"Oh, that's really sad," I said. "He wrote to me, offering me this job."

"I know. I was with him when he composed the letter. And I believe he sent you something else too. I hope you know how to make good use of it."

"Yes I do. It's already proved very effective." I smiled inwardly at the memory of Finsworthy's discomfort.

"Mr Corey is comforted to know you're here. I told him all about you, of course. It's very hard to find kindred spirits in the modern world. Some of us have to tread a lonely, difficult path. I think you understand what I mean."

"Yes, I do." I gazed across the hall at Antioch Corey's death-mask, at the shuttered eyes lit by the flickering blue flame. "I'm just wondering, why does Jabez Corey live in Massachusetts when the library is in London?"

"There are legal complications. Antioch Corey was born in America but he had many differences with his family, so he settled in England. He cut off all his family ties, apart from those with his great-nephew Jabez. Jabez still has connections with his home country and owns several properties....”

‘The Obeah man...’ I could only just hear Psyche now.

“I expect you’ve noticed that Psyche only has one song,” Llewellyn said. “And she never finishes it. But one day she will and a force will be unleashed strong enough to shake the whole of London. The Caribs are powerful people.”

“She’s a Carib? Like Tituba in the Salem witch trial?”

“Exactly.”

I glanced up at the gallery. “She’s gone,” I said. “Can’t you tell me what’s happened now?”

“Very well.” He lowered his voice. “You must tell no-one about this, but, out there in the square, I had to fight off a knife attack.”

“A knife?” I’d raised my voice in horror. “You could have been killed!”

“Jeanie! *Ssssh!*”

“Sorry. But,” I swallowed, “Shouldn’t you tell the police?”

“It’s not a matter for the police. And I will survive a few nicks and scratches.”

“But it’s more than that!”

“I admit it was a fairly frenzied assault, designed to get me to let go of my bag, even if it meant severing a finger or two. But I didn’t lose the bag and, as you can see, I still have all of my fingers.” He wiggled them playfully.

“And did you get the better of your attacker?”

“Oh yes. My assailant won’t be able to return.”

“Oh goodness, does that mean that you ...?”

“No.” He shook his head. “I haven’t killed anyone if that’s what you’re thinking. You can’t kill something that’s already dead.”

"Already ....*oh*!" My stomach flipped over. "What do you mean?"

"Sorry. I didn't mean to alarm you. And now, I can't say any more. There's much more to explain, but this isn't the place. Tomorrow, come to my office and...."

"Good evening."

I jumped, startled by that insidious voice. Clemency had done it again with her silent, sneaker-clad approach. Now she was gazing at us from the top of the staircase like a judge about to pronounce a heavy custodial sentence. Neither of us moved as she descended the stairs.

"Mr Llewellyn, you appear to have cut yourself." She stood in front of us. "Did you place your hand in a mincer?"

"I was rather careless." He spoke in a casual tone. "There was a smashed bottle on the entrance steps and I picked up all the pieces of broken glass with my fingers."

"You should be more careful." Clemency's voice oozed with false concern. "Cuts can become septic if they're not treated, you know. And then there's the risk of tetanus."

"I'm sure you're right, but I was worried about our readers, some of whom are quite elderly. One of them might have slipped on the debris. It wasn't easy to see it in the dark."

"How lucky that *you* saw it, then," she said. "Although how odd that you appear to have injured the back of your hand while your finger-tips appear to be unharmed. Also, you appear to have jabbed yourself in the neck."

"As I said, I was careless." He stood up. "Call it male clumsiness, if you like. Now, if you'll excuse me, I'm sure a lot of post must have arrived for me while I've been away."

"Before you go," Clemency was gazing hungrily at his bag. "Can we could talk about an issue that concerns me?

It seems to me that there are a number of valuable books that should be moved from the open shelves into the archives. I really would appreciate your support in this matter."

"I'll be delighted to discuss it tomorrow."

"I'd prefer to talk about it now." She blocked his path as he attempted to move towards the stairs. "It's not beyond the bounds of possibility that thieves could get into the library at night, intent on robbery. We can't take risks. This is urgent."

"So is my need to check my post and then get some rest." He spoke without rancour, but now there was a dangerous glint in his eye. "With respect, Miss Nantucket, I think you are being over-anxious. The building is secure at night. We have a night watchman who sees to that. I'm sorry if I sound abrupt, but I've spent several nights watching over a dying man, my old friend Jabez Corey, and then I had a very turbulent flight back from the States. I can't deal with this now. Why don't you send me a list of your proposals and concerns, Miss Nantucket, and I'll look them over them tomorrow."

"Is that your answer?"

"It is indeed."

"I see." Clemency tightened her lips. "Well, I suppose that will have to do. Good night, then. I'll be in the archive room until closing time if anyone needs me." She turned on her heel and left us, apparently accepting defeat.

"And now," Mr Llewellyn turned towards me. "You must excuse me too. Good night, Miss Gowdie."

"Good night," I said. I didn't want to leave, but it seemed I'd been dismissed. I stood for a moment, watching him as he went up the stairs, and then, unable to do more, I gathered up my things and, with considerable reluctance, went out into the night.

Fifteen

It was hardly surprising that I felt deeply troubled as I made my way home that night. I couldn't get the thought of Mr Llewellyn fighting off an attacker armed with a knife in a dark London square out of my mind, *an attacker who was already dead,* and as for Clemency's behaviour, that had been menacing to say the least. Was she involved in some way, could she be an accomplice? Certainly her comments about cuts turning septic had seemed deeply malicious. I must do something about that; there were certain folk remedies for treating wounds that I could take into work tomorrow. I would just have to persuade this unpredictable, elusive man to allow me to administer them. As for the rest, I wasn't at all convinced that the danger was past. A powerful protective spell was needed. But did I even know one?

I remembered, long ago, on Walpurgis Night, Nana telling me about the shield of Osiris and Anubis. She'd warned me to use it with extreme caution:

'Do not call upon these ancient gods for any trivial reason, Jeanie and never for your own safety. First, be aware that the gods named here are not our friendly, Celtic gods of nature and harvest, not Epona, or Lugh or Cernunnos; they are gods of the underworld, dealers in matters of life and death, and there could be unforeseen consequences if you summon them. You should only cast this spell when someone for whom you care is in extreme danger.

Your heart must be filled with anxious foreboding as you ache to protect that person at all cost. And it's not a spell for a novice.'

Aching? Anxious foreboding? Yes, I could relate to that. Whatever the dangers, if all else failed, I would try that spell.

It was a relief to be back in my basement flat; there'd been something strange in the air tonight, weird rustlings behind me as I walked along the road by the old cemetery, a feeling of being watched, although I told myself it must be my imagination. I locked my front door from inside, lit the black candles on the mantelpiece, changed into my kaftan and placed the pot of rosemary on the window sill beside my other herbs. Then I reached under my couch for my little brown suitcase. I remembered how relieved I'd been when they finally gave it back to me as I left Crowsmuir Hall; it seemed no-one had suspected the true identity of the objects in the old toffee tin. Perhaps, indeed, no-one had even opened the lid to examine them. Nana had disguised my apprentice tools well; only a fellow practitioner would see that the old butter knife with the scratches on the bone handle was a runic blade, the white stone was a vision charm, the metal dish was a scrying vessel and the candle-stub an everlasting light.

I laid a black cloth out on the carpet and arranged the objects in a semi-circle. I filled my scrying-vessel with water and sprinkled oil and hemlock seeds on the surface, then gazed into it for a full five minutes, before speaking the words of command: *Show me the danger that surrounds him. Tell me what I can do.* I knelt there for a very long time, until my back was stiff and my knees were aching, but not a single vision appeared. And then I started thinking about other things, speculating about the person who'd given me the pot of rosemary, reminding myself to call in to Pyewacket's to tell Dorian about that key... Stop this, Jeanie! I came back to my present task with a start. How could I have let my concentration drift so badly? Surely I, Jeanie Gowdie, the grand-daughter of Maudie Herrick, could do better than this? Flooded with shame, I gazed down at my apprentice tools. The fact that I was still using them meant I was still a novice, and that was the nub of the problem. The situation was desperate; I was only a few months away from twenty-first birthday, when I was supposed to have my Coming of Age ceremony and adopt my True Name. But I'd spent two years at Crowsmuir Hall, where it had been impossible to do any training for that day. And now time was running out. Still, I told myself, all would be well if Mr Llewellyn helped me, as I was certain he would. And now I must help him.

I stood up, holding my runic knife in my right hand. I hoped I could remember the invocation:

"Osiris, dark master of the underworld, Anubis, guardian of the passage of the dead, keep his enemies away and protect him with your power. Keep him safe. Let no wraiths or hop-goblins, no murderous assassins or evil spirits come near him. I, Mor--"

"Bloody hell, Gowdie! You'll have to do better than that."

Oh! I almost dropped my knife. That voice! Bushy's voice, here in the room with me. And this wasn't what I'd wanted. I hadn't intended to summon up the dead.

"Leave me alone, Bushy!" I felt indignant. "I've forgiven you for everything, but that doesn't give you the right to haunt me."

"Oh, is *that* who you think I am? Well, well...." The voice was both plaintive and insidious and now it occurred to me that it wasn't Bushy speaking to me from beyond the veil at all, but some clever imitation of his voice from an evil spirit. This was something beyond my capabilities. I had no idea what to do. I'd just have to improvise.

"Go away! This is my domain!" I whirled around, pointing my runic knife at the corners of the room. "Go! I conjure you to return to wherever you came from and..."

There was a crash as the pot of rosemary fell from the window sill. Now there was a mess of soil and shards of broken pottery scattered over the floorboards, but there was also silence. The spirit, whether it had been Bushy or an imposter, seemed to have departed.

I felt a mixture of disappointment and relief. The spell had been unsuccessful, but at least no real damage had been done, apart, of course, to the rosemary. With a sigh, I put down the knife and went to clear up the debris. And it was then that I saw just what had fallen out from the pot.

I knelt down, prodding the items with the tip of my finger, feeling a deep sense of distaste. These were not the things I'd have expected to find accompanying a welcome gift. The dried leg and webbed foot of an amphibian, probably a salamander, a piece of bone that was almost certainly of human origin, perhaps filched from a Bronze Age burial site by the light of a harvest moon, a yellowed, decayed tooth, and a square of snake skin. The significance was clear to me. These were tokens of malediction, designed to activate a spell against me. *Rosemary for remembrance.*

Of course! *Now* I understood. The words in that note, '*I hope you will be happy here'*, had been meant ironically. But who had written it? Surely it couldn't have been Psyche, I had no sense that she wished me any ill will. I didn't think it could be Clemency either; she was almost certainly opposed to magic and charms, and her puritan mind would baulk at resorting to them. But it seemed that someone in the library knew my secret and that person wanted to torment me with my past, perhaps even blackmail me. It was deeply unsettling; the curse seemed to be working. I'd done everything I could to put it all behind me, but now, unbidden, the memories were flooding back.

Sixteen

September 1970

"This lad you've been seeing, this Bushy," Nana Herrick knelt down on the rag-rug she'd brought out from the back parlour. "Are you sweet on him, Jeanie?" She took a wooden spoon from her apron pocket and made a shallow trench in the earth. "I think I'll plant some extra chervil and tarragon," she added. "Last year we ran short."

I stood on the path, ready to put our usual protections into place. Everything was prepared, the triangles of silver foil and bottle tops threaded on black cotton to deter the birds, the crushed egg-shells to keep the slugs at bay, the nets to place over the young shoots.

"Why don't we just protect the seeds with a charm?" I asked.

"That wouldn't be right, Jeanie. Haven't I told you that we must be careful about using our powers for own personal gain?"

"But this would be to benefit the plants."

"Here, in the garden, it's better to let nature take its course."

I nodded in agreement, although I'd often wondered whether Nana did use spells, secretly, when I wasn't looking. Her plants and herbs grew so prodigiously, a rampant proliferation of aromatic vegetation. She grew all the usual herbs for cooking, mint, tarragon, sage, basil and thyme, and others for medicinal and more arcane use. Borage to banish the black dog of melancholia, angelica root to dispel anxiety, feverfew to soothe headaches, catnip for animal pleasure, fenugreek for felicity. The darker stuff grew by the wall out of the sun. Belladonna and henbane, and something called Stinking Horus, and, most sinister of all, Asafoetida or the devil's dung, lurking in the dank area beneath the hemlock tree.

"Sometimes, of course we can intervene," Nana told me. "If a neighbour came to me and complained that her apple trees had been blighted by sawfly, or that her baby was grievously sick, then there are things I would do. But remember this. Never curse an enemy and never seek revenge for your own hurt. And if you ever fall in love, never try to ensnare the man with potions. He must care for you for your own sake. And the time must be right too. This is the best time for sowing, when the early frosts are over and the ground is warm and ready. And it's the same with love. Do you take my meaning?"

"I'm not sure that I do, Nana."

"I'm saying that green shoots are easily blighted by cold. It would be all too easy to give your heart when you're young and inexperienced. "

"Oh, I won't give my heart to Bushy," I assured her. "He's just a friend."

"Your mother had your confidence when she was your age." Nana sat back on her heels. "And then..." She shook her head.

"What happened to her, Nana? You've never told me."

"I don't care to speak of it. Now then, pass me the watering can. We must bed the seeds in and keep them moist if they're to prosper." She picked up a snail between her thumb and forefinger and carried across to the place where the dock leaves and the yarrow grew. "There's nothing wrong with becoming fond of a lad," she continued, "But you need to know your own mind. Bushy, that's rather an unusual name."

"It's the nickname they gave him at his old school," I said. "Because of his hair. It's thick and it sticks up all around his head like a dandelion clock."

Nana smiled at the description, but not unkindly.

"Are his parents good people?" she asked.

"I don't think so. His father walked out when he was a lot younger and his mother's usually drunk."

"That seems sad for him."

"I suppose it is. He's quite well off, though and he knows a lot of things. He's got books on astronomy and maths and physics and…all kinds of other stuff."

I was certain that Nana wouldn't like some of Bushy's reading material. There was that pile of old medical books under his bed that automatically fell open at the more explicit anatomical diagrams and the sections on venereal disease. He also had a copy of the *Kama Sutra*, and a translation of Sprenger and Kramer's *Malleus Malificarum,* with its stories about witches who stole men's private parts and hid them in bird's nests. I didn't much like that book myself. It was a vile work authored by vile men who'd done evil things and who described spell-craft in terms that were as far removed from everything I'd learnt from Nana as Neptune was from the sun.

"Well, Jeanie, I hope he's a good friend to you," Nana said.

"Oh, he is." Even as I said it, I wasn't sure it was true. Bushy was the first ally I'd ever had at St. Aggie's, but sometimes he made me feel uncomfortable. I was worried that he wanted more from me than I was prepared to give and there was something peculiarly needy about him. I didn't like that at all.

The day I met Bushy was the same day that something happened that led, indirectly but inexorably, to my incarceration at Crowsmuir Hall. I was in the school canteen, carrying my tray to a table when I slipped on a slick of boiled cabbage and fell down with a crash, twisting my ankle. The pain brought the tears to my eyes.

"Loser! Sticky-knickers! Bitch!" Chrissie Wilkinson, a girl who had never liked me, yelled.

As I struggled to my feet, I gazed back at her, hoping to appear cool and unmoved. Then one of Nana's sayings had come into my mind: '*Sticks and stones may break my bones, but at Lammas tide, cruel words will rebound on the giver*'. What happened next was as much a surprise to me as it must have been to Chrissie.

She made a strange noise, and then, soundlessly, she began to jerk up and down, one hand on her throat, the other waving her fork. At first, I thought this was all part of the mockery and then it became clear she was in distress. There was half a roasted potato on the fork she was waving in the air; the other half must be lodged in her throat. And now she was going blue.

Just as it seemed Chrissie might actually expire, the new Games Mistress, Miss Tolpuddle, a woman with beefy arms and a booming voice, rushed into the room and administered the Heimlich manoeuvre. Unfortunately, she did this with rather too much energy, dislodging the potato, but also breaking one of Chrissie's ribs. An ambulance was summoned; the school fell silent in shock. And then people started looking at me in a wary manner.

"Hey! Gowdie! I saw what you did!"

I lowered my racket. A tall, male person in shorts was staring at me through the wire fencing of the school tennis court. How dare he yell at me like that? Had he no manners? What he *did* have were legs like a stork and a voice like a strangulated cat.

I was tired of practising my serve all on my own, but this wasn't a welcome interruption. I was used to being bullied at St. Aggie's. It had started when I was in the first year, taunts shouted across the lacrosse-pitch, *'Hey, Gowdie, is it true about the bedbugs in your Dad's grotty old Guest House?'*, nasty whispers that I overheard in the gym changing room, '*That girl Jeanie Gowdie's got holes in her tights, and I bet she's got lice in her hair!'* And even now, in the lower sixth form, none of the girls liked me. But here was a boy, and I knew little about them, St Aggie's having only just become co-ed.

"Hey! Gowdie! That was a brilliant hex!" He seemed determined not to leave me alone.

Hex. I couldn't have words like that hurled in my direction. I ran out through the gate and ducked behind the rhododendron bush, pretending to be searching for a lost tennis ball. Over by the pavilion, I could see Angela Barnet and Venetia Carlisle talking in a conspiratorial huddle with some other girls. I knew what it must be; they were planning revenge.

I felt a jab on my shoulder.

"Hello, Gowdie."

"Go away."

"Don't be like that." The boy with the stork legs kicked at a stone with the toe of his tennis-shoe.

"You're very rude," I said.

"Rude? I didn't mean to be." He looked abashed.

I was almost beginning to feel sorry for him. He seemed to be a loner like me.

"You shouted," I said. "And you called me Gowdie."

"I thought that was your name. It's what everyone else calls you around here."

"Yes," I admitted. "They do. But that's because they don't like me. It's my surname. None of the other girls get called by their surname. Haven't you noticed?"

"I can't say that I have. I'm new here. But I saw what you did today in the dining hall. I thought you'd killed that girl for a minute. What's her name?"

"Chrissie Wilkinson." I said.

"Bet you feel like the cat who got the cream."

"I don't."

"I thought it was great, the way you hexed her," Bushy said.

"I never hexed her," I retorted. "It's wrong to hex people to the point of death."

"Oh." A smile spread across his face. "So you do know what 'hex' means. I thought you did. And where do you keep your *hexenbessen*, then?"

"This conversation is getting annoying," I said, moving away. I'd studied two languages at 'O' level and I knew perfectly well that *hexenbessen* was German for a traditional broomstick, but I wasn't going to encourage him.

"So, Gowdie, what's your first name then?" He followed me. "Is it Isobel?"

"No. Why should it be?"

"Don't you know about Isobel Gowdie?" He swung his tennis racket in a sweeping arc. "Isobel Gowdie was the greatest witch Scotland ever knew. But perhaps you're going to be even greater, doing a hex like that."

"Will you *please* stop saying that word!"

"I bet I'm not the only one who thinks you gave Chrissie Wilkinson the evil eye. I wish you'd teach me how to do a hex."

"I've had enough," I said. "Just go away."

"Oh, don't talk like that." He looked at me with big, pleading eyes. "I'm sorry. I was just trying to be friendly. Listen, it's boring as hell here. Why don't we both bunk off? It's last lesson after all. We could get away on your *hexenbessen* if you like. What do you say, Isobel?"

I glanced over to the pavilion and thought of the danger I might be in if I stayed. Venetia and Angela were Chrissie's friends; who knew what they might be planning? On the other hand, did I really want to play truant with this annoying boy?

"Nobody would miss us," he said. "Let's face it. We're spares as far as afternoon games are concerned."

"OK, then," I said, "Let's go."

"What's your name, then?" I asked, as we slipped out through the fence into the street.

"I'm Bushy," he said. "It's a nickname. But I prefer it to my real name."

"And what is your real name?"

"I'll show you." He pulled an exercise book out of his kitbag and pointed to the name 'James Finklebaum' that was scrawled across the front, alongside several cartoons of skulls and cross-bones and little stick figures fighting with hammers. "Take a look through this, if you like. It's got my essays in it. You can give it back tomorrow."

"All right." Hardly knowing why I'd agreed, I stuffed the exercise book into my bag.

"So." He pulled a handful of leaves off a privet hedge and threw them into the air. "Where are we going then? The chippie or the park?"

"Neither."

"Then come back to my house, I can show you the book I've got about Isobel Gowdie. Do you like books?"

Of course, I loved books. I was weakening, although I could hardly bear to admit it to myself.

"I hope you like books because I've got absolutely hundreds," he said. "I could lend some of them to you if you like. I can hardly move round my room because of all the books. They're stacked up everywhere. Come and see. It's not far from here. On the Fallowfield Estate."

Bushy's parents must be quite rich then. The Fallowfield estate had a gated entrance and there were red-brick executive-style houses with pitched roofs, large porches and dormer windows.

"Are you coming then?" he asked.

"All right," I shrugged. "But I won't be able to stay for very long."

The hallway in Bushy's house had dove-grey walls, a natural wood floor and a shelf of vases in various shades of mushroom, egg-shell and curdled white. It was a tasteful contrast to the hall at the Knox Hill Guest House with its swirly patterned carpet, disused fish-tank, concealed *breakfast ca...arrrrds* and framed religious texts. I didn't know whether to envy the elegance or be repelled by the cold sterility.

"Not in there." Bushy pulled a door shut, but not before I'd caught a glimpse of a woman lying semi-comatose on a taupe settee, her tight black dress hoicked up over her bare, bony thighs and an empty gin bottle on the floor beside her. "Up here." He led me to the stairs.

His room was at the top of the house. He had a desk, a cabin-bed and a wardrobe. There were none of the things

I might have expected in a boy's room, no model aeroplanes, no football regalia and no team photos. Instead, there was a poster of the planetary systems and a chart of the Periodic Table pinned to the pale-blue walls. It was more like a classroom than a place to sleep.

Bushy sat cross-legged on his bed, turning the pages of a large book. "Here she is. Isobel Gowdie." He held it out to me. "Don't you think she looks like you?"

I gazed at the picture. It appeared to be a print of a Victorian painting of a young woman in a long, green robe. She had staring eyes and her hair was a vivid red, quite unlike my stale-fudge frizz. She looked strong and self-willed. I didn't think she looked like me at all.

"Do you believe in reincarnation?" Bushy asked.

"I haven't thought about it," I said. This wasn't strictly true. Nana always said you shouldn't be upset if you accidentally stepped on an insect since that could mean you'd released some poor soul who was trying to work their way back up the chain of being to become human again.

"What about inherited genes?" Bushy said. "Your name's Gowdie and you *do* look like her. You could be her great, great, great, great, great, as many greats as you like, grand-daughter. Listen to this. '*Isobel Gowdie, born in 1630 or thereabouts, in Auldearn, Scotland, made four confessions of witchcraft in and around the year of Our Lord 1662. That she did consort with the devil who gave her a mark on her shoulder and who did make love to her, his semen cold as ice, that she could transform herself into a hare and into a cat, that she did lead a coven of thirteen witches and that she did enter a fairie-hill and saw elf-bulles that did rowle and startle her*'." He laid the book down on the bed. "Cool, eh?"

It did sound cool, but I hadn't much liked him mentioning icy semen. It was suggestive and I'd heard that when boys started talking like that, they had one particular thing on their mind. Well, if he was planning on making any advances, I was getting out of here. I didn't 'fancy' (to use an expression used by girls at St Aggie's) this boy at all.

"You know what puzzles me?" Bushy said. "Why did she confess? I mean, she wasn't being tortured or anything. A witch-finder hadn't been questioning her, making her sit up all night without sleep, or poking her with sharp instruments to find the devil's mark. And in Scotland, she could have been burned as a witch or at the very least, swum and then hanged. So why on earth did she *voluntarily* come out with all that stuff?"

I thought for a moment. A memory stirred. My father, spouting his fury by the witch stone: '*This is where they gathered the ungodly, sinning women. This is where they communed with evil spirits and practised their unholy rites. But this, too, is where they were righteously punished.*"

"Maybe she was taking the piss," I said.

"What?"

"She might have been taunting them," I said. "She knew they suspected her, so she told them what they wanted to hear. She embroidered all those details, made it all up, and she watched their faces as they believed her. And all the time, inside, she was laughing at them."

"But why?" Bushy leant forward, staring at me with an eager expression on his face. "Why would she do that?"

"Well," I examined the back of my hand, pausing for effect. "Perhaps the things that she'd really done were far worse than anything they could imagine."

"Far worse?" Bushy sounded incredulous. "Worse than having sex with the devil and letting him inject her with his icy semen?"

"Yes. She'd been her own person, with her own thoughts and ideas. I expect that was true of all the women they branded witches."

"Are you a feminist, Gowdie?" Bushy looked worried.

"I'm an individualist."

"What does that mean?"

"Work it out for yourself." I could see a dirty sock and several pairs of crumpled boxer shorts lying under the bed, next to a pink semi-triangular plastic object that, I could only suppose, a boy put down his trousers when playing cricket. I felt faintly repelled at the sight of these things.

"Well," Bushy continued, "The weird thing is, no-one knows what happened to Isobel Gowdie in the end. There's no record of her death or execution."

"Perhaps she got away. I expect she turned herself into a hare and went back into the hill to join the elf-bulles. Well, thank you for showing me the book. I've got to go now."

"Hang on. Don't rush off. Look, take the book with you. Borrow it. Give it back to me next week some time. Or keep it longer. For as long as you like."

He closed the book and held it out to me. I stared at the title embossed in gold on the cover: *The History of Witchcraft, Trials and Persecution in Great Britain, Europe and the New World 1400-1787.*

"I don't think I want to read a book like that," I said.

"Don't you? It's all in here, Sprenger and Kramer, and Matthew Hopkins, and the Salem Witch Trials. Did you know a woman was prosecuted under the Witchcraft Act as recently as 1944?"

"I didn't."

"One of the first rules of developing your power is to know the enemy. And they're still out there, the people who want to stamp out magic and destroy witches. They just use different terms of reference, that's all. You need to know this stuff, Gowdie, believe me. And you need a friend." He stood up and thrust the book into my arms. "See you again?"

"All right," I said.

Two simple words, easily said, but if I'd known that my association with Bushy was going to have such disastrous consequences for us both, I might have thought twice about saying them.

Seventeen

So my protection spell had been a failure and it seemed as though someone had attempted to put a memory curse on me. Never mind; I could still gather together some healing remedies to take into work tomorrow. In the meantime, what should I do with the salamander's leg, the ancient bone, the tooth and the snakeskin? My first instinct was to burn them, but then it occurred to me that I should keep these tokens if I wanted to find out who'd hidden them in that pot of rosemary. Cunning Murrell, the wizard of Essex, used witch-bottles filled with urine and nail-clippings to identify anyone who'd wished ill-luck on others: I could perform a similar summoning spell. Thus it was that I placed the bone and the other items in a jar with some garlic and salt and screwed the lid down tight. Tomorrow, I'd take this into the library too.

As I walked into the reading room, I noticed an elderly man in a stained trench coat sitting with his back to me by the window in the reading room. He'd broken up a piece of bread and now he was scattering crumbs on the sill. I remembered the conversation I'd had with Clemency in Psyche's place yesterday, when she'd referred to a 'filthy' old man who encouraged the pigeons. This, I supposed, must be the person she meant, but it hadn't been a fair description. Although his coat was scruffy and his boots were scuffed and down at heel, he wasn't smelly or unwashed. There was a scent of rose-water about his person and his long grey hair was clean.

"Good morning," I said. "I'm Jeanie Gowdie. I've just started work here and..."

"Sssh!" The man held up a warning hand as the pigeon with the dark plumage and raffish, sentient manner landed in front of him.

"It's very tame, isn't it?" I said, watching the bird taking bread from his outstretched fingers. I noticed that he was wearing a heavy silver ring in the shape of a snake swallowing its tail. *Ouroboros*. I knew about that symbolism, the eternal cycle of death and rebirth.

"*Tame*?" As he turned to face me, I saw that his left profile was covered from the tip of his eyebrow to the line of his jaw with a raised port-wine mark. It was as though a contour map of South America had been drawn on his face. "Nothing tame about this one," he said. "There's a difference between a living thing being tame and a living thing being bold. A grizzly bear might stand still and not run away when you meet it on a lonely path, but that doesn't make it tame." He crumbled up some more bread. "Far from it."

"Yes," I agreed. "I see what you mean. It certainly seems an unusual bird."

"It's a sport. Unique. Look how it behaves. Notice anything?"

"Well, it's pecking at the bread just like any bird would and..."

"Haven't you ever looked at the pigeons in London? The way they nod their heads forward with each step? Nod, jerk nod, jerk, but this one...this one keeps its head still. It moves with more dignity than your common avian creature."

"It certainly seems intelligent."

"Intelligent? Is that what you think? It may be a friend or a foe, but it's certainly not a circus exhibit. You'd do well to remember that. Are you familiar with the Egyptian Book of the Dead? Do you know about the 'ba', the bird of death that flies between this world and the next? Perhaps this clever bird has a message for us. I believe that one day many humble London creatures will enter a new cycle of evolution, developing human intelligence and....Why are you staring at me?" To my consternation, the man suddenly leapt to his feet.

"I wasn't...really I...I'm sorry." Oh no, I hadn't, I really hadn't, been staring at that birth mark. "I was just...I noticed your ring. I couldn't help admiring it. Does it have any particular significance or..."

"What makes you think you have the right to question me? Do I interrogate you about your personal accoutrements? Do I ask you why you dye your hair the colour of a lurid sunset or why you stand there, wearing a cloak that was not made for you? What is your game, exactly?"

"I really didn't mean to cause offence." My heart was thumping with alarm, but I was determined to be as conciliatory as possible. "And I don't have a game."

"Everyone has a game!" The man retorted. "Where did you get that cloak?"

"From a curio shop near where I live. Look, here's the label inside the lining, '*Avery's Tailoring, Bond Street.* I expect it was made- to- measure eighty or ninety years ago, but I thought it suited me and..."

"Enough!" He slammed down the window. "Wear borrowed clothes if you wish. It's entirely your affair. But you're very young, Miss Gowdie. My advice is that you don't try to run before you can walk."

"I don't think I quite understand what you mean. I haven't..."

"Good morning, everyone!"

Oh, what a relief! Here was Gerda. With a beaming smile, she dumped her bag on a table and began to unpack her things, some books, a vacuum flask, a wrapped loaf, a pencil case, a hair brush and an alarm clock.

"And a good morning to you, Professor." The man, suddenly calm, bowed to her with deference. "Forgive me if I do not stay. I have business to which I must attend."

"Of course! I too have much vork to do!" Gerda took off her knitted hat and flung it on to a chair. "I hope you have an enjoyable day, Konrad."

I waited until the man had gone, then turned to her.

"I offended him," I said. "I didn't mean to do it."

"Oh, you mustn't mind him," she shrugged. "Konrad, the bird man. His manners are abrupt but his heart is loyal. Tread carefully, and before long, he vill be your friend. He takes time to get used to newcomers, nothing more than that."

"That's good to know." I wasn't in the least reassured. "Have you seen Ernest this morning? The door to the parcels room is locked and..."

"Ah!" She nodded. "I am forgetting! Last night, he told me to tell you, your keys have arrived from the caretaker, look, they're in that in-tray on his desk."

"Oh, yes, thank you." I picked them up. "Gerda...I'm just wondering...is there someone here in the library who grows herbs?"

"At least fifty, I vould think! Vy do you ask?

"Oh, nothing in particular. Well, I'll let you get on."

I unlocked the parcels room, hung up my cloak and reached into my bag for the tokens of malediction and the card that had accompanied the rosemary. I re-read the message on the card and scrutinised the initial at the bottom. 'L'. But it wasn't an 'L' was it? Could it be 'C' for Clemency, 'P' for Psyche, or even a 'K'? There were so many possibilities.

I pulled open my desk drawer, placed the jar and the card behind a box of paper clips and turned the key in the lock. I might not even have to perform a spell. It might be that the power of the objects would attract my enemy all on its own. And, given that unsettling encounter with Konrad, it was quite possible that they already had.

"Good morning, Jeanie."

"Oh!" My stomach lurched. I'd been so deep in my thoughts I hadn't heard him approach, but here he was, Mr Llewellyn standing in the doorway. He looked exhausted, as if he'd been up all night, dark smudges under his eyes and with a general pallor that was worrying to me.

"I've come to see if you're happy with your working conditions," he said. "Is everything all right?" He closed the door behind him and, lowering his voice, added, "Also I wanted to remind you I need to see you in my office. In about half an hour?"

"I'll be there," I said. "I've brought in some special lotions to treat your..." I stopped, as he put a warning finger to his lips.

I glanced through to the reading room. Gerda was sitting at a desk with her back to us, and several other people were browsing the shelves, including a man in a light grey coat.

"You can't be too careful when handling *broken glass*," I said.

"Ah yes, my foolish accident with the *broken glass*." He nodded, then, in a louder tone, said, "Bring any postal loan requests to my office in about half an hour and I'll go through them with you."

"Of course, Mr Llewellyn."

"I'll see you soon, then. Oh, and Jeanie, there's no need to call me 'Mr' Llewellyn all the time. I hope we can be more intimate than that."

Intimate. The word was like a hook, making me feel hot all over and now he looked disconcerted too, as if he'd only just realised the implication of the word. "Less formal, I mean," he said. "Let's be on first name terms."

"OK. Only I don't know your first name. The letter you sent me was signed 'L.A. Llewellyn.' So, what does the 'L' stand for?"

"Strange as this is going to sound, it stands for 'Llewellyn'. My adopted parents were fervently Welsh and I suspect they wanted to make me doubly sure of my own nationality." He smiled. "But I do have a middle name, the one that I adopted when I was twenty one. If you prefer, you can use that."

"But I can't." I objected. "If you adopted the name when you were twenty one, then it must be..." I lowered your voice, "Your *true name*. You mustn't tell me that."

"I'm not sure I know what you mean."

"It would be bad luck for me to use your true name before I've adopted my own."

"Really?" He looked perplexed. "I've never heard that before. That sounds like some old superstition."

"Superstition?" I was shocked. "My Nana told me that! How can you possibly suggest the things that Nana taught me were *superstition?*"

"Oh Jeanie, I'm sorry, I didn't mean to criticise your grandmother. Let's not argue. But there's no need for 'Mr' from now on. Agreed?"

"Yes. Of course, Mr...that is, Llew.... *Of course.*" I could feel myself blushing.

I knew it was irrational and silly but the prospect of using his first name had made me feel quite flustered. *Llewellyn.* What was so difficult about saying that? All I had to do was drop the 'Mr' I'd been using from the outset. And yet I'd stumbled over my first attempt to do this simple thing. Besides, I liked calling him 'Mr Llewellyn'. It was the manner of address the heroine of a Jane Austen novel would use as she gazed at a man, fluttering her fan and enjoying the delicious *frisson* of social constraint. But I must get a grip on myself. This wouldn't do at all, I told myself firmly, as I knocked on his door.

"Come in!"

"Hello again." I bounced into the room, suddenly feeling jaunty and self-confident. "*Sir,*" I added. I closed the door behind me.

"Jeanie, you're incorrigible!" He laughed. "Are you always going to disregard my wishes like this?"

"You said I shouldn't call you 'Mr'," I retorted. "You never said anything about calling you 'sir'."

"And you say it very charmingly, but there's no need to be so deferential."

"Oh, I'm not deferring at all," I said. "Jane Eyre used to call Mr Rochester 'sir' and in my view, she always had the upper hand."

"I see." He paused, apparently reflecting on this. "Well, I'm afraid I'm going to be a sad disappointment if you want me to be Mr Rochester. I don't have a mad wife in the attic and I've never been tempted to commit bigamy."

"That's rather a relief," I said. "All things considered. Although, you know, Bertha Mason wasn't actually in an attic, just the upper floor at Thornfield Hall."

"I stand corrected." He smiled. "Well, sit down. We need to talk."

"And I can't wait to hear what you have to tell me," I said. "But I'm in charge right now. First, you must let me take a look at those cuts on your hand."

"There's really no need."

"Yes, there is. I doubt very much if you know anything about healing remedies and I just happen to be an expert." I took several little pots and jars out of my bag and arranged them on his desk. "And don't say anything about superstition, please."

"I wouldn't dream of it. Jeanie, what on earth is all this? You shouldn't have gone to so much trouble."

"Yes, I should. Wounded heroes deserve the best. So, let's see—I've got calendula for healing, agrimony to prevent renewed bleeding and arnica oil to soothe the discomfort. Now, this dressing might look a bit manky to you, but it's a length of Egyptian mummy-cloth impregnated with cobwebs and oil of cedar-wood."

"Egyptian mummy-cloth?" He sounded astonished. "I hope you didn't steal it from the British Museum."

"Of course not. I get these things by mail order. There's a senior hedge-witch who runs a little business in Pontefract. Nana used to get lots of supplies from there. Now, stop hiding your hand and let me see it properly."

"All right." With a pleasing meekness, he placed his hand palm-downwards on the desk.

"Oh!" As I unwound the handkerchief he'd used as a bandage, I was aghast at the sight of the bruising and inflammation. "This looks awful. It's so swollen and...You must be in pain."

"It *is* throbbing a little," he admitted.

"And what about the other cut, the one on your neck?"

"Oh, that's fine, that's nothing, I..."

"Please sit still. No arguments. I'll be as gentle as I can, but this is going to sting a bit."

"I'm completely at your mercy, Jeanie."

"Good."

I suppose I should have felt nothing but clinical detachment, but it was impossible not to enjoy the physical contact as I applied the ointments. I doubted if he was finding it pleasurable however; he winced several times as I used the cedar-wood spatula to push the healing juices deep into the wounds.

"Sorry," I said.

"I'm afraid I'm not the hero you think me," he said with a self-depreciating smile.

"Nonsense. You must have put up a brilliant fight. And this...thing....that you said wasn't even alive...it clearly meant business."

"Or rather the person who sent it did," he said. "The entity itself would just have been a weapon, controlled by some-one else. Someone who knew what I was carrying in my bag. Jeanie, is that *really* Egyptian mummy cloth you're putting round my hand?"

"Yes, it is. Special injuries require special treatment. You see, I don't think these cuts were made by an ordinary knife. The blade had been cursed."

"You think so?"

"Yes. But this will get better quickly now. There, I'm finished." I wound the last of the mummy cloth around his thumb and tied a knot. "I suggest you wear this glove to keep the dressing in place."

"Thank you. You're very efficient. You should work in a casualty department."

"Oh, you wouldn't have got this treatment in a conventional hospital."

"I suppose not."

"Although there are connections between orthodox medicine and natural healing. Nana Herrick told me that there were wise-women in Northumbria who were using their own form of penicillin in the sixteenth century. They knew everything there was to know about mould."

"Really?" Having slipped on the thin cotton glove, he flexed his fingers. "This feels so much more comfortable."

"I'm glad."

"So am I. Now, let's have some tea. Which mug would you like?" He pointed to an assortment on top of the filing cabinet.

"Definitely not this one!" I picked up one with a design of berries on the side.

"Why not?" he asked, "It's bone china and an antique."

"But it's got a long crack in it here, running right down the side."

"So it has." He peered at it. "Are you worried about germs?"

"I never worry about germs, at least not in the usual way. I was thinking of something far more sinister. Do you know those lines by W.H.Auden? *The crack in the tea-cup opens a lane to the land of the dead.* Poets always know the truth. Cracks are dangerous portals, whether they're in plastered walls or in china mugs."

"In that case, would you prefer a cup? I think there are some in that cupboard over there, although I never use them."

"No. I'm not fond of cups. I can't bear the fussiness of using a saucer. I prefer mugs."

"Oh, yes. A mug for me every time," he agreed fervently. "Although this *is* a rather grim collection I inherited from my predecessor. How about this one?" He held up a piece of heavy pottery that looked almost Neolithic.

"Perfect," I said. I was enjoying this silly, inconsequential conversation, it felt so relaxed and natural and if it hadn't been for the fact that I was anxious to hear the full story of what had happened to him last night, I'd have wanted to prolong it. Instead, I waited silently while he made the tea, a process that was fascinating in itself, as he was using a spirit stove that looked more than a little antique.

"So," he handed me the thick pottery mug. "I'm now going to tell you everything." He sat down opposite me. "And this is, of course, completely confidential."

"I understand."

"Well, as you've probably gathered, I was carrying something valuable in my bag last night. Jabez Corey gave it to me to safeguard. I thought bringing it back here to the library would be an uncomplicated matter, but the moment I left the Corey Mansion, I was sure I was being followed. But I couldn't see anyone...anything. I didn't dare sleep on the plane. I had to keep all my attention fixed on the overhead locker where I'd placed the bag. Then, when I arrived back in London, I took a taxi from the airport, and asked the driver to drop me at the entrance to the library, but the taxi broke down two streets away. I realise now that wasn't a coincidence."

"Was the taxi driver involved?"

"No. What I mean is that some-one else, unknown to him, had sabotaged the vehicle. So, I began to complete my journey on foot, and then some-one...*something*...called out my name as I was crossing the square. I turned. I saw the knife. And the faceless wraith-like entity that was wielding it."

"*Oh.*" I swallowed.

"Well, you know the rest. There was a struggle, but I defeated it. And the contents of my bag were saved."

"And who do you suppose sent this thing, this... *wraith*?"

"I don't know, except that it's clear we have enemies. These are critical times and I suspect that when Jabez Corey passes away, there will be those who will want to usurp his position and steal everything of value that we're keeping here. Oh, Jeanie," he sighed. "I really didn't want to involve you in this. I wanted you to be safe."

"But I want to help," I said. I paused, then added, "Can't you tell me what it was that Jabez Corey gave you to bring here?"

"Yes. I'm going to show you. It is his wish that I should."

He stood up, took a steel ruler from his desk drawer, crossed the room, knelt down and rolled back the worn Turkish rug. Using the ruler, he levered up one of the floorboards, revealing a black metal box with a numbered dial.

"Come and see," he said. "You'll need to memorise the sequence. Four numbers." I looked over his shoulder as he turned the dial to the left, then to the right, and then to the left and right again. "Have you remembered them?"

I nodded, repeating the sequence in my head: *one eight six one.*

"You put in the code seven times, and then the safe opens." He repeated the sequence just as he'd said and then opened the box. He took out a book with a green cover. "So here it is." He laid it on his desk.

"*Little Women,*" I read the title. "Why on earth would someone try and steal this at knifepoint?"

"Because it's not, in fact, a copy of *Little Women*. Look inside and you'll see what I mean."

I opened the book. Opposite the title page, there was a frontispiece, a colour plate of Jo, Amy and Meg gathered around Beth as she sat at the piano given to her by kind old Mr Lawrence. I turned to the next page and read the opening of the novel, as familiar and comforting to me as an old woollen glove: *'Christmas won't be Christmas without any presents,' grumbled Jo, lying on the rug.* But after that, there was no more of Louisa May Alcott's classic. The rest of the printed book had been cut out and something else put in its place, a parcel wrapped in stained cloth.

"Oh," I gasped. "How awful to cut up a book. If this was a copy of *The Wizard of Oz* I'd be really upset. That's my favourite book and..."

"Jeanie," he interrupted me gently. "I was sorry to see that Miss Alcott's work had been mutilated too, but without the disguise, this might not have survived." He unwrapped the parcel, revealing a hand-sewn manuscript. "This is what I was defending last night."

"Oh, goodness! What is it?"

"The title page explains it. Can you translate it?"

"I think so." I squinted at the minuscule hand-writing: *'Liber scriptus tenebris magus Antiochus Corey annum Iubileum MDCCCXCVII. Undeciphered manere donec septuagesimo post anno meum.'* It's slightly different Latin from the kind I know but I think...yes...*'The Book of Shadows of the adept Antioch Corey, written in this Year of the Jubilee, 1897, not to be deciphered until seventy years after my death.'*" Oh, this is amazing!"

"It's certainly unique. And now Jabez wants us to work on the translation together. I'm assuming you're familiar with the term 'Book of Shadows'?"

"Of course. It refers to a book in which an adept, a magus or a witch has recorded their secret rituals and magical procedures. It's often thought that the term was first used by the exponent of Wicca, Gerald Gardener, in the nineteen-forties, but I think it goes back much further than that. And it must do, if Antioch Corey wrote a *Book of Shadows* in the year that Queen Victoria celebrated her Diamond Jubilee. I've never seen one before. Oh, this is so exciting! There might be great and powerful magic in here, secret things, and together, we could try out the spells and rituals and..."

"Jeanie, no!" To my astonishment, he looked horrified. "This must remain an academic exercise, nothing more."

"But what would be the point of that?"

"It would be highly irresponsible of me to put you in any danger." He looked distinctly anxious. "I've thought about this, long and hard, and it seems to me that Antioch Corey must have had a good reason for insisting that his book shouldn't be translated until seventy years after his death. And why did he write it in a variety of ancient languages, not just Latin, and in certain codes of his own devising, making even that difficult? What if Antioch Corey discovered something that he didn't want to unleash on to the world until he was no longer around to witness the consequences, something that had the potential to be apocalyptic, the paranormal equivalent of the atom bomb?"

"Then he'd have ensured that the book came into the right hands. And Jabez Corey obviously thinks that you are the right person."

"But I'm not sure that I am. If I hadn't made a promise to Jabez, I might be tempted to destroy this book, but there's always the possibility there's a protective curse on it that could rebound on us both. Jeanie, listen, you don't have to agree to this. This is a burden that I'm prepared to carry on my own."

"Surely it's not a burden but a privilege," I said. "And we must be safe in here, inside the library, surely?"

"For the moment, yes." He looked at me with a grave expression. "But Jeanie, I don't want to sound patronising, but I do have to warn you. When you're young, the thought of experimenting with magic seems so exciting. But it's so easy to be drawn into danger, to overreach yourself and that leads to misery and loss and despair. When you've lived as long as I have..."

"Hey!" I was sure he was teasing me now. *Lived as long as I have*...how ridiculous! "You're talking to me like a middle-aged schoolmaster. And you're not even that old!"

He turned away from me. There was a long silence. Then he asked,

"And how old do you suppose I am, Jeanie?"

"Thirty five, no more than thirty six," I suggested. "Am I right?"

"In a way." He turned back to face me.

"What do you mean, *in a way*?"

"Jeanie, we're getting away from the subject in hand." He sounded impatient and dismissive. "Well," he began wrapping up the manuscript. "Then we'll carry out Jabez Corey's wishes. As long as you're really sure."

"Oh, I'm sure. It will be a pleasure, *sir*."

"I'm not sure it will be a pleasure for either of us. I'll be honest with you, Jeanie; I wish Jabez Corey hadn't burdened us with this. I'm concerned that there may be unforeseen consequences, hidden dangers. But I'll do my best. I shall endeavour to protect you."

Endeavour to protect you. I smiled inwardly. There was something rather charming about his formal way of speaking, his old-fashioned manners. I supposed it must be typical of adepts and the world they inhabited, so scholarly and set apart from ordinary life. Now I was filled with eager anticipation; we would be working together and I'd really get to know him. It didn't occur to me for a moment that I was stumbling blindly into a situation I might not be able to control. If only I'd remembered Nana Herrick's warning:

Take care where you step, Jeanie. Never let your heart rule your head. There are far more dangers out there than you might suppose. If you keep your head in the clouds, you won't see the poison frogs and vipers in your path.

Eighteen

Pyewacket's was still open even though it was nearly nine in the evening, and not only was it open, it was vibrant with vintage dance band music. As I walked in, I found Dorian, a long-handled feather duster in his hand, bee-bopping around to the rhythm of a scratchy record that was playing on an antique gramophone

"Greetings, Miss J. Gowdie." He flicked the duster at the ceiling. "And may I say how elegant you look in that cloak and those boots."

"Oh, you've remembered my name."

"Of course I have. I make it my business to know all my clients and your name was on the cheque you gave me. However, I must admit I don't know what the 'J' stands for."

"It's Jeanie," I said. "I like that, by the way."

"What, this old thing?" He waved the feather duster. "Genuine ostrich!"

"No, I meant the music."

"Ah! Yes! It's *Limehouse Blues,* from Andre Charlot's London Revue, 1924. Definitely a Chinese influence, wouldn't you say? The music of that period is one of my passions, love it, I'd have enjoyed being a flapper. Ah!" He poked the feather duster into a high corner. "There's another one! Would you believe I actually have cobwebs in here? It seems the spids have been crawling out of the dark recesses of old Rogers stock room in an attempt to colonise the shop."

"I don't mind spiders." I glanced upwards. "They're useful creatures."

"Perhaps, but they're not good for business." He shook his blond hair back from his face. "I have certain clients who are complete arachnophobes. Old Rogers might have thought big swags of spider-silk hanging everywhere made antiques look authentic, as if they'd come from Dracula's Castle, but I was trying for a more chic image. So," he put the feather duster down. "Are you here for a browse or are you looking for something in particular?"

"I came to show you something," I said. "The thing is, I've got it on my conscience."

"Ah-hah! Nothing as delicious as a guilty secret! So what is it?"

"This." I took the little jewelled key out of my bag. "I found it in the lining of the cloak you sold me. I wondered if it was valuable. I'm happy to pay you some more if you think it is." I handed it to him.

"Hmm." Dorian examined the key. "Middle or late Victorian, I'd say. I can't identify the precise maker; there were eight hundred and forty four master locksmiths registered in the Midlands in the eighteen-fifties. That was where most locks, keys and safes were being manufactured at the time."

"Could this have been the key to 23 Coleton Street?"

"No, it's far too small for a front door key of the period. I'd say this is the key to a small, ornamental box or casket, a jewel case, perhaps, or a musical box."

"You don't happen to have found anything like that, have you? Maybe marked with a monogram like the one on this key?"

"No, but I can keep looking. I've been through the stock books since I last saw you and I've discovered that old

Rogers got a lot of stuff from an auction after several houses in Coleton Street were demolished after the war. And, in fact, that's where he got that cheval mirror over there, the one I showed you before."

"Oh." I gazed at the pitted glass. "But you told me it came from a Bond Street store."

"Did I?" Dorian frowned. "It seems I was wrong. Sure I can't interest you in it? It's a lovely piece, like I said before."

"And also quite very expensive." I looked at the price tag.

"I'm reluctant to let it go for any less. But," he gave me back the little key, "as far as *this* is concerned, it's yours. Finder's weepers, as they say."

"Shouldn't that be 'finder's keepers'?"

"Should it? Rather depends on what you've found." He smiled playfully. "So, how are you doing with your research on 23 Coleton Street?"

"I have made a few inquiries. I'm just wondering, would it be possible to discover just who was living at a particular address in London in the late nineteenth century?"

"You'd need the census records," Dorian told me. "But those aren't released for a hundred years. The earliest ones you could access would be for 1871."

"Oh. Well, that could be useful. The thing is, I've heard a story, a kind of local legend, about two people who might have lived in the area nearly a century ago. Arthur Lewin and a woman called Mandy. The 'M' on this key, perhaps that stands for Mandy?"

"Mandy's a modern name," Dorian objected. "I don't think anyone was called 'Mandy' in Victorian times."

"Then it could be corruption of some kind. Maybe her name was Amanda, that name comes from an eighteenth century play. It's from the Latin, meaning loved. *Amare*. Or... here's a thought, what about 'Mandeep'? She could have been a woman of Indian origin. After all, Queen Victoria was made Empress of India in 1877 and people from the sub-continent must have come to England at that time."

"Hmm," Dorian mused. "Interesting speculations. I really think you should pursue your inquiries."

"I will. I'm going to take a look at the streets on the other side of the old cemetery. It's possible the house has gone, but there's a building there now that's supposed to be haunted."

"Haunted, eh?" Dorian raised his eyebrows. "I'd be careful of that. You might look for 'M' but she might find you first."

They still walk. Suddenly, I felt a frisson of something akin to fear.

"Sorry," Dorian grinned. "I wasn't trying to give you nightmares. Look, I might be reducing a few prices before Christmas, call back then." He pushed the cheval mirror back against the wall. "In the meantime, are you quite sure I can't tempt you to something today? Is there someone you'd like to give a present?"

"A present?" Now that was an idea. "Actually, I'd quite like to buy a mug. I know someone who doesn't have a decent one to his name."

"I don't have any mugs," Dorian said. "But how about this?" He picked up a piece of bone china crockery with a floral pattern. "This is rather charming and you *could* use it as a mug. It's a love tankard."

"I've never heard of such a thing."

"I'm not surprised. Very few of these were made. Look at the decoration. It's based on the Victorian language of flowers. Here on the outside, there's a pattern of purple lilac. That signifies the burgeoning of romance. And here's a yellow rose, symbolising falling in love. And around the rim, there's this circlet of ivy. That means that the love will endure. And if you look inside the mug, at the bottom, there's a red rose. And that signifies burning physical passion, something that's only revealed when you reach the depths. Those Victorians had to be outwardly decorous, but secretly, they were very erotic."

"It's rather lovely." I gazed at the tankard. "So roses mean courtship?"

"It depends on the colour. Roses are always a love token, but they're not necessarily romantic. White ones are for friendship or filial love; a father can give them to a daughter, or you could give them to a sibling. Of course, very few people outside of the antique trade would understand these meanings today. But if you were a young Victorian lady and a gentleman gave you this..." He winked knowingly. "Then you'd know you had an admirer."

"And if a young lady gave it to a gentleman?"

"Then she'd have to be a very fast young lady indeed! But, as I say, no-one speaks the language of flowers today. I'll sell this to you for a song," he beamed. "Or shall we say, three pounds?"

"Done!" What was I saying? Why did I always succumb to Dorian's sales talk?

"Do you want me to gift-wrap it for you?" he asked. "My gift-wrapping skills are second to none!"

"Thank you," I said. "Yes please. I'd like that."

"Oh, I forgot to mention," he added, as he placed the mug in a box. "I found some more vintage clothes. They're hanging on that stand over there. Take a look. That little black bodice is rather glamorous, don't you think? Genuine Edwardian."

"Yes," I agreed. "But I couldn't possibly wear it."

"Too saucy? Or do you have an objection to whalebone?"

"It's a shame about the poor whale, but it must have been harpooned a long time ago and there's nothing to be done about it now." I touched the bodice, fingering the satin and lace. "I don't even mind sauciness. But I can't wear sleeveless things."

"Why not?"

"There's a reason." My fingers strayed to my arm. "But I don't want to talk about it."

"Sorry. Didn't mean to probe. Well," he picked up a length of red ribbon. "You could wear the bodice under a jacket. What about that one, the embroidered Chinese silk? Just your size, I'd say and such a subtle shade of ivory. And there are a few other things too, that long velvet skirt and... well, why not try the clothes on in the back room? I'll be a while wrapping this."

"OK." I knew as soon as I agreed to his suggestion that once I'd put these things on, I wouldn't want to take them off. Dorian had a knack of finding just the right clothes for me, things made me feel transformed into someone beautiful and powerful. Some-one like the woman whose name began with the same letter as my true name. 'M', a woman with whom I was beginning to sense a very strong connection.

Nineteen

The following morning, as I sat on the tube on my way to the library, I suffered a crisis of confidence. The beautifully packaged tankard was in my bag but now I was thinking that I couldn't possibly give it to Llewellyn. I wasn't worried that he might know something about the Victorian language of flowers, but the flirtatious nature of Dorian's gift-wrapping was an embarrassment in itself. The paper he'd chosen was resplendent with images of hearts, roses and little cupids firing arrows and he'd tied up the parcel with festoons of red ribbon. It was so amorous and suggestive; it looked like a Valentine's Day gift. Whatever had Dorian been thinking? And, more importantly, how would Llewellyn interpret it?

I was still fretting over this when the train stopped between stations with such an abrupt jolt that my bag was almost catapulted off my lap. Minutes passed. There was no announcement, no explanation. A man on the opposite side of the carriage rattled his newspaper impatiently; someone said, "What, another bloody go-slow?" Others sat in stoical silence. I glanced at my watch. Unless we started moving again soon, I'd be late for work. I blinked, suddenly aware of a sharp prickling in my eye. I must have something in it, a smut perhaps blown in from the tunnel or an eyelash. I needed to examine it but...Of course, how could I forget? I had a mirror with me, the silver pocket mirror I'd bought from Dorian. I took it out of my bag and was just fumbling with the clasp when the carriage was plunged into darkness. What happened next was very disconcerting indeed.

One moment I was in my seat, the next I seemed to be out of my body, hovering close to the ceiling, looking down. I could see myself clearly, dressed in the clothes I'd bought the previous evening, the black bodice under the silk jacket, a long velvet skirt, my boots. I could even see the little droplets of rain in my hair.

The scene was lit by a preternatural blue glow, and—here was the most inexplicable and weirdest thing--*I was completely on my own*. I didn't understand. The carriage had been crammed with commuters a moment before; someone's briefcase had been banging against my knees, people were swaying awkwardly in the crush, enveloped in a fug of the smell of wet macs, after-shave and morning-breath. Now everything was silent and still but...*no!* Now I could hear voices, scratchy and malign, one voice chiming in after the other:

'Look at her. Thinks she's so clever. Thinks she's better than us. She must be tested. Put her through the fire again...'

"Through the fire, through the fire again..."

"Or water this time? Sink or swim, duck or drown?"

"Duck or drown, through the fire, through the fire..."

"Thinks she's so clever!"

"Mustn't be allowed..."

"I'll put a spoke in her wheel!"

Now the voices were coming all at once, spiralling into squeaky incoherence, like a record playing too fast:

"Duck or drown, through the fire, through the fire... through the fire again, sink or swim, sink or swim bring the water and..."

I had to get out of this. I had to return to reality. But how? *Help me, blessed Epona, goddess of the hills!*

I found myself being caught up in a sickening rush as if I was in a lift that was going down too swiftly. And then, as if nothing had happened, the normal lights were back on in the carriage and everything was just as it had been. I was back in my body, surrounded by the other commuters, all of us crammed in like pilchards in a tin.

"Apologies for the delay, ladies and gentle-spoons, we're being held by a red signal and will soon be on the move."

Gentle-spoons? Had that voice on the intercom really said *gentle-spoons*? I took several deep breaths, trying to quell a rising nausea. I was aware again of that uncomfortable prickling in my eye. The silver pocket mirror was still in my hand. I flipped it open and held it up to my face. *Oh!* What was this?

I couldn't see my reflection in the glass. All I could see was a thick, swirling mist. But now something was emerging, a face, but it wasn't my face and all I could see was the lower half of this face, a chin, a mouth, since the upper part was concealed behind a half-mask, a carnival mask, slit-eyed, decorated with feathers and diamante sparkles. I was still reeling inwardly with shock when the lips moved, mouthing a single word, just three syllables, but somehow I heard them as a whisper, right in my ear.

'Morgana....'

I closed the mirror with a snap and flung it back into my bag. I took several deep breaths and then, feeling calmer, I told myself that whatever had happened here was a good thing. It was exciting to discover there was magic in the mirror and that the spirit residing in the glass wanted to communicate with me. The only slightly worrying thing was that it—no, *she*—I was sure those red-painted lips had been those of a woman—knew my true name.

How reassuring it was to be back in the reading room, such a comfortingly eccentric place. There was Ernest's cumbersome old bicycle leaning against the radiator, Gerda at a table surrounded by books, Ernest himself hunched over a folded newspaper, tapping his front teeth with the top of his fountain pen, his brow furrowed with concentration. He must be doing the *Times* crossword, an activity that, from my observations, seemed to cause him very little pleasure and a considerable amount of anguish. No sooner had he written in the answer to a clue than he obliterated it, until the grid was such an inky mess he seemed to feel obliged to stuff the entire newspaper into the waste paper basket with an audible 'pah!' of despair.

"Good morning, Jeanie!" Gerda looked up from her note-taking. "And may I say vat a beautiful jacket? Such lovely ivory silk."

"Almost too good for a dusty old library," Ernest muttered, giving me a sidelong glance.

He gazed at his crossword again. "*Flirting goon pins confusion. Eight letters,*'" he announced in a sepulchral tone.

"Spooning," I said.

"This is my crossword!" He stabbed at his newspaper with his pen. "Why must you interfere?"

"I'm sorry," I said, abashed. "I thought I was being helpful."

There was a frenzied fluttering of wings as the dark-plumed pigeon arrived on the sill.

Gerda leaned towards it, holding out a piece of bread, but the bird ignored her, fixing me instead with an inquisitive stare.

"Yes! Yes, I see." Ernest put the pen down. "Thank you, Jeanie. But when I read out a clue, I'm thinking aloud. I don't want anyone to supply me with the answer."

"Yes. Of course. I didn't realise. I'll remember next time."

"No matter. Ignore my irritability." He ran his fingers through his toilet-brush hair as if attempting to tidy it. "Besides, you've given me the right answer. Impressive."

"I don't think I understand," Gerda said. "I am not a cryptic crossvord person."

"The word 'confusion' tells you it's an anagram," I explained. "So you rearrange the letters of 'goon spin' to make a word that means 'flirting'. Spooning."

"Spooning!" Gerda beamed. "Such an old-fashioned term. I suppose ven young people go courting these days, they don't call it spooning, perhaps they don't even say courting! Vould your boyfriend say 'courting', Jeanie?"

"I don't have a boyfriend."

"Ah! But you have an admirer, yes?"

"Not to my knowledge."

"I think you must have. Look in there, see?" She pointed to the parcels room.

My stomach flipped over. There, standing on my desk, clearly visible through the gothic windows, was a lead crystal vase containing a huge bunch of white roses and propped up against it, there was a heart-shaped piece of gold card.

As I walked into the parcels room, I was overcome by the gorgeous, heady scent. Even the feathery fern that had been placed behind the roses had an aromatic perfume. I touched the velvety petals with my finger tip. Could they be from *him*? There seemed, oddly, to be no message on the card. Still, who else would give me these? They must be from Llewellyn! I remembered what he'd said when I'd mentioned the rosemary: *Now I do feel remiss.* Well, he'd made up for the omission handsomely. Still, I mustn't stand here showing how overcome I was. Someone might be watching. I took a deep breath, moved the roses to the corner of my desk, sat down and turned my attention to the post.

There were several packages of returned books, but only one letter, a postal loan request.

I checked the name in the Directory of Life Members: Dr Hecate Burneside, Pendle, Lancashire. Yes, she'd been a subscriber for many years. I didn't recognise the title of the book and I was sure we didn't have it on the open shelves. I decided to consult Ernest.

"Let me see." He snatched the letter out of my hand. "Ah! Dr Hecate Burneside. I believe the book she wants is in the archive. Tell Miss Nantucket that it's for a subscriber whose requests are always honoured and ask her to find it for you. You might need to put a tin hat on before entering her sanctum. Rather you than me!"

The archive room was on the ground floor behind a green-painted door. I knocked and then, somewhat tentatively, pushed the door open and looked in. To my surprise, I couldn't see a single book, just ox-blood red walls, and three alcoves containing white marble busts of Roman emperors with hawk-like expressions. Clemency was sitting at a desk in the middle of the room, staring blankly into space.

"Can I help you?" Somehow, she managed to make this bland inquiry sound like a threat.

"I've come to collect a book for a postal loan," I said. "*The Salem Investigations*. Ernest said he thought it might be here."

"I believe it is, but books from the archives should never leave the building." Clemency frowned at me.

"But there are exceptions to that rule, aren't there?"

"Only in very particular circumstances."

"I see. Well, the book's been requested by Dr Hecate Burnside. She says in her letter that she's unable to leave her home these days."

"I'm not surprised. She's must be completely decrepit by now. There's no reason to give *her* special consideration, the appalling woman."

"Is she? Appalling, I mean?"

"Of course she is! What kind of person would call herself 'Hecate' and live in a place like Pendle? Haven't you read the Scottish play?"

"The...oh, you mean *Macbeth*. Yes, I know there's a character called Hecate in that, one of the witches and..." I broke off, afraid that I might be drifting into dangerous territory. "But surely Dr Burnside didn't choose her first name?"

"There are a number of people who *do* choose their names, replacing the ones they were given at birth." Clemency glared at me. "And the names they choose reflect their unhealthy preoccupations. Besides which, I know for a fact that Dr Burneside once borrowed a book and then used a knife covered in jam as a bookmark. If we send her this book, she'll drop tea leaves over it or worse still, allow a cat to vomit on it. I have a duty to preserve the archives."

"I do see that." I nodded. "But isn't it up to Mr Llewellyn whether books are sent out on loan or not? I'm sure that's what Ernest Brunswicker told me on my first day."

"That's true. More's the pity."

I looked around the room, at the ox-blood walls and the complete absence of books, wondering if I might find any evidence that Clemency was responsible for the pot of rosemary, the note and the memory curse. There was,

I noted, no sign of an old typewriter in here, although that proved nothing. Clemency could very well have composed her note at home.

"I'm fascinated to see how the archives are stored," I said.

"Oh, very well." She stood up and walked over to the left-hand wall. "You might as well know how to access the shelves. Here." She seized hold of one of the small wheels that were sticking out of the plaster at regular intervals and that I'd mistaken for a decorative flourish. She turned the wheel and a section of shelving began to emerge.

"You have to be careful with this system," she said. "Accidents can happen if more than one of these is pulled out at the same time and a person is in the way. No-one would want to see a reader crushed, would they?"

"I wouldn't have thought so, no."

"Well, here it is. *The Salem Investigations*." She held out a battered volume with a blue cover. "It will need to be packaged carefully. Three layers of non-acidic tissue minimum and then newspaper, lots of it. Then the thickest brown paper you can find. Write the label first and then stick it on, not the other way round. Even the slightest pressure from a pen could damage the book."

"Of course." I nodded. "I'll be as careful as possible." I reached out to take it from her.

"Ah!" She pulled her hand back. "You don't think I'm going to give it to you *now*, do you? That would be highly irresponsible. No, I'm not letting this book out of my sight until you bring a written letter of authority from Mr Llewellyn. You can also tell him from me that he can't make a habit of this kind of thing. He doesn't own this place. Not by any means. Custodians come and go, but the library will go on forever. Good morning, Miss Gowdie. Close the door on your way out!"

Twenty

I tried not to feel too unsettled by my encounter with Clemency, but it had been rather too much to bear on top of that weird experience on the underground. And now, back in the parcels room, another shock was waiting for me.

I was sure that I'd slipped that heart-shaped piece of card under the vase of white roses but now here it was, in the middle of my desk, on top of the ledger I'd been consulting, the *Directory of Life Members*. And as I picked it up, I saw that while I'd been right in thinking there was no message on the front, what I hadn't noticed was that there *was* one on the back. And very nasty it was too. The words and letters had been cut out of a newspaper, or possibly several newspapers, judging from the ill-matching typefaces, and pasted on to the card.

You would be mad to trust Llewellyn. He's not all he seems.

Ever yours,

A well-wisher.

A well-wisher? I knew that people who called themselves 'well-wishers' were anything but 'well-wishers'; they were motivated by spite, jealousy and a desire to cause trouble. This felt like the business of the rosemary all over again, a gift with a sting in the tail. And this time, the wielder of the poison pen had tried to soften me up with roses.

I remembered Dorian telling me that roses were always a love token. Well, these certainly weren't! Now, I could hardly bear their scent. I felt like dumping them in the bin, but I couldn't do that, not if I was going to find out who was behind this. I'd have to act cool and unconcerned, and pretend nothing was wrong.

I unlocked my desk drawer and slipped the card inside, next to the jar containing the maledictions and the other note. I was building up quite an interesting collection. *You would be mad to trust Llewellyn. He's not all he seems.* That just had to be nonsense, surely. But what if there was a grain of truth in it all? How did I know what to believe?

I knocked, with some trepidation, on the door of the Custodian's room.

"Come in!"

The moment I walked in, Llewellyn leapt up from his desk, his eyes hot with concern.

"Jeanie, what's wrong?"

"It's nothing. Nothing at all."

"Something's upset you, I can tell."

"I'm fine." I was trembling, despite myself. He was standing so close to me. I was fighting the urge to tell him everything, but the suspicion that had been planted in my mind was holding me back.

"Forgive me, but you don't look fine." He stepped back. "You look as though you've had a shock. Jeanie, if anyone... anything...threatens you in any way, you will tell me, won't you?"

"Please don't worry, I can look after myself." I pressed the flat of my hand against my stomach, trying to quell my nerves. This was ridiculous but what if Llewellyn really was untrustworthy? But no, he couldn't be, he was so kind and...

But he was almost certainly a spell-charmer and Nana had told me all about their deceits. *Oh!*

"Sit down" He brought a chair forward. "I'll make you some tea."

"Thank you." I put my bag down on the floor. The gift-wrapped tankard was inside and heaven only knew what had possessed me to bring it with me.

"Jeanie, is it something I've done?" He busied himself with the tea things. "If it is, then I'm sorry. I really didn't mean to upset you."

"No, it's not you." *I hope.*

"Good, I was afraid that I'd overstepped the mark. But I'm so grateful to you." He held up his bandaged hand. "This is healing so quickly." He smiled. "Here—your tea. I understand that for the English, tea is the perfect panacea for everything, including misunderstandings."

"Thank you." I took the tea from him. "Although I'm not sure I am completely English," I added. "My father was Scottish and my grandmother was born close to the border."

"So we both have Celtic roots. I've always felt Welsh to the core." He sat down at his desk.

"But you don't have a Welsh accent."

"That's because I didn't grow up there."

"Oh. Does that mean you don't speak Welsh?"

"Not at all. I do speak it. I was brought up bi-lingual."

"I wish I knew some of the language. I wouldn't know where to begin."

"Start with the Mabinogion. I can lend you a copy, a parallel text with English on one side and Welsh on the other."

"I'd like that. Thank you." This felt good. The tension was dissipating. "The reason I came to see you," I continued, "is that I need you to write a letter authorising me to send out a book from the archives. Here's the request." I handed him the letter.

"Ah." He skimmed through it. "Dr Hecate. Of course we must send her the book."

"I'm afraid Clemency wasn't very happy about the idea."

"Ah! So that's the trouble!" His face cleared. "I suppose Clemency spoke rather sharply to you. Take no notice, that's just her way. She does have the interests of the library at heart. And she's very protective when it comes to the archives."

"So I gathered. But she was rather critical of Dr Hecate."

"She doesn't know her. Dr Hecate is a dear friend of mine. She was very kind to me at an unhappy time in my life."

"An unhappy time?"

"Oh, you don't want to hear about that. Of course I'll write the letter. But perhaps we need to keep Clemency happy too."

Keep her happy*?* When had Clemency ever been happy? I decided not to express this thought out loud.

"I do know that Dr Hecate can be quite forgetful when it comes to returning books," he said. "She's getting on a bit now. You'd enjoy meeting her. So, we'll tell Clemency that you'll collect the book from Dr Hecate in person at the end of the loan period in the spring. Would that be all right? The library would pay your travel expenses, of course."

"Yes. That would be fine." I took a gulp of my tea. The warm liquid was settling my stomach and talking to him was making me feel better. How could I possibly doubt him?

"Now," he said. "There's something else to arrange; the practicalities concerning our work on the *Book of Shadows*."

"Are we going to start on it today?"

"No. I suggest we start tomorrow, at three o'clock; a regular, two hour session. But I'm still concerned about your safety. Someone, somewhere, knows about this book and is prepared to do anything to get their hands on it. People might ask you why you're spending time in my office and, of course, you won't be able to tell them the truth. So I'm going to suggest a cover story, one that won't be a lie. We must actually *do* some other work alongside deciphering the book and we must be seen to be doing it. Does that make sense?"

"I think so. What did you have in mind?"

"I'm thinking about the Cabinet of Curiosities. If we catalogue and research the collection, and exhibit a few pieces in the entrance hall for everyone to see, you can truthfully say you're working with me on Antioch Corey's legacy."

"That's a good idea. I'd love to find out more about these things." I glanced across at the cabinet, at the crowded shelves with the heaps of old pottery, the weird claws and feathers, and the jars of bloated, anaemic dead things drifting in their ancient formaldehyde. "Did Antioch Corey leave any notes describing his collection?"

"Yes, there's a box of index cards in the drawer at the bottom, but it's in a very poor condition. I must admit that I've got rather fond of this motley display. Antioch Corey travelled across North and South America as a young man, living with the indigenous tribes, engaging in their initiation rituals and learning about native magic. These activities didn't go down well with his more straight-laced relatives. He came from a very old family of early settlers, strict puritans, although strangely enough, one of his ancestors was executed as a witch at Salem."

"Giles Corey, I know, Gerda told me. So, these curiosities...when I came here for my interview, you mentioned a piece of sasquatch skin. Can I see it?"

"Yes. Of course." He unlocked the cabinet and took out what appeared to be a length of hairy old leather. "Take a look."

"The poor old sasquatch," I stroked the orange-brown hair with my forefinger. "I just hope the poor creature died of natural causes. It would be awful to kill such a rare beast."

"Quite. Although no doubt we'll discover this skin comes from a bear or a goat or some other kind of ordinary animal. Oh, Jeanie, how thoughtless of me, would you like to hang up your jacket? You'll get it dirty, handling all these grubby old things. Here, let me help you..."

"No, thank you."

"It's very warm in here and..."

"I said, no, thank you!" I folded my arms across my chest. "What are you trying to do to me?"

"Jeanie." He looked so shocked that I immediately felt stricken with remorse. What on earth was the matter with me, snapping at him like that? And how could he possibly know the reason that I…

"Jeanie, I wish you'd tell me what's wrong."

"Nothing's wrong. And I'm sorry I spoke to you like that." I bit my lip.

"Are you quite sure it isn't something I've done?"

"No! And just to apologise, I'm giving you this." I plonked the carrier bag on his desk. "Ignore the wrapping paper."

"But why should I ignore the paper?" He took out the box. "Oh. I see." He gazed at the little cupids with a bemused expression.

"I didn't choose it. It was the man in the shop."

"It's delightful. Should I open this now or save it for my birthday?"

"When is your birthday?"

"Months away."

"Then I think you should open it now."

"I will." He untied the ribbons with surprising deftness, removed the paper and opened the box. Then he took out the tankard and gazed at it in obvious astonishment.

"Heavens, Jeanie," he said. "This must have cost you a fortune. I haven't seen one of these in years. It's a Doughty. Oh, Jeanie, thank you so much. You really didn't need to do this."

"Yes, I did. That collection of mugs you've got over there is quite awful, especially the one with the crack in it. I don't know what you mean about a Doughty. The man in the shop never mentioned that. And I didn't pay *that* much for it."

"I'm relieved to hear it. I wouldn't want you to spend six months' salary on me. I'm not surprised the shopkeeper didn't realise it was a Doughty; the manufacturer's stamp at the base is almost rubbed out. But this china is very rare. All these lovely designs are based on the Victorian language of flowers. Did you know that?"

Oh! I was remembering what Dorian had told me. *Purple lilac...the burgeoning of romance...a yellow rose, someone is falling in love...a red rose.... burning physical passion.*

"I didn't," I said.

That wasn't really a lie was it? After all, I *hadn't* known anything about the symbolism until last night, even if I did know it now.

"I see." I thought I detected a flicker of disappointment in his expression. "Well," he added. "I'm just relieved to know you *do* like flowers. I was afraid you might dislike them for some reason. So I haven't offended you after all?"

"Offended me?"

"By giving you the roses."

"The roses? They *were* from you?"

"Yes. I suppose I should have left a note, but I thought you'd guess. They're to thank you for healing my hand."

"And they were beautiful," I said. "Thank you. You must have thought it was very rude of me not to say anything when I came in but thing is..."

"What?"

No, I wasn't going to do it. I wasn't going to tell him about the poison pen note.

"They're lovely," I said.

"Good. I'm just relieved you like them."

I did, of course, even though the roses were white. Pure virgin white, without a hint of romantic passion. And they'd been given to me by a man who, as it now transpired, knew all about the Victorian language of flowers. I tried not to feel too disappointed although, of course, I was.

Twenty One

"The Obeah man, he come, he come and take you away..."

Psyche was wiping her counter with dreamy inefficiency, smearing crumbs and spilled tea along its length with a damp dish-cloth. Behind her, a trolley of dirty plates waited forlornly for her attention. I sat at a corner table eating a slice of coconut cake, a battered second-hand copy of Charlotte Bronte's *Shirley* propped up in front of me: I had only just begun to read:

Calm your expectations; reduce them to a lowly standard. Something real, cool, and solid lies before you; something unromantic as Monday morning, when all who have work wake with the consciousness that they must rise and betake themselves thereto.

Oh dear. This was only the first page, but already it seemed *Shirley* was going to prove a considerable disappointment after the romantic excitement of *Jane Eyre,* the book that had fed my imagination in my teenage years, prompting me to dream of moody, troubled anti-heroes. I didn't want to read about something as dull as Monday morning, especially on such a grey, uninspiring day as this. I was feeling quite deflated as it was.

Almost the whole of November had gone past and I hadn't seen Llewellyn for days, although I was sure he was in the building. Something had gone wrong, I knew it, but I didn't know what the trouble could be, and, even before he started avoiding me, he'd become increasingly distracted and distant, although never anything but scrupulously polite. Too polite, in fact.

My sense of an anti-climax was intense. I'd fondly imagined those afternoons in his office, how we'd sit side by side, deciphering Antioch Corey's manuscript, exclaiming over our brilliant discoveries and beginning to experiment with the magic it contained, but it hadn't turned out like that at all. Instead, he'd been copying out several pages for me by hand before I arrived, and then he'd sit with the original manuscript in the opposite corner of the room, leafing through his dictionaries and not volunteering a single remark. The easy, light-heartedness that had begun to develop between us when I first came to work at the library, those jokes about mugs and cups and the exchange of gifts, had gone and constraint had taken its place. Sometimes, I'd look up from my work and catch him staring intently at me, but the moment our eyes met, he'd avert his gaze, murmuring an apology. I didn't understand his behaviour at all.

I'd been left to my own devices when it came to the work on the Cabinet of Curiosities too, and as for *The Book of Shadows,* that had also failed to meet my expectations. All I'd managed to translate from the Latin so far was a dull-as-ditch-water account of fiscal and legal affairs in the small New England town where Antioch Corey was born.

"I don't understand," I looked across the room at Llewellyn. "Why all the secrecy and the seventy year embargo if this is all it contains?"

"We should be grateful it's so banal." Llewellyn dismissed my concerns.

Grateful? But I wanted powerful spells, apocalyptic prophesies, a deep and dangerous delve into the dark side. I wanted something that would help me become a sorceress in my own right and I wanted him to show me the actual *Book of Shadows*, not guard it jealously and offer me nothing but a few transcribed pages. And now, just over a week ago, he'd suddenly announced that we needed to stop working on the book and the Cabinet of Curiosities altogether, giving me no explanation or indication of when we could start again.

"You see him soon, the obeah man..."

"Thank you, Psyche." I took my empty plate to the counter. "The cake was delicious. I was wondering, can I ask you something?"

Psyche stared back at me, her eyes milky and blank.

"It's about your song," I persisted. "What exactly do you mean, when you sing about the Obeah man?"

"*Him?*" She shrugged. "Why you ask? You want I summon him?"

"Summon him?" This was a startling offer. "But who is he?"

"When you see him, you'll *know*." She spat into her palm. "He'll come in the time of need."

I wanted to ask more, but she turned away, and with sudden vigour pushed the trolley into the kitchen area and slammed the door behind her. I heard the sound of rushing water and the crashing of crockery. The longest conversation I'd ever had with her was over.

I was about to leave when Gerda came through the door, carrying a stack of box files with a china pot filled with pens and pencils perched precariously on top. As she went to put them down, the pot skidded along the uppermost file and smashed on to the floor, scattering the contents everywhere.

"*Ach!* Such a good start to my day." Gerda smiled good-humouredly. "I should know better than to behave like a juggler."

"Let me help you." I bent down and began to pick up the pens and pencils. "I'm afraid your pot's badly chipped." I retrieved it from under a radiator.

"Vell," she shrugged. "It vas only an old marmalade jar after all! But I hope my Parker's in one piece. It vas a present from a dear friend."

"It seems to be intact." I handed her the fountain pen.

"Thank you." She removed the top and examined the nib. "Ah, it looks fine. A good omen." She sat down and began unwinding her long, multi-coloured scarf. "So, Jeanie, how is life treating you?"

"Very well," I lied. "And how's your research going?"

"Slowly, slowly. I have spent several days in the archives, reading in the presence of Miss you-know-who." She lowered her voice. "Tvice she varned me not to drop biscuit crumbs! And I had never intended to open my box of biscuits at all. So presumptuous of her. And the way she guards everything so jealously, as if she does not realise the material in the library belongs to us all. So different from you, Jeanie! You have done such good vork. I have enjoyed looking at your exhibition in the entrance hall. The notes on the sasquatch skin and the Sun Dance effigy-doll from Mexico vere most informative."

"Thank you."

"And you have been vorking on this vith our Custodian?"

"Yes." It seemed best to say no more.

"That must be very stimulating. I think it is an excellent thing that these items are now on display for all to enjoy. I daresay Miss Plymouth Rock vould not agree. Has she said anything to you about the vork ?"

"No."

"Then thank heaven for that! She told me once that, in her opinion, Antioch Corey's collection was a health hazard.

She mentioned the possibility of contracting anthrax from animal skins and suggested dust can cause asthma. In her opinion, the entire contents of the Cabinet of Curiosities should have been incinerated long ago. For my part, I am suspicious of people who vant to burn valuable things."

"Quite," I agreed.

"Her obsession vith hygiene must be a mental disorder," Gerda added. "But enough of her! Are you doing anything special today?"

"Yes, I'm heading for the stacks. My first visit. I'm looking forward to seeing them."

"Those stacks." Gerda rolled her eyes towards the ceiling. "Such a labyrinth. Ernest dislikes going up there, he tells me, all those old books and in such a muddle. Three whole floors. And so many of the lights don't vork. I hope you have a torch."

"Yes. Ernest's given me one." I took it out of my bag.

"Ach! The battery in that is almost expired! Vat on earth is Ernest thinking! You vill hardly be able to see a thing. And you shouldn't go up there in that lovely ivory silk jacket, so much dust and grime. But you vill find the stacks rewarding, I think, you could make some interesting discoveries. Perhaps even a forbidden volume or two."

"Forbidden? What do you mean?"

"Oh," she smiled. "There are always rumours about forbidden books in academic libraries, usually the allusion is to filthy porn! Here, they are supposed to be memoirs and biographies of those who have dabbled in necromancy and devil vorship. The books are said to be concealed in the stacks vith false covers. I have never discovered one, but then it is difficult to find anything up there."

"Oh dear. Then I might have a problem locating the book I need, *The Satanic Secrets of Charles Baudelaire.*

It's been requested by a Dr Deforest of Branksome Chine."

"Oh, I can help vith that!" Gerda assured me. "I happen to know there are some books on nineteenth-century French poets on the second level, just under the oriel window. But do take care up there and keep a tight hold on that torch!"

The stacks, as I'd been warned, were somewhat unnerving. The construction of the floors consisted of a heavy metal mesh that creaked alarmingly as I made my way along them, and where the light was a little brighter, you could see through to the lower level, so any woman worried that a Finsworthy type might be lurking below would be well-advised to wear jeans or trousers. But there was no Finsworthy here, or anyone else for that matter. I seemed to have the place to myself.

Gerda's remarks about the forbidden books had excited me. What if there was a memoir or a biography up here that might shed some light on the mysterious M'? Nasir's words were always echoing through my mind. *Arthur Lewin and Mandy. Bad people.* If anyone had dabbled in 'dark practices' it would be them. I was prepared to engage in a thorough search; Ernest had told me to take my time after all.

There was a thick smell of dust; a cobweb brushed against my face, there was mould on some of the walls. Remembering Gerda's warning, I took off my silk jacket and hung it over the back of a bentwood chair. Then I set off to find the book on Baudelaire.

I found it easily, it was exactly where Gerda said it would be; a slim volume in a grey paste-board cover, translated, I noticed, by a scholar at the Sorbonne. I slipped it into my bag, and continued along the row of shelves. Were any of these titles and covers false, I wondered? There were certainly some books here that I couldn't imagine any of our subscribers wanting to borrow; books on gardening, on waterways, on keeping tortoises and breeding guinea-pigs. I pulled one out at random; *A History of Bee-keeping in Sussex* and opened it. Oh. It really *was* about bee-keeping. No luck here then. I went up the spiral staircase to the next level.

I must have lost track of time. I was so absorbed in my search, pulling the books out methodically, examining each one, kneeling down to reach the bottom shelves. So many titles, and not a single one containing anything other than what it said on the cover: *The Afghan War: A soldier's story*, *Up the Creek without a Paddle*, *Humphrey Clinker*, *The Pilgrim's Progress*...I had to read each title in the feeble light from Ernest's torch. Very soon, I feared, the batteries would give up altogether.

And then I found it, inside a brown paper slip cover labelled *The Posthumous Papers of the Pickwick Club*; a thick book with a green leather cover and the title printed in gold: *Occult London, 1850-1900: With testimonies from witnesses.* I opened it, turning at once to the index at the back. There seemed no point trawling through all the m's, but what about Lewin as in Arthur? Could there be a reference here? I ran my finger down the page: *Lamp of Thoth, Levi, Levitation, Lewes....*

The metal floor creaked behind me, someone was approaching. I scrambled to my feet, dropping the book in my panic. *Oh!* Someone must have managed, unlike me, to find the cord to the overhead light, and now I was completely exposed, standing here without my jacket, my arm bare, fully visible. I heard a horrified gasp and then I saw Llewellyn, standing in front of me, an expression of what I took to be extreme disgust and revulsion on his face.

"What's happening?" I crossed my arms over my chest, defensive and shocked. "What are you doing?"

"Jeanie, I'm sorry," he sounded genuinely contrite. "I didn't mean to startle you."

"Why are up here? Were you following me?"

"Of course not. I was investigating a report from Miss Nantucket. She sent me a note saying that she suspected there were rats up in the stacks."

"And instead of a rat, you've seen *this.*" I held out my left arm, pointing to the livid, twisted, contracted, deformed flesh that I always hid from people. "And yes, I agree, it's revolting. I'm not surprised if it makes you feel sick." I was beginning to hyper-ventilate, making myself dizzy. "I need to get my jacket, please, my jacket, it's down there, I hung it up down there. Please, I must..." I tried to push past him.

"I'll fetch it." He spoke softly. "And Jeanie, it's all right. You don't have to hide those scars from me. They don't make you any less beautiful in my eyes."

He'd called me beautiful. I caught my breath.

"I'm not in the least beautiful," I said.

"But Jeanie, you are. It's something I struggle not to notice every day."

"I don't know what you mean. Now please, I have to go, I need to get my jacket..."

"We'll fetch it together." He spoke softly. "And Jeanie, listen, the only thing that's shocked me is the thought of how much physical suffering you must have undergone. It must have been an awful accident and..."

"It wasn't an accident," I said. "Not exactly."

"Not an accident?" He looked appalled. "You mean that someone actually...Jeanie, how..."

"I might as well tell you. It's a long story, but when I was eighteen, they tried to burn me as a witch."

Twenty Two

He unlocked his office and ushered me inside. I was feeling much calmer now, relieved to have the chance to tell my story to someone who would listen sympathetically. And he did seem sympathetic; he no longer seemed so cold and distant towards me. In some ways, he seemed more shaken than I was.

"Brandy." He put a tumbler into my hand and sat down at his desk. "I'm sorry I don't have a proper brandy glass but that is the very best Napoleon brandy."

"Thank you." I took a sip.

"You don't have to tell me anything. But if you've had enemies or people who haven't treated you well, then I do need to know. I want you to be safe here, I want to..."

"Protect me? You don't have to keep saying that. But yes, I want to tell you about it. This is the explanation for the two missing years on my CV, the time I spent in the institution."

"So what happened, Jeanie? Take your time. I'm here for you, please believe that."

"There was a boy I met when I was in the sixth form at school," I said. "I used to call him Bushy...."

Spring 1972

"This way, Gowdie!" Bushy yelled the words into the wind. "This must be the place!"

"Are you sure?" I gazed across the sodden fields.

"I'm two hundred and one percent certain! Come on!"

I stumbled after him as he crashed through the wet bracken like an over-enthusiastic dog. The waterproof cagoule I'd borrowed from the school's lost property box was flapping around my knees; my feet were skidding on the mud. It didn't help that I was wearing plimsolls a size too big for me, also from lost property, my father having refused to buy me new shoes. He'd said it was my fault that the sole had come off my last pair; I should have known better than to let Nana buy me such vanities, in patent leather and with straps, instead of laces. And now with Nana gone, I had to make do and mend.

"Come on, Gowdie!"

I grabbed hold of a bush, saving myself from falling headlong into the ditch but spiking my hand on a thorn. Bushy was oblivious to my wounded cry. He was yards ahead now, climbing over a five-bar gate into the open moorland. The rain continued to sheet down.

At least we'd survived the journey here. The tattooed lorry driver from whom we'd hitched a lift had driven so manically up the motorway, pulling out into the prohibited fast lane several times, that we were lucky not to have ended up on the central reservation with our necks broken.

"Over here!" Bushy waved frantically.

Why did he have to get so excited all the time? But that was Bushy all over. The scent of any kind of mystery, particularly if it related to witchcraft, was like a drug to him, giving him a buzz that made his eyes gleam. I hoped we weren't missing anything important in the Easter revision classes we were supposed to be attending; I wanted to get top grades in my A-levels. Leaving Knox Hill and running away to London dominated all my thoughts. I intended to go as soon as I got my exam results and I was determined to leave with honour.

"I can see it." Bushy was standing beside a dry stone wall, the toe of his boot nudging a steaming cow-pat. "There it is, over by that clump of gorse." He pointed across the field. "That's your Witch-Stone."

I wasn't at all sure that it was; we seemed to be in an entirely different place from the one I remembered from my thirteenth birthday.

"It looks smaller," I said. "And I'm sure it didn't tilt at that angle."

"Memory can be deceptive." Bushy took his camera out of his rucksack. "Right, come over here and I'll take a picture of you beside it."

"What if I don't want my photo taken?"

"Don't be a spoil-sport, Gowdie." He shielded the lens with his cupped hand. "What's the point of coming here if we don't make a record?"

"I wish I'd never told you about it," I said. "It's hardly one of my happiest memories."

"Oh, nonsense, Gowdie, don't you see? It was a significant moment in your life. A rite of passage."

We sheltered under a rowan tree to eat our packed lunch. I'd brought two apples and Bushy had made the sandwiches, filling them with a combination of his own invention, a gunge-like mixture of Marmite, sandwich spread and mashed hard-boiled egg. I found them deeply unappetising, but didn't have the heart to tell him. Luckily, he was too intent on his own food to notice how little I was eating.

"OK." Bushy munched eagerly. "Now that we're here, I'll tell you what I think. First off, your Dad's wrong about the witch-burnings."

"He's not my Dad, he's my father."

"Same difference." Bushy shrugged.

"You wouldn't say that if you knew him." I picked up a sandwich, lifted the top layer of bread and looked underneath. It was even worse than I'd feared; he'd added raw chopped onion to the mix. "A Dad is someone who's fun and tells jokes and who plays games and takes you to nice places and is soft and kind underneath, even when he's trying to be strict. My father is just strict."

"Interesting distinction," Bushy mused. "I haven't seen my father for years, so I wouldn't know. To tell the truth, I could manage perfectly well without parents."

"I suppose some of us have no choice." I took a disconsolate bite of my sandwich. "So, why do you think there weren't any witch burnings here?"

"There's no record of it. Most of the witch-burnings in Scotland took place in Edinburgh, near the castle. Besides, it doesn't make sense to burn people here. Why would you try and start a fire in the middle of a moor where it rains half the time? How would you keep the kindling dry?"

"I see." I felt somewhat repelled by his reference to such practical details.

"All the same," he continued. "It's no accident that the stone is here, not far from the border with Scotland. Strange things always happen on borderlands, and a dolmen, that's what stones like that are called, would have been erected in prehistoric times to keep out evil spirits. There's a legend about how the stone came to be here. What do you think that might be?"

"It was placed here by the devil?" I suggested. "Another story like the one about the sarsen stone that was dropped in the Severn on the way from Wales to Stonehenge?"

"Good suggestion, but no. This one's about a young woman who danced here on the Sabbath in the reign of James I. The local priest saw her, held up his Bible, and she was turned to stone on the spot. Not archaeologically accurate, of course. The stone was here long before the time of James I. This is almost certainly a pre-Roman Megalith, probably put here by the Beaker folk. The dancing on Sunday story is obviously a myth."

"A myth based on hate," I said.

"Hate?" Bushy picked up one of the apples and took a great bite. "Why do you say that?" He crunched noisily. The sound irritated me so much I wanted to scream.

"Only a man could have made up that story." I said. "There are some men who wouldn't want a woman to dance at all, whether it was Sunday or any other day of the week."

"Well, I didn't invent the story." Bushy grinned. "Don't have a go at me."

"I'm not having a go at *you*! I don't even think of you as a man."

"*What?*" He stared at me wide-eyed, his mouth full of half-chewed apple. There was something absurd about his wounded expression but all the same, I felt sorry that I'd offended him

"I only meant," I tried to make amends, "That you're not an adult. Not until your eighteenth birthday."

"I'm only a few months younger than you, Gowdie. I'll be eighteen in August. Actually, it's an educational disadvantage to be born in August. You have to compete with other kids who are a whole year older."

"So I've heard." I took a conciliatory bite of my gunge sandwich. "Sorry."

"Luckily," he flung his apple core away. "I've always been advanced for my age. Anyway, apart from the unlikelihood of the witch burnings, I do think certain rites must have been practised here, right up to the seventeenth century. Sabbats and magical ceremonies, like the ones your ancestor Isobel Gowdie boasted about attending."

"She wasn't my ancestor! Will you stop saying that?"

"You've got no proof whatsoever that you're not descended from her."

"It's impossible, don't you see? For one thing, Gowdie was my mother's married name, it's the name I inherited from my father. Can you imagine my father being the great-great-great-I don't know how many greats-grandson of a witch?"

"Why not? It might explain his fixation with this witch-stone. Anyway, you look like Isobel Gowdie. You're sexy like her." Bushy touched my cheek and leant forward, bringing his face close to mine. I leapt to my feet as startled as if a wasp had buzzed in my ear.

"Leave me alone!"

I ran, stumbling over the uneven ground in my too-long, flapping waterproof. There were tears and drops of rain on my cheeks, and my plimsolls felt as though they were beginning to disintegrate. At last I fell against the dry stone wall, gasping for breath. I imagined Isobel Gowdie standing with her head held high, out-facing her accusers. She'd have given it to them straight: '*Yes, I'm a witch. I can turn myself into a hare. I can turn myself into a bird. I've been to faerie-land. I've danced widdershins around the church with the Man in Black, so stick that in your pipes and smoke it!*'

"Gowdie?" Bushy appeared beside me, a puzzled expression on his face. "What's wrong?"

"You wouldn't understand." I brushed the wet from my face.

"I might. Look, I think I get it. You haven't got over your Nan, have you? It must have been a shock, her taking her own life like that."

"She didn't 'take her own life'," I retorted. "She went to join the seal people. She passed into the Summer Lands."

"So it's true?" His eyes widened. "Your Nan really was a pagan, following the Old Religion, hexing the weather and casting spells, and worshipping the Horned God?"

"I don't want to talk about it."

"But you must! Don't you see? You're her heir! You have to step into her shoes. I can help you. I've read about initiation ceremonies. We have to perform one to put you on the right path."

"Not yet we don't. Nana told me that I wouldn't have my Coming of Age until I was twenty one."

"That can't be right," he objected. "That's old-fashioned. It must be eighteen now, the same as in the conventional world. Anyway, you have to make a start. And you need someone to help you. And that's me!" He ripped off his anorak and pulled open his shirt. "See?"

He pointed to his bony, hairless chest. Just above the breast-bone there was a red, livid geometric shape with five distinct points. A pentacle. I could see that it was very recent and almost certainly self-inflicted, probably made with a penknife and the point of a pair of school compasses. I didn't know whether to laugh or cry.

"I think you should put some TCP on that," I said.

"Why should I? I was born with this mark!"

"So," I hesitated. "If you were born with it, how come it's bleeding?"

"Because," Bushy said proudly, "it's a magical mark and it bleeds every full moon, and there's a full moon tonight. This is the mark of the intermediary, the Holy Fool. Gowdie, we'll do the ceremony the day we get our A-level results. That will be the perfect time."

Twenty Three

Bushy stared up at the Knox Hill Guest House. He didn't seem impressed by the pebble-dash façade, mock Tudor gables, monkey puzzle tree and the swinging sign reading 'Vacancies'

"So at last I get to see where you live, Gowdie," he said.

He sounded slightly disgusted and I didn't blame him. However, the knowledge that I was about to leave made the ugliness of my so-called home suddenly irrelevant. My A level results were just as good as I'd hoped they'd be and tomorrow, I was going to run away to London.

"Come in, quietly," I whispered. "We don't want to wake my father. He's out in the back kitchen."

I'd checked on him half an hour earlier and found the man who objected to *in-eeeeee-briation* slumped over the kitchen table, his head resting on his folded arms as he snored loudly, an oil lamp and an empty bottle of Scotch next to him. There was a good chance he wouldn't wake up until morning, but I'd closed the door very quietly just in case.

The situation at Knox Hill was desperate now. My father no longer spoke to me, not even to threaten me with the fulminations of the prophet Amos. He'd stopped washing, not that he'd ever been particularly conscientious when it came to personal hygiene. There were dirty finger marks all over the old Bible that he leafed through so frequently.

A week ago, our electricity had been cut off. The rates were overdue. The telephone was out of order. Mrs Wallace still called in from time to time, but not to work, since there were no wages for her. She'd taken a job serving in a fruit and veg shop. In her view, my father was 'not himself', but it seemed to me that he was more himself than usual, yelling Biblical quotations out of the window at passing squirrels and cursing the world.

"OK," Bushy sat down in the guest lounge and opened his rucksack. "Here's what I've brought. First, some alcohol." He took out two bottles of cider. "Also some herbal smokes, candles, a *lot* of candles, matches of course, some red ribbon and—" he paused, apparently for dramatic effect. "This!" He produced a small book.

I gazed at it. Just like the so-called 'mark of the intermediary', it was an obvious fake. I could see that the cover was one of the hymn books from school, but with a different title pasted on the front: *The Grimoire of Invergrerey.* I decided to play along with the deceit; poor Bushy had apparently gone to a considerable amount of trouble to impress me, creating those old pages by soaking paper in tea and singeing the edges with a match. And he had been rather moody lately, slamming his fists against walls and bruising his knuckles. It was better not to upset him.

"Wow! Where did you get hold of that?" I exclaimed with fake enthusiasm

"Well, that's the weird thing," Bushy told me. "I was in that second-hand bookshop, you know, the one by the market? I'd picked up a different book and the shop-keeper asked me if I'd like it wrapped, and I said I would, and then he went out into the back and came back with a parcel and said, "Are you sure you want this book?" I said 'yes' and he handed it to me, and when I got home and opened the package, instead of *Birds of the Hebrides*, I found this!"

"Why did the shopkeeper make that mistake?"

"Gowdie, don't you get it? He didn't make a mistake at all. It was a magical transaction; I was destined to be the new owner of the grimoire."

"The grimoire?"

"A grimoire," Bushy explained patiently, "is a book of magical rituals. And here," he turned the pages, "is an account of the ritual that must take place when a novice witch reaches the age of eighteen. Shall I read it to you? The writing's very difficult to decipher."

"All right, go ahead." I tried not to sound too cynical and weary.

"Right!" He held the book up to his face. "Here's what it says: *'Gather ye greenerie of laurel and ivy and make ye a crowne to place about her head. Make ye the pentacle of red ribbon and laye it on ye grounde. Make a circle of lights. The acolytes must goe sky-cladde as they repeat the dark mantra: 'Eco, eco...'* Oops, no, I'll stop there. I'd better not say the name of the spirits out loud until we're ready. Anyway, we have to go sky-clad and..."

"Sky-clad," I repeated. "That means naked. You must be joking."

"I thought you might say that, so I've come prepared. I brought this." With an air of triumph, he pulled a white nylon nightie out of his rucksack. "You can wear this. It's a bit diaphanous so you'll still be semi-sky clad, as long as you take off your underwear."

"Thank you," I said faintly. "That's very thoughtful of you." *Oh no.*

We cleared a space, pushing the old horse-hair settee and the fake leather arm chairs with the splitting seams up against the walls. I felt hot and uncomfortable. It was one of those muggy, overcast summer evenings when the air is full of midges.

I went outside and collected some laurel and ivy. Fortunately, there was a lot of it growing in our gloomy back yard amongst the bins and all the discarded ironmongery; an old tin bath, a rusting length of pipe, and a wheelbarrow that had lost its wheel. I found a length of gardening wire and made a frame for the wreath. Then I went back into the house and up to my room where I changed into my costume. I gazed at myself in the mirror and oddly enough, found I rather liked my appearance, the leaves around my head and the floating, synthetic garment falling to my ankles. Perhaps it wouldn't be too revealing if I made sure I wasn't standing with the light behind me. Besides, whatever Bushy said, I certainly wasn't going to remove all my underwear.

"Ready?" Bushy asked. "OK. Now let's light all these candles. No, don't draw the curtains; we have to keep them open to let in the moonlight."

"There isn't any moonlight."

"There will be later. Also, we need some air." He pulled up the big sash window.

Bushy's preparations took another twenty minutes as he made the pentacle from the ribbon, cutting it into lengths and arranging the pieces on the carpet, and then placing candles all around the room. After this, he sat cross-legged on the floor with his eyes closed indulging in five minutes meditation, as he called it. Then he instructed me to stand in the pentacle with my arms outstretched as he began to walk around the room in an anti-clockwise direction reciting what he called 'the dark mantra'. This consisted of the words 'ecco, ecco' followed by names that he claimed were those of the fallen angels mentioned in the Talmud. The words sounded vaguely familiar and I'd just realised where they really came from, when I heard stifled giggling.

I spun round, and saw they were standing just outside, by the open window, Chrissie Wilkinson and her cronies, Venetia Carlisle and Angela Barnet and some others I didn't recognise. Chrissie had a bottle in her hand; it looked like vodka. They were high, I could tell; they'd obviously been celebrating their disappointing A-level results with expensive substances.

"Go away!" I shouted at them. "School's over. You can't do anything to me now."

"Is that so, *witch*?" Chrissie Wilkinson swayed slightly, but her tone was defiant. "You think we don't know? Your boyfriend told us, didn't he? About the rag dolls and the pins you stick in them and the people you hurt and the hexes you do."

"Bushy?" I turned to him. He'd stopped his recitation and was now standing with his back against the wall, shielding himself with a cushion as he stared back at the girls. "Surely you didn't say that about me?"

"Yeh! I told them you were brilliant! I told them they'd better leave you alone."

"But it isn't true! I've never...."

"'Get her! Get the witch!" The chanting started quietly at first.

"You...don't...scare...me." I could hardly get the words out; my chest felt so tight.

"*Get her! Get her! Get the witch!*" The voices were louder now, gathering momentum.

"Clear off!" I yelled. It wasn't a very subtle response, I realised, but it was the best I could do at that moment.

"Think we won't do it?" Angela Barnett produced something from her bag. "Do you want me to light this, witch?" she said. "Well, do you?"

She was holding a large firework. I could guess where she'd got it from; her father was in charge of the closing display at the local fete every year.

"Do your worst," Bushy leaned out of the window. "I have all the demons from the Talmud on my side."

Of all the ill-judged lies he could have told them, this was possibly the worst. Besides, he didn't even know the names of any ancient demons. Those words he'd been chanting had been lifted straight from the lyrics of a song by Dave Dee, Dozy, Beaky, Mick and Titch, something about *Zabarak,* no, that wasn't quite right..*Ka...*

"Don't be so stupid!" I grabbed his arm. "Come away from the window!"

"*Burn the witch!*"

Everything was quiet for a moment, and then Angela lifted up her arm. A second later, the firework hurtled through the window and hit a plate on the dresser. There was a sizzle, and then it exploded in a shower of gold. The cheap nylon carpet, with its design of purple, red and yellow whirls that resembled psychedelic dog-turds, started to melt. I'd have been pleased to see the back of such an unloved monstrosity if it hadn't been for the danger we were in.

"Burn the witch!"

More smoke and now a candle had ignited the filthy old curtains.

"Bushy! Help me!" I pulled at them but they wouldn't come away from the old metal runners.

"Geronimo!" Bushy was leaping from foot to foot, knocking over more candles, his eyes gleaming with insane joy. What was the matter with him? What had he taken?

Flames licked at the plaster ducks on the wall. Billows of black, choking smoke gushed out across the room from the burning armchairs. I clapped my hand over my mouth, eyes watering, and managed to grab Bushy's arm, dragging him into the hallway.

"Get out!" I pushed him towards the front door and without waiting to see whether he went out or not, I ran back to the kitchen. My father was still slumped at the table, but the snoring had stopped. I was sure he must be dead, that he must have been dead for some time. There was no smoke in here, not yet; his death could have nothing to do with the fire. A stroke perhaps, a heart attack... I didn't know, but that stillness, that lumpen immobility could only mean one thing.

I felt neither shock nor grief, but I did feel a duty to behave decently. I couldn't leave my father here to suffer an unofficial cremation. He'd always expressed a wish to be buried. But he was a big, heavy man and I couldn't move him and now the smoke was coming into the kitchen, and I knew I had to get out.

I ran out of the back door and round to the front of the house. I couldn't believe how fast the fire was spreading. The first floor was blazing now. I could hear a fire engine in the distance and someone must have called the police, because there was Bushy with a blanket around him, standing by a police car. The moment he saw me, he started shouting, "Hey, Gowdie, we did it, we raised a fire demon!" and he shouted that again and again, and the neighbours who'd gathered were staring at us both. So I told the police there was a body inside and then the fire-engine arrived and...Of course, there was no sign of Chrissie Wilkinson or any of her accomplices.

And then I remembered my suitcases, the ones I'd packed ready for the next day. The big one was full of my clothes and things that could be replaced, but the other one, the small, battered brown one, contained things that were sacred to me, things that Nana had given me, a book that had belonged to my mother, my apprentice tools, other stuff...So I had to go back in. I had to save it.

Someone tried to stop me, but I was too quick and I ran round to the back of the house and up the fire-escape. I remembered that I'd left the door at the top propped open. That had been part of my escape plan for my flight to London. So I got back into my attic bedroom, and I found the little case and I was about to leave but the flames and the smoke had reached the upper storey of the house, and as I was coming out of my room, I looked at my nylon nightie and saw that the sleeve was melting into my skin...and it didn't even hurt at first, that was the odd thing, but then..."

I broke off, gasping. To my shame, I could feel tears in my eyes.

"Take your time, Jeanie," Llewellyn said. "You don't have to say any more just yet."

"But I must finish." I took a deep breath. "I have to get to the ending. So, I got out of the house, but my arm was badly burnt and I was in a hospital at first. And then, before my arm was properly healed, I was taken to a place called Crowsmuir Hall. They kept me there for two years. I was assumed to be guilty."

"Guilty?" Llewellyn frowned at me. "Guilty of what?"

"Arson and attempted manslaughter. What else? But I didn't do it. I didn't do any of it. And you're the only person in the world who's ever believed me."

Twenty Four

"Fire. You passed through fire." Llewellyn's voice was husky and there was a strange look in his eyes. "Oh, Jeanie, that is so...you see, I've also..." He stood up and walked over to the window. "But this isn't about me. Thank you for telling me everything."

Not quite everything. There were certain details that I'd omitted out of sheer embarrassment. I hadn't mentioned that during the so-called ceremony, Bushy had insisted on being fully 'sky-clad'. That was, of course, the reason he'd grabbed a cushion to shield himself when those girls appeared. And earlier, when I'd come downstairs after putting on the nylon nightie I'd found him standing in the middle of the room completely naked with his arms stretched out in a crucifixion pose.

"As you can see, I've been circumcised!" he announced. I was so startled to find him displaying his naked parts like a man on a deli counter selling salami that I hadn't known what to say, although I did choose not to look too closely.

"I don't understand why people assumed you'd started the fire," Llewellyn turned back to face me. "It was those girls who threw in the firework."

"Yes, but we'd lit the candles. And there was something else. It turned out that there were rags soaked in paraffin shoved into the gaps in the skirting boards in the front room of Knox Hill. We were blamed for that, but I've often wondered if my father was responsible. In his madness, he might have been planning a big conflagration, the cleansing fire of Jehovah, the smiting of Sodom and Gomorrah. Or maybe he was just planning an insurance fraud. Anyway, it was assumed that Bushy and I had done that. It didn't help that Bushy kept yelling that we'd raised a fire demon. 'We', he would keep saying 'we'. So it was hardly surprising everyone thought we were responsible."

"But what about those girls? Surely they were mentioned in court?"

"There was no trial or hearing. I was in the hospital and then they took me to Crowsmuir."

"Really?" He frowned. "That doesn't sound right."

"I suppose it wasn't right, but I didn't question it at the time. After all, I'd been interviewed by the police. They didn't believe me when I said Angela Barnett had lit the firework. They didn't even believe those girls were there, they all had alibis for that night. Their parents were adamant that they'd been at home and no-one doubted the word of such prominent people. Chrissie's father was a councillor, Angela's was a solicitor, Venetia Barnett's father was the chief of the local police and all three of the men were Freemasons."

"Of course they were." Llewellyn's expression was grim. "And this boy, Bushy, what happened to him?"

"No-one would ever tell me. I think he must have been sent away, to a borstal or some kind of detention centre. Or possibly a mental hospital. Anyway, now he's dead."

"He died?" He sounded surprised. "How do you know that?"

"Nana told me that when a rabble of rooks settle in a yew tree and begin to caw in unison, it means they're telling you about a death. You just have to close your eyes, and the name of the person who's passed away will come into your head. It happened when I'd been at Croswmuir for nearly a year. I saw the rooks, and I closed my eyes, and Bushy's name came to me, so I knew that he had gone."

"Poor Bushy." Llewellyn shook his head. "I can't help feeling considerable sympathy for this young man. He must have felt very sad about what he'd done. He boasted about you, wanting to convince those girls that you were a powerful witch, and brought the catastrophe down on you both."

"I doubt if he even realised he was responsible. Bushy was never strong on self-reflection."

"All the same, I think he cared about you very much. In fact, I think he was in love with you."

"In love!" I was horrified by this suggestion. "But he was just a boy! He was seventeen."

"And that's just the age when those feelings are the most intense and hurt the most."

Could this be true? I'd always believed that teenage boys were far less romantic than girls, but now I was remembering Bushy's behaviour during those last months before we took our 'A' levels. There was that day in the recreation ground when he asked if he could kiss me. He said, "I've never kissed a girl and I'd quite like to try it, if it's all the same with you." It had felt so wrong. Heathcliff would never have spoken like that to Cathy and I didn't want my first kiss there, by the swings and the jungle gym. I didn't want to be kissed by Bushy at all and I was just trying to think of a tactful response when he caught me by the shoulders and gave me a wet, slobbery, open-mouthed kiss, all tongues and clashing teeth. I thought it would never be over.

"There," Bushy said at last. "Now, if either of us should ever meet someone and fall in love, we'll know what to do, won't we?"

Would we? I didn't want him to see me wiping my face, but as he'd dribbled on my chin I had no option. Luckily, he'd turned away; he was hanging on to the fence, gulping in deep breaths. I couldn't think what was wrong with him but I was determined never to let him do anything like that again.

"I used to feel angry with Bushy," I said. "But now I've forgiven him. In his way, he was trying to do something for me that night."

"Yes, it sounds as though he was." Llewellyn nodded. He paused for a moment, and then asked, "Tell me, what do you remember about being taken to this place, Crowsmuir Hall?"

"There were two people in dark suits, a man and a woman. They came to the hospital and told me to come with them and I thought they were taking me to another part of the hospital for burns treatment, but instead, they told me to bring my things and then I was taken away in a black car. It was a long journey, to somewhere in the North, past Inverness, I think. I don't know who they were."

"Has it ever occurred to you they might have been witch-finders."

"*Witch-finders?*" I repeated, incredulous. "In England? In the twentieth century?"

"I'm afraid the witch-finders have never gone away. They use different job titles now, and they work through the channels of the conventional world, the law, politics, the police, freemasonry and even the church."

"But no-one ever asked me about spells or occult ceremonies."

"Perhaps this boy, Bushy, had said enough for both of you."

"Yes, perhaps he had." I nodded. "But *witch-finders*...I can't believe that."

"I'm afraid that I can. Jeanie, would you mind very much if I looked into this, made some inquiries about this place, Crowsmuir Hall?"

"No, I don't mind at all. And, of course, although I was locked up for two years, they *did* let me go in the end."

"Did they give you unconditional freedom?"

"Well no, I suppose they didn't. They told me where I was to live, where I was to work. But now I've successfully left both places! So, it's all in the past now, surely?"

"I sincerely hope so, but you can't be too careful." He walked over to the Cabinet of Curiosities, unlocked one of the drawers and took out a narrow black box. "Jeanie, I want to give you something." He opened the box and hooked out a necklace, a string of small black stones secured by a silver clasp. "This is obsidian." He laid the jewellery on the palm of his hand for me to see. "These stones are known as Apache tears. There's a legend about some Apache warriors who rode deliberately to their death, launching themselves off a steep mountain side rather than face defeat against the US cavalry. The women who loved the warriors cried and their tears turned to precious stones and so all the sorrow of a wounded nation became transformed into something beautiful."

"It's lovely." I gazed at the necklace, at the way the stones glimmered as the light fell on them. I felt sure they contained powerful magic.

"I'm glad you think so. Jeanie, I want you to wear this."

"Oh, but I can't take it," I protested. "It must be so valuable and surely it belongs to the Library if it's from Antioch Corey's collection?"

"Jabez Corey would be more than happy for you to have it. Please, won't you accept this?"

"Oh, but I..." I hardly knew what to say. "The clasp looks so delicate. I'm afraid I'd break it."

"Then I'll put it on for you, if you'll allow me."

"Yes. Thank you." My heart was beating very fast. He stood behind me, lifted my hair and fastened the clasp in a surprisingly expert manner, without any of the clumsy fumbling I might have expected from a man.

"Thank you."

"Oh, Jeanie, it suits you." He gazed at me. "It suits you so well."

Our eyes locked. There was a knot in my stomach. He was looking at me as though he wanted to kiss me, and I realised that I wanted that to happen, I wanted that so very much. But if that happened, where would it lead? Was I even ready for...*Get a grip, Jeanie! Don't think like this! Oh, but he called me beautiful and now....*

"Jeanie," he spoke softly, "I want you to know that I am determined to ensure that no harm like that ever comes to you again. And if you ever need my help, you only have to ask."

Ah! Here was my opportunity to mention the subject that had been occupying my thoughts all these weeks. Up until now, I hadn't known how to broach the subject, especially not over the past weeks when he'd become so strange and distant. But now, there seemed to be a new understanding between us. This must be the time.

"I *do* need your help," I said. "It's about my Coming of Age. When I was at Crowsmuir, I couldn't do anything to prepare for it, and it was the same when I first came to London. But now I'm here, and I've met you, and I know you're an adept, so I want you to teach me advanced magic and help me to arrange the Ceremony."

There was a long silence. Then,

"I'm sorry, Jeanie," he said. "But I can't do that."

"*What*?" I felt as startled as if he'd just slapped my face. "But you can't mean it! Nana Herrick told me to come to London, to find those of our own kind, and when I met you, I was sure that you were the person who..." I broke off, unable to continue.

"I'm not the right person, Jeanie. And I can't do what you ask. I'd be putting you in terrible danger. And I've sworn to protect you."

"I don't want to be protected!" My shock and hurt gave way to fury. "I'm not a child! I'm nearly twenty one, about to come of age and..."

"You have a very independent spirit. But you don't realise how vulnerable you are."

"Vulnerable?" I felt stung. "I've looked after myself so far. They didn't destroy me at Knox Hill, they didn't destroy me at Crowsmuir and now here I am, in London, living my own life. Have you any idea of how patronising you sound?"

"I don't mean to be. Listen, Jeanie, I do have an idea. I think it would be useful if you visited Dr Hecate in the spring, in April. You must miss your Nana very much and Dr Hecate..."

"Next April will be too late," I interrupted him. "My birthday is in March. The ceremony has to take place before then. If it's delayed, then I'll never fulfil my destiny. Why are you doing this to me? *Why* are you refusing to help me? When I first came here, you asked me about spells and shape-shifting and I told you my Nana was a wise-woman. I thought you understood."

"Jeanie, we mustn't quarrel." He sounded genuinely distressed. "Of course I understand. But..."

"But what?"

He took a deep breath. "I don't practise magic any more. I relinquished it many years ago."

I was too shocked to speak at first.

"But that can't be true," I said at last. "Out in the square that night, how did you manage to defeat that thing, that wraith or whatever it was, if you didn't use magic?"

"That was different. It was a matter of survival and keeping my promise to Jabez Corey. Jeanie, I just want you to be safe."

"And I don't want to be 'safe'!" All the disappointment and anger spilled out of me in a rush. "I came to London to achieve my destiny. I wanted to learn the skills that would help me to become a powerful sorceress. I thought you were going to help me. And now you tell me you don't practise magic anymore. How pathetic! I thought you were someone special, but now...now I know you're not the person I thought you were. And if you must know, all this business with *The Book of Shadows* has been a complete disappointment. I don't think you're even been giving me the real pages to translate."

"You think I'd deceive you to that extent?" He looked so hurt that I almost wanted to take back my words, but I was too angry. There could be no mending this.

"I don't know what you might do," I said. "You haven't been honest with me. There are things you're hiding from me. I don't even know if I can trust you."

"You must trust me."

"Must?"

"Jeanie," He ran his fingers through his hair. "There are things you don't understand. If I was even to *think* of arranging a Coming of Age ceremony for you, the consequences could be catastrophic. I am not the right person and magic, real magic, involves far more than the simple folk customs your Nana taught you. There's more harm in it than healing, it leads to pain and loss and suffering...I'm sorry, I've said too much. But now I've given you that necklace, you'll be protected as long as you wear it."

"*What!*" I touched the apache tears. "These are for my protection? But I thought you'd given them to me as a ..." *As a love token.* I couldn't say the words; it would be too humiliating to admit what I'd been thinking. My fingers were trembling as I felt for the clasp of the necklace. "You'd better take these back."

"No, Jeanie, no! You must keep them."

"But I don't want them now. Everything's spoiled!"

"Oh, *Jeanie*." He sounded completely wretched but I was too fired up now to feel any sympathy. "You don't understand. I..."

"There!" I dropped the necklace on his desk. "Please, no more explanations. And now I'm going."

"Jeanie, please..."

"If you really cared," I struggled to keep the tremble out of my voice, "You wouldn't be treating me like a naïve girl. You wouldn't be telling me you don't practise magic any more. Even if that was true, now that I've asked for your help, you'd take it up again. You'd do it to prove that you're a man, and not just any man, but an adept. And you'd do it for me. Good-bye!"

I didn't mean to slam the door quite as hard as I did as I left but I enjoyed the resounding crash all the same. *And whist to that man*, as Nana would have said.

Twenty Five

I sat at my desk, closed my eyes and attempted to repeat the old Wiccan charm against anger that Nana taught me but as I struggled to remember the words, I realised I was enjoying all the negative energy that was coursing through me. I felt resolute and empowered. So Llewellyn had given up magic, had he, and wasn't prepared to help me with my Coming of Age? Then I'd take charge of my destiny without him. There must be some other way to learn the powerful magic I needed. There was, for example, 'M'.

I took the monogrammed mirror and the little key out of my bag and laid them in front of me on the desk. *Are you there? Can I find you? You know my true name... Tell me yours.* I sighed. Nothing was happening; perhaps the conditions here weren't right. Well, I must just get on with my everyday work.

First, there was the postal loan for Dr DeForrest of Branksome Chine to despatch. I laid the copy of *The Satanic Secrets of Charles Bauldelaire* on a length of brown paper and reached into my desk drawer for the string and sealing wax. *Ow!* I sucked the tip of my thumb. What was a loose drawing pin doing in there? Oh, curses!

There was a loud bang as a cascade of shattered glass fell on to my desk. I jumped up; startled. Blessed Epona, there was even a sliver of glass in my hair. I picked it out carefully and dropped it in the bin.

"Problem?" Ernest looked in through the door.

"No....that is..." I looked up at the ceiling. "Nothing really, except the light bulb up there just exploded."

"Quite a common occurrence. Happens a lot here!" Ernest picked up the bin and began sweeping the fragments away with the back of his hand. "The old place hates the new wiring."

"New wiring?"

"Yes. It was put in here in the nineteen-fifties, I understand. Better order a new bulb. Just pop a note in the box for Jim the caretaker."

"I wonder if Jim could get me an oil lamp," I mused. "I think I might prefer it to an electric light."

"Oh, Jim will get you anything you want." Ernest flexed his knuckles. "He's very accommodating for an invisible man."

"Long time, no see!" Nasir grinned at me as I walked into Mustafa's. "Don't tell me you need to use our phone again. What have I told you about getting one of your own?"

"I don't need the phone." I closed the door behind me. "I've come for supper. Is there time for that before you lock up?"

"Any other customer, I might say no." He glanced up at the clock. "But in your case, I'll say yes. After all, you've never come in for supper before. It'll be my honour to serve you one of our specials. So, why haven't you been in here for so long?"

"I started a new job and I got into the habit of getting to work early."

"A new job?"

"Yes. As a matter of fact I found the advert for the vacancy in here."

"In here?" he frowned.

"Yes." I looked around at the custard yellow walls, the steamed-up windows and the twin bottles of red and brown sauce on each table, reflecting, once again, on the mysteries of fate. "It was on a torn bit of newspaper that was sticking to my saucer."

"Blimey!" Nasir rolled his eyes. "That was a piece of luck. Anyway," he pointed to the chalk board on the wall. "What about our all-day breakfast? Bubble and squeak, beans, mushrooms, fried slice, fried eggs, black pudding and bacon?"

"I missed lunch, so yes. I'll have it all, except for the bacon."

"What's wrong with our bacon?" He cocked his head to one side. "Or do you have religious reasons?"

"No, not at all. It's just that bacon isn't my thing." I felt a flash of nausea, remembering the smell that used to pervade the Knox Hill Guest House.

"You don't know what you're missing," he grinned. Want a drink while you're waiting?"

"Yes. A coffee, please."

"Coming up!"

I sat down at my usual table and flicked idly through an evening paper that someone had left there. I never bought a paper for myself and I didn't regret knowing so little about current affairs. Politics, sport, TV shows, so-called famous people, they all seemed so irrelevant to me although sometimes I found it informative to dip into that other, outside world.

"Brown sauce?" Nasir put the steaming plate down in front of me.

"Yes, please. Lovely." I'd never touched brown sauce in my life. Time to be more adventurous.

"Here you are then, new bottle. Tuck in."

"Thanks." I picked up my knife and fork. "Nasir, have you got a moment? I wanted to finish the conversation we were having the last time I was in here."

"You'll have to remind me what we were chatting about." Nasir walked over to the door and turned the sign to 'closed'.

"You were telling me about a pub, near Coleton House. There was a man who used to talk to your auntie in there. He told her ghost stories, about a woman called Mandy, and a man called..."

"Oh, yeh! Right!" Nasir nodded vigorously. "Creepy stuff! Well, I can remember something. The old bloke said that the pub was named after this Mandy. It had some quite ordinary name when it was first built, but then a new brewery took it over in the sixties."

"And called the pub Mandy?"

"No. It was called *The Sorceress.*"

"*Oh!*" Now this was exciting! "And did you go there?"

"'Course I did. I used to stand outside on summer evenings with a bag of crisps and a lemonade while my auntie was inside. The sign was from some old painting. A bloke stuck up in a tree and a weird woman in a clingy green dress holding a book and giving him the glad-eye. And he's looking at her as though he wants to rip her clothes off, if you'll excuse the expression."

"I think I know that picture," I said. "It's called *The Beguiling of Merlin.* It's by Sir Edward Burne-Jones, based on an Arthurian legend."

"Come again?"

"You must have heard of Merlin? He was a powerful wizard in King Arthur's court, but then he became infatuated with the sorceress Nimue, and she imprisoned him in a hawthorn tree. Her magic proved stronger than his because he was weakened by love."

"Right!" Nasir snorted. "Typical woman, always wanting to get the better of a bloke. And then I bet she went off with someone else."

"She did. King Pelleas."

"Poor old Merlin. Ooops, I can smell burning. Must've left something on the stove, 'scuse me."

I finished everything on my plate, and then took my mirror out of my bag and flipped it open, ready to re-apply my lipstick. It was then that I saw her, the old woman to whom I'd given my mac all those weeks ago. She was out in the street, staring in at me, her face pressed up against the window. And her expression was far from friendly.

I got up from the table, opened the door and leaned out.

"Can I help you?" I asked.

The old woman pursed her lips but didn't reply.

"I gave you my mac," I said. "Do you remember?"

"Charity handouts." She bent over her trolley, rearranging the contents, the piles of old shoes, the carrier bags stuffed with paper. "What makes you think I want them?"

I noticed her feet. Those worn-out bedroom slippers could hardly be providing protection from the cold, especially not with her toes, complete with gnarled yellow toenails, sticking out through the holes.

"Why don't you come in out of the cold?" I said.

"Not likely." She pulled her moth-eaten cardigan round her shoulders. "Once you're in, they'll never let you out again. You should know that."

"I don't understand."

"Don't you? But I know what you want." She plucked at my cloak. "You want to find *her*. Lady M. She's got what you need. But she won't give in to you easily. You'll regret it if you upset her. Through the fire, through the fire and through the fire again!"

A chill ran through me. How did this old woman know those words? This couldn't be a coincidence; there must be some connection between her and that strange experience I'd had on the underground. And what else did she know? I had to question her further, although I had the distinct impression she wasn't going to welcome any probing on my part.

"Did you know this 'Lady M?" I asked. "Do you know what the 'M' stood for? Could it have been Mandy?"

"That's for you to find out," the old woman muttered. "Not for me to tell. But she's waiting for you." The old woman waved her arms wildly in the air. "Over there, all amongst the angels and the tombs."

"Over there? You mean in the old cemetery? Are you saying she's buried there?"

"Buried? You won't find her lying in the earth, under the ground. Not her." The woman gave a hawking cough and spat copiously on the pavement.

"But what do you mean? Are you saying that...?"

"Hello, Nora." Nasir came out of the café carrying a white plastic bag. "Plenty of leftovers for you tonight."

The woman seized the bag, looked inside, gave a grunt and flung it into her trolley.

"I'm off," she said. "But *she* wants to watch it." She pointed to me. "Find her yourself. And gawd help you when you do!"

"London's full of mad old bats." Nasir took my money, rang up the till and handed me my change. "You don't want to take any notice of nutty Nora."

"Is that her name? Nora? It doesn't seem very kind to call her nutty."

"No, you're right, but it's what everyone says. She's been wandering around here for years. Story is that she got bombed out in the war and has never been the same since. She comes round at closing time and we give her some food. She can be a bit aggressive. Standing out in the street, shouting a load of gibberish."

"I'm not sure that everything she said just now was gibberish. I think she knows something."

"I doubt it." He slammed the till drawer shut. "Old Nora's off her rocker. Start listening to her and you'll go off your rocker too."

"But if she was here during the war, and maybe even before that, she must know some local stories? She mentioned 'Lady M.' and I think she might have meant Mandy. And she said something about angels and tombs. And if these people, this Arthur Lewin and Mandy, really did live around here, isn't it likely that when they died, they were interred in the old cemetery?"

"Could be." He nodded.

"But the thing is," I persisted. "Nora said, 'You won't find her in the earth, lying under the ground'. Was she trying to tell me that she's still alive?"

"If she was talking about 'Mandy', she'd have to be about a hundred and fifty," Nasir laughed. "No, she's dead all right. And she could still be in the cemetery even if she isn't buried in a grave."

"What do you mean?"

"Haven't you seen those tombs that look like little houses? The ones where the coffins are stacked up inside on shelves."

"The family mausoleums?"

"Is that what they're called? Yeh, she could be in one of them."

"Of course! Yes, that makes sense!"

"All I know," Nasir said. "Is that old cemetery's a spooky place. When we were kids, we used to dare each other to go in when it was getting dark and we'd look for ghosts. We used to run round the graves anti-clockwise and call out 'Is anybody there?' And we'd peep through the grilles and look inside those mausoleum things and we'd try and get into the catacombs. *Whoo-hoo*!" He flapped his arms. "And we weren't the only ones. Some really weird people used to hang around in there too, holding séances and stuff, even hunting for vampires."

"Really?"

"Oh yes. Anyway, sorry to hurry you, but it's time to lock up."

"Of course. I'll be on my way."

"Well, be careful on your way home. There are some strange people about."

"Oh, I don't mind that," I told him. "I quite like strange people. In fact, I might even be one myself."

Twenty Six

"Just arrived for you," Ernest handed me a bulky brown envelope. "Special delivery."

"Special delivery?" I looked at the printed label bearing my name. "You mean, through the post?"

"Internal mail."

"I didn't know that there was an internal mail."

"There isn't. Just being facetious. Never mind, just take this."

"Thank you."

I went through to the parcels room and closed the door. My hands were trembling as I opened the package and took out a familiar narrow box. I lifted the lid and gazed at the necklace of apache tears that was nestling on a wad of padded silk. I couldn't help feeling a pang of regret. What on earth had come over me yesterday, rejecting this lovely gift? I'd been in such a rage, as if I'd been possessed. There was a folded piece of cream note-paper tucked inside the box. I took it out to read.

Dear Jeanie,

I've been called away on urgent business. In the meantime, the work that we were engaged upon is, of course, suspended. Please believe me when I say that you <u>*must*</u> *wear this necklace for your own protection. I wish I could tell you more, but I think that would be unwise. Forget that I was the person who gave this to you. I don't blame you for your anger. I am a brute and you are quite right to despise me.*

Yours,

L.

I couldn't help smiling. *A brute!* What an archaic word. His self-depreciating apology was like that of a character in a nineteenth century novel, Laurie in *Little Women* or Eugene Wrayburn, one of my favourite literary crushes, in *Our Mutual Friend.* I didn't feel angry any more, but equally, I wasn't ready to wear the apache tears. I'd take them back to my flat and keep them somewhere safe, perhaps in my case under the couch. I certainly wouldn't lock them in my desk drawer, not next to the things I'd found buried in the pot of rosemary...Ah! I'd just remembered something!

That book, *Occult London*. I'd left it lying on the floor up in the stacks. I hoped it was still there. I must go up and retrieve it. I couldn't believe I'd been so careless; there I'd been, possibly on the brink of a really exciting discovery, and then Llewellyn had come along....*Oh!* Suppose he'd known what I'd been doing? Suppose his arrival hadn't been a coincidence at all, and his excuse for being there had been a ruse, and all the time he'd been trying to prevent me from....No, I mustn't start being suspicious of him. I must just go up to the stacks and find that book.

I knelt down on the metal floor, torch in hand. How very kind of Gerda to bring in some new batteries; it was working well now. However, I was having difficulty finding the book and yet I was sure this was the place where I'd found it. Had someone had taken the book away or put it back in a different place? That seemed unlikely as so few people ever came up here. I shone the torch along the shelf, examining the titles: *Steam Boats of the Mississippi, Sewing the American Quilt, The Gold Rush Years.* I didn't remember any of these books from yesterday.

As I edged along the creaking floor, I wondered about the weight of all these books. Just how strong were these shelves? I had a vision of them collapsing like a pack of cards, burying me under a morass of obscure writing. And now there was something wrong with the torch after all. It was flickering and... *oh!* I gasped as something hairy brushed up against my left ankle.

Was that a rat? At that moment, my torch went out.

Hell! This wasn't good. As far as I remembered, there were no light-cords that worked on this level. And then I heard something, a rustling, as if someone wearing a full-length garment was approaching and then...

'Morgana...'

The voice was little more than a sigh, but I'd heard it clearly. I knelt there on the metal floor, my heart thumping.

"Yes, I'm here," I whispered. "Can you help me?"

'Fool!'

"Oh, I'm not a fool." I said. "I'm a seeker after truth. *Da mihi quod postulo scientia.* Give me the knowledge that I need."

'Ha!'

There was a sudden flash of light, then darkness, and then the lights began to flash on and off as if a delinquent child was pulling at the cords. A rush of wind came out of nowhere and books began crashing down from the shelves in a cacophony of thuds and cracking spines. I put my arms over my head. There must be a charm against poltergeist activity, but I didn't know one.I'd just have to improvise once again.

"Quietus! In nomine senex deorum..."

Everything was suddenly still. I pressed the switch, found my torch was working again and shone it on the floor around me, discovering, to my consternation, that I was surrounded by splayed-out books and torn-out pages. As I began to gather them up, I saw that some of the loose pages were from *Occult London.*

"Hello? What's going on up there?" *Clemency.* The very last person I wanted to see, especially when kneeling on the floor surrounded by mutilated books.

"Nothing. That is..." I quickly thrust as many pages into my bag as possible.

"Jeez, what happened here?" The light cord that hadn't worked for me had worked for Clemency, and now here she was, standing in front of me, gazing at the mess. "Did you do this, Jeanie Gowdie? This is completely unacceptable! So destructive, so..."

"It wasn't me." I tried to hide my panic. "I just found this. It could have been rats. Didn't you make a report about them?"

"I did. But rats chew the edges of books; they don't rip out pages in this manner." She stared accusingly at the devastation.

"It could have been an accident," I suggested. "Someone must have left a window open and..."

"A window? There are no windows on this level."

"From somewhere downstairs, I mean. There was a gust of wind..."

"I didn't hear anything." Clemency's eyes narrowed. "There's obviously a vandal in this library and they must be dealt with. I shall be reporting this to the trustees. And in the meantime, please be more careful when you're up in the stacks."

"Of course." I smiled at her as politely as I could.

*

I drew the curtains of my basement room, lit a black candle, and laid out the pages I'd brought home from the stacks. I'd been waiting all day for this, for the chance to examine them in private. I picked one up at random; a fragment from a book entitled *Table Rappers and Conjurors.* The typeface was very small and the text was stained in places:

'*...quite similar to the exploits of Daniel Dunglass Hume who enacted celebrated feats of levitation and tricks with burning coals. There were, however, allegations of trickery, such as muslin disguised as ectoplasm, servant girls jumping out of cabinets dressed in ethereal white, and ghostly hands made of plaster grasping those of the living. Others, however, including Abraham Matthewson, claimed Hume was a genuine magician with paranormal powers. Matthewson himself produced remarkable...*Here the fragment ended.

I picked up two more pages; these were from *Occult London*. Here was some more information about Matthewson. First, a detailed bibliography of books in Greek and Latin that were believed to be lost when a library in Prague burned down in 1658 but that were later found in his possession. Then there was an eyewitness account of one of Matthewson's spells:

In 1857, Matthewson, the celebrated adept and necromancer, was seen to summon the dead by means of a spell known as 'The Beckoning'. Using a mirror that had belonged to the deceased, he filled the room with the smoke from coiled incense burners such as those used in Chinese temples, then took hemlock and the seeds from a laburnum tree, together with a rotting skull dug from a churchyard at full moon and the caul from a baby who was born with twelve toes. After he had uttered the invocation, the dead woman appeared in the room as a corporeal presence and was seen to take snuff before leaving through the window, floating at a height of sixty feet above the ground.

This, of course, can be construed as a fanciful account, but the use of a mirror that has captured the reflection of the deceased cannot be discounted as an instrument of psychic power. The words of the invocation follow here...

My excitement grew as I read on to the end. *A mirror that belonged to the deceased.* Oh!

Why didn't I try a beckoning spell right now? I didn't have a rotting skull or the caul of a baby with twelve toes of course, but I did have plenty of hemlock and laburnum seeds, and most significantly, I had the mirror that had belonged to 'M' and that I believed to contain a spirit. Perhaps even *her* spirit. I remembered my recent encounter with old Nora. What was it she'd said? *She's got what you need. She won't give in to you easily.* That was it! I must beckon 'M'. I'd already received two communications that seemed to be from her, one on the underground and another up in the stacks. Now I must be the one to initiate contact.

I placed the mirror on my black cloth, surrounded it with scattered seeds and filled my scrying vessel with oil and water. I lit the incense and sat cross-legged on the floor. Then, with what I hoped was due solemnity, I began my invocation:

"I beckon thee, she whose name begins with 'M', whether sorceress, witch, angel or demon. Let she who once owned this glass show herself to me. I, Jeanie Gowdie, soon to adopt her true name of Morg..."

There was a sudden, frantic knocking at my door. *Damn!* Who on earth was being so inconsiderate at this time of night? So much for my Beckoning Spell. And before I'd even got properly started too!

No-one ever knocked on my door, apart from the occasional meter reader. Even the postman left parcels on the step. I wasn't at all sure it would be wise to respond. I'd heard reports of thieves who forced their way in when unsuspecting householders opened the door. But it might just be a group of young carol singers who'd started the season early and were poised to burst into an off-key rendition of *Away in a Manger* the moment I appeared. Even so, I wasn't in the mood for Christmas yet.

There was a momentary silence, and then the knocking was renewed with such violence, I wondered if it was someone in desperate need of help. Perhaps a woman had been attacked by one of those legendary 'flashers' that Doris at the hostel had warned me about. I couldn't ignore such an urgent summons. I took the precaution of opening the door on the chain.

"*So* sorry to disturb you." The woman had a deep, sultry voice. She was painfully thin, virtually skeletal and was dressed in a little black cocktail dress that might even be an original Coco Chanel. Her arms and legs were bare and she wasn't wearing a coat. That seemed quite unsuitable for a cold November night. My first thought was that she was an upper class prostitute who had become too old and haggard to earn much money on the game and so had taken to begging. Or perhaps she was an actress, or a local eccentric. I told myself that she was probably more vulnerable than threatening. I unfastened the chain.

"Can I help you?" I asked.

"I hope so." Her mouth was a slash of crimson lipstick, cutting across her face like a wound. "I'm collecting the names of people who would be interested in subscribing to *Cat Lovers' Monthly.*"

"Sorry. Not really my kind of thing."

"We begin publication next month." Undeterred, she edged forward. "It's a new and very lovely glossy magazine, full of useful hints on looking after our feline friends. There will be beautiful photographs of cats, including a centre-fold 'Moggy of the Month' that can be pulled out and displayed on your wall."

"I'm afraid I'm not very interested in cats."

"No?" She pointed to the bottom of my door. "But you have a cat-flap!"

"Yes," I agreed. "That belonged to the previous tenant. But I keep it locked."

"Locked?" She looked appalled. "But suppose a dear little kitty wanted to get in?"

"I don't want any stray animals in my flat," I said. "To tell the truth, I'm not fond of cats."

"Not fond of cats?" She held up her hands in a rather shocking display of spidery fingers with bright crimson nails. "But everyone loves cats."

"Not me. Now, if you'll excuse me..." I went to close the door.

"Do tell me more." She stepped forward. Oh, no! She was practically over my threshold and now I wasn't at all convinced she *was* harmless. "This is fascinating. I've never met a person before who has openly admitted to hating our feline friends and wanting to cut off their paws!"

"Good heavens, I never said that!" I was horrified by the way she'd twisted my words. "I wouldn't dream of ill-treating a cat."

"But would it be fair to say, you hate them?"

Oh dear, would I never get rid of her?

"Not hate, no," I explained. "But I don't trust them. Cats are sly, predatory creatures. It's horrible to see a cat stalking a beautiful bird that's innocently pecking around on a lawn.

And they take fledglings out of their nests too. And as for the way they treat poor little mice, batting them with their paws for hours and torturing them, it's cruel. I love birds and little furry mice. My Nana and I used to do everything we could to keep cats out of her garden."

"So I can't persuade you to subscribe to *Cat Lovers' Monthly?*"

"I'm afraid not."

"I see. Then I won't trouble you any further." She stepped back. "Although," she gazed at me with narrowed eyes. "I can't help feeling you've just made a serious mistake."

"Good night." I slammed the door.

I waited to hear the sound of her stilettos clicking up the area steps, but there was an unnerving silence. Either she was still lurking out there, or she'd taken off her shoes and walked away in bare feet. Anything was possible. My hands were shaking as I secured the chain. How foolish of me; I should have asked for her name. Without knowing that, I couldn't put a protection spell in place to keep her away from my door. And whoever that woman was, I never wanted to see her again.

Twenty Seven

"Good morning, Jeanie." Gerda looked up from her work as I came into the reading room. "Are you looking forvard to the Yule tide vacation?"

"Of course," I said.

This wasn't entirely true. The library was due to close from Christmas Eve to the beginning of the New Year. I'd never have been given such generous leave at the insurance office, but I had mixed feelings about the prospect of being away from this place for so long. I was going to miss the company; Gerda, Ernest, Psyche and the regular readers I'd come to know. And most of all I was missing Llewellyn. Was he even going to return before the break?

Ever since that weird woman had knocked at my door, I'd been feeling edgy and quite unlike myself. I hadn't been sleeping well and a number of disturbances in my flat at night had worried me. I'd heard footsteps on the area steps, scratching behind the skirting board and strange, subdued laughter that seemed to be coming from the pipes. And then, this morning, I'd found a mutilated bird on the door step, a mess of black feathers, bones and intestines that could only be a message of ill-will. It was this last incident that had convinced me to start wearing the necklace of apache tears. I was wearing it right now, discreetly concealed under a silky, gold-threaded scarf. I didn't want Clemency Nantucket to see; there was still the faint possibility she was responsible for the memory curse and if she guessed that Llewellyn had given me something to keep from Antioch Corey's collection, she would almost certainly object.

"Vell, I rather dread the so-called festivities." Gerda took off her glasses and laid them on the open book in front of her. "Such an interruption of my vork and there are tiresome family obligations. I shall be going to my sister's in Innsbruck. First, ve vill fall into each other's arms, then, after a few days, ve shall not be getting along. She vill force me to eat too much stollen, she vill tell me that I am a mad old academic and I vill be driven mad by her *hausfrau* ways. At last, I vill return to London, determined to avoid her invitation next year but knowing I von't have the courage." She sighed. "And you, Jeanie, do you have family to visit?"

"No, none at all."

"Ach! I hope you vill not be lonely. Vill you be going to any parties?"

"I don't think so."

"But you vill at least come to the party here?" She smiled encouragingly. "Ve have it in Psyche's place, staff and regular readers, before ve all part company for the year. It is a tradition. I am the organiser."

"That will be on Monday, then?" I glanced at the calendar pinned to the wall.

"Yes, and the library vill stay open late especially for our party. Isn't that right, Ernest?"

"Indeed!" He jumped up from his desk. "The Yule-Tide gathering. Chocolate log. Plenty of holly. Greenery. Mistletoe. Bring a gateau." He jerked his head towards me. "Or a quiche."

"All the pagan trimmings then!" I joked.

"Traditional." He nodded. "One year we performed a New England Mummers play."

"A New England Mummers play?" I repeated "I didn't know there was such a thing."

"Oh, indeed there is!" Ernest attempted a smile, baring his teeth like a shy shark hoping to find friends. "And Psyche makes punch. Don't drink too much. Lethal!"

"I'll bear that in mind," I said. "I'm just wondering, what's the tradition here about cards and presents?"

"Cards but no presents! Definitely no presents, not between staff. Embarrassing. Awkward." Ernest curled his hands into fists and began rubbing his nails together frenziedly. "No presents, definitely no presents!"

"Ah, but I have an idea!" Gerda beamed. "This year, there *vill* be presents. I am organising a St Nicholas Bran Tub."

"A 'St Nicholas Bran Tub'!" Ernest sounded aghast. "What in the name of thunder is a St Nicholas Bran Tub?"

"It is a simple but ingenious idea," Gerda explained. "You must have seen a lucky dip? A big barrel or tea-chest filled vith bran in vich gifts are hidden? This is just the same. You dip in and see vat you get. It is fun."

"And who is going to supply these gifts?" He sounded unconvinced.

Gerda reached into her bag and took out a large brown envelope. "I have prepared some cards," she explained. "Each vun has the name of a person here at the Library. You dip into the envelope and take a card at random, and buy a present suitable for the person you've drawn. So, if someone draws 'Gerda', they go, I hope, to Knightsbridge, to Harrods, to buy a small box of my favourite chocolates, *Mozartkugeln.* I joke, of course! So, the present is vrapped, the giver puts only the name of the recipient on it and the parcel is popped into the bran tub! At the party, each person gets a gift from St Nicholas!"

"Sounds childish. Won't work." Ernest cast an anxious look at his bicycle. "We're not always sure who's coming to the party. Sometimes readers who haven't been here for months turn up. How are you going to be sure there's a present for everyone?"

"Have faith Ernest. I have thought of that. Some of the cards vill be blank for unmarked presents that vill be distributed last. If you draw vun of those blank cards from my envelope, you simply buy a gift that any person, man or voman, could enjoy."

"But how could there be such a present?" Ernest looked bewildered. "Men and women are so different!"

"Humph!" Gerda shrugged. "Doesn't everyone like chocolate?"

"But men like plain chocolate with hard centres and women eat milk-coated truffles!" He thrust his fingers into his unruly hair. "I really can't see how it's going to work!"

"It vill," Gerda assured him, "And it vill be fun. Jeanie, vill you pick a card now?"

"Of course." I reached into the envelope. The moment I read the name on the card, my heart sank.

"Something wrong?" Gerda frowned at me.

"Oh, no. It's fine." I adopted what I hoped was a carefree smile. I knew it was wrong to harbour mean-spirited thoughts in this season of goodwill, but of all the names I could have drawn, this was the one I wanted least:

Clemency Nantucket.

Saturday 21st December. The shortest day of the year, the winter solstice, and the beginning of the old feast of Yule. I'd planned to call in at Pyewackets, but first, I had to buy Clemency's present for the St Nicholas Bran Tub. This was an irksome obligation; I'd much rather be choosing a present for a friend, venturing over to Knightsbridge in search of those *Mozartkugeln* Gerda mentioned, or finding something Ernest might like, perhaps a scarf or a book of crosswords. I had no idea what kind of thing would appeal to Clemency. No doubt she would despise anything she considered frivolous, so no vanity bags, nail polish, lace hankies, bangles, trinkets, little china ornaments or scent for her. There was also the possibility that she didn't eat sweets or chocolate because they were fattening and bad for your teeth. As for a bottle of sherry, the word 'teetotal' probably ran through her as indelibly as the place name in a stick of seaside rock. I supposed it would be best to get her a practical item. A pair of good, thick tights. Some carbolic soap. A gingham apron with pockets for stout wooden pegs. An axe to chop down the trees. Oh, dear, I must stop! This was supposed to be the season of goodwill.

I gazed in at the window of a fancy goods shop where there was a display marked 'Gifts for her'. Perhaps a box of those lemon-shaped soaps might be suitable, given Clemency's obsession with hygiene? I doubted if she'd like any of that lacy underwear or a pair of sheer stockings complete with a sexy garter. But what about gloves? There was a good assortment here, leather ones, stripy ones, mittens and zany ones with different coloured fingers. Then I noticed a pair of thick grey woollen ones with a snowflake pattern on the back. Ah! Now *those* were perfect for Clemency. Practical, homely and offering warm protection from the freezing winter mornings. I went in and bought them straight away. Thank goodness that task was accomplished. Now for my visit to Pyewackets.

"It's Jeanie Gowdie!" Dorian looked up from his perusal of *Antique Dealers News* with a grin. "I was sure you'd be back here before Christmas and now here you are. So, are you now looking for a Christmas present for the man who has everything? I expect he's getting something wonderful for you."

"There is no 'he'," I assured him.

"Tut, tut." Dorian gave me a sympathetic smile. "Lovers tiff, eh? In that case, I think you should cheer yourself up by buying something for yourself."

"As a matter of fact, I've come to make you an offer. Remember that cheval mirror, the gothic revival one? The one that came from Coleton Street? I'd be interested in buying it after all."

It was something that had occurred to me, late last night when I'd been re-reading the description of Abraham Matthewson using a mirror that had belonged to the dead person. The prospect of another attempt at the beckoning spell frightened me just a little, but I was determined to try again. And this time, I was planning to use a larger mirror, one that might prove to be a more powerful conduit for the magic.

"Oh dear." Dorian shook his head. "I haven't got it anymore. It was sold a week ago. Hey, you look really disappointed. I *am* sorry. Is there anything else you'd like?"

"Not really." I stared disconsolately at the other items ranged around the shop, the ladder-backed chairs and the umbrella stands, the vases, the rugs and the pictures, all of them delightful but none of them suitable for my purpose.

"Such bad luck," Dorian said. "I don't even know who bought it. I wasn't here. I'd gone up to Mayfair for an auction and a friend was standing in for me. I was actually rather put out when I discovered he'd let the mirror go to this person, whoever it was. I knew you were interested in things from the Coleton Street sale and I thought perhaps you might come in and bargain for it. I often give good customers discounts before Christmas. My fault; I should have put it to one side for you."

"Did your friend describe the person who bought the mirror?"

"Apparently it was a man. Rather scruffy man, apparently, but he had a lot of money on him. Paid in cash. Anyway, all is not lost. He might have been a dealer, not a private collector. The mirror might soon be on sale again, in another London shop. Give me a few weeks and I'll see if I can trace it."

"Thanks. I'd appreciate that. You see, I really need that mirror."

"Need it?" He cocked his head on one side, looking at me quizzically. "And what are you planning to do with it, if you don't mind my asking?"

"Oh, I'll just put it a corner of my room," I said. *And utter a few invocations to beckon the dead.*

"Well," he beamed at me. "I'll do my best. And in the meantime, maybe I could interest you in something else? I *have* got something new in stock. Just look." He reached under the counter. "What do you think of this? It's a cat basket!"

"A cat basket?" I stared at it, a long bamboo container with a mesh door at one end and a handle at the top.

"Perhaps I should say it's a cat-carrier," Dorian said. "The Rolls Royce of cat transporters. It was hand-made in Ceylon at the turn of the century. The handle is made of ivory and the interior is padded purple brocade. Puss must have been pampered, don't you think?"

"But I don't need a cat basket," I objected. "I have no wish to own a cat."

"They can be very good companions. And this, let me tell you, was the property of Carmelia Grande. You must have heard of her."

"I'm afraid I haven't."

"Really?" He sounded surprised. "She was a silent screen actress. She used to play ageing ladies of ill-repute and aristocratic countesses. She was famous for carrying her black cat around with her everywhere, on to film sets, at First Nights, and into the dining room of the Algonquin Hotel in Manhattan. She said the cat brought her luck, and legend had it that Carmelia Grande was a witch. Every good witch should have a cat. Don't you think?"

"Not necessarily. Toads can make excellent familiars too."

"Ha!" he laughed. "Brilliant. Well, if you change your mind about this cat basket, you know where it is. So, can't I tempt you to anything at all? A little Christmas gift for that special someone in your life?"

"I don't know why you think there's a special someone."

"Well," Dorian smiled. "I seem to remember selling you a rather beautiful love tankard a while back."

"Oh. Yes. You did." My fingers strayed back to the apache tears. The poor, silly man; I was almost ready to forgive him. Perhaps I would buy a small peace offering and give it to Llewellyn at the Yule Tide party. Assuming, that was, he'd be there.

"I remember seeing a brandy glass in the window," I said. "Do you still have it?"

"I'm afraid not." He shook his head. "But I could easily get another one like it. Can you call in again, maybe on Monday morning? I'll be opening early as it's nearly Christmas. Is it going to be a gift?"

"Um...yes, it is."

"Then I shall put it in a special box and tie it with ribbon. And I predict your offering will prompt a declaration of love. And if not," he winked in a playful manner and pointed to the basket, "you could always get a cat."

Dusk was gathering as I made my way down the road, heading for the area on the other side of the cemetery. My failure to acquire the cheval mirror had been deeply disappointing, but I could still take a look at Coleton House and have a search for *The Sorceress. Arthur Lewin and Mandy...bad people...they still walk.* That was so intriguing. I was clinging to the idea that 'Mandy' had been a powerful sorceress and had left a trace of magic in these streets.

The main road on the other side of the cemetery was dense with exhaust fumes and the congestion of slow moving traffic. There was a parade of somewhat uninspiring-looking shops, a launderette, a newsagent's, a take-away food outlet with a greasy-looking doner-kebab turning on a spit in the window, a small greengrocer's with a display of fruit that looked past its best. I crossed by the lights and went into the newsagent's. It was a cluttered, chaotic place, selling groceries as well as newspapers and sweets, and nothing seemed to be in any logical order.

I picked up a bag of peanuts in their shells and held it out to the burly middle- aged man behind the counter. It seemed rude to come in without buying anything and this shop keeper had rather a forbidding look.

"Do you know Collyaton Road?" I asked.

"Twenty pence." The man took my money and then turned his back, busying himself with rearranging the cigarette packets on the shelf behind the counter. It seemed he was eager to get rid of me.

"I'm sorry to trouble you," I persisted. "But I'm looking for Collyaton Road. I was wondering if you knew it."

"Second turning on the left, past the barbers." He didn't look round. "But I'd be careful about going down that road on your own, especially now it's getting dark."

"Oh!" I felt a stirring of excitement. "Then you've heard about the ghosts?"

"Ghosts?" He spun round to face me. "No, I was thinking of the drug addicts and the prostitutes. This was a nice area before the war but now look at it. If it's ghosts you're wanting, I'd try the cemetery." He let out a loud guffaw.

"Well, thank you for your help." I said politely.

"Don't mention it. And if you do go into the cemetery, remember you have to watch out for the living in there too."

"You mean there are muggers?"

"No. It's a gay cruising area. You might stumble upon something you don't want to see."

"I'm sure I can cope with anything like that."

"Yeh? Well, don't say you haven't been warned."

Collyaton Road was dull, not a place of beauty but rather of urban decay. Several old shop premises were boarded up, as was the only pub. The sign had gone, so I had no way of knowing if it had once been *The Sorceress.* I quickly found Coleton House where Nasir's auntie once lived, an unprepossessing red-brick nineteen-fifties building; three storeys, long balconies, green front doors and louvre windows. Further on from the council flats, there was a small convenience store and a fish and chip shop. Litter careered along the pavement. There was nothing remotely spooky about this street. If Arthur Lewin and 'Mandy' really did *still walk*, I couldn't imagine why they'd choose to haunt a place like this.

I retraced my steps, planning to return home, but then I stopped by the gates of the old cemetery. I had, of course, intended to go in there sooner or later, to have a search through the tombs, but this didn't seem a good time, not when it was getting dark and I had no torch, and the cemetery office was closed. But now, through some compulsion, I stepped inside.

There was something rather soothing about all these extravagant monuments of mourning set amongst the overhanging trees. Stone angels stood with their heads lowered in respectful grief, their arms encircling marble crosses; cherubic figures on the graves of children peeped out from the undergrowth. There were broken columns encased in ivy, signifying lives that had been cut short prematurely, and imposing mausoleums on either side of the wide, central path. And there were crows everywhere, circling in the air, pecking at the gravel and strutting across the grass. Such dignified birds, so self-possessed in their fine glossy plumage. The denizens of the underworld. I rejoiced at the sight.

I sat down on a seat under a sycamore tree and took out the bag of monkey nuts that I'd bought at the newsagent's. I wasn't particularly fond of this kind of nut, but the birds might like them. There was a sign warning against feeding the wildlife but I couldn't see how nuts could do them any harm. I began cracking open the shells and scattering the nuts around a nearby gravestone. The inscription was well-preserved: *'Samuel Greatorex, 1860-1912, Beloved father, much esteemed founder of the Society for the Conversion of the Heathen. A pillar of the Community'*. Pillar of the Community? What had the poor 'heathen' done to deserve his interference? I could just imagine the stiff, upright collar that Samuel must have worn as he administered his self-righteous zeal.

A crow began to peck at the scattered nuts. Two men walked past me, one of them in jeans and a bomber jacket, the other in a dark suit. "What a beautiful tie you're wearing," the man in the bomber jacket remarked to the other, and then they took each other by the hand, and cruised off towards the trees. The crow perched up on top of Samuel Greatorex's headstone, and stayed there, as if watching me.

I took the silver mirror out of my bag, snapped it open and gazed into the glass. *Are you here, 'M', in this place, resting in one of those mausoleums?* There were so many of them; I wouldn't have time to examine all the inscriptions today.

A bell began to toll. The sound was coming from the chapel at the far end of the cemetery. How strange; my eyelids were feeling heavy. The cemetery was no place to sleep, I thought, as I slipped the mirror back into my bag. A mist was rising all around me and I could hardly see beyond the nearest gravestones. I was so cold; I must get out of here. But I felt too sleepy to move and before I knew it, I'd slipped into oblivion.

"The Lady Mandragora, who wouldn't envy her, loved by the most powerful adept in London?"

"And such a gorgeous man, too."

"But he wouldn't be interested in *us*, sweetie; he's no Mary-Ann!"

The two young men, deep in their conversation, were walking towards me down the path, both of them wearing brown suits and bowler hats, one of them whirling a cane in the air. They resembled two late-nineteenth century clerks, Lupin Pooter and Murray Posh from *The Diary of a Nobody,* perhaps. The mist was clearing and now I could see that the cemetery looked different, tidier and less over-grown, with newly planted trees. And, most tellingly of all, the gravestone of Samuel Greatorex, who departed this life in 1912, had disappeared. *Toto, I have a feeling we're not in 1974 any more.*

"Come to find him, have you?" She came down the path towards me, old Nora in her worn-out slippers, but she didn't have her supermarket trolley. Instead, she was pushing an antique pram filled to the brim with old rags and with a cylinder gramophone perched on the top. Her clothes too, had changed; that long black dress and cap was the uniform of a servant from a century ago.

"Him?" I repeated. "No, I wasn't looking for a man."

"But a man might be looking for you!" She leered at me. "You knew this was the trysting place, didn't you? Some won't be happy and may the devil take the hindmost! Well he's here, so get a move on."

"I don't understand. Who do you mean?"

"Over there. *Him*." She pointed towards a huddle of yew trees.

As I looked over to them, Llewellyn stepped out of the darkness. He was dressed in an ebony-black evening suit with a starched white shirt and a velvet bow-tie, and he had a white fringed silk scarf slung loosely around his neck. I'd never seen him looking so desirable. He stood there, gazing at me with such a passionate expression that I was quite terrified for a moment. Then, with a sleight of hand that took my breath away, he reached up and plucked a blood-red rose out of thin air.

"Hello Jeanie," he said.

Twenty Eight

I stood up slowly, half in a trance. I knew this wasn't a dream, not with the taste of mist on my tongue and my feet planted on the solid ground, but I also knew that reality had shifted, here in this domain of the dead where so many memorials spoke of resurrection and a life to come. For a moment, I couldn't speak, and then when I did, I found myself saying something entirely inconsequential.

"The old woman," I looked around for Nora. "Where has she gone?"

"I didn't see an old woman." Llewellyn turned the stem of the rose around in his fingers. "All I saw was *you.* Jeanie Gowdie, who tortures my sleep and fills my every waking thought, and for whom I yearn so much it's like a knife twisting in my heart."

"*Oh.*" I was so startled by this confession that I was unable to say anything more. If any other man had spoken those words, I would have assumed it was a thumping lie or even a joke. But Llewellyn wasn't any other man and besides, I wanted to believe him.

"Didn't you guess?" He stepped towards me.

"No. That is..." I could hear the sound of horses' hooves and the light beyond the cemetery gates was from gas-lamps. "What's happening? What year is this?"

"It both is, and isn't, 1897."

"I don't understand."

"It's a spell, Jeanie. You said that if I cared about you, I'd take up magic again. And that I'd do it for you. And so, you see, that's exactly what I've done."

"But you've brought me here without asking my permission." I couldn't think why I'd said that. It must have sounded deeply ungrateful.

"But you did give me your permission." He smiled at me with a teasing expression. "However, if you've changed your mind, then I can transport you back. You'll wake on that bench and you won't even remember this ever happened."

"Oh, but I want to stay," I assured him. "This is what I've been wanting for so long. For you to show me true magic."

"In that case, Jeanie," he held out his arm. "Will you do me the very great honour of having supper with me tonight?"

"But I'm not dressed for 1897. And you look as though you're going to the opera."

"Your dress and cloak are perfect. And you're wearing the necklace I gave you."

"Yes. The apache tears. And now I'll always wear them."

"You must. You look lovely, Jeanie. I can suggest only one improvement. Will you permit me to put this rose in your hair?"

"Oh, yes." I stood very still, trying not to tremble. *We are together; we are properly together. It's beginning; he'll tell me everything now. He'll tell me about himself, his life and who he really is. He'll tell me everything I want to know.*

"There." He stepped back. "That's perfect. Now let me take you out of the cold. The London fog is bad for the lungs. Or at least it would be, if it was real."

I took his arm and he led me towards the cemetery gates. The earthy mounds of newly-made graves loomed up in the moonlight; an owl hooted. The quality of the light was so different from that of the London I knew; I was reminded of the *Nocturnes* of Whistler or one of the moonlit scenes of Atkinson Grimshaw. We were dowsed in a spectral glow.

"So if it's 1897," I said. "Does that mean we can call a hansom cab and go into the West End to see Henry Irving in a play at the Lyceum?"

"I'm afraid not," he said. "This spell doesn't extend that far. You must understand that this isn't time travel. It's an illusion."

"And yet everything feels so real." I marvelled. "Look, there's even horse manure in the road."

"Perhaps I've overdone things." He smiled apologetically.

"No! I love it. This is such a wonderful period of history and...Oh!" I pointed to the sign on the wall, lit up in the gaslight: *Coleton Street*. It was here, in front of us, a terrace of elegant houses, old Coleton Street, before the houses were demolished and the council renamed it. A street from the past, where straw was strewn in the road to protect the sick and dying from the disturbance of the clatter of carriage wheels, where barefoot children sold matches and posies, and where city workers returned to their homes after long hours of filling ledgers with beautiful copper-plate writing.

"Can we go down here?" I asked.

"No. That's the wrong way." There was a slight warning note in his voice. "Our destination is down here."

We had arrived at a Victorian public house. The sign, *The Red Dragon*, was swinging gently in the slight breeze and a dim light was burning behind the frosted windows. He took a key from his pocket, opened the side door and led me up a dark staircase. The walls were covered in a dark crimson cloth, the stair carpet was soft and luxurious and I guessed he was taking me to a private room.

"Here." He pushed open an oak door.

We stepped into a room that was opulent and gas-lit, dominated by an ornate fire-place with a surround carved with fantastic, faun-like figures. There were mirrors in baroque frames and green velvet curtains looped across the windows and tied up with gold tasselled cord. The air was suffused with sandalwood and musk and all around the walls there were black and white pictures that I recognised, Beardsley's designs for Oscar Wilde's *Salome*. A table in an alcove was set for supper; there was a bottle of champagne in an ice bucket, a starched white cloth, two lead crystal glasses and a domed silver dish.

"I hope you like oysters." He took my cloak and hung it on a bentwood stand, then pulled out a chair for me.

"I bought some tinned ones once. They were rather grey and sludgy."

"These are fresh and far better. They taste of the sea." He lifted up the domed lid, revealing the circlet of little shells, each one with an oyster glimmering under a sprig of parsley, seasoned with a sprinkling of paprika and a slice of lemon. "And they're all for you."

"Don't you want any?"

"No, but we'll both have the champagne." He picked up a starched cloth and wrapped it around the neck of the bottle. The cork came away with an extravagant pop but he didn't spill a drop as he filled two glasses to the brim and handed one to me. "Shall I propose a toast?"

"Oh yes."

"I'd like to drink to your future, Jeanie." He raised his glass.

"Thank you." I chinked my glass against his. "And now it's my turn. I want us to drink to no more secrets."

"No more secrets?"

"Yes. I told you the secrets of my past, all about Bushy and the last night at Knox Hill and how I came to be in Crowsmuir Hall. Now there are things you need to share with me. You never speak about your past life and yet I'm ready to trust you with all my heart as long as you open up to me."

"You're asking me to risk a very great deal, Jeanie." He looked serious. "If you knew everything, you might never want to have anything to do with me again."

"You think my feelings would change if you told me?" I said. "But what can you possibly have done that would be so bad? You're a good person, I just know that."

"Even those you call good people are capable of bad acts."

"Well, perhaps. But we have to be honest with each other. So let's drink to no more secrets."

"To no more secrets." He was looking at me steadily as he raised his glass, but his hand was shaking as he placed it down again on the table-cloth.

I had never eaten oysters before or drunk champagne. The aphrodisiac associations weren't lost on me but if this was a seduction, then I was ready for it. We were sitting side by side on the red plush banquette and I could see our reflections in the glass opposite, and we looked like a man and a woman from the eighteen-nineties, enjoying a secret liaison. *Fin de siècle.* That was what this period had been called, a time of delicious decadence.

"Have you ever done a spell like this for anyone before?" I asked.

"No, Jeanie. You're the first."

"Really? But in your life, before this, you must have had..." I didn't quite know how to finish the sentence.

Other women, other relationships... I both did and didn't want to know the truth about that. "You can't have lived like a monk."

"No, I've certainly never lived as a monk." He picked up a fork, turning it over and over in his hand. "But I'm not proud of my past. Jeanie, there's so much I need to tell you, but I hardly know where to start." He took a deep breath. "How much do you know about the people who practise magic?"

"Nana said there were two kinds of practitioners, those who used their magic to help others and those who use it to dominate and destroy," I launched into my peroration. "She told me there were people like herself, hedge-witches, wise women and cunning men who work alone, passing on the folk wisdom that had been handed down to them. Then there were the practitioners of higher magic, the adepts, the sorcerers and the magi, and some of those are dangerous, the spell-charmers, the warlocks, the necromancers, the shape-shifters and the purveyors of glamour."

"And where do you suppose I fit in to all that?"

"I was hoping you would tell me."

"And I will, only...I'm not sure how to begin."

"Then why don't I ask you some questions? I'll start with something quite ordinary. Tell me about where you live."

"There are two places." He put the fork down. "One is where I stay in London during the week. It's not a very nice place, a rented room in King's Cross, above a turf accountants shop. I'd be ashamed for you to see it."

"Goodness!" I laughed. "I'd have imagined something more impressive, like a penthouse flat overlooking the river, or a big house by Regents Park."

"I'm not rich, Jeanie. But I do have another home, my real home. It's in mid-Wales, in the Black Mountains. It's very beautiful there, not far from Offa's Dyke. There are ravens and goats and when the moon rises over top of the peaks, the hills look like a silver sea. I lived there on my own for a long time. It was the place where I found peace. I inherited it from my adoptive parents."

"Oh, I'd love to see it! You say you were adopted?"

"Yes, from a very young age. The people who brought me up were highly erudite and skilled, members of a particular order. They taught me the things that have set me apart." He held up his hand; the eye of his dragon ring glinted in the gas-light. "And then, when the time was considered right, I came to London as a student."

"A student of magic?"

"Yes. Later, I came of age and adopted my true name. But then...things happened and it's a long story, and not a very pleasant one."

"But I'm ready to hear it."

"It will spoil tonight if I tell you now. Tonight is about the... feelings I have for you. But Jeanie, I'm sorry, tonight can never happen again."

"Why not?" My heart was thumping.

"Because nothing must ever come of my feelings for you, not in the ordinary, everyday world. And you must never get to care for me the way I care for you. That could destroy us both."

"I don't understamd."

"Jeanie, listen." I sensed his agitation. "I'm not a good person. I've done things of which I'm thoroughly ashamed. There was one thing, one particular thing that...

"Oh, stop this!" I began to laugh. My head was swimming with the champagne and I was too intoxicated with excitement to take him seriously. "That's quite enough. I know what it is you're going to tell me."

"You can't possibly know."

"Yes I can. You're going to tell me you're a spell-charmer. Well, I don't care. Nana told me to be wary of spell-charmers, but I'm not afraid of you. I couldn't be. Whatever you've done, it doesn't matter. You're the loveliest man I've ever met, and this is the first date I've ever had, I don't count the times I spent with Bushy. This my best evening ever, I'm impressed, no-one has ever transported me to another dimension in a magically-recreated version of the past before or given me oysters.. But just because this is 1897, you don't have to start talking like the wicked Lord in a Victorian melodrama."

"Oh, Jeanie!" To my relief, he was smiling. "You're wonderful. No-one's ever talked to me like this. You bring me down to earth and you make me feel alive again. For years I felt numb and hopeless and... But it would be so wrong of me to take advantage of you. I promised I'd tell you the truth and there's something I realise I must tell you now, something that I'm afraid is going to shock you terribly and..."

"Kiss me first! Tell me afterwards!"

"Oh, *Jeanie.*" He gazed at me with so much emotion that I could hardly believe it was real. Could he really care for me that much? He must do, he thought I was beautiful, the poor deluded man. As he leant forward and took hold of my hands, I tilted my face towards him, closing my eyes. This was it then, this was going to be the moment, at last, and...

There was a sudden, violent cracking sound. I sat up sharply, opening my eyes, jerked out of the reverie that had hardly begun. And then I saw, to my horror, that the walls around us were moving, the floor was tipping up away from us, and there were showers of plaster coming from the ceiling. The whole place was falling apart.

"What's happening?" I gasped.

"The spell's breaking up." His eyes flashed with anger. "Someone's working against us. Someone doesn't want us here. Come. We must leave." As he pulled me to my feet, all the gorgeous fittings around us began to disintegrate in a cloud of choking dust. Paint peeled, plaster cracked, and the old world elegance began to give way to the draughty dereliction of bare wood, flaking plaster and crumbling brick.

"Look out!" He pulled me to one side, as the chandelier crashed to the floor, only just missing us. "I have to get you out of here. Hold tight." His arms were round me, then, with an effortlessness that was quite astonishing, he lifted me up. Debris swirled around us; he shouted words in a language I didn't recognise, his evening shoes clattered on the disintegrating staircase as he carried me down. And then, suddenly, we were outside, back in the London of 1974, with its exhaust fumes and neon signs and rubbish bins.

"I'm so sorry." Gasping, he set me down then bent over, breathing deeply. When he finally looked up, his face was ashen and he looked as though he'd aged ten years. "I've failed you."

"What happened just now wasn't your fault," I said.

"Wasn't it?" The bitterness in his tone was only too evident. "I should have cast a stronger spell than that. No-one should have been able to get near us."

"It doesn't matter." I touched his sleeve. "Listen, my flat isn't far away. Why don't you come back there with me now? We could talk. We could...that is, you could..."

"No, Jeanie." He shook his head. "No. I told you. We can't ever be together in that way in the real world. Look what's happened already. You don't know what we're up against."

"Then tell me!" I insisted. "Tell me what this is all about."

"Not now. This isn't the time. Look, your transport has arrived."

"My transport?"

"Yes. I have to be sure you get home safely."

A black limousine had pulled up to the kerb alongside us, a vintage vehicle with long running boards and huge headlamps. As the driver turned to look at me, I recognised him. There was no mistaking that elongated birth mark on the left hand side of his face.

"It's Konrad." I was astonished. "What's he doing here?"

"He's come to take you home."

"Konrad owns that car?"

"No, it's my car. Listen, you must go with him."

"But I don't want to go without you."

"You must. On Monday, we'll meet in my office, but we mustn't talk directly about tonight. We can only refer to it in hints and allusions because the magic that has made this possible is fragile. Do you understand?"

"No, I don't , I really don't...but I'll do what you say."

"Then good-night, Jeanie." He opened the rear door of the car. "And please take care." He stood, watching me as I got in, and then closed the door behind me. He didn't wait to see me go; he simply walked rapidly away and I felt bewildered and on the verge of heartbreak.

"Good evening, Miss Gowdie." Konrad's tone was cold and unwelcoming.

"Hello, Konrad." I was forced to address the back of his head. "This is very kind of you."

"Kind?" He pulled away from the kerb. "I can assure you this wasn't my idea. And I hope you understand that any conversation between us would be inappropriate."

"But why?

"It's not my place to explain. I do, however, have one question for you. Would you take pleasure in wounding a man who has already been hurt beyond endurance?"

"Absolutely not!" I was shocked by his question. "Konrad, what do you mean?"

"You've done enough damage already." He swung the car around a corner too fast. "I have nothing more to say."

I was stunned into silence. What had I done, why such antagonism? I took the rose from my hair, and laid it in my lap. The petals were beginning to drop and wither and my heart was aching. I was beginning to fear that I was destined to be left in ignorance forever.

Twenty Nine

There was a verse Nana used to sing to herself while she was working in her garden:

Hemlock in the morning,
Aconite on the afternoon,
Mandragora by moonlight,
A potion for a lover and a fool.

When I asked her what the words meant, she said it was a warning about love and that was the reason the names of three strong poisons appeared in it. A lover was invariably a fool although it was possible to be a fool without being a lover. But love was a folly that turned the cleverest person's brain to mush. And love was bound to bring pain, just as you could never expect to find a rose without a thorn. You were better off avoiding such complications.

I wanted to ask Nana if she'd ever been in love, but didn't feel I could, but from the hints she dropped from time to time, I guessed she'd never been married. It seemed my mother's birth had been the result of some brief and unsatisfactory liaison with a man who was best forgotten. Nana, I was sure, mistrusted men, and who was to say she was wrong?

*

"Party day!" Gerda exclaimed as I came into the reading room. "But, in the meantime, as you see," she encompassed the room with a sweep of her arm, "Business as usual."

I was rather relieved to see it. I could just imagine the semi-drunken silliness that must be going on at the insurance office, Finsworthy, perhaps, armed with a plastic sprig of mistletoe, doing his best to make the festive season intolerable for any woman who didn't find either him or his Fishermen's Friends breath alluring. Here, everything was calm and soothingly studious. Ernest, frowning and inky, engrossed in his crossword and several of the regular readers working quietly at the tables.

"Don't vorry," Gerda added, "Things vill liven up later once ve all have had some of Psyche's celebrated punch. Are you all prepared for tonight?"

"Oh yes." I'd brought my own contribution for the feast, some mince pies made according to Nana's special recipe, and later, I was going to change into a black silk dress with a full, floaty skirt and some peep-toe high heeled shoes. I'd never been to a Yuletide party before; I felt childishly excited, especially at the thought that Llewellyn would be there.

"And did you bring the gift for the St Nicholas Bran Tub?" Gerda asked.

"I did." I handed her Clemency's gloves, still in their original brown paper bag. "I'm afraid I forgot to buy any Christmas wrapping paper."

"Don't vorry, I vill deal with that! Oh, and Jeanie, good news. Mr Llewellyn has returned."

"Oh, really?" I tried to sound casual. "Did he say where he'd been?"

"I didn't ask. I suspect he may have been to America. Vith Mr Jabez Corey so very ill and..."

"Good morning!" Clemency flung open the door and burst into the room with surprising force, a contrast to her usual silent approach. "I am now officially at the end of my tether! Does anyone here know how to contact pest control?"

"Pest control?" I repeated.

"Yes. First rats in the stacks, and now I've just seen another cockroach in the archives."

"A cockroach?" Gerda's expression suggested she was suppressing the urge to laugh

"Cockroaches are a hazard to health," Clemency informed her. "I've reported this before, but the caretaker appears to have done nothing. So now I intend calling in pest control."

"Oh, you mustn't call those people," I said. "They'll use poison. There's no need to kill cockroaches. You simply ask them politely to move on."

"I beg your pardon?" She turned her withering gaze on me.

"You scatter salt," I said. "And you repeat the rhyme: '*Hie, hence, hie hence, little roach/ Never, never again approach/There's a place where you can go/ Across the field where the winds do blow'*." And once you've said that, they'll never trouble you again."

"Are you trying to be amusing?" She looked at me as though she'd just caught a whiff of a particularly bad smell.

"No," I said. "I'm just concerned for the poor little insects. They do a lot of good, you know, clearing up waste material. But if you really don't want cockroaches, try the rhyme."

"What utter..."

"I think Jeanie is trying to be helpful," Gerda intervened. "It's just a little folk superstition, but it might vork."

"You seriously think I would engage in such pagan filth?" Clemency glared at us. "Have you both gone mad? Are you laughing at me?"

"Of course not," Gerda said. "But Yule is almost upon us. Ve are feeling light-hearted. I'm sorry, Miss Nantucket, I don't intend to offend you."

"It offends me," Clemency's eyes narrowed. "When certain readers drop the remnants of their packed lunches in amongst the book shelves and encourage the cockroaches. Well, it seems I'll get no help here!" With a toss of her head, she turned on her heel and stalked off, slamming the reading room door behind her.

"Oh dear," I said. "She doesn't seem very happy."

"No," Gerda agreed. "And she never vill be. But vat do ve care? I'm afraid to say I have no interest in pleasing Miss Plymouth Rock! And now, if I vere you, I'd take a look in the parcels room. Be prepared for a delightful surprise."

I gazed with joy at the huge bunch of mistletoe that was hanging from the ceiling. It wasn't the tacky plastic stuff from Woolworths, it was real mistletoe, the kind the Druids would have gathered in the oak groves, loaded with shining globes of white berries and glistening green leaves. Beautiful. It must be from *him*.

Filled with happiness, I turned to the pile of white envelopes in my in-tray and began to open them. Christmas cards. Of course! I was so unused to receiving them that I hadn't realised what the envelopes were likely to contain. And these were lovely, several from scholars who regularly came to the reading room, one from Ernest (featuring a gloomy-looking snowman), and another from Gerda, a traditional snow scene scattered with glitter.

"Now your room is really festive!" Gerda looked round the door, beaming approvingly.

"Yes," I agreed. "Thank you so much for the lovely card. I've got some for everyone too. I'm bringing them to the party. Um...the mistletoe...did you see who put it here?"

"I did not." Gerda shook her head. "But if you want my opinion, then I think it is your admirer."

"My admirer?"

"Someone here in the library is carrying a torch for you, Jeanie! Don't tell me you didn't guess. Haven't you received certain tokens before? I seem to remember some roses. Vell, perhaps there vill be more mistletoe hanging up in Psyche's place tonight. I vouldn't be surprised if your devoted follower isn't about to declare his intentions!"

I had to remind myself to walk down the corridor in a steady manner. No-one must suspect my excitement. I must look as though I was on official business, carrying a pile of papers that needed to be signed by the custodian. Inside, I was brimming with happiness. *Tonight*, I thought, *tonight,* although I could get no further than that, except that I was sure I was blushing. *Mistletoe.* That was so romantic! But then I remembered what Llewellyn had said about only referring to the events of Saturday night in hints and allusions, and I knew I had to be circumspect, even now.

"Come in!" He responded immediately to my knock.

"Good morning, sir." I closed the door of the Custodian's door behind me.

"Good morning, Miss Gowdie." His greeting was formal but his expression was light and playful. "I trust you had an enjoyable weekend?"

"I did. I discovered that champagne and oysters are excellent at this time of year."

"And I saw a beautiful girl with a rose in her hair."

"But one should be careful of the fog."

"And be particularly mindful of falling chandeliers." He smiled, but then his expression became serious. "Jeanie, as you can see, I'm just on my way out. We can't talk now."

"Oh." I was disappointed. "I thought you were wearing your coat because you'd just arrived."

"No, but I'll try to be back later."

The brandy glass, I thought, it was here in my bag. I'd collected it from Pyewacket's that morning. Dorian had placed it a gold box, tied with a red ribbon. Perhaps now was a good time to give it to him. Better to do it here, privately.

"Jeanie," Llewellyn was peering at me with a bemused expression. "There's a speck of something on your cheek. It looks like glitter."

"Glitter? Oh, that must be from Gerda's card." I took out my mirror and flipped it open. "Yes, I'll just..."

"My God, Jeanie!" His voice was suddenly harsh and shockingly unfamiliar. "Where the hell did you get that?" He reached forward, making a grab for the mirror. I pulled back, startled, then his fingers circled my wrist and I felt a searing pain, as if I'd just come into contact with a branding iron.

"*Ow!*" The tears sprung into my eyes. "That hurt!"

"I'm sorry," he gasped, releasing me at once. "I'm so sorry. I didn't mean...I can't have...Oh, good grief." The colour leeched from his face as he stared at the livid red mark on the underside of my wrist. "Witch-hazel...I'm sure I had some..." He pulled open his desk drawer, rummaging through the contents in a frantic manner. "I'm so sorry, I...it was an accident. The witch hazel...I can't find it. I was sure I had some." He pulled a handkerchief out of his pocket and dipped it in the jug of water by the window. "Here, take this, put it on the place." I could see he was distraught; his eyes were wet.

"It's all right." I waved the handkerchief away. "It's not painful now."

"Oh thank goodness. You must know I'd never want to hurt you."

"And yet you told me that you might do it all the same."

"Yes, I did." He looked abject. "And it seems I've been proved right."

"But this wasn't you." I pointed to the mark. "It was your ring, wasn't it? There's magic in that ring, isn't there?"

"Yes, there is," he admitted. "But you were holding a magic artefact too. When certain conduits of power connect, it's like putting live electric wires together. Jeanie, you must give me that mirror."

I felt a sudden flash of anger. What right did he have to issue this instruction?

"And what would you do with it if I did?" I demanded to know.

"I'd put it in a sealed box, utter the correct incantations and throw it into the Thames." He was grim and tight-lipped. "It's quite obviously lethal."

"Lethal or not, it's my property now." I told him. "And I was destined to find it."

"Why do you think that?"

"I'd rather not say. All right, I'll let you take a closer look, but promise me you won't destroy it."

"Thank you. Don't put it straight into my hand. Just place it on my desk."

"Here, then." I did as he said.

"Good grief!" He stared at it, transfixed. "This is even worse than I feared. Jeanie, please tell where you got this."

"I bought it from an antique shop near where I live. It used to be an awful old junk shop but since Dorian took the place over..."

"Dorian?"

"Dorian Pyewacket."

"There's a man calling himself Dorian Pyewacket selling antiques in West London?"

"Yes."

"And this Dorian, he wouldn't have blond hair and look like a chorus boy from the Alhambra, by any chance?"

"The Alhambra?" I repeated, puzzled. "Wasn't that a London theatre that was demolished decades ago?"

"Yes, I daresay. It was just a figure of speech."

"Are you saying that you know Dorian?"

"I may know something *of* him. There's a possibility that our paths may have crossed at some time." There was a distinct coldness about his tone of voice. "And now I'd very much like to know what game he thinks he's playing."

"I don't think Dorian's playing a game at all. I was the one who found the mirror. It was in an old trunk. He had no idea it was there."

"Is that what he told you?" He sounded unconvinced. "Tell me, have you experienced any disturbances since you've had this object in your possession?"

"No." I tried to sound nonchalant, but I was trembling inside as I told this lie. That morning on the tube, that voice speaking my true name; of course I'd experienced disturbances. *Through the fire, through the fire and through the fire again* . Part of me wanted to tell him, but another part of me felt compelled to hold back.

"Jeanie, why aren't you being honest with me?" He sounded more sad than angry.

"Why are you keeping so many things from me?" I countered.

"Oh Jeanie....I don't think you realise just how much danger there is all around you. There's so much you don't know."

"Then tell me! Stop hinting at things, stop keeping me in the dark! Didn't we agree? No more secrets?"

"And I *will* explain everything." He put his handkerchief away. "But there isn't time now. I have to act quickly. And if you won't let me destroy this mirror, allow me to borrow it. Please trust me to do the right thing. You do trust me, don't you?"

If he'd asked me this only a few minutes earlier, I would have said yes without hesitation. But now, doubts were beginning to creep into my mind all over again. Perhaps he was the one who was playing games. But if I didn't trust him, what was left for me? I so wanted to believe in him; I must take that leap of faith. After all, Nana might not have known everything there was to know about spell-charmers.

"Yes," I took a deep breath. "I trust you."

"Good." He put on a pair of leather gloves and picked up the mirror. "And now, I have to go."

"But...won't you be back for the party?"

"Party?" He looked puzzled.

"Yes, Gerda's been organising it and..."

"I don't know. I really don't. I'm not much of a party person."

"But surely you need to be there, as Custodian of the library?"

"I usually look in for a few minutes but...perhaps this year, I could stay longer...I shall do my best...but I can't promise...I'm going to do what I can to make things safe for you, for both of us and it may take a considerable time. And there is a slight danger, only very slight of course..."

"Then let me come with you!"

"No, that's impossible I'm afraid. But there is one thing. Remember when we talked about true names? You said I shouldn't tell you mine, but you *should* know it, there might come a time when you might need to call me from a long, long distance away. If you were ever in mortal danger, if your life was threatened, and you spoke my true name, you'd reach me wherever I was."

"I would? Then you'd better tell it to me." I remembered sitting with Nana on our last day on the beach. "Whisper it in my ear," I said. "Even those pigeons on the window sill could be spies."

Thirty

Psyche's place had been transformed into a yule-tide grotto with greenery, red ribbons and candles. A small potted pine tree, sprinkled with silvery dust, stood in the corner. Scholarly, polite conversations were in progress as people circulated with glasses in their hands while others were loading their plates with mince pies and sandwiches from the buffet table. Light glinted on the cut glass bowl from which Psyche was serving punch. I noticed she was using an earthenware cup rather than a ladle; I wondered if that was in deference to the spoon-phobia that, according to Clemency, who was lurking by the door, a disapproving expression on her face, afflicted Ernest Brunswicker. Deciding to keep my distance from her, I collected a glass of punch and went to join Ernest, who was over by the wall, clinging to his bicycle.

"Are you staying in London for the holiday?" I asked.

"No." He shook his head violently. "I'm going on a retreat. Not religious, just for people seeking peace. It's in Kent, near the sea. I shall be doing a lot of reading. Proust, Descartes, the history of the railways."

"That sounds very restful."

"It will be. And what about you, Jeanie?"

"Well, it'll be my first Christmas in London. I shall certainly go to Trafalgar Square to see the Norwegian tree. Apart from that, I haven't any other plans."

I glanced towards the door. I was beginning to be worried about Llewellyn. If only he'd told me where he was going when he left the library that morning. Any number of disasters could have befallen him. He might have been hit by a bus or a taxi as he crossed a busy street in a distracted state of mind. The underground was a hazard too. You could trip and fall down the escalator or be pushed on to the line by a drunken reveller. And then, of course, he could have been attacked by a malevolent entity or sub-human spirit from hell. Anything was possible.

"Ernest," I turned to him. "You don't seem to have a glass of punch. Would you like me to get you one? I rather fancy another one myself."

"Thank you. That's kind." Poor Ernest. He wasn't looking in the least relaxed. Like Llewellyn, he didn't seem to be a party person either.

I was on way back to Ernest carrying the drinks when Clemency intercepted me.

"Can I give you some advice?" She knocked my elbow; it was difficult to tell whether she'd done it on purpose but I almost spilled some of the punch.

"I'd really rather you didn't." Oh dear, alcohol had loosened my tongue.

"Really?" She frowned at me. "You are getting too full of yourself these days. But your comeuppance is coming soon, believe me!"

"Goodness." I attempted to change the subject. "This punch is strong. What do you suppose Psyche's put in it? White rum, I expect, probably pineapple juice, grenadine, and I think I can detect just a hint of brandy. It's very potent, I don't think I'd better drink too much of this, otherwise I'll soon be talking as much gibberish as you!"

What on earth had possessed me to say that? At first, I thought she hadn't heard me. But then, "I suppose you think you're *so* clever, don't you?" she hissed. "But I know what's been going on. And don't think you'll get away with it. Like hell you will!"

"I'm not sure I know what you're talking about."

"I'm talking about you and Mr Llewellyn. *Working together*. Well, that's one way to describe your schemes! And now, where is he? I expect you're hoping he hasn't had an accident. Perhaps you've been imagining the type of accident he might have had. Well, all I can say is, he deserves to have an accident, the way he's been behaving!" As she leant towards me, I noticed a pastry crumb stuck to her chin, next to a small spot that she'd attempted to hide with a blob of concealer. I was so mesmerised by the sight that I almost forgot to feel menaced. Now I was wondering if Clemency was the enemy who'd placed the poison-pen note by the roses. Perhaps this wasn't a good moment to show that I had the measure of her.

"Great party!" I said. "Will Santa Claus be coming to town?"

"You need to be careful." The pastry crumb dropped off Clemency's chin as she breathed mince-pie fumes into my face. "You need to be very careful." She paused, bit her lip, and then added. "*Witch!*"

"Sorry?" I was genuinely surprised. "Did you just call me a..."

"St Nicholas Bran Tub time!" Gerda clapped her hands, beaming expansively. "Take your seats, everyone."

Ernest was sitting in a corner, twisting his hands in his lap, an anguished look on his face. "Presents," he muttered. "Embarrassing."

"It's just a bit of fun," I said. I wished there was a better way to reassure him; Ernest probably had very little concept of fun.

"I pick first," Gerda announced. She thrust her arm into the tub and pulled out a parcel wrapped in red paper. "Ah! This is for Psyche, the provider of the feast."

"You see?" I turned to Ernest as Psyche tore the wrappings off her gift, revealing a colourful apron. "Everyone's enjoying themselves. Look, Psyche's pulling out a parcel now."

"Miss Nantucket," Psyche announced.

Oh, those gloves! I just hoped that if Clemency didn't like them, she'd never find out that I was the one who'd bought them. She could twist anything, even a kind gesture, however half-hearted, into an attack.

"Thank you." Clemency accepted the parcel. "I hope you will forgive me if I don't unwrap this now. It's not my custom to open anything before Christmas Day, whatever heathen practices others may enjoy."

"Dear God! The woman's insufferable!" Ernest muttered. "And who bought that apron for Psyche? It's covered in pictures of pineapples. Stereotyping!"

"Well, not really," I whispered. "I think she enjoys cooking and it does look like a good quality apron and there were matching oven gloves and..."

"*Jeanie Gowdie.*" Clemency contrived to make my name sound like an insult. "A somewhat unusual wrapping, very ingenious, although I'm not sure it's entirely clean." She held out a square package measuring about six inches by four.

"Thank you." I took it from her and pulled the next gift out of the tub, something for Gerda which looked very much like the *Mozartkugeln* she'd wanted. Then I went back to my seat to examine my present more closely.

The wrapping was, indeed, unusual, a piece of hessian, tied together with garden twine, just a little stained but with little fragments of leaf-mould and sticks with berries stuck to it. I could see why Clemency had disapproved, but my heart was racing. This was the kind of wrapping that Nana would have used; whoever it was who'd selected this gift for me must know something about natural magic. I put the package into my bag; like Clemency, I was going to save the pleasure of opening it for Christmas Day.

"Ernest, for you!" Gerda held out a long, thin package. He sped forward, grabbed it and tore off the paper. A moment later, the object he'd unwrapped clattered to the floor as he dropped it, a look of horror on his face.

"Ernest?" I bent down to pick it up. "Oh, this is really rather nice. They call this a 'love-spoon' in Wales. They're carved out of wood and decorated with..." I stopped. Ernest was looking so pale I was afraid he was about to pass out. It would indeed have been a charming gift for the right person, but when it came to spoons, I remembered, Ernest was anything but the right person.

"Ach!" Gerda seized the spoon and shoved it into her bag. "Just vat I need! And for you Ernest, in exchange, you take my present, a dear little box of *Mozartkugeln.* If you can't eat chocolates at Christmas, ven can you?"

"But I bought you those. I was the one who drew your name." Ernest protested. "I wanted you to have them."

"Never mind!" Gerda beamed. "I am just happy to know that you thought of me. Please, take."

"Thank you." He stretched out his long bony fingers to grab the box. "And now if you'll excuse me..." He began wheeling his bike towards the door. "Have to go, have to go."

"But you have to pull out the next parcel out of the bran tub first," Clemency objected.

"No, he does not!" Gerda retorted. "There are no more gifts! At least, there is one more, but the recipient, sadly, is absent. Good-bye, Ernest, ve vill see you in the New Year. An unfortunate mistake," she muttered in my ear. "I hope."

"I hope so too," I said. "But wouldn't everyone have known that a present like that for Ernest was a bad idea?"

"Quite possibly. But if someone vanted to be deliberately unkind, who knows?" She spoke in a low voice. "There are unkind people everywhere. Even here, in the Antioch Corey Library." She pointed surreptitiously at Clemency who was standing with her back to us, deep in conversation with Dr Beyton, a scholar who specialised in the history of the covered bridges of New England.

"You think it was *her?*" I whispered.

"Who knows?" Gerda shrugged. "Not all the parcels were handed to me. Some were placed straight into the tub."

"Well, whoever it was, I think it was mean. With Ernest suffering from such a dreadful spoon phobia."

"Spoon phobia?" Gerda looked astonished. "Is that vy ve alvays see Ernest stirring his tea with a biro?"

"Yes, I believe so."

"Poor man! And now his fear has been compounded by something else too. This is vat has added to his distress." She pulled the spoon out of her bag. "The writing on the handle. See?"

I did see. The words were clearly visible, written in poker work. *I curse you and wish you a painful death.*

"That's appalling!" I said. "Why on earth would a Welsh love spoon be made with a message like that?"

"Perhaps it is a mistake," Gerda suggested. "Perhaps this vas made in Hong Kong, by someone who didn't speak English and picked up the wrong phrase book."

Or perhaps someone really hates Ernest. And all of us. I looked across at Clemency and shuddered.

"Well," I said. "I think I'll be leaving too. I don't want to miss the last tube home. Have a good holiday and I'll see you in the New Year."

I tried to sound cheerful, but I was woozy from Psyche's potent punch and deeply disappointed. And as I thought of the brandy glass in its gold box, still at the bottom of my bag, unclaimed by its intended recipient, I felt childishly close to tears.

Thirty One

I opened my eyes with a start. This was dreadful. I had no memory of walking to the underground, or getting on the tube and yet here I was in an empty carriage, in a train that was pulling out of Wimbledon station. I couldn't understand it. How could I possibly have allowed myself to drink so much at the party that I'd fallen asleep on the District Line? Anyone could have snatched my bag while I was slumped in this corner seat (thank goodness, my bag was still on my lap) or I could even have been arrested. Had someone, Clemency perhaps, spiked my drink? I had no idea. I only knew that I'd missed my stop, that I'd have to get out at the next station, cross over to the opposite platform and...But, no, this wasn't right! Surely Wimbledon was the *last* station on this branch of the District Line? How could it be that the train was gathering speed? It wasn't making the return journey towards Earls Court but was hurtling along in the same direction as before. This didn't make sense; there couldn't be any track after the end of the line.

And now we were moving at an unnatural, astonishing, rattling speed.

I was more than a little alarmed but couldn't help being aware of the irony. I'd wanted to experience a magical transportation ever since I was a child, *Whish! Down the rabbit hole like Alice! Across the London skies with Peter*

Pan and straight on until morning, but this was one was making me feel dizzy and I just wanted it to stop.

At last, the train began to slow down and then came to a halt after a backwards and forwards juddering that made my brain feel like a wobbling blancmange. The doors opened. I got up, groped my way forward and stepped out into darkness.

Here was the strangest thing. London is never pitch-dark; there are always street lamps and lights from buildings creating that familiar urban glow. But now I could hardly see a thing. I supposed that I must be on a station platform, but what station? It couldn't be Wimbledon Park, the stop I *would* have reached had the train reversed and gone northwards in the direction of Earls Court, Olympia or to the relative civilization of Edgware Road. Perhaps this was a disused station. Where was the exit?

As I stood there, trying to get my bearings, I became aware of the beam of a lantern ahead of me. Other lights appeared, breaking into the soupy gloom, and then several figures emerged. First, an old woman in a white bonnet and a long sackcloth dress and apron; she had a bunch of herbs hanging from a string around her neck. There were others behind her, men and women, all of them elderly, some carrying primitive farm implements as well as lanterns. As a group, they were weird, archaic and menacing. I stood my ground, but nevertheless felt more than a little disconcerted.

"You've come too far," a voice muttered close to my ear, "You didn't buy a ticket for this zone."

"And we weren't expecting you so soon," another voice added.

"I just need to get back to West Brompton," I said. "Can I get a taxi from here? Where's the ticket barrier?"

"Barriers! Do you speak of the gateways?" An old woman spat the words at me, the hairs on her chin quivering as if to emphasise her disgust. "You must be purified in the Beltane fire before you can pass through those."

"On such a night as this, Antioch Corey sold his soul to the devil." A wrinkled-faced man holding up a pitchfork stepped in front of me. "What say you to that?"

"I've had a long day," I said. "Normally, I'd be delighted to discuss this but the thing is..."

"Answer his question." The old woman with the herbs around her neck elbowed the man aside. "He asked you what you had to say about Antioch Corey selling his soul to the devil. Give us your reply!"

"There's no such person as the Devil," I said. "There's only the Horned God of the Old Religion. The Great God Pan is very far from dead."

"A pretty speech." The old woman pursed her lips. "And just what might be expected from the grand-daughter of a hedge-witch. You think yourself clever, but your knowledge is limited. As for the way out, you must find it for yourself. If you apply yourself, you will have learned your craft by Lammas Tide. All true witches must suffer. And they must study!" She grabbed my arm; I winced as her horny fingernails dug into my skin. "And what have you done?"

"Would you mind letting go of me?" Despite the pain, I tried to sound polite.

"We summoned you to the library," the old woman continued, tightening her grip. "But what did you do? You wasted your time fretting over a man, and not just any man, but the adept, Llewellyn Arawn Llewellyn, a man of overweening pride whose sins will never be expunged. Do you fancy yourself in love with him? Answer me, Jeanie Morgana Gowdie!"

"You know our true names." Now this *had* startled me. "How can that be?"

"We, the Elders, know everything. And you know so little." The woman gave my arm a violent shake. "Don't you know how much you have offended us by failing to do our work?"

"*Your* work? I don't understand."

"Antioch Corey is flesh of our flesh, bone of our bone, a descendent of our loins." The wrinkled faced man intoned, banging the end of his pitchfork on the ground. "His legacy is *our* legacy. You have a duty to perform. Tell me this, Morgana Gowdie, what should matter to a true witch, becoming mistress of her craft, or mooning over a man?"

"I can't answer that. I don't see why there has to be a choice, surely I can...be careful!" I flinched as the tines of the pitchfork hovered within an inch of my eyes.

"We are angry with the adept Llewellyn Arawn Llewellyn for distracting you with his romantic nonsense," the old man said. "But fear not, *we* will not punish him. There is another who will dispense justice."

"Punish him? What do you mean? What's happened to him?"

"That is not your concern. Forget him!"

"This is outrageous!" At last, I managed to extricate myself from the old woman's grip. "I can't allow this. And you're wrong. My first concern was always to achieve my destiny. But if anyone's hurt the man I love..."

"Love? What sentimental twaddle!" The old woman ripped the bunch of herbs from her neck. "You have no time to waste on love. Do you suppose a spell-charmer is capable of love? Do you know nothing of the lies they will tell, the tricks they will play? Now go back, Missy, and do our work. And be quick about it!"

My eyes stung as she flung the herbs in my face and gave a loud, mocking laugh. And then I fell into darkness.

I was lying on the couch, in my flat. My head was resting on one of my velvet cushions, a sandalwood joss stick was smoking in the holder on the window sill, the black candles were flickering on the mantelpiece, my velvet cloak was hanging on the hook on the back of the door, my bag was on the table and the security chain was in place across the door. This was both comforting and alarming since I couldn't remember how I'd got here.

So now I had amnesia. I'd heard about this kind of thing, people drinking so much that it left a gaping black hole in their memory. *In-eeeeeeeeeeeebriation*, as Angus Gowdie would have said. But I hadn't drunk too much of Psyche's punch, had I? It must have been Clemency, spiking my drink when I wasn't looking

So what had happened? Perhaps I'd become drowsy on the tube, got off at the right station and walked home in an alcoholic daze. I pictured myself staggering along the street from the station, perhaps even tripping over the kerb. But at least I *had* got home. And *then* I must have fallen asleep again on my couch and had that surreal dream about the Elders. How had my subconscious thrown up an idea like that? Maybe it was something to do with trying to translate Antioch Corey's *Book of Shadows*. Whatever the reason, at least I was safe.

But what if I'd lost something? I jumped up, grabbed my bag and scrabbled through the contents. Methodically, I placed each item on the table; my purse, my keys, my travel card, the gift-wrapped brandy glass, the intriguing parcel from the St Nicholas bran tub. Thank goodness, nothing had been lost. But, oh heavens, what was this?

I gazed at my arm. There were two half-moon marks, red and raw, marks that could only have been made by fingernails. The old woman with the herbs! She'd held me in a ferocious grip while she was whispering all those veiled threats in my ear; *Purified in the Beltane fire...Learn your craft by Lammas-Tide...punish him.* I could hardly believe it possible, but it seemed there was no room for doubt. The Elders were real.

I needed a stiff drink. Since I felt completely sober, without a hint of a headache, I couldn't see that it would do me any harm. I took a bottle of brandy I'd bought a few weeks ago out of the cupboard and looked around for a glass. *Ha!* My eyes focused on the gold box on the table.

I undid the red ribbon with grim determination. What had the Elders said? *Do you really suppose a spell-charmer is capable of love? Do you know nothing of the lies they will tell, the tricks they will play?* What if they were right? What if he'd tricked me into giving him the mirror and was going to use it in some way that wouldn't benefit me at all?

If that was the case, I'd deal with it! I'd been self-sufficient before, I could be self-sufficient again. I took the brandy glass out of the box and filled it to the brim.

"Happy Yule-tide, Jeanie," I said. I lifted the glass high in the air. And then I saw the cat at the window.

Thirty Two

Even I, with my reservations about cats, could see that this was a fine-looking feline. It wasn't the skinny, insidious-looking type of cat; it had solidity, elegance and dignity. He (I was certain from the build and the shape of the face that the animal *was* male) had glossy black fur and a brilliant white bib with a curious black splodge under the chin like a bow tie, an appearance that suggested a raffish, improvident Victorian gentleman whose once-expensive evening clothes had been rendered shiny with age. A charming sponger who'd cadge a few drinks and enjoy particular success with women, who'd take him in, feed him, and let him wind them round his little finger. The cad! The bounder! Well, I was made of stronger stuff. I refused to be exploited by either man or cat. I went over to the window and tapped on the glass. The cat didn't move. I knocked harder. The cat stared back at me, unblinking. I lifted up the window.

"You have to go," I said.

The cat remained where it was. I had to admire its impudence.

"If you're a stray," I continued, "there's bound to be someone round here who takes in cats. Only I'm not one of them. Good-night."

I closed the window and pulled the curtain across. What an unsettling night this had been. I picked up my brandy and my copy of *The Wizard of Oz* and settled down on my couch to seek out the company of the Scarecrow, the Tin Man and the Cowardly Lion. I soon forgot about the cat.

The shutters had been pulled down over Pyewackets plate glass window and there was a sign on the door:

Hello Folks! Shut happens! Open again after Christmas. D. Pyewacket.

This was puzzling. Why on earth would Dorian close the shop on Christmas Eve, when there'd be customers in search of last-minute presents? Well, never mind. It was very unlikely he'd discovered the whereabouts of the cheval mirror just yet. In the mean-time, I'd go to Mustafa's for breakfast.

I sat at my usual table, sipping scalding hot tea and leafing idly through a tabloid newspaper that someone had left tucked behind a bottle of tomato sauce. The headline on the front page was *Pull Down your Pants, you Prat!* I didn't follow the news but even I'd heard about the Conservative minister who was missing, assumed drowned. Now it seemed he'd been discovered alive and well with his mistress in Australia, having faked his own death. At first the police suspected him of being another missing man, a murderous aristocrat with a long scar on his thigh, so they'd asked him to lower his trousers to identify himself. I might have found this grimly amusing if the subject of male disappearances hadn't been a sensitive one for me just then. I quickly turned the page.

The rest of the newspaper wasn't very edifying. There was a photograph of a bare-busted woman wearing a Santa Claus hat, alongside several stories about seasonal tragedies, a car crash caused by drink-driving, a house set on fire by Christmas tree lights, and a man who choked to death on the sixpence in a Christmas pudding. And a merry Christmas to all our readers! I folded up the paper and pushed it away from me in despair.

"Here we are." Nasir placed the plate in front of me. "Bubble and squeak, beans, mushrooms, sausage, fried slice, sunny-side up eggs, black pudding, everything except the bacon. Are you all right? You look a bit gloomy."

"No, I'm absolutely fine. Thanks, this looks good."

"Any more tea?"

"Not just now, thanks." I picked up my fork and speared a mushroom.

"Going away anywhere?"

"No. I'll be spending Christmas in London, being pestered by a stray cat."

"Pestered?"

"Yes. It's refusing to leave my window sill. It appeared there last night and I told it to go away, but it was still there this morning."

"Must be getting hungry," Nasir mused. "Stuck out there like that."

"It doesn't have to stay there," I said. "Couldn't it go and raid a dustbin? I thought cats were supposed to be resourceful."

"Perhaps it's not used to being homeless. Skinny, mangy-looking thing, is it?"

"Well, no." I dipped a corner of fried bread into an egg yolk. "Now that you come to mention it, it isn't. If anything, it's rather a well-groomed cat."

"You know what I think?" Nasir began wiping the tables with a greasy-looking cloth. "I reckon it belonged to some old woman. She pampered it and called it darling Tiddles and all that, but now she's snuffed it and her relatives don't give a stuff about poor old moggy. They'll have thrown it out in the hope that it'll get run over."

"*Oh!*" I almost choked on my tea. "That's a horrible thought."

"People can be cruel," Nasir shrugged. "But that's life."

Yes, I thought, it is.

This was going to be my first Christmas in my own flat and despite recent events, I determined to make the most of it. I'd spent two Christmases at Crowsmuir Hall and very bleak that had been too. Only one person from the outside world came to see me, and that was Mrs Wallace, on the first Christmas Eve. Visitors were allowed to bring fruit, magazines, fancy toiletries and chocolate but all Mrs. Wallace had to offer were recriminations. She sat in front of me, refusing to take off her winter coat, even though the room was warm. Then she told me I was ungrateful.

"Ach, Jeanie," she said, "How could you do such a thing? Your own father, such an upright, God-fearing man. I blame your Nana. She turned your head with all that nonsense of hers."

She'd put on even more weight and dyed her perm orange. Her plaid coat, garish hair and wobbling jowls gave her the appearance of an orang-utan who'd been brought to Scotland from the wilds of Borneo and learned to speak in a Caledonian accent. I didn't bother to protest my innocence, guessing that would be pointless, but there was one thing I did want to know.

"What did they do to Bushy?" I asked, picking at the bobbles on the scratchy, ugly jumper they'd given me to wear.

"Do to him?" She stared at me. "What do you mean 'do to him'?"

"I mean, has something happened to him? I'm afraid that he might have been....hurt."

"Hurt? That's one way of putting it. Although they don't hang young offenders in this country." Mrs.Wallace adjusted her tea cosy hat. "More's the pity," she added, with a sniff.

My happiest Christmases had been when I was allowed to stay with Nana. We'd decorate Cliff Cottage with greenery; holly, trailing ivy, a bunch of mistletoe, and small pine branches, all tied up with red ribbon. We'd light our candles and bless the house in the name of all the pagan gods of the Old Religion. Then we'd make cake and fruit punch and sing the old songs. My favourite was 'The Two Magicians' about the courtship of two shape-shifters: '*She became a rose, a rose all in the wood/ and he became a bumble-bee and kissed her where she stood.'* Nana told me that some people thought the man in the song was bad, forcing himself on the woman against her will and always getting the better of her no matter how many times she transformed herself, but that wasn't right. The two magicians were lovers, spurred on by mutual desire. '*She became a corpse, a corpse all in the ground, and he became the cold clay and covered her all around...'* That ending always made me shiver.

We'd open our presents the moment Christmas Day arrived after the stroke of midnight. Nana's presents were always hand-crafted; little rag dolls or shell pictures or boxes made from papier-mâché containing amulets and special coins, and she made her own wrapping paper too. It was comforting to me that the present I'd received out of the St. Nicholas Bran Tub looked so much like one of Nana's gifts. I'd be opening that as soon as Christmas Day began, in the first seconds after midnight. It was exciting, the first Christmas present I'd had since Nana passed into the Summer Lands.

After leaving Mustafa's, I went to Kosminsky's and bought some food and drink for the holiday;smoked salmon, pate, pickles, cheeses, bagels and a bottle of sherry. Then I went to the market to buy greenery to decorate my flat. I was hoping against hope that Llewellyn would still appear. In one of my wilder fantasies, I imagined Konrad pulling up outside in his limousine, ready to drive us both down to the special place in Wales. Nothing like that happened, of course and deep down, I knew it wouldn't.

Just as dusk was falling, I decided to return to the old cemetery. Perhaps if I sat on the same bench and waited, Llewellyn might reappear. The gates wouldn't be locked for another hour; it was certainly worth trying. I put on my cloak and ventured out, filled with renewed hope.

The windows of the tall houses that backed on to the cemetery were all lit up. I gazed up at them, imagining the preparations that must be taking place inside those homes, the stockings that were being hung up by children, the huge tins of Cadbury's Roses that were being opened, the TV schedules that were being checked, the sherry glasses that were being filled. I assumed those were the kind of things people did in the everyday world on Christmas Eve. But here I was, sitting on a bench by the grave of that pillar of the community, Samuel Greatorex, waiting for a man who was always eluding me.

Oh, Llewellyn Arawn Llewellyn, where did you go? I knew I couldn't summon him by calling his true name since my life wasn't actually in danger, although perhaps it *would* be if I sat here all night in the cold. But that would be a ridiculous, self-inflicted jeopardy. Best get moving.

I stood up, and began making my way down the path, stopping to read the inscription on one of the family tombs;

three generations, it seemed, of a prominent banking dynasty. No sign of 'M' or 'Mandy' here. *You won't find her underground.* It was then, just as I was reflecting on old Nora's words, that I noticed another mausoleum in an overgrown area not from the perimeter wall. I could just make out the roof sticking up above the laurel bushes, with a thick cluster of dark yews behind it. Something about it seemed familiar; yes, that was it, I'd seen it before, from the road, when I was running home in that thunderstorm, weeks ago. I decided to take a closer look.

I had to leave the path to reach it, making my way through tall clumps of grass and doing my best to avoid the brambles. At last, I was standing in front of it. It was an impressive if neglected structure with three stone steps leading up to a copper door embellished with metal lilies. There was a statue on either side of this entrance; one in white marble, the other in sandstone. The marble figure was on the right, an angel wearing long robes and holding a sword with both hands, the head raised, eyes cast towards the sky, as if preparing to ascend to the heavens. The sandstone figure on the left had a grotesque, snarling face, and the body was in a crouched position as if preparing to attack. Two guardians, one malevolent and menacing, like a creature from hell, the other, calm and celestial. A Manichean polarity and something disturbingly different from anything I'd ever seen before in a Victorian cemetery.

I read the inscription on the plaque beside the door:

Abraham Matthewson 1793-1888. Alchemist, Inventor Poet
Also daughter of the above, Mary,
otherwise Mandragora Carfax
Departed that life January 10th 1901.
'Judge not, lest ye be judged'.

Abraham Matthewson? Surely this must be the same Matthewson who'd summoned the dead as described in that fragment from *Occult London* So he'd had a daughter, a woman who'd begun life as plain Mary, but who had adopted a more exotic name. *Mandragora.* That name was so evocative, redolent of hallucinogenic potions, reminding me of Nana's rhyme: *Hemlock in the morning, Aconite in the afternoon, Mandragora by moonlight....*

Mandy...Mandragora I felt a shiver of excitement. There just had to be a connection here! I began exploring the area around the mausoleum, my feet sinking uncomfortably into the uneven ground. That was an odd phrase on the inscription, wasn't it, 'departed that life'. Surely it should be 'this life'? As I looked down at the ground, I saw that someone had been here before me and quite recently too, judging from the row of tea-lights at the bottom of the left hand side wall. They'd been snuffed out, but there was still a lingering smell of melted wax, and here, too, scattered in the long grass, were several fragments of charred paper and a small metal dish. I remembered Nasir telling me about the weird people who used to hang around in the cemetery trying to hold séances. What people, I wondered? Just teenagers who'd seen too many horror films or people who knew exactly what they were doing? I bent down to pick up the metal dish, wondering if there might be marks on it or....*aaaagh!*

It came at me from nowhere, a huge, dark, flapping thing that wrapped itself around my head, covering my mouth and nose. I couldn't scream; it felt as though the shock had sucked all the breath out of my lungs. I tore at the thing frantically, staggering back and tripping over a fallen headstone. I couldn't breathe...I couldn't...oh, thank goodness, I'd got the horror off my face but now it had wrapped itself around my arm, clinging on like a spectral hand.

I managed to sit up, and then, to my relief, the thing dropped to the ground and I saw it for what it was; nothing more than a torn piece of a refuse sack that must have been caught in a sudden gust of wind. Except that there'd been no wind.

I took a deep breath and got to my feet, and then I saw it, on the apex of the mausoleum roof. The letter 'M', cast in wrought iron, identical in style to the monogram on the key and the mirror, So, I had definitely found her! I'd found 'M'. And, just as old Nora said, she wasn't underground. She was there, in that tomb, the 'M' who had lived in Coleton Street. 'Mandy' otherwise known as Mandragora Carfax, born Mary Matthewson, daughter of the adept Abraham Matthewson, dead since 1901, but, it seemed, very far from departed. And it was clear she didn't want me here. Too bad, I'd be coming back. And next time, I'd come prepared.

Back in my flat, I poured myself a stiff brandy, and picked up the parcel that I'd left on the table.

Hessian, berries, leaf mould and garden twine, not at all the kind of wrapping I'd have expected Clemency to use. So, thank goodness, at least she wasn't involved. As I turned the package over, I noticed a piece of yellow card sticking out from under the twine. The message had been written in red ink:

For Miss Jeanie Gowdie, otherwise the sorceress Morgana. Avoid cracks in the tea cups and the soft blandishments of false lovers. Be wary and do our work. Attend to the wisdom of the Elders who have sent you this gift.

The Elders? A tingling sensation ran up my arm and I dropped the card with a gasp. Oh, good grief! How could this be? How on earth could one of those archaic persons I'd met on a dark station beyond Wimbledon have infiltrated Gerda's bran tub? I was still puzzling over this perplexing matter when I heard a scratching at the window.

"Who's that? "I tugged at the curtains.

Oh, no. Not that cat again. Why on earth wouldn't it go away?

I lifted up the sash window.

"This is getting beyond a joke," I told it.

The cat stared back at me. There were beads of rain on its fur and although its expression was patient, I thought I could also detect a certain desperation there too, a pained look in its eyes. It must be very cold and very hungry by now, the silly thing. There was nothing for it; I was going to have to let it in.

"All right." I raised the window higher. "You win. It's Christmas Eve and I can't leave you out there to starve."

"That's awfully decent of you," the cat said, jumping in. "I'm down on my luck, don't cha-know, and I'm looking for a berth."

"Do you want some food?"

"To tell the truth, I *am* just a trifle peckish. Haven't eaten a thing for a long time, although, of course, I don't want you to put yourself out."

"It's all right." I took a packet of smoked salmon out of my shopping bag. "I can't be cruel to the needy at Christmas."

"Dear me," the cat demurred. "I couldn't possibly take that. I expect you bought that as your treat for Christmas Day."

"I did. But you can have some," I said. "Then I'll send you on your way."

"Oh dash it!" The cat protested. "But I've got nowhere else to go!"

Of course, the cat didn't *actually* say any of those things. That was simply what I *imagined* it would have said if the legend that animals are given the gift of human speech on Christmas Eve had been true. I was impressed, however, by its behaviour. One of the things I've never really liked about cats is the way they make such a scene when they're about to be fed, yowling and rubbing themselves around your legs, creating such an insincere, fawning display. This cat, although almost certainly ravenous, had impeccable manners. He stood waiting politely, as I filled a dish with salmon, and then gave me what seemed to be a grateful look before beginning to feed.

At that moment, the musical hall song about the man from the East End who aspired to be an elegant man-about-town popped into my head. Burlington Bertie. That was what I'd call this cat if I was forced to keep him. Keep him? What on earth was I thinking? This was a *cat.* I didn't want a cat!

"You can stay here for now," I told it. "After Christmas, I'll look for your owner. Right. Ground rules. First, as I said before, I'm not really a cat person, at least, I'm not soppy about them the way some people are, so please don't think you can get too familiar. So, no jumping on my lap, no sticking your claws in my knee, no sleeping on my bed. No bringing dead mice in here please, no killing of *any* mice, and if I look out of the window and see you stalking any birds, expect to be sprayed with water! And there must *definitely* be no landing on my chest like an incubus in the middle of the night! Now this," I walked over to the door, "as you probably know, is a cat-flap. I am going to unlock it for you, and you can come and go as you please. Oh, and one last thing, mind the road. There are some rough lads who speed up and down on chopper bikes and one of them hit a tabby last week. I can't afford vet's bills and besides, although you're here on sufferance, I'd hate to see you hurt."

What a very attentive cat. He seemed to have listened to every word. Perhaps he'd be a useful companion after all, especially considering I'd otherwise have been spending the holiday on my own.

At that moment, the clock on my mantelpiece chimed midnight, signalling the start of Christmas Day. According to traditional lore, animals could no longer speak, but it *was* time to open my mysterious present.

Part Two

The Guidance of Goodwife Gurlie

Thirty Three

"What do you suppose this might be, Bertie?" I turned to the cat. "Well, it's officially Christmas Day, so now's the time to find out just what's under these wrappings."

I picked up my nail scissors, snipped through the garden twine, and carefully unfolded the stained hessian cloth. Then I stared at the item I'd found inside, immediately convinced that there was something ominous about it. It was a thick block of yellowed paper measuring about four inches by seven, secured by two gold rings at the top and mounted on a dark wood stand. There was an inscription on the cover sheet in Gothic lettering:

Goodwife Gurlie's Guidance Calendar
A page a day.

Take careful heed of what we say
Or there'll be a beavy price to pay.

I took a deep breath and flipped the cover sheet over to view the first page. Hmm. This seemed harmless enough, a head and shoulders portrait of a smiling young woman in a mob-cap framed by a border of entwined ivy and climbing roses. The eponymous Goodwife Gurlie, I assumed. Some homely advice was printed next to the portrait:

January 1st. *Always bake home- made cherry pie, do not buy it from others, if you want to gain the respect of your neighbours. First pick fresh cherries. Stone them when the moon is full. Then you must roll out your pastry, taking care to....*

I turned over to the next page, expecting to find the rest of the recipe, but instead the words '*She who peeps too far into the future will be punished for her impatience!'* jumped out at me, quivering in the air. This weird vision was accompanied by a loud cackling that filled the room. *Oh!* I dropped the calendar on the table with a shriek. These Elders! Just why were they doing this to me?

As the days passed, it occurred to me that I might keep Burlington Bertie after all. I'd had no luck tracing his owners and besides, he was anything but a nuisance. It certainly helped that he didn't exhibit any of the behaviour that I'd always found rather off-putting in cats. No dead mice or dead birds had been brought into the flat and presented to me as trophies, he didn't jump on my lap or stick his tail in my face, he hadn't clawed the furniture or made irritating yowling noises and, remarkable at it seemed, he'd even respected my privacy, leaving the room whenever I was dressing or undressing. He was such a solemn, dignified animal, reassuringly un-cat-like, in fact, but more of a familiar spirit. Perhaps, I thought, I could adopt him, and have him as a companion. It wasn't such a bad idea.

On New Year's Eve, I was pleased to find Pyewackets open again with Dorian there, rearranging the window display. He seemed to have acquired some new stock; a nineteenth century wash-stand, an ormolu clock, a wind-up gramophone, an oriental cabinet, a stuffed heron inside a glass dome, a copper coal scuttle, a pile of vintage magazines.

"Ah! It's Jeanie Gowdie." He came to the door to greet me. "Good to see one of my most discerning customers again. Did you have a nice Christmas? Any plans for tonight?"

"Christmas was fine." I stepped into the shop. "And tonight, I'm just going to have a quiet New Year's Eve at home." *Casting a few spells to prepare for this special year, the year of my Coming of Age. Looking into my scrying vessel for a glimpse of my future. Pouring a libation of brandy mixed with wormwood on the doorstep to welcome the New Year.* It wouldn't do to share these plans.

"A quiet night?" He sounded dubious.

"Yes, a quiet night. I'll listen to the chimes of Big Ben on the radio and toast the New Year in with a glass of sherry," I said. "What about you?"

"Oh, I shall party!" He flicked at his feathered earring. "Go to a few bars and then head down to Trafalgar Square to sing *Auld Lang Syne*. You should try it."

"I'm much happier at home."

"You don't know what you're missing." He smiled. "Well, do feel free to browse. Or are you looking for anything in particular?"

"There *is* something I might like to buy. But first, I wanted to ask about something. Did anyone come in here, a man, just before Christmas, asking you about the things you sold me? And, in particular, mentioning the little mirror with the monogram engraved on it?"

"The spirit glass? No." He shook his head. "No, no-one's been in here asking questions like that. In fact, hardly anyone *did* come in here after the twenty third. You came to collect the brandy glass and then it all went very quiet.

Business was surprisingly slow, and I decided to cut my losses and I went to Paris."

"Yes, I noticed you weren't open on Christmas Eve. I was rather surprised."

"Oh well..." He shrugged. "You win some, you lose some. And Paris was magical. Now, what was the thing you wanted to buy?"

"The cat-basket. The one you showed me before Christmas that belonged to a woman called Carmelia Grande that you said was the Rolls Royce of cat carriers Do you still have it?"

"Indeed I do."

"Then I would like it. Because, you see, I've acquired a cat."

"Really? How did that come about?"

"It wasn't something I planned. At first, I thought it was a stray, so I looked at all the missing cat notices in the newsagents' windows around here, but no-one seemed to have lost one meeting its description. Someone suggested to me that the owner might have died, and that seems likely. So it looks as though I'll have to keep it."

"Splendid." He winked knowingly as he reached under the counter for the basket. "As I said before, every good witch should have a cat."

Nana taught me that each day of the week has its distinct character. Some days tend to be lucky, others less so, and much depends on whether the day happens to be named after a particular god. Fridays, for example, can be felicitous, despite the popular prejudice against the thirteenth, since the day is protected by the benevolence of the goddess Freyja. Saturdays, under the auspices of Saturn, are joyful. Wednesdays, on the other hand, can be so full of pitfalls and pratfalls it might be better to stay in bed:

'*Never cast a spell on a Wednesday, Jeanie,*" Nana said. "*Never marry or buy shoes on that day. The shoes will squeak, the marriage will be unhappy and the spell will rebound on you. Wednesdays are dressed in sackcloth. Woden's day is a day for mourning. Woden's day, Ash Wednesday, black Wednesday, Wednesday's child is full of woe. And remember in particular to take extra care if the first day of the year is a Wednesday. That is the unluckiest day of all.'*

Some might call this superstition, but all I know is that the date the Antioch Corey Memorial Library reopened after the Yule Tide holiday was Wednesday the first of January, and everything that happened only served to confirm Nana's warnings about the day dedicated to the one-eyed Nordic god.

I'd got up early, chosen one of my favourite velvet dresses, splashed on perfume and put on my necklace of apache tears. It never occurred to me that Llewellyn wouldn't be at the library and I was wondering whether I should pretend to be furious with him for not having contacted me. But perhaps, I thought, he had a good explanation for his absence. He might have been taken ill with 'flu (poor love!) and spent Christmas confined to that dreary place in King's Cross he'd described or perhaps he'd been summoned to New England to Jabez Corey's death bed. Well, now at last, the wait for an explanation was over.

"Why have you brung that cat into work?"

I froze with my key in the lock of the reading room door. *Brung*? Who was this person with shaky grammar and no handkerchief who'd just snuck up behind me and asked that question in a depressed, nasal tone?

I spun round. A pasty-faced girl with strawberry blonde hair was leaning up against the wall, gazing at me with a mournful expression. Her arms were covered in goose bumps; her bare legs were like two sticks of spaghetti. She looked no more than fourteen.

"Can I help you?" I asked.

The girl sniffed, a long, bubbling snort that was painful to hear. "You what?" She wiped her nose with the back of her hand.

"I was wondering who you are and what you're doing here."

"I'm Cazzie Tank. Is that your cat?" She pointed at Burlington Bertie, snugly ensconced inside his wicker basket.

"Yes," I said. "I've brought him into work as he's not used to being in my flat on his own." Oh goodness, I sounded ridiculous! "I'm sorry to ask again, but what are *you* doing here?"

"I'm on work experience."

"Work experience? What's that?"

"It's what we get at my school. They send us out to places when we're in the fourth year. I was supposed to come here before Christmas. But I weren't well. I've still got a bit of a sniffle."

So I've noticed. It occurred to me that it wasn't surprising she'd caught cold, dressed in that micro skirt and skimpy top, but perhaps those zip-up, sheepskin ankle boots that looked as though they belonged to a much older woman would save her from chilblains. I was surprised no-one had told me to expect this girl. Ernest certainly hadn't mentioned it.

"Well, it's nice to meet you Cazzie." I picked up the cat basket. "Come through to the reading room."

"Blimey." Having followed me in with an air of discontent, all drooping mouth and hunched shoulders, Cazzie stared at the shelves. "It's a bit old and spooky in here, innit?"

"I like it," I said.

"I don't. I hate books."

"You hate books?" I tried not to sound as appalled as I felt. "That's a shame. Books are the most wonderful things. They take you to different worlds and into the minds of other people, and..."

"I wanted to go to one of those modern offices in the city."

"I see." I shuddered inwardly, imagining all that glass and noise and the prowling behaviour of men like Derek Finsworthy. "Well, I think if you give the library a chance, you might find it interesting. I work through there." I pointed to the parcels room. "This way, let me show you."

"Right." Cazzie's lack of enthusiasm hung like a dead weight in the air.

"One thing's puzzling me." I unlocked the parcels room door. "You say you've been sent here by your school but surely it's the school holidays right now? I thought schools didn't go back until the fifth or sixth of January."

"It's coz I missed the proper time last term." Cazzie slumped against the stationery cupboard. "So they said I'd got to come now. Fing is, me attendance record is a bit crap." She wrinkled her nose and gave another lengthy snort.

"Here." I pulled open my desk drawer and took out a box of tissues. "Help yourself."

"Fanks, but no fanks." Cazzie dismissed the box with a flap of her hand. "Can't use them."

"No?"

"No. I had an ear operation when I was little and now, if I try to blow me nose, it feels like me head's going to explode."

"Oh dear." I reminded myself that this disability was far worse for her than it was for me.

I opened my bag and began to unpack my things, arranging them on my desk; a new pen, a bag of mint imperials, a mandala woven from rushes to bless the start of the year.

"So, Cazzie," I tried to sound encouraging, "How long will you be working here?"

"A few weeks. The bloke told me you needed an assistant."

"Bloke? Do you mean Mr Brunswicker?"

"No. That weren't his name. He said he was the chief custard."

"I think you mean the Custodian." Oh, thank goodness! My stomach flipped over with joy. So he *had* returned! "You mean Mr Llewellyn."

"Llewellyn?" Cazzie shook her head. "Nah, that weren't his name."

"Are you sure?" I swallowed, all my delight evaporating in an instant.

"Yes. He was wearing jack-ups."

"Jack-ups?" I repeated. "Sorry, but what are...?"

"You know, *jack-ups*. Trousers what..."

"Good morning, colleagues." With a slow, lumbering gait a man in a baggy grey suit was advancing towards us across the reading room. He was a large person with short grey hair and a long, putty-coloured face that ended in a goatee beard. His eyes were as cold as frogspawn and his feet, encased in square-toed shoes, seemed too large, while his trousers were definitely too short. Now I knew what Cazzie had meant by 'jack-ups'. His trousers weren't speaking to his boots, as Nana would have said.

"Allow me to introduce myself." He ducked as he came through the doorway. "I am Malachi Hopkins, the new Custodian. And you, I assume, are Miss Jeanie Gowdie?"

"Yes." I nodded. "I am. But I don't understand. Why are you...?"

"It's quite simple," Frogspawn Eyes informed me. "Miss Providence Corey and Miss Salutation Corey have appointed me. I am now in charge of the library."

"But Mr Llewellyn is the custodian. Jabez Corey..."

"Jabez Corey's wishes are no longer of any significance. He is deceased. He died on Boxing Day."

"Oh! That's so sad." Although I'd never met Jabez, I felt genuinely distressed by this news. "So I assume Mr Llewellyn's staying in New England for the funeral and you're here on a temporary basis?"

"Wr-rong." The way Hopkins pronounced the word made me think of the verse in *Corinthians* about sounding brass and tinkling cymbals. "My appointment is permanent."

"Permanent?" I was bewildered. "But what about Mr Llewellyn? Where is he?"

"Now that is an interesting question." A distinctly nasty edge crept into his voice. "But rest assured, the Antioch Corey Memorial Library now has a custodian who will insist on certain standards."

"Standards?" My chest felt tight; this was a nightmare. This just couldn't be happening.

"I will be implementing a new system. Purification and Progress is my motto." Hopkins tilted his head back, narrowed his eyes and looked down his long nose at me. It was like being judged by a self-righteous old goat.

"And I do not think we need mourn the passing of Jabez Corey who, I understand, was an ungodly and blasphemous person." He uttered a dry cough and tugged at the waistband of his trousers, pulling the garment upwards as if hoping to bring it up to his armpits. "I must also inform you that Ernest Brunswicker has been dismissed."

"Ernest?" Could this get any worse? "But why?"

"I have it on the best authority that the man was a neurotic."

"He was a good librarian." I retorted. "The readers respected him."

"I have to say I find that difficult to believe. Miss Clemency Nantucket has given me an entirely different account of the man. But I'm delighted to tell you that if you play your cards right, you could take Mr Brunswicker's place."

"But I don't want to take his place," I protested. "I think of him as a friend and..."

"It would be a promotion for you, Miss Gowdie. You are supposed to feel flattered and gratified." Hopkins tilted his head, treating me once again to the old goat treatment. "Are you usually this argumentative?"

I didn't trust myself to speak. I knew that if I did, I'd be unable to control the torrent of fury and ill-considered words that were bubbling up inside me, so I simply stood there, clenching my fists behind my back. Cazzie, I noticed, had moved her position so that she was standing in front of the cat basket, keeping Burlington Bertie safe from view.

"Has Ernest been given any redundancy money?" I said at last.

"That is not your concern. For now, you are responsible for both the reading room and the parcels room. Fortunately, you have Miss Tank to assist you with the more menial tasks."

"But what about..."

"Enough!" He raised his voice suddenly, making me jump. "Now Miss Gowdie," he resumed in a quiet drawl. "I don't want to take up any more of your time at this moment but be so good as to come to my office at eleven o'clock. I wish to brief you on a number of essential matters. Good morning."

As he turned on his heel and lumbered off, I noticed, with some distaste, that he had a sagging, low-slung bottom. In a nice man, such a feature might have made him seem lovable and bear-like, but it was clear that Hopkins was not a nice man. Cazzie waited until he was gone, then made a disparaging sound. I believe she'd have described it as 'kissing your teeth'.

"What an old tosser," she said.

She might be a rough diamond and her sniffing was intolerable, but I was beginning to warm to Cazzie Tank.

I hardly knew what to do with myself; my mind was reeling with the horror of this situation. Eventually, I set Cazzie the task of tidying the stationery cupboard, and went through to the reading room, where I began a desultory rearranging of the shelves. What I really wanted to do was burst into furious shouts of rage, but that simply wouldn't do. My throat felt as though it had a large lump of rock lodged in it. Then, to my relief, Gerda arrived.

"Happy New Year!" She entered the reading room in her customary breezy manner, a large plastic box in her hands. "I bring you the spoils of the Yuletide feast. I have stollen and strudel and a special almond and honey cake I made myself and..." She stopped, staring at me. "But vat has happened? You look so upset, Jeanie."

"Oh, Gerda." I wailed, unable to contain my emotions a moment longer. "I'm afraid this is going to be anything but a happy new year!"

Thirty Four

"Wotcha." Cazzie grinned, emerging from the parcels room with a rubber band stretched between her thumb and forefinger. It seemed that instead of tidying the cupboard, she'd been spending her time making paper pellets and pinging them into the bin, but I felt too depressed to reprimand her.

"Hello my dear." Gerda put the box of pastries down and held out her hand in greeting. "I don't think ve have met. Pleased to meet you."

"Gerda, this is Cazzie," I said. "She's been sent here by her school on work experience. Cazzie, this is Professor Gerda Goldfarb."

"Professor?" Cazzie sniffed loudly. "I don't get it. Aren't Professors blokes?"

"Not all of them, my dear." Gerda smiled. "Velcome to the library. How long vill you be staying vith us?"

"Dunno. I feel like bunking off right now, if you wants the truth. I can hardly breave in 'ere. All the dust is getting up me nose."

"Listen, Cazzie," I seized this opportunity to talk privately to Gerda. "If you need some fresh air, why don't you take Bertie out for me? You could give him some exercise in the square."

"'Spose he runs off?" Cazzie looked dubious.

"He won't," I assured her. "He's a remarkably well-behaved cat and he'll go back into the basket when you call him. Just make sure you don't let him out until you're in the middle of the grass and be careful of any dogs."

"I'll do me best."

"You have a cat now?" Gerda peered through the grille at Burlington Bertie. "I didn't know you vere fond of cats."

"I wasn't, but this one behaves himself. It's almost as though he knows he's a guest and has to be on his best behaviour."

"He's really very handsome." Gerda nodded approvingly. "For a cat. But I mustn't get too close. Much as I like cats, I am allergic to them. As a child I suffered badly from asthma and even now, the fur might set me off."

"Oh goodness, I hadn't thought of that! Maybe other readers will feel the same. Although I'm glad to say this cat doesn't seem to be given to moulting."

"Right, then I'll be off." Cazzie moved towards the door.

"My dear child," Gerda protested. "Do you not have a coat? You vill freeze out there."

"'S'allright," Cazzie shrugged. "I don't feel the cold. At least, not much. See ya."

"Vat a little urchin." Gerda turned to me the moment she was gone. "Vere is she from?"

"I don't know the name of the school."

"But I have never known a school send a pupil here. It is most odd."

"That's not the only thing that's odd," I said. "I think we'd better go into the parcels room and close the door. Gerda, I've got some terrible, terrible news."

Having listened intently to my account of the morning's events, interspersing it with gasps and violent shakes of her head, Gerda's expression was one of deep perplexity

"How can this be?" she mused. "Our dear friend Ernest sacked, our distinguished Custodian removed from his position, and an unpleasant man who is unable to vear his trousers properly here in his stead. Ach! It is an outrage."

"It's horrible. And I don't know what I can do about it."

"Ve must think of something. This interloper, vat do you say his name is?"

"Hopkins."

"Hopkins? Mein Gotte! That is a cursed name! Along vith Sprenger and Kramer and all the others who have been persecutors of independent vimmen and vitches throughout the ages. And another thing, vat proof is there that he speaks the truth about being the new Custodian? Could he be an imposter?"

"He says he was appointed by Salutation and Providence Corey."

"So the puritans have seized power! No doubt Miss Plymouth Rock will be delighted."

"I expect she will. But I can't understand why Jabez Corey didn't do something to prevent something like this happening before he died. He must have left a will."

"Ach." She shuddered. "Ve are talking America here, a land of opportunity, a fine place in many vays, but also the abode of lawyers. There are more lawyers per square foot in America than there are spiders. There must have been so many legal loop-holes and these cousins have exploited them."

"Yes, I expect they have. And, oh, Gerda, what do you suppose has become of Mr Llewellyn?"

"That is something ve must discover at all costs. I remember how he never came to the party that night.

I remember thinking that was strange. Alvays, in the past, he has come and spoken to people, even if he never stayed long. And after the party, I made a disturbing discovery. About the St Nicholas Bran Tub."

"The St. Nicholas Bran Tub?"

"Yes. There had been a mix up vith the labels. That spoon with the threatening message, it vas not intended for Ernest at all. For him, someone had bought a book of crossword puzzles; I found it after he'd gone. I'm afraid that the spoon, a *Velsh* love spoon remember, vas meant for someone else. And I think you can guess vat I mean."

"You mean it was meant for Mr Llewellyn?"

"Indeed. Someone must have had a serious grudge against him. Remember those vords on the handle. *I curse you and...*"

"Oh, Gerda, don't go on! I can't bear it." I felt sick to my stomach.

"Yes, it's no good crying over the milk that has been spilt. But ve must take action. First, ve must contact Mr Llewellyn."

"But I don't know where he lives."

"No?" She raised her eyebrows. "Did he never tell you? But now I think of it, he never told me. But you, my dear, you vere close to him, I felt and..." She broke off.

"He mentioned a home in Wales and a room in Kings Cross, but I don't have the address of either."

"And vat about Ernest?"

"I only know that he lives somewhere in Southwark. Clemency mentioned that when I came here for my interview."

"But there must be a list of staff addresses. Perhaps Ernest has it? Vat about searching his desk? It vill not be pleasant looking inside those drawers as he used to throw in the crusts from his sandwiches, but that is the most likely place to find such information."

"Yes," I agreed. "Let's look there. It won't be prying, because according to this awful Hopkins man, that's actually *my* desk now. Not that I want it to be." I went over to the desk. The top drawer was stuck and it took several vigorous yanks to get it open. "Oh dear," I peered inside. "What an awful mess. I'm not sure I want to explore in here with my bare hands. There are little brown things with legs running about and...*ouch!*" I sucked my finger. "I think something just bit me."

"That must have been an earvig," Gerda said.

"Well, whatever it was, there's nothing useful in here, just crumpled balls of paper and indigestion pills, and paper clips that have been twisted out of shape."

"Yes. How Ernest used to set my nerves on edge ven he vould clean his ears vith them!"

"Well, I just wish he was here, doing that right now."

"So do I," Gerda nodded. "To hear the clank of that bicycle on the stairs vould be music to my ears. It vould give me joy to see him inking in the crossvord and hear him rubbing his fingernails together." She sighed. "But no time for nostalgia. Try the other drawer."

"It's locked. No, wait, I think I remember he kept the key in this little pot. Yes, here it is." I turned the key in the lock. "*Oh!*" I stared at the only item in the drawer, a small white envelope, marked *Private and Confidential: To be handed to Jeanie Gowdie in the event of my disappearance.* "Oh, Gerda, this is Llewellyn's handwriting."

"I see. Then I must let you read that letter undisturbed. It is clearly a personal communication."

"Yes." I slipped the letter into my bag. My heart was beating very fast.

"And in the meantime, I vill find Ernest's address. There can't be many Brunsvickers in the telephone book."

"Ernest might not even have a telephone."

"Then he must be on the Electoral roll. Don't vorry. I vill find him."

"Thanks Gerda. But oh, this is so awful! And now," I looked at my watch, "just to make matters worse, it's nearly eleven o'clock and I've got an appointment with that dreadful man Hopkins."

"Chin up!" Gerda said. "Remember that you are a resourceful young voman, and together, ve can do much to defeat this vile man!"

"Come in, Miss Gowdie, take a pew! Eleven o'clock on the dot. How admirably punctual you are."

It was horrible to see Hopkins behind Llewellyn's desk, drinking tea and beaming at me as though we were old friends. At least he wasn't using the love tankard. He'd provided himself with a blue willow pattern tea service and how incongruous he looked with that delicate cup and saucer in his large hands, crooking his little finger and pursing his ugly lips. I felt obliged to sit down in front of him, although I would have preferred to stand. Sitting felt like an act of subjugation.

"Are you familiar with this room, Miss Gowdie?" He took a sip of tea, closed his eyes and clacked his cup down into the saucer as if to emphasise the point. *Sip, clack.* The sound set my teeth on edge.

"Familiar with it?" My mouth felt dry.

"Yes. Familiar." He opened his eyes and looked at me with the keen gaze of a myopic reptile who had suddenly been provided with spectacles. "I understand from Miss Nantucket that you spent a considerable amount of time working in here. Strange, when it was your brief to look after the parcels room."

"I was helping Mr Llewellyn catalogue the cabinet of curiosities."

"Ah yes, the cabinet of curiosities." He turned to look at it. "A collection of unhygienic junk, wouldn't you say? You may be interested to know that I intend to have this room thoroughly fumigated." Hopkins lifted his cup to his lips. *Sip, clack.* "Oh, and by the way, Miss Gowdie, when we were speaking earlier today, I thought I caught a glimpse of a creature that looked remarkably like a cat. A live one, unlike that monstrosity, which is, mercifully, very dead." He pointed to the two headed specimen in the cabinet. "Can you shed any light on this matter?"

"None whatsoever, I'm sorry. I have no idea where Antioch Corey found that mummified cat."

"Please don't be satirical with me, Miss Gowdie." He looked down his nose. "And, let me add, you'd be well advised to keep any live cat out of my sight. I have a horror of them. In fact, if I saw a cat about to fall out of the window of a high building, I'd make no attempt to save it. I hope you take my meaning?"

I did. Although I made a great effort to look innocent, my stomach was twisting in horror at this murderous innuendo. Hopkins lifted his cup, took another sip of tea and replaced the cup in the saucer with that dreadful clacking sound.

"Well, to business," he continued. "As I said before, I know nothing of the whereabouts of my predecessor. But it occurs to me, having reflected on the matter, that perhaps you do?"

"No. No I don't. When I said I thought Mr Llewellyn had gone to New England, I was simply assuming..."

"Yes, I realise that. And I would have known if he was there. But he is not. And we, that is Salutation and Providence Corey and myself, are anxious to locate him. He is facing disciplinary charges."

"*Disciplinary charges!*" The words burst out of me before I could stop myself. "But what on earth do you mean? Mr Llewellyn has done nothing wrong."

"Hasn't he? I have it on the very best authority that when Mr. L.A. Llewellyn visited the Corey mansion in the autumn of last year, he stole a very valuable item."

"I find it difficult to imagine Mr Llewellyn as a thief." I tried to sound calm.

"I'm not asking you to *imagine* it, Miss Gowdie. I'm telling you this as a fact." He lifted his teacup. *Sip, clack.* Ugh! "Now, I wonder if he confided in you. Perhaps you know the whereabouts of this purloined item?

"I don't know what you mean." I lied.

"Don't you? I suspect you already know, but just to elucidate, it was a book. A book in manuscript form."

I mustn't look, I told myself. I mustn't look at his big, ugly feet or start visualising what's lying under the floorboards just beneath them. He's only inches away from Antioch Corey's *Book of Shadows.* And I mustn't say anything about it at all. I mustn't say that I happen to know Jabez Corey entrusted the manuscript to Llewellyn. I mustn't say a thing. I must look as innocent as possible. I mustn't even think about it. This horrible man might even be a mind reader.

"And theft may be only one of his crimes." *Sip, clack.*

"I don't understand." *And by the way, you've dripped tea on the front of your shirt. Ha!*

"Don't you? I'm afraid that everything my predecessor has been doing here has been in direct opposition to the wishes of Miss Salutation and Miss Providence Corey. But you can dismiss the previous regime from your mind. You will answer to me and to my deputy, Miss Clemency Nantucket now. Purification and Progress. That is to be our mission statement. Is there anything you wish to say about that?"

"No. Nothing at all." Another lie.

"Then you may go." *Sip, clack.* "For the time being, that is," he added.

I sat down at my desk in the parcels room, trying to control the rage that threatened to overwhelm me. That man! That awful man! This was worse, far worse, than anything I'd had to endure from Derek Finsworthy, and it was going to take far more sophisticated weaponry to defeat him, I knew that. But I wasn't going to let Hopkins get the better of me, definitely not. *You'll get your comeuppance, Mr Jack-Ups, believe me...*But I had to think very carefully about what to do, there was no point charging in like a bull at a gate. That would be counter-productive, and besides, I knew so little about this man. For all I knew, he might be in league with the people who'd sent me to Crowsmuir Hall.

I took Llewellyn's letter out of my bag. I just hoped he'd left me some advice. My hands were trembling as I slit open the envelope:

My dear Jeanie,

If you are reading this, it means that the very worst has happened and I have failed in my attempt to make the situation safe for us. Accept the possibility that we will never see each other again. Ernest Brunswicker has instructions to hand you this letter in the New Year if I have not returned. He knows nothing of the business I'm engaged in but I trust his discretion.

Perhaps you know how I met my end or perhaps you are still wondering what has happened. Perhaps you aren't worried about me at all and in many ways, I hope that's the case; I don't want you to ~~suffer the agonies of separation~~. be unhappy in any way. At least we had some time together, and I was able to tell you something of my feelings, but it was selfish of me to burden you with them. You are too young to be encumbered with me. But thank you for brightening my life and restoring my hopes. Forget me. My fate is unimportant. If you knew everything about me and I promise I would have told you when the time was right, you might never have wanted to see me again in any case.

What on earth did this last sentence mean? Why was he so fond of these dark hints? Puzzled, and more than a little frustrated, I returned to the letter:

Forget about me. The most important thing now is for you to achieve your destiny. I have, perhaps wrongly, tried to protect you from its dangers, but I see now it is your right to develop your skills in magic and adopt your true name. There is only one person who can help you; her name is Dr Hecate Burneside. We've already spoken of her; I wish we could have visited her together. We would have had a wonderful time, picnicking on Pendle Hill and I'd have ~~kissed you, made love to you, let you renew my~~ Dr Hecate will instruct you on how to undertake your Coming of Age ceremony. As you rightly said, this must take place in the year of your twenty first birthday.

Please go to Dr Hecate as soon as possible, darling Jeanie; you will need to stay with her for at least a week to complete your instruction. She will be expecting you and Jabez Corey will give you leave of absence. No need to ask him; he will know. Don't waste any of your precious skills searching for me. I may be dead or I may be alive, but I will be beyond your reach. There's only one thing to say now and that is that I love you with all my heart and soul and very being, no woman has ever made me feel the way you do and if only I had been able to love you properly, ~~consummate my desires and...~~

Sorry. No more time. Thank you, Jeanie, for helping me to feel alive again.

With my undying love,
Llewellyn Arawn Llewellyn.

This was all too much; the tears began coursing down my cheeks. Fortunately, Gerda had gone and Cazzie, returned from the square with Burlington Bertie, was in the reading room, playing with the date stamp and making herself a necklace out of paperclips, so there was no-one to witness my distress.

"What an awful day, Bertie." I put the cat basket down on my rug, and secured the chain on my door. "What an absolutely...*Oh!*"

I stared at the calendar. The portrait of the smiling, homely Goodwife Gurlie had gone, and in its place there was a picture of a sunken-jawed crone framed by a border of thorns and cobwebs. This wasn't the only startling transformation. There, beside the portrait of the crone, was a text that had nothing to do with cherry pie:

Curse the man with the frog-like eye,
Stick him with pins and by and by
He whose trousers are too short
Will soon develop a genital wart.

Heed the words of Grandma Gandy on this day, Jan. 1st in the year one thousand seven hundred and five.

Well, well, well. The Elders certainly had a grim sense of humour. I wasn't at all sure it would be ethical or advisable to carry out these instructions to the letter, but this was certainly a very encouraging call to arms. I was beginning to feel better already.

Thirty Five

To prevent net curtains yellowing in the sun, wash them three minutes before dawn in the milk of an ageing ewe. Add the saliva of a possum and all will be well.

Goodwife Gurlie's Guidance for this day, Jan 2nd

"Looks like Goodwife Gurlie's back." I told the cat. "But I wouldn't be surprised if Grandma Gandy's just biding her time. Or perhaps they're just two sides of the same person? Now listen Bertie, you have to stay here today. It's far too dangerous for you at the library. No, don't look at me like that, I mean what I say. Yes, I'm sure you'd like to help me, but Hopkins has already threatened you. But don't worry, I'm going to get rid of the horrible man. I just need to work out how. Any ideas?"

It seemed such a pity Bertie *couldn't* actually speak; he might have the answer to my problems. He certainly had a remarkably intelligent appearance. And now he was sitting on the rug, staring up at me, as if he was really listening, and had something to communicate.

"I've been thinking about this a lot," I said. "And I'm absolutely sure Llewellyn's hasn't come to any real harm. I'd know if anything serious had happened. He's alive somewhere and when he can, he'll come back. In the meantime," I touched the apache tears with my fingertips, "I'm going to do what he advised. Go and see Dr Hecate.

She'll help me, I'm sure of it. And then once I've had my Coming of Age ceremony, I'll have so much more power. The only thing is, I don't know how I'm going to get leave of absence now that Hopkins is in charge. I'll have to think about that one. Well, I'd better get to work now. I'm leaving the cat flap unlocked, but you must only go out if it's *really* necessary. Got that? Good. I'll see you later."

"Good morning, Miss Gowdie." Malachi Hopkins, he of the frog-like eyes and the vertically-challenged trousers, lumbered towards me across the entrance hall, a large cardboard box in his arms. "Just having a clear out."

"Really?" I feigned a neutral interest. "May I see?"

"If you insist." He lowered the box.

I gazed, appalled, at the contents. He'd filled the box with items from the cabinet of curiosities. Here was the mummified, two-headed cat, and the enormous claw that I'd identified as a relic of the Aepyornis, the extinct, flightless bird of Madagascar. Here, too was the sasquatch skin, along with several little Aztec figures, an American Indian mask carved from redwood and some jars of preserved Amazonian insects.

"But those are things from Antioch Corey's collection," I protested.

"So I believe, Miss Gowdie, but ancient pieces of taxidermy such these," he prodded the two-headed cat with his forefinger, "can harbour mites. I'm afraid I don't wish to share my office with such an unhygienic display. All this vile stuff must be incinerated by the caretaker."

"But some of it could be of interest to our scholars," I objected.

"Nonsense! It is trash. Now, let us not waste time discussing such a trivial matter. There are several more pressing concerns. There is much to be done to modernise this benighted place."

"Modernise?"

"Of course." His eyes narrowed. "Can you not see that the systems here are archaic to say the least? Old ledgers with hand-written entries, we cannot have that! Records must be placed on microfiche. And it seems there has been no means of checking the work of staff or readers. I shall be introducing reviews and assessment for all. It is vital that we bring the Antioch Corey Library into line with the twentieth century."

"But..."

"Do I detect a note of dissent? Is there something you wish to say, Miss Gowdie? Do feel free to share your thoughts with me. I like to think I am a receptive listener."

I took a deep breath. I couldn't possibly stay silent, whatever the risk.

"It seems to me," I began, "That the library is perfect as it is. It's how the readers like it. It's the way Jabez Corey intended it to be, a memorial to Antioch Corey."

"Hmm." He tilted his head in his judgemental old goat style. "An interesting position, but as I have informed you, Jabez Corey is deceased. We must move on. And in some cases, some people must move out."

"Move out?"

"Yes. I've discussed this matter in some detail with Miss Nantucket. I believe that this library is supporting what I can only describe as human parasites."

"Parasites?"

"Yes. People who are obsessed with undesirable subjects and who have no useful contribution to make. I shall be requesting that members of the library who claim to be engaged in research submit samples of their work to me and if I judge that work to be lacking in worth, I will see to it that their membership is cancelled."

"I don't quite see how that will work," I said. "Economically, I mean. If we lose subscribers, then we lose funds and..."

"Ah!" He beamed. "But I shall be replacing the dead wood with new blood. Other, more worthy, scholars will be joining us after this purge. We will have new sponsors. And I expect you to support my new initiative."

"That's a tautology." The words were out of my mouth before I could stop myself.

"I beg your pardon?"

"'New initiatives', it's a tautology." I felt forced to explain, even though I knew I shouldn't. "An initiative is, by definition, new. So you don't have to qualify the word in that way."

"I see." He pursed his lips. "I expect you think you're very clever, Miss Gowdie, but believe me, it's possible to be too clever sometimes."

"I was trying to be helpful."

"Really? Then you can help by paying attention to the document on your desk. By which I mean, the desk in the reading room that, I understand, was once used by Mr Brunswicker. It is your desk now, and I require that you use it. And please read the document carefully. Good day, Miss Gowdie."

A folder marked *Purification and Progress: The Library Development Plan* was indeed lying on Ernest's desk. With considerable unease, I flipped it open and skimmed through the closely typed pages. There were a number of headings, such as *Initiatives, Proposals, Action Plan*, *Management Directives* and *Restructuring*. There was more, much more. It was all depressingly reminiscent of the insurance office but even more nit-picking and futile. I could only assume that Hopkins was set on destroying the library from within. This kind of regimentation would drive all the readers away and turn the place into an empty shell. The question was, why was he doing this? Was his motivation pure self-aggrandisement and pig-headedness or did he have some darker purpose? Since it seemed he'd formed an alliance with Clemency, I had a terrible feeling that I already knew the answer to that.

Cazzie opened her bread roll and began picking out the thin stalks of mustard and cress, putting them to the side of her plate. Her pale fingers moved rapidly and almost obsessively and try as I might, I couldn't help finding her behaviour peculiar. There was something very worrying about Cazzie; she was such a waif, as Gerda had said, so pale and undernourished-looking and I wasn't even sure whether to believe her story about work experience. Not a word from her school had I received.

"I'm just wondering," I said. "Why did you ask Psyche for an egg and cress roll when you don't like cress?"

"She don't do egg and cress without the cress." Cazzie continued to remove more pieces of the offending salad item.

"I'm sure she would if you asked," I said.

"Doubt it. She's a bit weird, isn't she? Why does she sing that mad song all the time?"

"*Sshh!*" I shot her a warning glance.

"She can't hear me." Cazzie sounded unperturbed. "She's gone out the back."

"Yes, I know but there's no reason to be unkind about her."

"But you don't mind me slagging off old Jack-Ups?"

"Listen," I lowered my voice. "I just think you should be careful about what you say. You don't know who might be listening."

"You think there's spies?" Cazzie looked excited. "It don't matter, do it? I can talk about old Jack-ups as much as I like, because even if he heard us, old Jack-ups wouldn't know he *was* old Jack-ups and he'd think I was talking about someone else."

"All the same, I think you should be careful."

"We had a teacher like him once." Having cleansed her roll of cress, she took a large bite. "Like old Jack-Ups. We got him in the end. 'Spose we shouldn't have done it, but the pompous git had it coming to him."

"I don't think you've told me the name of your school."

"It's Bog Street Comprehensive. Nah, not really! Your face!"

"You need to tell me the real name of your school," I said. "Won't your teachers be coming here to see how you're getting on?"

"Bloody hope not!" She laughed. "Anyway, we got rid of him. This teacher, I mean."

"Got rid of him? How did you do that?" Despite my better instincts, my curiosity was aroused.

"We never murdered him, worse luck. We just drove him mad with all kinds of tricks. And he thought we was fick. But fick people can get the better of clever people all the time, by pretending to be even more fick."

"I don't think you should call people 'thick'."

"Why not? I know I'm fick. And I'm pig ignorant. I ain't never done good." She opened her roll, stuck her finger into the mashed egg mix, licked it off and sniffed loudly.

Poor Cazzie's sniffing was getting worse. I hoped she wasn't actually swallowing all that catarrh; that wouldn't do her any good at all. I remembered one of Nana's remedies, an inhalant made from olbas oil to which had been added a sprig of thyme, a spoonful of powdered moss scraped from the grave-stone of a drowned sailor, and a charm uttered at sunrise. Perhaps I could bring something like that in for her, although getting hold of the moss might be difficult. I wasn't sure that the mail order company that Nana had always used would have any in stock.

"I don't suppose you are 'thick', Cazzie," I said. "I just think no-one's ever given you a chance."

"I can look after meself."

"Yes, I'm sure you can," I said. "But you could do so well. You just have to decide what it is you want to do. Don't you have any ambitions, things that you're interested in, maybe things that aren't taught in school but that you could study all on your own?"

"Like what?" Cazzie gave another lengthy snort. The sooner I mixed that inhalant for her the better.

"Well, I don't know....music, perhaps, or fashion or..."

"I think it would be cool to do magic," Cazzie announced.

"You do?" Now this *was* encouraging.

"Yeh." She rubbed her nose with her finger. "Like on the stage at the Palladium. When the bloke in the evening suit saws a woman in half or pulls a rabbit out of a hat."

"Oh, I see." I felt disappointed. "That's not really magic. That's just conjuring. Illusions."

"You mean there's some other sort of magic?" Cazzie gawped at me. "Like *real* magic? You're having a laugh, right?"

I considered my reply. Tempting as it was to open up some new horizons to Cazzie, perhaps now wasn't a good time to start talking about spells and charms. Particularly as Clemency Nantucket had just entered the room.

"There you are." Ignoring me, she strode towards Cazzie.

"Happy New Year, Clemency." I did my best to smile, but I was startled by her appearance. Both her hands were encased in bandages that extended several inches above her wrists; it was like being confronted by a reanimated Egyptian mummy from a horror film. I didn't know whether to express concern or pretend not to have noticed. In the event, she made the decision for me.

"I expect you're wondering about *this*." She held out her hands. "Well, so I am. It can't have happened by accident."

"But what has happened?" I asked. "I do hope it's not too painful."

"For your information, it's an agonising, itchy rash and at the hospital, they said they'd never seen anything like it. I'd sure as hell like to find the person who bought me those gloves!"

"Gloves," I repeated. My mouth felt suddenly dry.

"On Christmas Day," Clemency continued. "I unwrapped the present I'd been given from the St. Nicholas Bran Tub. It was a pair of woollen gloves. Perfectly fine, I thought. Swell design. Warm. But then I put them on when I went out for a walk and within a few hours my hands were lobster-red and covered in disgusting lumps. And then the infection started spreading up my arms."

My stomach was churning with fright. This was the Chrissie Wilkinson incident all over again and who knew what the consequences would be this time? Clemency would be relentless; she would be making rigorous inquiries throughout the library and if she found out that I was the person who'd bought those gloves, the consequences would be severe. But I hadn't done anything! I hadn't cursed those gloves, had I? But what if things like this just happened, against my will, what if I had certain powers that I couldn't control, what if...*no!* Surely not!

"Oh dear." I tried to hide my dismay. "I suppose you must be allergic to wool."

"No. I've never been allergic to wool. *Never*."

"Perhaps it was nothing to do with the gloves," I suggested. "A cleaning fluid you used, perhaps or a new brand of soap? Or biological detergent or..."

"It was the gloves." She glowered at me.

"My mum's allergic to wool," Cazzie announced. "It can come on any time."

"You reckon?" Clemency turned to her. "Actually, you were the person I wanted to see. Would you be interested in helping me in the archive room this afternoon?" she asked.

"'Fanks, but I'm not interested in some old room." Cazzie took a large bite of her roll.

"This isn't an invitation, it's an instruction," Clemency hissed. "Are you always this rude?"

"Rude?" Cazzie sounded genuinely puzzled. "You asked if I was interested and I told you I weren't. If I *had* to come, you should have said so."

"You're very impertinent!"

"Nah." Cazzie grinned. "I'm just fick."

I spent the afternoon dealing with the requests for postal loans that had accumulated over the holiday period. I'd hoped that reading the letters and searching for some of the more obscure books would distract me but all it did was increase my anxiety. All I could think about were the dreadful changes that would take place if Hopkins got his way. Dr A. Harmsworth of Bexhill on Sea, for example, had asked to borrow one of the books that had been dictated to the medium Ethan Crowley Jnr. What if Clemency persuaded Hopkins that such 'blasphemous nonsense' should be removed from the shelves and Hopkins agreed and cancelled Dr Harmsworth's membership at the same time? Something must be done to prevent Hopkins from interfering with this quiet, scholarly haven and destroying its special quality.

Well, there was one thing I could do right now. I could rescue those items from the Cabinet of Curiosities that Hopkins had taken down to the caretaker's room. Since the mysterious Jim didn't clock in until late, nothing would have been incinerated yet. With any luck, I could even retrieve the box before he saw it.

I waited until locking-up time and then took the lift to the basement. Psyche's place was closed by now, so there was no light coming from the far end of the corridor, just one low, red night-light glimmering by the exit doors. I could barely see where I was going. I was aware of a heady, fragrant smell, one that I recognised from the hostel in Upminster. But who on earth would have the nerve to smoke weed in the nether regions of the Antioch Corey Library now that Hopkins was in charge?

I was feeling just a little apprehensive; there was something unsettling about the place, all those pipes running along the low ceiling and the insidious humming sound that was probably only the boiler, but which was drilling into my ears like a subtle torture. I arrived at the door marked 'Caretaker' but there was no sign of the box standing outside. Perhaps Hopkins had placed it somewhere else, by those big industrial bins in the yard for example. I moved towards the fire doors. Then I realised I was being watched.

I have a sixth sense about this kind of thing. Before I walk into a bathroom, I'll know if there's a spider in the sink. I'm not afraid of discovering one; it's just that I can sense when I'm not alone. And I knew I wasn't alone now. Someone *or something* was down here with me.

"Anyone there?"

No response.

"Hello?"

I could hear breathing. Now I was completely spooked. It had better not be Hopkins lurking down here. Or Clemency. Or the entity that had attacked Llewellyn when he was bringing the *Book of Shadows* to the library. Oh! The *Book of Shadows*! What if Hopkins got his hands on *that* in the course of clearing out the office? I must do something to stop that happening too! But right now, my main priority was to get out of here before I was attacked by my stalker.

"OK." I tried to sound like someone who was unconcernedly speaking their thoughts out loud. "Looks like Jim the Caretaker's not here. Pity, I need him to fix that wonky door on the stationery cupboard. Never mind, I can always come back tomorrow and put a note in the request box. Well, I'm off!" I headed towards the lift.

"Gotcha!" Two wiry arms grabbed me from behind, holding me in a strong grip.

"Let go of me!" I struggled furiously.

"Keep cool. I'm not going to hurt you." The person let me go.

I whirled round to face my assailant. A light was snapped on, and I was confronted by a tall figure in brown overalls.

"What are you playing at?" I demanded. "If you're Jim, I can only say that..."

"Sorry. Couldn't resist."

"Resist? Are you mad?"

"Hello, Gowdie. Don't you recognise me?"

I stared at the man, at the knitted bobble hat pulled down low over his forehead, at his over-bright eyes. For a moment, I couldn't make any sense of this situation, but then, as he whipped off his hat, *I knew.*

"Oh good grief!" I gasped, hardly able to believe it possible. "*Bushy!*"

Thirty Six

"I can't quite take this in." I shifted my position, trying to get comfortable on the bean bag on the cold stone floor. "I thought you were dead."

"Dead?" Bushy grinned. "Not me. As you can see, I'm very much alive. Fig roll?" He held out a half-empty packet.

"No thank you. I don't really like them," I told him. "I ate far too many of those squidgy things once so as not to offend you, but now we meet again, I'm going to be honest with you. Even when it comes to biscuits."

"Not true. You used to love them." Bushy took a fig roll for himself and stuffed the packet back into the pocket of his overalls.

"I didn't. I really didn't."

"If you say so." He shrugged. "Coffee's on its way. Make yourself at home."

I looked around me. The caretaker's room was a gloomy cavern, lit by a single sixty watt bulb and smelling faintly of damp. There was an upturned tea-chest that was being used as a table, a settee without legs, a camp bed and a primus stove together with a pile of random stuff heaped up in one corner, clothes, saucepans, crockery and books. Bushy's worldly possessions, I assumed, although it looked more like a collection for a jumble sale.

"Are you living down here?" I asked.

"Yes." He nodded. "Since the summer. Got chucked out of my flat. Well, it was more of a squat really."

"Oh dear. Sorry to hear that."

"Don't worry, I prefer it down here. At night, I have the whole building to myself. I've got all the keys and I just roam around, monarch of all I survey. Never short of anything to read either. Suits me. Now, tell me, Gowdie, are you pleased to see me?"

"I'm relieved to find you're still alive. But I don't understand. If you've been here all this time, why have you been hiding from me? You must have known I was here. I sent a note, just before Christmas, when I needed a new light for the parcels room. I signed my name. Why didn't you contact me?"

"What makes you think I didn't?" He spooned coffee powder into two thick white china mugs, and picked up a bottle of milk. "Oh, bad luck. I think this milk might be a bit off." He sniffed at it. "But it's all I've got." He took the kettle off the primus stove. "Sugar?"

"No. I don't take sugar. Don't you remember?"

"Sometimes people's habits change over the years. Here." He handed me one of the mugs. "Hope this won't make you puke."

"It'll be fine," I gazed with some apprehension at the greasy globules floating on the surface of the muddy brown liquid. "Bushy, I've got to ask you this. What happened to you after that night at Knox Hill?"

"Oh." He looked sheepish. "I got sectioned."

"*Sectioned*?"

"Yes, sectioned. Sent to the loony bin, a high security ward. They said I'd be locked up for seven years, but I managed to get out before that. But seven's a good number, don't you think? Seven for a secret never to be told. I strode across the seven hills of Rome in my seven league boots. Seven stars, seven seas, seven samurai. Do you know the old border ballad? *'Now ye maun go with me, /True Thomas/Ye maun go with me/And ye maun serve me seven years/ Through weal or woe as it may be.'"*

"Yes. I know it," I said. "*Thomas the Rhymer*. He was kidnapped by a faerie queen."

"And here I am, Gowdie. Back again, from the land of fairie. And I'm your true Thomas. And I won't desert you again. "So," he took a gulp of his coffee. "What made you think I was dead?"

"I had a kind of premonition. But it seems I made a mistake."

"Maybe you didn't. You see, technically speaking, I *have* been a bit dead."

"What on earth do you mean?"

"It was when I first came to London. I fell off a bus. I saw the ticket inspector coming and, of course, I hadn't got a ticket, so I decided to leg it. I jumped off the platform and the bus was still moving, going really fast, and I went sprawling and hit my head on the pavement. I was unconscious, I got some kind of blood clot on the brain, and they operated and in the middle of the op., my heart stopped. For a full two minutes."

"Oh, how *awful.*"

"No, it was great." He grinned. "I saw stuff. Visions. And then, once I was conscious again, I felt stronger. I felt like Gandalf after he returned from the mines of Moria. Know what I mean?"

"Not entirely but I'm glad you recovered."

"I felt different, so I decided to reinvent myself. I changed my name to Jim Findus."

"Findus?"

"First thing that came into my head. I was in a shop, buying fish fingers. And it was a kind of joke. You know 'find us' because I didn't *want* anyone to find me. And then I got this job and that happened in a weird way too. I was in the job centre, and they said they hadn't got anything for me, but this old guy came up to me, and said he could get me work as a caretaker, in a library, taking over from his brother. I was told to come to the rear entrance, late at night, and I met the caretaker who was retiring, he showed me the ropes, and I've been here ever since. The old caretaker's name was Jim too, so I expect a lot of people upstairs in the library think I'm him."

"But that's not possible, surely?" I really didn't know how much of Bushy's story to believe; it seemed to be getting stranger by the minute. "I mean, what about your wages, surely they're paid into your bank account and..."

"No bank account. I get paid in cash. An envelope appears in my tray, every Friday."

"Right." I nodded. "So you've been down here all on your own, seeing no-one. Haven't you been lonely?"

"Not in the least. I've never been that great with people. Never even wanted to be with them. Apart from you, Gowdie."

"Oh." I didn't know whether to be touched or appalled.

"Those were the best days of my life, when we were hanging out together. Remember that day when we went to find the Witch Stone and that night when we did the ceremony at Knox Hill? Great times, eh?"

Great times? I ran my finger-tips down my arm, picturing the livid and ugly scars that lay under the fabric of my sleeve. I felt slightly sick.

"Things went very badly wrong that night." I spoke quietly, but I could feel renewed anger coiling up in the pit of my stomach.

"Yes. I know." He nodded. "But it was all right at first. And at least I managed to raise a fire-demon, didn't I?"

"Bushy." I struggled to be patient. "There *was* no fire-demon. There was only the firework that those girls threw in through the window, and the paraffin-soaked rags and the candles."

"Of course there was a fire-demon!" He thumped his fist against the wall. "I saw it! It was like a Chinese dragon with knobs on! It was moving all around the room, thrashing its tail. I summoned it up out of the ether. I did all the incantations; I had the power. You think I can't do anything, don't you? You think I'm useless! But I'm as good as any of them, I am, I am!"

"Calm down!" I was alarmed by the wild look in his eyes and the way his voice had risen to a strangulated screech. "Perhaps it's better if we don't talk about that night. Not if it's going to lead to an argument."

"I don't want to argue with you, Gowdie." His voice was quieter now. "You were my only friend. Look, I'm sorry about what happened, the house burning down and your Dad and everything." He slumped down on the floor, seemingly contrite.

"I don't think the fire killed my father," I said. "I think he'd had a heart attack or a stroke before the fire broke out. And I know you meant well." *In your way.*

"So you're not going to turn me into a toad then?"

"Bushy," I smiled at him. "I have no idea how to turn people into toads."

"Don't you?" He looked genuinely disappointed. "I thought you'd be a fully-fledged witch by now."

"I'm afraid not. Listen, you still haven't explained why you've taken so long to let me know you were here."

"But I *did* let you know. I gave a welcoming gift on your very first day."

"A gift?"

"I put it on your desk. And I typed a note. Can't remember exactly what I said, but it was something like *Welcome to the library, I hope you'll be happy here*."

"The rosemary." I stared at him. "*You* did that? You buried those things in the soil, those awful things. What were you thinking of, trying to put a memory curse on me?"

"A curse?" He sounded astonished. "Of course it wasn't a curse. But I *did* want you to remember me. Just in case you'd forgotten."

"You really thought I would forget you after everything that happened? After..." *After Knox Hill burned down. After my father died. After they said I'd tried to kill him. After I was physically marked for life. After I was locked up in Crowsmuir Hall for two years.*

"I sent you other stuff too." Bushy picked up his mug again and took a gulp of coffee. It must have been stone cold by then. "Mistletoe at Christmas. Did you like it?"

"I..." I stopped. I didn't have the heart to tell him that I'd wanted it to be from someone else.

"And before that," he continued. "I sent you a note warning you about Llewellyn. I stuck it by his creepy bunch of roses."

"That was you as well! That horrible message? Bushy, how *could* you?"

"I had to warn you."

"But it was like a poison pen letter! Telling me not to trust him. And I *do* trust Llewellyn. He's clever and kind and sensitive, he's so courteous and touchingly old-fashioned and he's lonely and sad inside, and I care about him and now he's disappeared and..."

"God almighty!" Bushy jumped to his feet, hurling his coffee mug to the floor.

"What's wrong with you?" I gazed at the rivulets of coffee trickling amongst the pieces of shattered pottery.

"What's wrong with *you*, caring about a man like that?" He kicked at the mess on the floor. "Don't tell me you're in love with the bastard!"

"Bastard? Don't call him that."

"Why not? It's what he is, both literally and figuratively."

"I can't think what you mean."

"Listen, Gowdie." He squatted down in front of me. "What makes you think your precious Llewellyn is good enough for you? *I'm* back, and *I'm* the person who can help you. As for Llewellyn, quite apart from his questionable character, he's far too old for you."

"He's thirty six, that's not so much older than me."

"He told you he was thirty six?"

"More or less."

Bushy burst into a hysterical gale of mirth. He rolled his eyes, he rocked backwards and forwards. Then, as he recovered from his fit of hilarity, he delivered his final blow.

"Ha!" he chortled, "The bloody liar. He's not thirty six. He's closer to a hundred and thirty six. He's been on this planet since Victoria was on the throne. Oh, don't look at me like that, Gowdie. Anyone would think you didn't believe me."

Thirty Seven

"Of course I don't believe you." I tried to conceal the tremble in my voice. I didn't want him to see how much he'd upset me. "I've never heard such a ridiculous thing. Well," I got to my feet. "Thanks for the coffee but I think I'm going to have to go now. I'd like to talk to you some more, but I can't stay here right now, not if you're going to start talking nonsense."

"It isn't nonsense, Gowdie." Bushy assured me. "It's true. Would I make something like this up?"

"Yes, you would. You know you would!" I'd intended to stay calm, but my indignation was getting the better of me. "You were always inventing things. What about the mark of the Holy Fool, and the *Grimoire of Invergrerey,* and all that stuff about me being a reincarnation of Isobel Gowdie?"

"Ah!" Bushy held up his right forefinger, a triumphant look on his face. "I'm still convinced that *last* thing is partly true. You might not be the reincarnation of Isobel Gowdie, but you're definitely her descendent."

"You've no proof of that."

"I don't need proof, it's obvious. And I *can* prove that what I'm telling you about your precious Llewellyn is true. He's a Cursed Immortal."

"I've never even heard of a Cursed Immortal!"

"Haven't you? And I thought that you'd have twigged by now, working in this place. Well, they were an exclusive, secret cult, established in the late nineteenth century. They were scholars of the occult who underwent a ritual to cheat death and outlive their contemporaries. And many of them are still around today."

"That can't be true."

"Can't it? The evidence is right here, in the library. Ever seen those names in the ledgers, names of people whose dates of birth suggest they shouldn't still be alive?"

My stomach flipped over. Of course I'd seen them. *Clarence Galsworthy, Blavatsky Cummings, Annie Kensington....*What had Ernest said about the library not giving up all its secrets at once?

"Think about it Gowdie," Bushy was insistent. "Just how much has Llewellen Arawn Llewellyn told you about himself?"

"Oh. You know his true name." I had a cold feeling in the pit of my stomach. What if there was some truth in all this? I was remembered that night at the Red Dragon and the confession that Llewellyn had been on the verge of making, just before the spell broke up around us: '*There's something I have to tell you, something I'm afraid is going to shock you terribly...'*

"Yes, I know his true name," Bushy looked smug. "And I also know his true age. And I'm going to prove it to you."

"I don't want you to do that. Look, I'm going. I can't take any more of this." I moved towards the door.

"But you'll come back tomorrow, won't you, Gowdie?" Bushy looked at me with a pleading expression. "Now that I've found you again, we have to talk. You will come back?"

I took a deep breath.

"I'll have to think about it," I said.

"Bertie?"

I peered under the couch, pulled back the curtain in the alcove and looked into the bathroom. No sign of him. The cat definitely wasn't here. I knew from Kipling that cats walked by themselves, that they were fickle and if someone offered them better pickings, they'd simply transfer their allegiance to another household. But I felt rather upset. Strange as it seemed, I was almost getting fond of that cat, relying on his reassuring company.

Well, no point fretting. Best relax and try and enjoy the evening, despite the series of shocks I'd received. I changed into my kaftan and took the calendar off the mantelpiece. Ha! So Grandma Gandy was back! And tonight, she had an intriguing story to tell:

In 1648, Old Mother Sumppit hearde that the witch-finder, Thomas Kilgarreth, was coming to her village. Hide she didde in the privie, but hee did kicke down the door, and didde swim her in the ducke pond, whereupon she sunke and drowned. Going downe the third tyme, she cried out 'Lucifer will rotte your manhood!' and within a daye, his balles had shrunk away to a size no bigger than two grains of rice and no issue did he bear and no woman, nor manne, nor even himself, did he ever pleasure againe. As for Old Mother Sumppit, she swum to the bank and lived another dozen years in anothere parishe. '

Heed the words of Grandma Gandy on this day, Jan. 2nd in the year one thousand seven hundred and five.

Hmm. I was relieved to learn that Old Mother Sumppit hadn't actually drowned and it was deeply comforting to think of the downfall of the witch-finder right now. But I wasn't at all sure that this grimly comic anecdote was going to be much help in defeating Malachi Hopkins and saving the Antioch Corey Library.

Thirty Eight

I unlocked the reading room and raised the blinds. The place was unnaturally quiet. None of the regular readers, some of whom would usually be waiting to be admitted by this time, had arrived. I looked disconsolately at Ernest's empty desk. So Hopkins 'required' me to use it, did he? Well, too bad. As far as I was concerned, my desk was in the parcels room. That was where I wrapped up the postal loans, checked the returns and wrote letters to the subscribers with the ledgers at my elbow. I wasn't going to comply with all his petty orders and I was prepared to defend the Antioch Corey Library to the death. *Take that, Mr Jack-Ups!*

I was feeling more than a little unsettled after my reunion with Bushy but I was determined not to think about it for a while. I must simply get on with some work. Tackling some routine tasks would be a calming activity. How about chasing up some overdue loans? I began a letter to a Mr James R. Woolf of New Orleans who'd borrowed, but not returned, a biography of Abraham Lincoln that he'd taken out in 1965.

Dear Mr Woolf,

Abraham Lincoln: Man, martyr or magician by Thelonius T.Houseman. publ. Yale 1910 It has come to my attention that your five year loan period for the above item expired a considerable time ago and I do apologise for troubling you but another reader has now put in a request and....

I stopped writing, struck by a sudden thought. Of course! I'd been wracking my brains for an excuse to leave the library for a week to visit Dr Hecate, a destination that I couldn't possibly disclose to Hopkins, and now, at last, I had an idea. It was a bold scheme, but it might just work. And angry as I was with Bushy, he might just be the person who could help.

"Jeanie?" Gerda appeared in the doorway. She seemed very far from her usual exuberant self, anxious, subdued, almost furtive, glancing over her shoulder as if she was afraid she was being followed. "Is it safe to talk?"

"I hope so," I said.

"Thank you." She sank down on a chair by the window. "I'm afraid all the vorry is getting to me. If this place is going to change out of all recognition, my vorld falls apart."

"Mine too," I said. "But the library won't be destroyed while we're here to fight for it." I placed my unfinished letter to James Woolf under my blotter.

"I, too, vill resist! But I have come to tell you vat I did yesterday. I vent to find Ernest. I tried making inquiries in his area, Southwark, you told me, I tried various newsagents, thinking that vun of them might be in the habit of delivering his newspapers, and at last, I thought of the obvious thing, the thing I should have done in the first place, look him up in the London telephone directory. There vere only two E. Brunsvickers, vun was a voman, a brassy blonde who was running a so-called massage parlour, and the other vas an elderly man called Edvard who lives in a small terrace house not far from Borough Market. You were right, our Ernest is not on the telephone. But Mr Edvard Brunsvicker was able to tell me where Ernest lives, because very occasionally, Ernest's post had been mistakenly delivered to him, and Ernest had discovered this, and had arrived at the house, leaning on his bicycle, of course...but perhaps I do not need to explain all this."

"No, go on. This sounds like great detective work."

"Perhaps, but I do not have a good ending, I'm afraid. So I find Ernest's flat, it is above a greengrocer's, I knock, but there is no reply. And the neighbours tell me that they haven't seen Ernest since Christmas. He has gone avay, they don't know vere. So I am no further forvard, and..." She broke off suddenly, her eyes widening. "Ach!" Her voice sunk to a whisper. "No more just now. Like the ghost of Hamlet's father, look vere it comes again."

"Good morning." Cup and saucer in hand, Hopkins entered the parcels room. "I don't believe we've been introduced." He frowned at Gerda, blew on his tea, took a sip, and then put the cup down on the saucer. *Sip, clack.* That harmless sound was now as pleasant to me as the whirr of a dentist's drill.

"I believe not," Gerda returned his gaze, as if defying him to ask for any further information.

"I wish to be acquainted with all those who frequent this place," Hopkins told her. "I shall be asking to see your credentials in due course." He turned to look at me. "Miss Gowdie, do you happen to know where your young assistant is this morning? You might like to remind her that punctuality is a priceless commodity." He took another sip of tea.

"I believe she's helping Miss Nantucket in the archives," I said.

"I see." *Sip, clack.*

"Excuse me." Gerda got to her feet. "I am going back to the reading room, but first, I vish to ask a question."

"Indeed?" Hopkins looked down his nose.

"I have an acquaintance," Gerda said. "His name is Konrad. He used to sit over there, by the vindow. I am vondering if you have seen him? There vas a pigeon, a really unusual one vith black plumage, that he used to feed and..."

"No pigeons will come here now," Hopkins informed her. "I am having spikes of broken glass placed on the window sills to keep such filthy visitors away."

"It was only one pigeon," I said. "And it seemed to be intelligent. A rare species. I would think a bird like that should be encouraged. Suppose it wasn't entirely of this world."

Hopkins laughed. It was not a pleasant laugh, rather more of the pained, feral scream of a hyena with haemorrhoids.

"Miss Gowdie, you worry me," he said. "You seem to have some very strange ideas. No doubt you paid too much attention to the eccentricity of the previous custodian. Let me remind you again that I am in charge now. And you," he turned back to Gerda. "I assume you are a member here? If so, I require a detailed report from you, explaining your research work. You have until four thirty p.m today to produce it. Good day." He turned on his heel and left us.

"Intolerable!" Gerda rolled her eyes. "Stop your ears, Jeanie. I am about to say some vords in German that are so rude, I have never spoken them out loud although I vonce read them on a lavatory door in Stuttgart." She took a deep breath. "*Up deinen haarigen arsh!*"

"I agree, Gerda," I said. "I agree completely. You know, I did a little German at school. So up his hairy arse indeed."

As soon as I'd finished my day's work, I went down to the caretaker's room. Bushy was in there reading with the door open;he jumped up as soon as he saw me.

"Hello, Gowdie." He ushered me inside and closed the door behind us. "I knew you'd be back."

"Yes, I'm back."

"Let me guess. You need my help."

"Yes, I need your help. And I'm really glad you're not dead."

"Don't mention it. Now, tell me what I can do, and I'll do it. If I foul up this time, I promise you I'll get out of your life for ever. But I *won't* foul up because I'm going to get it right this time. I want to prove myself to you."

"OK," I said. "But no more sending me anonymous notes, right? We have to be upfront and honest with each other."

"Promise. Scouts honour."

"And can we please *not* talk about the things you were saying yesterday? About..."

"The Cursed Immortals? I'll do my best although you'll have to face the truth sooner or later. So, what's troubling you, Gowdie?"

"It's this man who's taken over the library," I said. "This Malachi Hopkins. Have you met him?"

"No. With any luck, he won't bother me."

"But soon he might. He's embarked on a programme of what he calls 'Purification and Progress'. He's started clearing things out, in fact, he told me he was sending some things down here for you to burn, exhibits from the Cabinet of Curiosities. Have you seen them?"

"No. Nothing like that has appeared down here."

"Then I suspect he was lying, that's he's stolen them for his own purposes. Bushy, listen, he's dangerous. He might even be a witch-finder. Do you believe in witch-finders?"

"Of course I do. I warned you about them years ago when I lent you that book, the very first day we met. I knew they weren't just in history."

"I don't think I believed you at the time. But now I do. Even if Hopkins isn't a witch-finder, I'm absolutely convinced he's going to destroy the library. He's sacked my colleague, Ernest Brunswicker, he's started driving the regular readers away...And there's something else. He's looking for a certain book, a very important book."

"A book?"

"Yes. It would be a disaster if Hopkins got his hands on it. And the thing is, I know where it is, it's right beneath his feet, it's in the custodian's office, under the floorboards, under the rug, in a locked box. We have to get it out of there. I thought perhaps that you...After all, you've got all the keys."

"You want me to go into the office and retrieve this book?"

"Yes. Yes I do. Late at night, when there's no-one else around."

"I could do that. So what is this book?"

I thought for a moment. Perhaps it wouldn't be a good idea to tell him too much.

"It's a copy of *Little Women,*" I said.

"What?" Bushy gawped at me. "You're kidding me, right? A copy of *Little Women* is so important it has to be locked in a box under the floorboards in the custodian's office?"

"It's a first edition," I improvised wildly. "It's worth a lot of money. There are people who'd go to great lengths to get their hands on it."

"Really?"

"Yes. You said you wanted to prove yourself to me. Well, this is your test. But please be careful, getting hold of this book is more dangerous than you might think."

"Anyone who messes with me will regret it, Gowdie. I've learnt judo." He flexed a skinny arm. "Tomorrow morning, when you get into work, I promise you, *Little Women* will be on your desk."

"Oh, goodness no, you mustn't leave it lying about! You need to hide it somewhere and then bring it to me in person. And that can't happen here. We should meet somewhere else, away from the library."

"Where?"

I thought for a moment. It was Saturday tomorrow, and it wasn't my shift, although with Ernest gone, I couldn't imagine who was going to open up the reading room. Not really my problem though; there were far more pressing things on my mind.

"There's a café near where I live, Mustafa's," I said. "Cranston Street, SW10. Can you meet me there tomorrow morning at about seven? Bring me the book and I'll buy you breakfast. And then I'll tell you about the rest of my plans."

"Sounds intriguing. So what about this book? You say it's in a locked box. I can get into the custodian's room, no problem, but I don't have a key for the box."

"The box doesn't open with a key. It's a combination. You turn a dial, like on a safe. I'll write the number down for you." I took a biro out of my bag. "Do you have a scrap of paper?"

"Write it on my hand." He held out his left one. "Go on."

"Is that a good idea? Suppose someone sees it?"

"I'll put my gloves on when you've finished." He produced a fingerless pair out of the pocket of his jeans.

"OK." I wrote the number a little shakily. As Bushy gazed down at his hand, a slow smile spread across his face.

"Did *he* choose this combination?" he asked. "Your beloved Llewellyn?"

"Yes, as it happens," I said. "But it's just four random numbers."

"You think so? Those aren't random numbers; that's a date. Ha!" He let out a derisory snort. "1861. The year he was bloody well born! *Now* do you believe me?"

Thirty Nine

'Never allow dust to accumulate under the bed. It will form into balls of fluff out of which will be engendered the spiders of lust from which you will never be free. So sweep well and sleep well and always keep your heart pure. Then you might just avoid tragedy, but do not bank on it.'

Goodwife Gurlie's Guidance for this day January 4th

With a sigh, I placed the calendar back on the mantelpiece. *Spiders of lust?* What absolute nonsense. What was it with these Elders? Had they nothing more useful to say? Didn't they know I was in desperate need of guidance? Hopkins had seized power at the library, Llewellyn had disappeared, my cat was missing and I needed to get to Dr Hecate as a matter of urgency. Thank goodness for Bushy; with all his faults, he was going to be of more practical help. I couldn't wait to tell him about the scheme I'd planned. It might just work.

I was glad to see the café was crowded this morning; perhaps that meant we wouldn't be too conspicuous. Bushy was sitting at a corner table, hunched over a newspaper, a hot drink in a steaming mug at his elbow.

"Hi!" He looked up with a grin as I approached. "I'd like faggots, gravy, mash and marrow-fat peas since you're buying."

"You want all that for breakfast?" I felt faintly nauseous at the thought.

"You're forgetting," he grinned. "I work nights. This is my supper."

"Oh. Right. Yes, of course."

A girl in an overall appeared beside our table, pad in hand. She had short dark hair and was wearing pink plastic hooped earrings, and her manner, as she wrote down our order, clutching her biro in a ham-fisted way, suggested she was terminally bored.

"Isn't Nasir here today?" I asked her.

"Who?" The girl looked at me blankly.

"Nasir," I said. "I come in here quite a lot and he's always behind the counter."

"Dunno." She rubbed her nose on the back of her hand. "I've only been here since Wednesday."

"Oh." I looked around me. "Perhaps he's taking a break then." Everything in here seemed much the same with the custard-yellow walls and the lino the colour of baked beans but now here was this somewhat hostile and uncomprehending girl. It was just a little disconcerting.

"Aren't you hot in that anorak?" I asked Bushy. I slipped off my cloak and folded it carefully over the back of my chair. "It's very oppressive in here."

"Doesn't bother me." He shrugged. "Besides, there's a reason. Mission accomplished. I've got it." He unzipped his anorak, revealing a package sticking out of the large inside pocket. "But I'm not at all sure you ought to have this. You haven't played straight with me, have you?"

"I don't know what you mean."

"Yes, you do. You accused *me* of making things up and all the time, you've told a big fat porkie yourself."

"A porkie?"

"Porkie pie, lie. Or to put it more elegantly, you've been economical with the truth. You told me that the book you wanted me to rescue was a first edition of *Little Women.* But what I've got here isn't some morally uplifting story about young ladies distributing oat cakes to the poor. This isn't *Little Women,* is it? This is Antioch Corey's *Book of Shad...*"

"Sssh! Keep your voice down!" I grabbed at his sleeve.

"Keep calm, Gowdie." He patted my hand. "No-one in here knows what I'm talking about."

"I wouldn't be so sure of that." I glanced over my shoulder. Was anyone eavesdropping? I couldn't tell although I didn't like the look of a man who was sitting two tables behind. He was wearing a pin-striped suit and was quite unlike the usual customer, and now he'd folded up his newspaper and was writing something in the margin.

"This is amazing," Bushy said. "To think that Antioch Corey's *Book of..."*

"*Sssh!* Let's talk about Louisa May Alcott and *Little Women.*"

"Not sure I've read it."

"Yes you have." I raised my voice. "Tell me, do you think she should have let Jo marry Professor Bhaer? I quite like him, personally, but other people, particularly feminist critics, have said..."

"Faggots." The girl with the pink earrings slapped a thick white china plate in front of Bushy. I noticed that her nails were far from clean.

"Great!" It was touching to see how Bushy's eyes lit up at the sight of what looked like rancid fat floating in grey sludge. He picked up his fork and started shovelling mashed potato into his mouth, eating with the rapidity of someone with a train to catch.

"Slow down," I said. "It isn't a race."

"Sorry. I'm starving. Anyway," he wiped his mouth with the back of his hand. "Never mind Louisa May Alcott, what about Antioch..."

"Eat your breakfast. Please." I gave him a warning glance. "After this, we're going somewhere else. And then we'll talk. In the meantime, just try to be a little discreet."

"Nice place you've got here, Gowdie." Bushy looked around my tiny living space with evident approval. "Not sure why you had to bring me on such a roundabout way to get here, though. We must have gone down at least ten of the wrong streets, then doubling back on ourselves and diving down alleyways...it was crazy."

"I was afraid that someone might be following us." I secured the chain on the door and pulled the curtains across. "Did you see anyone?"

"Not just now, no. But some weird stuff did happen to me after I left the library. I'd got hold of the book, and put everything back, the box, the floorboards and the rug. But then, when I was getting the bus, I kept seeing it out of the corner of my eye. A hunched figure with a hood over its head."

"Oh, I expect that was just a beggar or some poor homeless person." I didn't believe what I was saying, of course.

"Don't patronise me, Gowdie." He spoke mildly enough, but I sensed a certain degree of resentment. "We both know it was some kind of wraith or infernal guardian."

"Do we?"

"Yes, we do. Gowdie, when you asked me to save that book, you should have told me what it was. How about trusting me a bit more?"

"I'm sorry. I realise now I should have been more honest."

"To tell the truth, I guessed you were hiding something. And you did hint there might be some danger." He sat down on the floor and took the book out of his anorak pocket. "Well, I can see why you didn't want this Hopkins man to get his hands on this. Hot property, eh? Bet there's some dangerous stuff in these pages!"

"Quite possibly there is. Most of it hasn't been translated yet."

"I don't suppose it has. I couldn't make much sense of the bits I looked at, apart from some Latin that I remembered from school. So, is it likely that when Antioch Corey wrote this he also put a curse on it, with the intention of destroying anyone who stole the book?"

"I don't think so. If there is a curse, it won't be from Antioch Corey. You weren't stealing it. You were bringing it to me for safe-keeping and I was one of the two people who were asked to translate it. The other one, if you must know, was Mr Llewellyn and he didn't steal it either. Jabez Corey entrusted him with the book."

"He told you that? You believe him?"

"Yes I do. I know for a fact that he defended it at considerable personal cost; he was attacked by an entity on his way to the library and nearly had his fingers cut off."

"Bloody hell, Gowdie!" Bushy was wide-eyed. "Don't tell me you're planning to keep this book here, in your flat?"

"Yes, I am. It'll be fine. I shall put some protections in place. I shall wrap it in a special antique black cloth along with some hemlock seeds and a talisman that Jabez Corey gave me and cast a spell using my runic knife. It'll be safe here."

"If you say so, Gowdie." He looked dubious. "But I can't say I like this."

"Don't worry about me, I'll be fine. Now listen, I need your help with something else."

"Shoot! Tell me!"

"There's someone I need to visit. Her name's Dr Hecate Burneside and she lives in Pendle, Lancashire and I'll need to stay with her for at least a week. And I have to go soon. But there's a problem. I'm not due for any leave and I can't possibly let Hopkins know where I'm going, and besides, he would never give me permission."

"You could always ring in sick, say you've got flu, and then go off on this trip instead."

"I can't do that. It's bad luck to lie about illness. If you pretend to have a headache, then you get one. Nana taught me that."

"Really? I was always bunking off games with fake ailments when I was a kid and nothing ever... Oh, no, wait a minute, there was that time when I said I had hay fever and..."

"Bushy," I interrupted him. "Please listen. The reason I want to stay with Dr Hecate is to prepare for my Coming of Age ceremony."

"But I could help you with that."

"No!" I hoped I hadn't spoken too sharply. "It has to be Dr Hecate. But I need an excuse, to visit her. So this is my plan. And I think it'll work if we're careful."

"Right." He nodded.

"Well, this is it. One of my jobs at the library is to chase up loans that are long overdue, often years overdue. And sometimes, although I've never done it, some of these books have to be collected in person. What if we prepared a list of subscribers who live scattered all over the country, from here to Inverness, down to the tip of Cornwall and out to the Scilly Isles? We can tell Hopkins they've had valuable books out on loan for years. The subscribers will all be fictional of course, but the books will be real. At night, when no-one's around, you could remove the actual books, so that there are gaps on the shelves where they *should* be, and you could hide them. Then you could forge the entries in the ledgers in the parcels room, making it look as though these books *were* borrowed years ago. Then all I have to do is take the ledgers to Hopkins and offer to retrieve the overdue books, tell him it's going to take me at least a week. I'll say I've been inspired by his plans to reform the library."

"Great idea! Flatter the bugger and appeal to his vanity. We could even invent some books too. Make them sound pornographic. A man like Hopkins would love pornography, trust me."

"Would he?"

"Oh yes. All puritans have secretly filthy minds."

"I'll take your word for it. But look, we've got to be careful, like I said. After today, we mustn't meet in person, not even outside the library. Write to me, though, post letters to me here. No-one must suspect we know each other. There's always the possibility that Hopkins has a spy, someone in the library who's working with him. I'm thinking it might be Clemency Nantucket."

"Oh, I won't have any difficulty keeping out of *her* way. Little does she know how often I've been browsing in the archive room at night."

"You didn't eat biscuits in there, did you?"

"I might have done." He shrugged. "Why?"

"Just something I heard her complain about once. I strongly suggest you don't do it again. You mustn't leave a trail."

"I won't. But this is exciting! Gowdie, I love this!" He leapt to his feet, his eyes wild with excitement. "Time to live dangerously! Give me a week or so, and I'll sort out the whole thing. Trust the ingenuity of your True Thomas! Now we're really in business!"

Forty

I do not advise the keeping of cattes within the house place where they wille spreade their fleas and make unholie mess. The barne is the best place for such creatures and when they falle sick, they can be quickly dispatched with a blunderbuss or a mallet to the head. Flinche not from this taske. It is the kindest waye.

Goodwife Gurlie's Guidance for this day in January

I can't say that I felt greatly cheered by this latest piece of macabre advice from Goodwife Gurlie. Bertie was still missing and I, in turn, was missing Bertie. If, in the way of cats, he'd found a more comfortable berth than the one I had to offer, then that was his choice but I now felt an urge to lure him home. To this end, I took to placing dishes of enticing food out on the window sill; tinned oysters, deluxe chicken mixes, even some left-over smoked salmon from Kosminsky's, but he hadn't reappeared. What an ungrateful creature!

On a more encouraging note, Bushy was making excellent progress with our scheme to outwit Hopkins. Each morning, as soon as I arrived at the library, I consulted the ledgers and found new entries that gave every appearance of being old. Bushy's forgery skills had obviously become far more sophisticated since our sixth form days. He must be using the oldest of inks and the scratchiest of vintage dip pens to write in those names, dates and titles in perfect italic script. In addition, his selection of books was diverse, imaginative and occasionally racy, including an early edition of the *Malleus Mallificarum,* a large tome on the development of the US Federal Civil Service and a novel, *Naughty Nights in Nebraska* by an obscure cousin of Abraham Lincoln.

At the end of the second week, I received a note through the post:

All done, Yours, True Thomas.

With it, there was a detailed itinerary of a journey that would, purportedly, take me around all round Britain, starting with a visit to an elderly academic in Penzance and ending in Inverness. And so, armed with this programme and a few of the ledgers, I headed for the Custodian's office.

"This is an extraordinary request, Miss Gowdie." Hopkins frowned at me. "I can't imagine why you think I can spare you from the library at such a busy time."

"A busy time?" I repeated. "But there's hardly been anyone in the reading room for days."

"That is not a relevant observation." He picked up his tea cup. "When I say 'a busy time' I am referring to all the reorganising and rationalisation that has to be done. Stock-taking. Re-cataloguing." *Sip, clack.* "Making an inventory of everything on the shelves and removing any pernicious items to name but a few of the tasks ahead."

"And that's precisely why I want to chase up these missing loans," I said, leaning forward in what I hoped would be perceived as a display of eagerness. "I think that some of these books need to be examined urgently. And others are so valuable that we can't afford to lose them. I've written several letters to these subscribers requesting their return and I've come to the conclusion that the only way we're going to get them back is if I retrieve them in person."

"I see." He tilted his head back and looked down his nose at me, old-goat style. "And who do you suggest should supervise the reading room in your absence?"

"I can ask Professor Goldfarb to keep an eye on things. And there's Cazzie, if Miss Nantucket can spare her."

"Hmm. I'm not sure I share your faith in Professor Goldfarb. But certainly we should be giving more responsibility to Miss Tank, a most promising young person. Let me have a look at those ledgers."

"Certainly." I placed them on his desk. "I've put ribbons in to mark the relevant pages."

He took an inordinate time going through the entries, peering through a magnifying glass at some of them, pursing his fleshy lips, and uttering odd noises that might have meant anything from suspicion to approval. I tried to look as neutral as possible, terrified as I was that Bushy might have made a slip-up somewhere, and that our ruse would be rumbled.

"Well, Miss Gowdie," he said at last. "I do have a few questions. For example, this man who lives on the Isle of Man, Dr Neil O'Claggart, who borrowed *My Life amongst the Bull-whips of Laredo* ten years ago. Is he an undesirable character?"

"I really couldn't say."

"It's concerning to find one of our subscribers borrowing a book with such a suggestive title. And what about the author, Madame Pom Pom de Vere? That sounds like a harlot."

"It's a respectable book," I assured him. "A rare American classic. Mentioned by Herman Melville in a letter, but lost to the world for nearly a century. It's exciting to discover there was a copy in the Antioch Corey Library."

"Hmmm. And you say many of these other books are similarly valuable?"

"Several of them, yes, I believe so."

"Well," he mused. "Perhaps I could stretch a point and release you from your usual duties. Although I hope you don't expect to travel first class and stay in five star hotels at the library's expense."

"Oh no!" I exclaimed. "I don't want to claim expenses. In fact, I'm happy to take unpaid leave."

"Really?" He raised his eyebrows. "Are you doing this for *love*, Miss Gowdie?"

I flinched. There had been something unnecessarily salacious about the way he'd pronounced the word.

"For free, yes," I said. "You see, I was really inspired by your *Library Development Plan.*"

"That's gratifying." He seemed to have swallowed the bait. "I still find it strange that you don't appear to want any payment. But be that as it may, now that I come to think of it, your absence could be convenient. The refurbishment and clearance of the parcels room can begin while you're away."

Oh no. I'd played right into his hands.

"I wouldn't want to put you to any trouble," I said. "I like my parcels room just as it is."

"But it's not *your* parcels room, is it, Miss Gowdie? It belongs to the Antioch Corey Memorial Library."

"Oh, goodness, yes! I only meant...that is...of course... I agree."

"I hope you do. Please take more care about how you express yourself in future, Miss Gowdie." He picked up a paper knife, turning it over in his hands, and then pointed it towards me, weapon-like. "I *am* prepared to authorise your absence but I will expect a full audit on your return of all the books you've managed to retrieve."

"Of course."

"And there's one other thing." He paused. "I don't take kindly to dishonesty."

"Oh?" I tried to sound casual, but now I was really uneasy. Did he suspect something?

"You look somewhat alarmed, Miss Gowdie. Do you really not know to what I refer?"

"No. I...I really don't."

"Don't you? Well, a number of possibilities spring to mind. For example, if it should transpire that any of these overdue, valuable books have been sold for profit, that would be a criminal offence and must be reported to me at once. Similarly, there will be severe penalties meted out to any subscribers who have actually *lost* any of these books. I hope you understand. Can I trust you to deal with any of these misdemeanours?"

"Of course."

"Good. And then if you were to take advantage of my generosity...if things should transpire to be not as they seem..." He turned the paper knife over in his other hand. "But of course, this is a *bona fide* exercise, isn't it? You can assure me of that, can't you?"

"Of course." My heart was beating fast. "When can I go?"

"Oh, feel free to depart this weekend, Miss Gowdie. At least that will ensure two fewer working days are lost. I shall expect you back in a week. Good-day!"

As I sat down at my desk; preparing to write to Dr Hecate, my feelings were somewhat mixed. It was clear to me that, even if he had fallen for my subterfuge, Hopkins had an ulterior motive for giving in to my request. Who knew how much havoc he'd create in my absence? But I couldn't spend time worrying about that. I had to prepare for my trip.

I posted my letter on the way home, hoping it would get there before me. The next day, Friday, I made a special trip to Euston to buy my train ticket and then went home to pack. Should I take the *Book of Shadows* with me? *No,* I decided, it was far too dangerous, I didn't want to run the risk of being followed by hunched, hooded figures, or attacked by a wraith armed with a spectral blade and it would certainly be unfair to inflict such hazards on my hostess. The book must remain where it was, hidden behind the panelling in my flat, wrapped in mummy cloth. I would, however, take the tin containing my apprentice tools and *Goodwife Gurlie's Guidance Calendar*. Then I took the gold key marked with Mandragora's monogram out of my bag and hung it around my neck on a long piece of velvet ribbon, tucking it out of sight under my blouse. It was a matter of deep regret to me that I no longer had the mirror in my possession: I felt sure that Dr Hecate would have been able to instruct me in the correct use of a spirit glass. I went to bed early, that night, but was so excited I didn't get to sleep for hours.

I woke again at six. I got up quickly, washed and dressed, gulped down a mug of tea and reached for my case. And at that moment, Bertie came through the cat flap.

"Bertie?" I was shocked by his appearance. He seemed to be in a dreadful state, limping, bedraggled and miserable; as I bent down to examine him, he turned his head away as if ashamed of his condition. "What's happened to you?"

I touched his fur with the tip of my forefinger; it felt cold and damp, and it was stuck all over with leaf mould. It seemed he'd been wandering around in the open for days. I filled a bowl with cream, but he simply stared at it, dull-eyed. Oh heavens, I thought, I know nothing about treating sick cats and this one looked in urgent need of a vet. Perhaps

Dr Hecate would know what to do. Yes, she was bound to be a cat expert.

"OK, Bertie," I reached for the cat basket. "There's nothing for it. You'll have to come to Pendle with me."

According to my false itinerary, I was going to start at Paddington, heading for Penzance to visit a Professor Trehearne who'd purloined the entire works of H.P. Lovecraft in a Japanese language edition. How dreadful it would be if Hopkins discovered me here at Euston instead. As I sat on my train, waiting for its departure, I suddenly had a vision of him appearing on the platform, cup and saucer in hand like a refugee from the Mad Hatter's tea party, and looking at me accusingly with his frog-spawn eyes. '*How very strange to find you here, Miss Gowdie.*' Sip, clack. *'This isn't the way to Cornwall.'*

I peered out of the window. There was nothing suspicious out there, only ordinary travellers and a porter pushing a trolley. I glanced at my watch; the train was due to leave in a few minutes and...Oh, good grief! What was *he* doing here? A familiar, lanky figure in jeans, a thick sweater and a bobble hat was advancing towards my carriage.

"Bushy!" I lifted up the window. "What is it? Is something wrong?"

"Hope not." He beamed. "I've come to see you off, that's all."

"But we shouldn't be seen together. I told you."

"Hardly matters now, does it? You're on your way to Dr Hecate."

"Sssh!"

"For heavens' sake, Gowdie," Bushy peered through the window. "Why are you taking that cat with you?"

"I can't leave him behind."

"But won't it get in the way? I could keep it in the caretaker's room until you get back."

"It wouldn't be safe. Hopkins hates cats. And if he should find him..." I shuddered inwardly. *They can be quickly dispatched with a blunderbuss or a mallet to the head.*

"Well, anyway, I've got something for you." He reached into his satchel. "Perfect reading matter for the train. It's the proof I promised you."

"Proof? Proof of what?"

"Proof that your precious Llewellyn is a Cursed Immortal." He held up a slim volume, bound in black leather. "Privately printed in Paris, the only remaining copy. I found it up in the stacks."

"But I don't want..." I was interrupted by the guard's whistle.

"Take it!" Bushy jogged alongside the train as it began to move. "It's for you." He flung the book through the window with expert aim. "A charming tale of perversion, devil worship and the seduction of young virgins. Enjoy!"

Forty One

As the book landed in my lap, my first impulse was to hurl it straight back out of the window. *Perversion, devil worship, and the seduction of young virgins.* That was just the sort of scandalous farrago Bushy *would* invent to discredit Llewellyn in my eyes. But it was too late; the train was gathering speed and Bushy's waving figure was receding rapidly into the distance. Well, I might as well take a look at this so-called memoir, even if I did suspect a forgery.

I gazed at the cover, at the exquisitely tooled leather binding and the image of the plumed dragon, identical to the one on Llewellyn's ring, stamped in gold on the front. I turned to the title page:

My Life in the Magical Arts: A Confession.

Llewellyn A. Llewellyn.

Paris MCMXXXIX

This rough magic I do abjure, I'll break my staff
Bury it in certain fathoms of the earth,
And, deeper than did ever plummet sound
I'll drown my book.

I'd never liked those lines from *The Tempest*. It always seemed to me to be the height of selfishness for Prospero to jettison his magical artefacts in that way. If he hadn't wanted to be an adept any more, then he should have passed his staff and his book to Miranda, so that she could become a sorceress in her own right. I remember expressing that opinion in an essay I wrote at school. The English teacher put a thick red line through the entire paragraph accompanied by the comment, *Nonsense!* I suppose I couldn't have expected a teacher at St. Aggie's to understand. And I hadn't understood why Llewellyn would ever have wanted to give up magic either. But if this book was genuine, *if* it was, then I might be about to find out the truth. I turned the page and began to read:

I, Llewellyn Arawn Llewellyn, cursed immortal and spell-charmer, a man for whom the joys of life are dead, write these words as the world stands on the brink of another terrible war. I write in a spirit of shame and contrition but not, I hope, in self-indulgence but rather in the desire that this account of my life will serve as a warning to all those who may be tempted to indulge in the darker forms of magic. This coming war will be the apocalypse. Millions will die, as those of us who have practised magic have foreseen, although we are powerless to prevent the coming destruction. Magic can only do so much. And it is magic that I now renounce. And if I should perish in the forthcoming conflict, then that will be for the best. I have outlived my time.

Oh, good grief! Bushy could never have written this. This was real; it had to be. I could hardly breathe as I read on:

Practising the supernatural arts is a drug that destroys the soul. I was once young and arrogant and thought myself invincible, but now, as a result of the path I chose, many of my dearest friends are lost to me. The woman I thought I loved died cursing my name. I was forced to leave my home and now I live on in the loneliness of exile. The seeds of my downfall were sown from my earliest years. To explain,I will begin my account in 1861, the year of my birth.

I have, of course, no memory of the London Foundling Hospital where I was taken when only a few days old, but it is clear the circumstances of my birth were irregular. My mother offered me for adoption, placing with me a token by which I might recognise her one day but, as in all sad cases of this kind, I was never to see her again. Two benefactors of the hospital, Ann and Richard Lewellyn, saw the token, a gold signet ring bearing the stamp of a plumed dragon and instantly recognised the insignia of the secret occult society of which they were members, the Order of the Red Dragon, founded by the magus Rhys Ap Howell in 1711. Their investigations revealed that my father had been a renegade member of the order who had been expelled from the society for vicious practises and who later drowned in the Bristol Channel when attempting to escape from his creditors and that my mother had been a servant girl whom he seduced. They were never able to trace her.

Thus Ann and Richard Llewellyn took me back to live with them. They are not to blame for the direction my life has taken. They were right to teach me the things they knew and many of the slanders that have been disseminated concerning the Society of the Red Dragon are false. There was no devil worship. There were no orgies, although equally, there was daring, and the philosophy of the order was based on an individualism that ran counter to traditional theology. But Ann and Richard were kind and loving step-parents and without them, I would have foundered far sooner than I did.

As I grew up, I studied the magical arts while enjoying the ordinary pursuits of any other young person of my age. I learned to swim, to ride and to fish under the tutelage of my manservant, Konrad, the most loyal companion I have ever had. It was Konrad who rescued me when I was chased by a stampeding bull at the age of five and who nursed me through several dangerous fevers; without him, I would surely have died.

If I became ambitious and arrogant as I grew older, it was through no-one's fault but my own. At thirteen, I was sent to London and apprenticed to the adept Abraham Matthewson. He was an old man, eighty two, but still sharp and vigorous of intellect. Inevitably, I became infatuated with his beautiful daughter, Mary, who had by then adopted her true name of Mandragora. She was a wild and powerful sorceress, accomplished in shape-shifting and the subtle arts. Before long, she had taken me into her bed. I was fourteen. Although I did not know it, she was almost forty.

I stopped reading, appalled. This was a shocking revelation! The cradle-snatching bitch! Here was a reason to hate Mary Matthewson, otherwise known as Mandragora Carfax with a passion! And to think I had wanted to be like her, and had tried to summon her with that beckoning spell. Thank goodness my attempt had been unsuccessful. She didn't sound like the sort of person I'd want to emulate at all.

I took a deep breath before continuing:

I truly believed I was her first lover, and I believed too that she was no more than six years older than I was myself. Soon, she owned me, body and soul. Others who have been enslaved by physical passion will understand how she became the centre of my world, but we were no ordinary lovers. We were shape-shifters and practitioners of magic;

nightly, we explored the world in the form of other beings. Wolves were heard to howl over Hampstead Heath, owls flew together over St. Paul's, a bear was seen crossing the common in Lewisham; these were ourselves. Those who saw us in these forms never suspected our true identity. We knew we were playing a dangerous game, but we were reckless and the magic we practised crossed many boundaries that would have horrified my adoptive parents had they been alive to see it.

In 1888, at the age of 95, Abraham Matthewson passed into the other world. His time had come after a rich and powerful life. He had been preparing for death for several years, having commissioned the building of his tomb, a structure which embodied many secret symbols. His funeral was attended by every prominent adept in Europe and amongst them, the warlock Ivanov Pietrovich Raspartin who had travelled all the way from St Petersburg. From him, I first learned of the existence of the cult of the Cursed Immortals.

Abraham Matthewson bestowed his entire estate on me, on the condition that I never desert Mandragora. I could not have foreseen how this would become an onerous commitment. For so long, I had believed we were happy together. We voyaged to America and on our return, we moved to a house in Coleton Street, West London, where our salon became celebrated. Many famous figures of our day, poets, actors and adepts, flocked to our door. And then came that fatal night, the night of our initiation into the cult of the Cursed Immortals.

It was 1897. I was thirty six years of age.

Thirty six. Of course. So he hadn't lied to me, not entirely. And neither, I realised to my horror, had Bushy.

It would be false to claim that no self-interest inspired my actions. I was deeply attracted by the prospect of remaining in the prime of life for decades to come. To have a face that remained unlined, limbs that remained supple, a mind that would stay sharp and a body that would always be strong, was an alluring prospect, worth the losing of my soul, a concept in which I was not even sure I believed. But there was another consideration that was uppermost in my mind and that was to please Mandragora.

She had begun to change towards me; there was often a harsh, mocking tone in her voice. I had angered her by discovering, quite accidentally, the record of her birth. Now the effects of ageing caused her anguish. I tried to assure her she was still a beautiful woman, as indeed she was, even though she was now in her sixties, but our relationship was troubled. I knew she was no longer faithful to me. There were several men and boys, some no more than fifteen years old, others far older, who were constantly in the house. There was a young actor, for example, and the aristocrat, Lord Carfax. And then I met Raspartin and I knew there was one way to please her; I would invite him to Coleton Street and ask him to perform the ritual through which we, and a select group of our friends, would become cursed immortals.

Ten of us gathered in the house to learn about the ritual including the friends of my wife, the young actor and Lord Carfax. My manservant, Konrad, now in his early seventies was also there. He had no personal wish to become an immortal but he refused to allow me to undergo such a dangerous procedure without his protection and had decided to accompany me. As always, his first thought was for my welfare.

Raspartin stood before us and explained the implications of our request. No-one, he explained, would be rejuvenated and no-one would live forever. A cursed immortal can die like any other person, through injury, disease and decay, but if a person was healthy, in body, mind and soul when they passed through the cleansing fire, then their life span would be extended far beyond what is considered usual, and the process of ageing could be delayed for more than a century. Each one of us must prepare assiduously for the ritual over a period of three days; there must be fasting, humbling of mind and body, and a full confession of sins, no matter how trivial.

On the fourth day, dressed in white robes, we gathered in our octagonal chamber in Coleton Street. The room was filled with the perfume of smouldering incense and herbs. Raspartin beat the gong and demanded that we empty our minds. As we began the ritual chant, he lit the fire in a deep, earthenware brazier in the centre of the room. The fire flamed like no other fire I had ever seen, giving out no heat, but a cold, piercing, light and reaching up to the ceiling which remained untouched by flame or soot. As each of us passed through the fire, one by one, and emerged untouched, singeing not so much as a hair, I marvelled at the skill of the adept. Mandragora had elected to go last. Raspartin demanded to know if she had anything yet to confess.

"Nothing." She spoke the words proudly and clearly, her head held high. "I am ready to enter the fire."

"Are you sure, my sister?" Raspartin's voice was as cold as the piercing light of the fire. "If you tell falsehoods before this gathering, then the consequences could be severe."

"I am certain." She stepped forward.

"Then go forward."

As Mandragora stepped into the fire, the flames changed, burning suddenly hot and yellow; we were all driven back by the heat. And then she screamed, dreadful screams that haunt me to this day; she fell to the ground, horribly burned. A little maidservant who had witnessed the whole scene, watching through a keyhole,rushed in to douse her with water. But the damage was done.

It was useless for Raspartin to assure me that I could not be blamed, that Mandragora alone bore responsibility for this catastrophe, having failed to confess all the secrets of her heart. Her rage against me was complete. And I... ashamed as I am to say it, for a while, the shock drove me out of my right mind. I was confined to my room, raving and drugged, tended to by Konrad and the little maidservant.

Thus it was that nine of us, not the ten that we intended, became cursed immortals that night. Lord Carfax took Mandragora to his country estate where he remained in constant attendance. A defrocked priest performed a marriage ceremony and he became her husband and the heir to her fortune. Four years later, I received a letter summoning me to come to her; she was dying.

I entered her room, hoping for forgiveness and reconciliation, only to find damnation as Mandragora cursed me on her death-bed, "Never forget I am a sorceress and my magic is older and more powerful than yours," she said. "Even from beyond the grave, I will come after you, if you ever dare to love another woman. You are mine for eternity and I will make you suffer. I will kill you both, if need be. I will mar your every chance of happiness." Even after she was laid in her father's tomb, she appeared to me, reflected in mirrors, pursuing me, leaving me hag-ridden. I believe that even to this day, her spirit is not at rest.

Of the nine of us who became cursed immortals that night, seven remain. Lord Carfax was killed in the Great War and another died of a lingering disease the spores of which had always been present in his body. I continue to walk the earth, outwardly the man I was on that day in 1897, inwardly, feeling old before my time. I now know the true meaning of the words 'cursed immortal'. It is not a question of losing your soul. It is to live on, tired and jaded, losing the friends you loved and finding the world alien and unforgiving. That, indeed, is a curse and not worth the pain of seeking immortality.

Llewellyn Arawn Llewellyn *September 1939*

Forty Two

The train had passed through Watford Junction, Tamworth, Stafford and Crewe, but I'd barely noticed the stations, so deep had I been in these pages. After reading the opening chapter, I'd skimmed through some of the subsequent sections; they contained detailed descriptions of meetings with other adepts and histories of various occult orders but it was these personal, first pages that had given me so much cause for reflection. The emotions I experienced as I read them were powerful and distressing; anger, shock, grief, incredulity and above all, despair at my own naivety. So the truth had been staring me in the face all the time and I'd been too obtuse to make the connection. Arthur Lewin and Mandy. *Arawn Llewellyn and Mandragora Carfax.* And Bushy was right. Llewellyn was a cursed immortal. How dare he be right!

The train was slowing down; I saw that we were approaching Lancaster. I just hoped there was a convenient bus service to Pendle, a taxi might prove expensive.

"We're here, Bertie." I pulled my bag down from the rack and bent down to pick up the cat basket. "Oh dear, you do look poorly."

Now I felt guilty. I'd hardly looked at the cat during the journey, immersed as I'd been in my reading and there he was, slumped in a heap, like a discarded fur stole at the bottom of the basket, barely moving. Nana had taught me nothing about cats, except how to discourage them from entering the garden and raiding bird's nests, so I had no idea what to do with a sick one. Perhaps I should have bought a copy of *Cat Lover's Monthly* after all.

As I came out of the station, squinting against the winter sun, I was startled by the sudden blast of a car horn.

"Jeanie Gowdie! Over here!"

An old woman, hunched like a tortoise over the steering wheel of a dumpy-looking green car, (an Austin A30 as I later learned), was waving at me in a frantic manner. I knew at once that this must be Dr Hecate Burneside. She was exactly as I might have imagined, ancient and eccentric, with wild hair like a birds' nest and eyes as acute as a hovering raptor.

"Get in." She leant across the front seat and flung open the passenger door. "My dear girl, thank goodness you had the sense to come to me. We have no time to lose."

"You got my letter then?"

"Letters? I don't rely on such mundane methods of communication. No, your letter has yet to arrive, but I saw you in my scrying vessel as you boarded your train in London and I knew you were in trouble. Now, of course, the nature of the trouble is only too clear. Well, it was bound to happen sooner or later. But I shall do my best."

"I'm not sure I know what you mean."

"Oh, *do* get in! Don't just stand there. I suggest you get into the back seat with your luggage. Clamber across! There's no time to waste. I'm afraid this car has no seat-belts, hold on to that strap. And make sure you close the door properly; it'll rattle all the way if you don't bang it firmly. Are you ready? Then let's go."

"It's really very kind of you to come and collect me, Dr Hecate."

"Kind? Kindness has nothing to do with it." The engine roared as she pulled out the choke and pumped the accelerator vigorously. "This is a matter of urgency. What a sorry situation. I knew, of course, that a dreadful man called Hopkins had seized control of the library, but I knew nothing of *this* latest catastrophe! Well, I hope you'll like our country-side. We'll be going through the Trough of Bowland and over Dunsop Bridge. You should see it in the late summer when the heather's out. But forgive me if I don't talk any more until we get to Gibbet Lane. I need to concentrate on the road. My eye-sight isn't quite what it was and if I engage in any deep debate, I'm afraid I might run the car into a ditch."

Forced to be patient, despite all the questions I was longing to ask, I settled down on the leather seat, holding on to the cat basket with one hand and clinging to the strap with the other. Dr Hecate drove very fast. A succession of images flashed past me; a glimpse of a snake curled up on a rock under a clump of bracken, a little waterfall gushing from the bottom of a dry stone wall, a stoat scampering safely across the road and disappearing into a hedge. As we came into Clitheroe, a flock of rooks rose up from a bare tree and spread themselves in an elongated pattern across the grey sky. I had several reasons for feeling apprehensive, not least because of my suspicion that Dr Hecate had never passed a driving test. Even if she had, her comments about her eyesight were hardly reassuring.

Hemlock Cottage was a low, white-washed building half-hidden amongst rowan trees and gloomy pines. It had a slate roof and the lattice windows were dirty and cracked, but the garden appeared to be well-kept. There were herb patches and snowdrops, some espaliers for fruit trees and a neat little greenhouse filled to bursting with potted vegetation.

"Here we are." Dr Hecate brought the car to a halt by the gate. "Take care as you get out. There are a number of toads in the grass and I don't want them stepped upon."

She unlocked the sun-blistered front door and ushered me into a dimly-lit sitting room with a kitchen area at one end. There was a low, beamed ceiling; books and tapestry cushions were scattered everywhere. I noticed a row of statuettes displayed on the sideboard representing various Egyptian deities.

"Can you name these?" Dr Hecate pointed to them.

"Um...Anubis, Sekmet, Ra...I'm not sure of the rest."

"Dear, dear, a gap in your knowledge, and I was told you were astonishingly erudite. Well, sit down!" She thumped the cushions of a threadbare, floral settee. "I'll put the kettle on the range. You must need something after your journey."

"Thank you. Dr Hecate, do you know anything about cats? I'm rather worried about..."

"I should think you are!" She picked up a cake tin and pulled off the lid with unnecessary force. "Dundee or cherry? The cherry's in here, the Dundee's on that plate by the skirting board."

"Cherry, please." I said, making a choice in order to be polite although neither of the cakes looked appetising, especially not the dusty one on the floor that looked as if it had been nibbled by mice. I sat down on the edge of the settee.

"Are you in that picture, Dr Hecate?" I pointed to the framed photograph above the fireplace, a sepia image of a group of young women dressed in the fashion of the 1920s, standing in front of an imposing building.

"Yes, indeed. Third on the left, front row." She tapped the glass with the cake knife. "Girton College. I had an affair with Bertrand Russell, but then every blue stocking girl did in those days. But he was such a rationalist, it didn't last. Of course, I've known most of the great thinkers and magicians in my time; Aleister Crowley was a disgusting man, he used to pick his nose with a cake fork. Oddly enough, I remember that with more revulsion than I do his dabbling in devil-worship. Your cake, my dear. And your tea."

"Thank you." I took a small bite of the cake; it tasted of cloves and something else that I couldn't identify, except that I was aware it was rather unpleasant. I took a gulp of the tea, hoping to wash away the taste, but that was even worse and made me choke.

"And now we must get straight to work." Dr Hecate sat down in the high-backed chair by the hearth. "But first, tell me if you have tried any procedures."

"Procedures?"

"Spells, incantations, anything of that kind?"

"I attempted a beckoning."

"A beckoning?" She sounded appalled. "Good grief, what possessed you to do such a reckless thing? A novice should never contact spirits!"

"But the spirit had already contacted me, through a mirror I bought in a curio shop and..."

"Stop there." She held up her hand. "I don't need the details just now. "But," she flapped her hand in the direction of the cat basket. "What made you suppose a beckoning was the way to deal with such a serious transmogrification?"

"Trans....?"

"I need to know the facts. How long has he been in that shape?"

"Poorly, you mean? I don't know. You see, he was missing for a while, and then, when he came back this morning, Burlington Bertie seemed..."

"*Burlington Bertie!*" She rolled her eyes towards the ceiling. "What on earth possessed you to call him that?"

"When I first saw the cat, I thought he resembled a gentleman in an evening suit," I explained. "And he has such impeccable manners. He doesn't behave like a cat at all. He's so dignified. He turned up on my window sill just before Christmas and..."

"For the love of the goddess Bastet!" Dr Hecate clapped her hand to her forehead. "Just before Christmas! You mean this has been going on for weeks?"

"What's been going on? I don't understand."

"Are you really that imperceptive? Don't tell me you haven't noticed!" She leapt to her feet and picked up the cat basket. "To think you've been calling him Burlington Bertie, as if he were a music hall joke. My dear girl, if that cat had appeared on my window sill, I wouldn't have called him Burlington Bertie. The first thing I'd have done, even *before* attempting an urgent shape-shifting reversal spell, was restore his dignity and call him Llewellyn."

Forty Three

"But...I don't understand." I swallowed. "Dr Hecate, you can't possibly mean...are you saying that...this cat is actually....but that's impossible."

"If you don't believe me, look at his eyes," she insisted. "Did it never occur to you that while most black cats have yellow eyes this one has eyes of an exceptional green? Did you never stop to wonder why instead of behaving like a cat, this animal was behaving like a perfect gentleman?"

Green eyes? A perfect gentleman? Surely this was a joke? But what had I just been reading on the train, what about the shape-shifting that Mandragora Carfax....?

"Dr Hecate," my mouth felt dry. "You must be pulling my leg."

"I only wish I was, my dear.

Oh! The room was spinning; I felt as though I was being sucked into a centrifugal force. I had to close my eyes, I was so dizzy.

"I'm so sorry I had to drug your tea, my dear." Dr Hecate's voice seemed to come from a long distance away. "But it's for the best. Much as it might be useful for your education to witness this procedure, I'm afraid it might not work and could end in disaster. I wouldn't want you to be too distressed."

*

When I finally came back to consciousness, groggy and confused with a crick in my neck, it was very dark; I could just about make out the vague shapes of Dr Hecate's high-backed arm-chair, the fireplace and the coal scuttle.

I sat up slowly. I was feeling far from well. If I didn't concentrate, I might be sick.

Perhaps the cherry cake had upset me. Dr Hecate might be a graduate of Girton College, a skilled witch and an ex-mistress of Bertrand Russell but I had severe doubts about her baking. And then there had been the tea...the drugged tea. Oh! It was all coming back to me. Just before I'd passed out, she'd been telling me a ridiculous story about... but what if everything she'd been saying had been true?

I staggered to my feet. Where was the light switch? Did Dr Hecate even have electricity in her cottage? Probably not. I groped my way to the window and pulled open the thick curtains.

The garden was bathed in moonlight so preternaturally bright that it looked like a stage set, artificially-lit and unreal. Some hollyhocks were nodding in a faint breeze and a hedgehog was sitting on the grass. I opened the window and leant out, taking in big gulps of the night air. Then I climbed over the window sill and stepped into the garden. *Careful you don't step on the toads.*

"Jeanie..." The voice drifted towards me.

I looked across the grass. There he was, at the end of the path, one hand resting on the trunk of a rowan tree. He was dressed in his evening suit, but he looked far from elegant. His clothes were crumpled, his hair was damp and plastered against his forehead and his feet were bare. His voice sounded odd too, faint and wavering, as if he hadn't spoken for a long time. Which, of course, I realised, in human terms, he hadn't.

You might think that, on seeing the man I loved, standing before me in his true form at last, I was overwhelmed with joy. Perhaps another woman would have run to him, embraced him, kissed him and wept with relief. I'm afraid I didn't. I was incandescent with rage.

"How dare you!" I yelled. "How dare you play a trick like that on me, you and your shape-shifting!"

"I didn't..." He bent over, taking great, heaving breaths. His face looked unnaturally pale; I assumed that was the effect of the moonlight.

"I know all about it now," I continued, getting into my stride. "I've read your *Confession*. I know all about the life you led with Mandragora Carfax! What were you doing, trying to relive the times you had with her? Here I've been, thinking you'd abandoned me, when all the time, you've been lurking in my flat, spying on me and pretending to be a bloody cat. How pervy can you get?"

"I..." With a groan, he sunk to the ground.

"Get up, for goodness sake! What's wrong with you?" I demanded. "If you think you can impress me by fooling around and..." I stopped. He was lying flat out on the grass, his eyes were closed, and he wasn't moving.

"Are you all right?" My voice sounded very small to me.

"Does he look as if he's all right?" Dr Hecate came round from the back of the cottage, a large bucket in her hand. "Must you shout at him when he's in agony?"

"*Agony?*"

"Yes, agony." Dr Hecate set the bucket down on the ground. "His head will be banging like a thousand anvils, his every muscle must be tortured by pain and his body is being consumed by fever. I have done my best, but I fear the damage has already been done. Such a prolonged transmogrification can be fatal."

"Fatal?" I stared at her, aghast. "Then what on earth possessed him to do it?"

"You surely don't think he did this to himself?" She sounded incredulous. "You think he would be such a fool? Of course he wouldn't. *She* has kept her death-bed promise. She said she would destroy him if he ever looked at another woman and now she has. This is the curse of Mandragora Carfax."

It would an understatement to say that I felt flooded with guilt. I was distraught. I fell on my knees beside him, cradling him in my arms, attempting to mop his brow with the hem of my skirt. "Dr Hecate," I wailed. "We must call an ambulance."

"An ambulance?" She repeated, sounding as puzzled as if I'd just used a word from an obscure foreign tongue. "What good would that do?"

"We've got to get help! Look at him!"

"We will do what we can," Dr Hecate assured me. "All is not lost. But I'm rather surprised you think there's anything to be gained by dialling 999. Quite apart from the fact that the nearest telephone box is two miles down the road, I think you'll find the National Health Service, despite its undoubted merits, is powerless when it comes to healing those suffering from paranormal afflictions."

"Oh, I can't bear it," I wailed. "To think that the last thing he'll have heard on this earth was me yelling at him."

"You mustn't blame yourself too much." Dr Hecate patted me on the shoulder. "But Bastet only knows who could have been so foolish as to raise Mandragora's spirit, thus enabling her to return through the astral planes and wreak her vengeance."

"Dr Hecate." I swallowed. "I'm very much afraid that was me."

"Really?" She looked intrigued.

"Yes...the beckoning. I thought my spell had been unsuccessful but....oh!"

With sickening clarity, the memory of that night flashed into my mind, that woman with her sharp red nails and her little black dress, her decayed grandeur and her insidious manners. '*Can I interest you in subscribing to Cat Lovers Monthly?'*

"Remembered something?" Dr Hecate looked at me with a knowing expression.

"Yes. I tried the spell and...I used *her* mirror and... then a woman knocked on my door, and I opened it and..."

"You failed to recognise Mandragora Carfax."

"Yes." The realisation was a dead weight in the pit of my stomach.

"You mustn't feel this is all your fault. I wouldn't be surprised to learn that the Carfax woman was on the move from the moment you and Arawn Llewellyn first met. No time to lose. We must take some practical steps to remedy this woeful situation. Do you have any ideas?"

"My grandmother, Nana Herrick, was a hedge-witch and she trained me in the healing arts. Feverfew for headache, hoodwort and valerian to induce untroubled sleep, meadow-sweet to soothe the stomach and echinacea for the restoration of strength."

"All of which are readily available from my garden." She nodded. "And in addition," she pointed to the bucket, "I've brought water from my well, which is fed by a spring blessed by the Druids and ideal for cooling a fever. These simple medicaments will be palliative, but something more is required for a full cure."

"Tell me what to do. Please."

"An ancient text describes how the wizard Merlin fell sick of a grievous ailment and was restored to health by receiving the ministrations of a young novice witch while lying half-naked on a bed of goose-down. Certain incantations were said, invoking Khonsu, the Egyptian god of the moon. I do have a copy of the incantation, fortunately, but I'm afraid some of the other conditions might be more difficult to meet. For one thing, the young witch has to be a virgin."

"Actually," I could feel myself blushing. "I don't think that's going to be a problem."

"Ah! I see!" Dr Hecate beamed at me. "How very refreshing in this day and age. So, let us waste no more time. I hardly think we should leave him here on the wet grass. Let's get him indoors. And then it's up to you, my dear. I take it you love him?"

"I think I do."

"Splendid! Then I'm sure you will do your best. You must be hopeful, but you must also be prepared for the worst. I cannot say more than that."

He became a corpse, a corpse all in the ground...

Was that voice real or was I dreaming? I hadn't meant to go to sleep, but by five in the morning I had become so drowsy that my eyes had finally closed. Now I opened them with difficulty and saw the dawn light leaking through a gap in the blue gingham curtains. I had sat all night in this chair by the bed, long hours, sponging his body with the water from the well, administering to him, whispering words he didn't seem to hear. So we'd spent the night together but he'd been completely unaware of my presence. It had been akin to a wedding night, but without any hope of consummation.

I went over to him, and touched his bare shoulder with my fingertips; he was so perfect, so beautiful, so unblemished, perhaps the best preserved centenarian on the planet. He didn't stir, but I could tell his fever was gone.

He became a corpse, a corpse all in the ground

And they were lost forever with the cold clay all around.

Was I imagining it, that mocking, sly woman's voice, twisting the words of the old song I used to sing with Nana Herrick?

He'll never have your maidenhead that you have kept so long!

I crossed the room and flung open the lattice window.

"If that's you, Mandragora Carfax," I called out, "Then you should take care. I'm alive and you're dead and I'll win in the end, see if I don't!

A violent wind shook the branches of the yew tree at the edge of the garden. I leaned out and shouted again, and then everything was still. But she hadn't gone, I knew it, she was just biding her time, playing with me. Soon, I'd have to deal with her properly, and I guessed she wouldn't give in without a fight.

I went through to Dr Hecate's tiny bathroom, with its sloping ceiling and bare wooden floor. There was a hip bath and a Victorian wash stand and a row of china frogs on the window sill. The sanitation was primitive; there was only one cold water tap. I splashed some water on my face, dragged a brush through my tangled hair and went downstairs.

Dr Hecate didn't seem to be here, although the table had been set for breakfast. I took a pair of kitchen scissors out of the drawer, picked up a wooden trug and some gardening gloves and went out into the garden. I'd gathered plenty of healing herbs last night, but now I needed to find some protection for the house against the spirit of Mandragora. *Allium ursinum* with its pungent, garlicky stench was a good weapon against evil incursions, but that didn't usually appear until April. White snakeroot and South American monkshood, also useful, were unlikely to be found growing in England. As I looked around, I quickly realised that Dr Hecate's garden was unaffected by seasonal and geographical considerations. There were plenty of exotic plants growing here, including generous clumps of *Aconitum Satanica,* and several spikey things that I suspected of being insectivorous and dangerous. I cut some *heracleum mantegazzium*, using the gloves to protect my skin from the deadly sap, and then opened the gate and went out into the lane. A gentle mist was rising; a white horse was standing alone by a stile. And there, in the field opposite, were some juniper bushes. Perfect! A few sprigs hanging above the threshold would add to my protective measures.

I set off across the field, luxuriating in the feel of the soft, dewy grass underfoot. Everything around me, the hedgerows, the trees, the white horse, the unnaturally blue sky, was clear and shining. I was filled with optimism. Everything was going to be all right. And now that I had Dr Hecate as my mentor, I would have my Coming of Age ceremony. Perhaps it could take place here, under Pendle Hill. And *he* would be with me. And then...and then who knew what we might achieve together? I could hardly breathe for excitement as I anticipated the future Nana Herrick had predicted for me.

"She became a rose, a rose all in the wood,

And he became a bumble bee and kissed her where she stood...'

Singing to myself, I snapped off some juniper and tied the pieces together with long grass. The sun was rising in the sky; I could feel the warmth on the back of my neck. I wandered on a little further, picking some yarrow and stopping to greet a hedgehog that peered out of a bush. My feet were soaked; I should have known better than to come out in these thin, canvas slippers. I was just bending down to pick a sprig of coltsfoot, when I heard the slam of a car door in the distance. I looked up and saw the vintage limousine outside the cottage. Konrad was at the wheel and a figure was slumped in the back seat. A moment later, I heard the roar of the engine.

"Wait!" I began to run back across the field, stumbling over the tussocks of grass. What was happening? "Stop!" I reached the gate, gasping for breath. "Please!"

I was too late. The car was already climbing the hill and within moments it was over the crest and out of sight.

Forty Four

A clever woman can live without the love of a manne, but with the right manne, she can be stronger. But howe can there be a manne whose love is untainted by self-interest? Be prepared to walke through several miles of broken glass to finde such a one, otherwise, continue alone.

The Guidance of Goodwife Gurlie for this daye and every daye

"Goodness." Dr Hecate looked up from the stove where she was stirring a pot of porridge."Are you a believer in an early morning jog? If so, I really think you need better running shoes than those." She looked down at my Chinese slippers.

"I saw the car," I panted. "What's happened? How did Konrad come to be here? Where are they going?"

"Too many questions, my dear, and I'm not prepared to answer any of them just now. I don't mean to sound harsh, but you must dismiss all thoughts of Arawn Llewellyn from your mind for the time being."

"I can't do that! What if he's dying? What if....?"

"Calm yourself, Jeanie Gowdie. We have work to do, preparing for your Coming of Age, and we must focus on that. You have no time for romantic entanglements of any kind. That kind of thing will only serve to cloud your judgement."

I gazed at the breakfast table, at the homely brown teapot, the blue and white striped milk jug, the chunky pottery porridge bowls. I didn't know whether to feel comforted or completely bereft.

"That's what the Elders told me," I said.

"You've seen the Elders?" Dr Hecate's face brightened. "They have communicated with you?"

"Yes."

"Then you have been summoned, and it is imperative that you attend to the task they have given you. Now, the porridge is ready and the tea is brewed. First, we'll have breakfast and then you must change your footwear. You'd better borrow a pair of my walking boots. Do you have any apprentice tools?"

"Yes, they're in my luggage."

"Good. Then bring them with you. Your instruction starts today and you will need to give me your full attention."

"Here we are." Dr Hecate leant against the trunk of a lone, withered tree, catching her breath. "Top of the hill. I used to run up here when I was a girl but now, even a steady trudge makes my heart leap in my chest like a wounded salmon. See the path over there?" She pointed with her stick. "Do you know what it is?"

"I'm afraid not."

"That is the Salter Fell Track where they were led to their imprisonment and death. Chattox and Demdike, Device, Redfern and the rest. The women they called the Lancashire witches. What do you know about them?"

"Only that they may not have been witches at all, but just unfortunate women who were victimised for no reason except that they were poor and old."

"Or they could, indeed, have been a primitive pagan coven. We can never be certain."

"But what do you think, Dr Hecate?"

"I strongly suspect that the Old Religion was widely practised in this part of Lancashire. I have no doubt the Malkin Tower, the place where Demdike and her associates met, was an epicentre of ancient power. They exist all over Britain, on ley lines, in stone circles and dolmens, in any place where humankind has connected with elemental forces. Perhaps you are familiar with this notion?"

"Yes, my grandmother often spoke about it."

"Good. Then you will understand why I have brought you here. Now let's sit." She unrolled a blanket and laid it on the ground. "We'll be here for a while. Now, let me see those apprentice tools of yours."

"Here they are." I took the toffee tin out of my bag, and laid the objects out on the grass.

"Good." She turned them over, the knife, the stone, the candle stub and the dish, examining each item with evident approval. "Your grandmother chose well. But soon, you must be prepared to relinquish these things. Once you have had your Coming of Age ceremony, you must bury them in a place such as this."

"Bury them?" I was aghast. "But Nana Herrick left me these when she passed into the Summer-lands. I promised myself that I'd never lose them."

"You will not be losing them. You can take comfort in the knowledge that you will always know where they are."

"But..."

"These are just apprentice tools even if they do have sentimental value. At your Coming of Age you must take possession of a new set of magical artefacts, tools that you must either inherit or win from a powerful practitioner of magic."

"But how...?"

"No!" she held up her hand. "We will not speak of that just now. First, there is something I have to reveal to you, a crucial fact concerning your identity of which I believe you are unaware. Perhaps you should brace yourself. Are you ready?"

"I think so, but what...?"

"You're a heritant, Jeanie. The first to be born in England for over a century."

"But I don't even know what that means." I stared at her.

"A heritant is one who carries the blood-line of the practitioners of the Old Religion," Dr Hecate explained. "In some cases, the imprint might go back as far as pre-Roman days. Did you never suspect this?"

"Nana Herrick told me I was born to the Craft. I assumed she meant I'd inherited her gift for folk magic and healing."

"As no doubt you have, but I suspect your legacy came to you through the paternal line."

"But how can that be? My father was so opposed to magic, and surely no-one in his family..." My stomach flipped over. *Isobel Gowdie*. What if Bushy had been right after all? How delighted he'd be if I told him. Then I *won't* tell him, I decided.

"I must warn you that to be a heritant is more of a curse than a blessing," Dr Hecate continued. "It is a curse because it makes you vulnerable. The enemies of magic will spurn you and persecute you. No doubt you have already encountered hostility in your life."

"Yes, I have." *Chrissie Wilkinson and her cronies, the Governor at Crowsmuir, those girls at the hostel, Clemency Nantucket, Malachi Hopkins....*

"But," Dr Hecate assured me. "It can also be a blessing. Certain skills that take others years to develop will come instinctively to you. You have many gifts. Let me demonstrate. Take that stone, and lay it on the palm of your left hand. Now close your fingers over it and open your eyes."

"But my eyes are already..."

"I'm speaking figuratively, Jeanie. Just do as I say."

I took hold of the stone, gripping it tight. Nothing happened for a moment, but then the landscape began to undergo a transformation before my eyes. The clouds, the dry stone walls, the heather and the bracken all shimmered in an unnatural light and then everything was magnified. I could see every leaf, every blade of grass, every tiny insect crawling on the ground and then the surface of the earth peeled back and I could see the world beneath, the burrowing creatures, the clay, the peat and bedrock until finally I was staring into the pulsing, molten heart of the planet itself.

"*Oh!*" I dropped the stone on the ground. "This is too much! I don't want this!"

"Visions are always a shock at first," Dr Hecate said in a matter-of-fact voice. "You will become accustomed to them in time and will learn how to switch them on and off at will. We will work on training all your senses in the course of this week. We will work on many skills but there is one thing I advise against. Shape-shifting is to be avoided at all costs." She reached into her capacious haversack and took out a large lunch tin with a hinged lid. "First, we'll eat. I've made two kinds of sandwiches, tinned meat and egg mayonnaise. Which would you prefer?"

Those five days I spent with Dr Hecate reminded me of the times I'd spent with Nana, although she proved to be a far sterner teacher. Some of the things she taught me made me feel half-ashamed, as I realised how much I'd stumbled around in my naivety, creating havoc where I should have exercised control.

"Your grandmother, it seems, brought you up mainly in the traditions of old British magic," she told me. "That has its roots in folk lore, herbal healing and Druidic wisdom, in the cult of the Great Earth Mother, the Horned God and the Celtic wheel of the year but there are so many other disciplines you will need to study, Nordic, Sufi, Greek and African. Much can be learned, too, from the practices of the medieval alchemists, the shamans of the Americas and the holy men of the Russian steppes."

"And how did you become a practitioner of magic, Dr Hecate?" I asked.

"Through long study and against considerable parental opposition," she told me. "Believe it or not, I was a rector's daughter, brought up in the Lincolnshire Wolds. As you can imagine, I wasn't christened 'Hecate'; that was the name I took at my Coming of Age ceremony. My field, when I went up to the 'varsity, was Egyptology and Folklore. I still have a grudging respect for those ancient gods and goddesses; I often consult Anubis over a thorny problem or two!"

"My grandmother taught me a spell evoking the Egyptian gods," I said "I tried it once, but I don't think I can have done it properly as it didn't work."

"Are you sure of that? You've already told me how you attempted a beckoning that you thought was a failure and look what power you actually unleashed! Now, what did your grandmother tell you about your Coming of Age ceremony?"

"Just that on that day, I would adopt my true name, the one she'd whispered in my ear."

"And you haven't shared that name with anyone since that day, I hope?"

"No, I haven't, although I've used it when alone, attempting a spell."

"That is permitted. Now, regarding the ceremony, did your grandmother mention the spell you must cast, or explain about the summoning of the seven?"

"No. She didn't have time to instruct me any further. She was called back to the Summer-lands."

"Ah, I see. Well, then, let me explain. There are certain vital elements in a Coming of Age ceremony. First, as I have already explained, there is the adoption of a new set of magical artefacts and the declaration of your true name. Then you must cast a spell."

"What kind of spell?"

"I leave that to your discretion. You could, for example, create a beautiful summer's day in the midst of winter, or you might conjure up the spirit of a powerful necromancer from the time of the Black Death. However, I advise against such frivolity. Now," she took an ebony box out of her haversack. "This contains a pack of cards known as the Arcana Magi. It's somewhat like the Tarot, but much older. These cards will play an important part in the arranging of your Coming of Age ceremony. Let me explain. For the summoning of the seven, you must first choose seven of these cards at random. I will lay them face down in the shape of a pentacle. Now pay careful attention to my instructions..."

On the final evening at Hemlock Cottage, Dr Hecate prepared a special supper that we ate by candle-light. It looked like an ordinary vegetable bake, but I could tell it contained certain hallucinatory ingredients that are not for sale in an ordinary supermarket. We drank home brewed wine and laughed a lot; outside the window, the yews were bathed in moonlight and the hedgehogs kept watch.

"And now, my dear," Dr Hecate said. "I will answer any questions you might have about Arawn Llewellyn. You have been very good this week; you haven't mentioned him once. I hope you haven't been brooding over his fate."

"I did my best not to do so."

"Good. Rest assured, he is safe. Konrad will have known what to do, and where to take him."

"But where was that?"

"That I am not free to disclose. He's in a place that only you can find, using the skills you have developed this week. Don't look so crestfallen, my dear, you can do this. Remember what I've taught you about guardians, gate keepers, tokens and portals. You already had an intuitive understanding of these things even before I began to instruct you. You will succeed."

"I hope so." I paused, then asked. "Llewellyn told me you'd been a friend of his for many years. How did you meet him? Was it at the library?"

"No. It was many years ago, during his long exile in the gloomy, soggy valleys of Wales."

"The gloomy, soggy valleys? But Llewellyn told me that his home in the Black Mountains was beautiful."

"Ha!" Dr Hecate gave a short laugh. "It rained non-stop when I was there, but perhaps it was an exceptionally wet summer! I'd just retired from my lecturing post, so it must have been the late nineteen-fifties. I was on a walking tour and was just descending the Skirrid Mountain when I fell and twisted my ankle very badly. A young man, or rather a person who I *took* to be a young man, came running to my rescue. It was the first time I'd ever seen him and I didn't know who he was Nor did I know that he wasn't quite as young as he seemed." She smiled. "I was, of course, astonished when I discovered the truth. I'd heard very bad things about spell-charmers and cursed immortals, and yet here was one offering me kindness and friendship."

"My grandmother warned me against spell-charmers too."

"And not without reason. I'm afraid they can be very easily tempted into the darker realms of magic. Now, you should know that Arawn Llewellyn wrote to me last October, asking my advice about you. As an adept, he had recognised you immediately as a heritant and this knowledge presented him with a dilemma. He didn't know whether to keep you in ignorance of the fact, the silly man! I wrote back urging him to be completely honest with you about everything, including telling you his past. I take it he didn't do what I advised?"

"I think he *would* have told me about his past eventually but he didn't..." I hesitated. "Get the opportunity. I only learned the truth about him when I was on the train coming here. I read his memoir, his *Confessions.* Someone gave it to me. To discredit him, I think."

"I see. I'm surprised a copy has been found. I thought they'd all been destroyed years ago. Well, I, too, have read that somewhat self-lacerating document. Please don't judge the man too severely; he's lived long enough to regret the excesses of his early years. He paid his dues with his war service, of course."

"He was in the war? You mean the Second World War?"

"I mean both wars, my dear, serving as an ambulance driver in the Great War, and then working with the Resistance in France in the second. Arawn Llewellyn can be a hero when the need arises, although I fear he has lost his way somewhat. My dear, I believe you are the only person who can persuade him to return to the fight. I have every reason to believe that it was Jabez Corey's wish that Llewellyn should inherit the role of Magus after his passing. So, return he must, to eject this man Hopkins who has usurped his position."

"But I can't persuade Llewellyn to return if I don't know where he is."

"Only you can find him. You will need magic to get there. You will need to locate the gatekeeper and ask to be admitted though the portal, using the right words. I can't guide you every step of the way, Jeanie Gowdie."

"No. I understand. And the thing is..." I hesitated. "There's something I haven't told you. about Mandragora Carfax. You see, I've got...here, I'll show you." I pulled the velvet ribbon out from under my blouse and held up the little gold key.

"Hmm." Dr Hecate frowned. "And where did you get that?"

"From a curio and antique shop, near where I live. The owner sold me several other things that must have belonged to her, a cloak, some boots, and that mirror I mentioned. He said he knew nothing about where they'd come from or who'd once owned them."

"Do you suppose he was telling the truth?"

"I have the feeling now that he wasn't."

"I see. And what became of the mirror?"

"After I used it for the beckoning, I gave it to Llewellyn. He was horrified when he saw me with it."

"I imagine that he would have been! And, in my view, the foolish man should have told you why. Well, I think I can guess what happened then. He used the mirror to contact Mandragora, he would have visited her tomb and... Well, I think we can guess the rest."

"Her magic proved too strong for him."

"As will yours be, my dear, once you've come of age." She gave me a sly wink. "Well, Jeanie Gowdie, now you have the key, you must find the box it fits. And that box, I'm sure, will contain the artefacts you need to win. And you must fix this everything, Jeanie Gowdie, you, the last heritant. Tomorrow, as soon as you get back to London, you must make contact with Llewellyn and persuade him to join you in the fight. This isn't just about your Coming of Age ceremony. You are no ordinary novice, and you have a witch-finder to defeat and the legacy of Antioch Corey to save."

Forty Five

Love is a distraction and a curse. No true witche should indulge in it. Continue to courte your familiars instead, and cherish toades and sprites before any manne born of woman.

The words of Grandma Gandy, written downe in the yeare 1696

I could only assume there'd been a power failure since the street lights were out in my road and all the houses were dark. I could only just make out where I was going because of the residual urban glow from the surrounding area. I took extra care as I went down the area steps, clinging to the hand rail and would have reached the bottom without mishap had it not been for the person huddled up on the last step with their back against the railings.

"Ah!" I stumbled and crashed into the door.

"Wotcha, Gowdie." A hand seized my arm, pulling me to my feet. "Sorry, look, I'll put my torch on. Don't panic, it's only me."

"Bushy! You nearly gave me a heart attack. I didn't even see you. Why didn't you say something when you heard me coming?"

"I didn't hear you. Must have nodded off."

"I wasn't expecting you." I fumbled in my bag for my key. "Why are you lurking here?"

"Well, for a start," he held up a carrier bag, "I've brought all these books. I figured that if you were going to be coming back to the library tomorrow, there was a fair chance Hopkins might waylay you as soon as you came into the building, demanding to see all the outstanding loans you'd collected on your supposed tour of England. I thought it would be handy if you could produce some of them right away."

"That's good thinking on your part. Thank you." I unlocked the door and stepped inside, reaching for the light switch. "Oh, hell, the electricity *is* off. Never mind, I've got plenty of candles, provided I can find the matches."

"Can I come in? I've been freezing my bollocks off out here."

"Of course you can come in. Although I *am* wondering why you're not at work."

"Ah well, that's the thing. That pompous bugger Hopkins has given me the sack and made me hand in all my keys."

"Oh, *no!* Why?"

"Long story. So where are those matches?"

"I thought they were here in front of the fireplace." I scrabbled around trying to find them. "But I must have put them somewhere else."

"Why do you need candles anyway? You've just spent a week being instructed in witch-craft. Can't you rustle us up a corpse-light or two?"

"No," I told him. "Magic should never be used for simple domestic convenience. Ah, here are the matches." I struck one and began to light the candles. The light glimmered eerily against the old brown wallpaper. *Bushy, matches and candles*. Not, perhaps, the best combination.

"Any chance of tea?" He sat down, cross-legged on the floor.

"Yes. I have a primus stove. So tea is possible, if you don't mind the herbal kind. But Bushy, this is a disaster. If Hopkins has sacked you and you've had to give in your keys..."

"Oh, I've still got keys," he assured me. "Months ago, I got duplicates cut. I can still get into the library. Hopkins won't get the better of me."

"I hope not. But what on earth happened? Why did he sack you?"

"Cost cutting, he said. He put on a sickening display of regret, practically shedding crocodile tears of remorse. Apparently, and I don't believe this, there are no longer any funds to pay a full time caretaker and night watchman. Well, I didn't say anything, just kept schtum. Pretended I understood and didn't mind at all."

"When did this happen?"

"It was last night. I was doing a round of the building when I ran into him. He was coming out of the archive room. *"Ah, it's Jim isn't? So glad I bumped into you. I deeply regret to say your services are no longer required."* Well, you can imagine how I felt."

"Of course I can."

"So the upshot is, the situation at the library's been dire. Hopkins and Nantucket have been going round removing all kinds of books from the shelves and now they're all piled up in the yard. Looks like they're planning a bonfire, but it's a bit early for Guy Fawkes."

"This sounds awful. How about Gerda? Is she all right?"

"As far as I know. Look, Gowdie, I want to hear about your trip to see Dr Hecate. What about your Coming of Age?"

"It'll have to wait until later. I have to go out."

"Now? But you only just got here."

"I know, but I really must go. It's urgent."

"Urgent? Can't I come with you?"

"No. You can't. You really can't. I have to do this on my own. But you can stay here. Make yourself some herbal tea. Sleep on my couch but *please* be careful of the candles. No trying to raise any fire demons while I'm away. Just take care of the place. I may not be back until late."

The street that ran alongside the old cemetery was deserted. A gust of wind caught an empty plastic bag and blew it into my path; I heard a tube train rattling along the over-ground tracks in the near distance. I stopped at the locked side gates and gazed through the railings at the gravestone of Samuel Greatorex, preacher to the heathen. There was the bench where I'd sat on Christmas Eve, filled with yearning, longing for Llewellyn's return, and not far away from there, through the undergrowth, was Mandragora's tomb. Now I knew what must have happened. He'd come here, that time before Christmas; he'd laid out those tea-lights and beckoned her spirit, using the mirror and casting a spell of some kind. Perhaps he'd asked her forgiveness and begged her to move on. But she'd been too full of anger and she'd humiliated him and then sent him back to me in the shape of a creature she knew I was likely to reject. She couldn't have been more spiteful. Soon, however, she'd have to reckon with me. I was the last heritant. She would regret messing with me!

I walked on to the main road on the other side of the old cemetery, to the launderette and the kebab shop and all the unromantic trappings of 1970s urban life. I crossed by the lights, and turned into Collyaton Road and the flats where Nasir's auntie had lived. I heard the sound of a barrel organ; I recognised the melody, *Take a Pair of Sparkling Eyes* from *The Gondoliers.* The instrument was somewhat out of key, and yet the music still seemed evocative, sentimental perhaps but also full of nostalgia for a past that I'd only visited once in my life. And then there she was, old Nora, wearing the mac I'd given her, operating the barrel organ outside the boarded-up pub.

"So you're here." She stopped turning the handle.

"Yes, I'm here."

"And what do you want with me?"

"Nora, I believe I know who you are," I said. "You were the maidservant at No 23 Coleton Street. You looked through the keyhole on that awful night, you came into the room and you threw water..."

"I never threw any water. He conjured it out of the air."

"He? Who do you mean?"

"Your precious erstwhile lover. The one who takes you to supper at the Red Dragon and puts roses in your hair. I saw the pair of you, didn't I? Back there, meeting amongst the tombs. Yes, I knew that house. My mother swept and scrubbed their floors and when I was a child, I played with the black beetles that crawled out from under the kitchen skirting board. And yes, I knew them, Arawn Llewellyn and Mandragora Carfax, when they were the most powerful adepts in London."

"And what were they like?"

"*He* was kind. *She* never even noticed me." She spat on the pavement.

"I want to go to that house now, please," I told her. "Can you help me get there?"

"And what makes you think I can do that?"

"You're the gatekeeper, aren't you?"

"I might be." She squinted at me. "But I won't do it for nothing. You have to pay a toll."

"You want money?"

"No." She shook her head. "I need something more personal. You must give me your necklace."

"I can't give this to you." I put my hand up, touching the apache tears that I'd worn every day since just before Christmas. "I'll give you anything else. Anything at all."

"Nothing else will do. I want those stones."

"But..."

"My final offer. Give them up or stayed locked out of his life forever."

"All right." Flooded with dismay, I undid the clasp and held out the necklace.

"*His* gift. Taken and given away!" She snatched it out of my hands. "Oh, you're so easily fooled!"

"Fooled? Is this a trick?"

"Oh, it might be. Still, I'll send you to the house. Just close your eyes and repeat the words of ingress. Don't you know what they are?"

"No, I don't."

"I told you once, do you never listen? Very well, I'll say them for you. *Through the fire, through the fire, and through the fire again.*"

A rushing sound filled my ears; it was like the sound of water a drowning person must hear when they've been knocked down by a breaking wave and they're sinking into the sand, unable to extricate themselves. I tried not to panic, but I felt unable to breathe, and the sensation of hopelessness and terror seemed to go on forever. At last there was silence and I felt steady enough to open my eyes. And now I found myself in the Coleton Street of the eighteen-nineties. The flats were gone and there were the tall, elegant houses with their stucco porches and their spiked iron railings. Number twenty three was right in front of me. I went up the steps and reached for the bell pull.

"The Master is severely indisposed and can see no-one, least of all you."

Konrad stood before me, dressed in a tail coat, starched shirt, black trousers and white gloves and with a dark plumed pigeon perched on his wrist.

"I must see him," I said. "I want to help."

"Help? You?" His eyes were cold and unforgiving. "With respect, *you* are the person who is responsible for this catastrophe. He would never have taken up magic again if it hadn't been for you. You flaunted your attractions, forcing him to hunger again for that most illusory of commodities, the love of a woman, and then you meddled in things you didn't understand and brought the past crashing down on him. I tried to warn him about you, but to no avail. But at last he's here, in a place of safety. Now go away and leave him in peace."

"Listen, Konrad," I said. "I know you've been a faithful friend to him all these years, but I care too. In fact, I think I love him."

"Love him? What do you know about love? You're very young, Miss Gowdie, and for the last English Heritant, you are astonishingly naïve. You have made some serious blunders."

"I realise that," I said. "And now I want to put things right. Please let me come in. We can't talk properly while I'm here, out on the porch."

"I have no great wish to talk with you at all, but I agree that an altercation on the door step would be undignified. Very well." He stepped back, ushering me in with very little grace. "You may as well see the damage you've done."

I stepped into an opulent hallway. There were huge ferns in Italian pots, gold curtains, fringed lampshades and oriental rugs and it might have been the home of any prosperous late-Victorian family had it not been for all the occult symbols, the floor tiles decorated with zodiac signs and pentacles, the tapestry of the cabbalistic Tree of Life on the wall, the images of mythical creatures, dragons, basilisks and chimera, painted on the door panels. The atmosphere was suffocating, airless and suffused with the smell of pure beeswax. Was this really a place of safety, or was it a prison?

"Where is he?" My legs felt weak; I was suddenly afraid. Nothing about this felt right.

"You'll find him in the Peacock Chamber. On the first floor, turn right, the door at the very end. Please don't tire him and leave as soon as you can."

The upstairs passage was dark, lit only by a few candles; phantasmal shadows flickered on the walls. There was music, *Come into the garden Maud,* playing, it seemed, on an old cylinder, a tinny sound that still brought tears to my eyes. *I am here at the gate alone.* Ah! Those words! They made me think of being kissed in a garden filled with the scent of lilies. Kissed by someone who was soon to leave me, perhaps succumbing to consumption, or dying in a foreign war.

I had come to a pair of panelled doors, each bearing a design of a silver peacock with an emerald for its eyes. I pushed them open. The room was full of smoke; wispy tendrils pluming up to the ceiling and irritating my eyes, making them water. And there was an odd smell that had neither the pungent, herby smell of pot nor the ethereal quality of church incense but which suggested something narcotic and dangerous. I looked around at the azure hangings looped over the walls, the red paper lanterns hanging from the ceiling, the Chinese rugs and ebony cabinets and the pipes laid out on a low table. I had stumbled into a gentleman's personal opium den.

Llewellyn was there, lolling back against the cushions on the bed in the centre of the room, a four poster with a high headboard in the design of peacock's fantail, picked out in green, blue and gold. He was barefoot, wearing a loose white shirt and dark trousers and he would have looked astonishingly handsome with his hair falling over his forehead, had his eyes not been so alarmingly blank.

"What on earth are you doing?" I demanded to know. "This won't do you any good at all. You have to listen to me. I've done what you said. I've spent a week with Dr Hecate, and she's prepared me for my Coming of Age. I've made all the plans; I'll have the Ceremony in the library, and I'll get rid of Hopkins and save the library at the same time. But you *must* be there too. You're supposed to be the Magus, not some washed up drug fiend. Come with me now! You have to get out of here."

"*Oh, God.*" He rocked forward, burying his head in his hands.

"What it is?" I went over to him and sat down on the edge of the bed. "Are you in pain?"

"The Greek army," he mumbled. "Marching through my head. Troy, Thermopylae and Marathon. They'll never stop now. And you must go. I'm waiting for Jeanie Gowdie."

"But I *am* Jeanie. Look at me!"

"No more thought." He turned his face away. "Just oblivion."

"You must get out of here," I shook him by the shoulder. "You're supposed to be protecting Antioch Corey's legacy. I need your help!"

"Jeanie." He gazed at me with dilated eyes. "If only Jeanie were here."

"I *am* here!" I felt like screaming with frustration. "And you must listen. This man, Hopkins, he's a witch-finder, I'm sure of it. He won't be satisfied until he's got rid of us all."

"Where did I lose them?" He picked up a cushion and cradled it to his chest. "Like Orlando, searching for his lost wits in the waters of the moon. *Mare frigoris, mare vaporum, oceanus procellaum*....disgrace and failure...she mustn't come here, she mustn't see..."

"I *have* come here. And if you can do nothing else for me, tell me where it is, Mandragora's casket. Is it here, in Coleton Street? This is 1897, right? Did she leave her casket here? Look, I've got the key." I pulled it out from under my blouse.

"*Weave a circle round him thrice/And close your eyes with holy dread...His flashing eyes, his floating hair, for he on honeydew has fed...*"

"Pull yourself together!"

"*And drunk the milk of paradise....*"

"That's enough!" I headed for the door. "I don't have time for this. If you prefer to addle your brain with opium, that's your problem. I'm going. I've got things to do. I'm going to have my Coming of Age ceremony without you. And I'll defeat Hopkins on my own. And for your information, I love you, Arawn Llewellyn, I love you so much it hurts, but quite frankly, you're behaving like a complete arse!"

And with those words, choking with rage and frustration, I fled from the room, slamming the double doors behind me.

Forty Six

"Don't you think that was a little harsh?" Konrad looked at me askance. He was on the landing, ostensibly watering a potted fern but I suspected he had an ulterior motive for positioning himself there.

"Were you eavesdropping?" I gazed at him coldly. I didn't want him to see that I was feeling a certain degree of remorse. *Arse.* Had I really said 'arse'?

"I couldn't help overhearing." He put down the indoor watering can. "You raised your voice somewhat. I warned you that the Master was seriously indisposed, but you wouldn't listen to me."

"He might be indisposed as you put it, but it seems he's brought it on himself."

"You think so?" Konrad's expression was deeply reproachful. "Tell me, how much do you understand about the condition known as melancholia? Do you suppose anyone chooses to suffer such grief and pain? Yes, a considerable amount of narcotic poppy has been imbibed, certainly, but I administered that to him myself in the hope of providing a sedative."

"I see," I said. "And was that really such a good idea? Will that help him to recover?"

"He has no wish to recover. He has suffered too many humiliations for a proud man and he now yearns for his long life to come to an end."

"You can't allow that!"

"I only wish to serve my Master as I have always done. As for you, Miss Gowdie, I believe that this love for him that you profess is tinged by self-interest. All you want, really, is to achieve your ambitions. Am I right?"

"No. You're wrong. Yes, I want to become a powerful sorceress, that's my destiny, but I'm prepared to work for the good of every adept and cursed immortal in London. Look," I reached for the gold key. "I have *this.* Konrad, please help me. Show me where it is, the casket containing Mandragora's artefacts of power. I need it. It's in this house, isn't it?"

"No, it is not." He flung open a door behind him. "You're welcome to search, but you won't find it. Go in, look for yourself."

I stepped into the room, a lady's dressing chamber. There were gold silk curtains, an Empire-style couch, a bentwood chair, and a rococo dressing table. The scent of musk and jasmine was overwhelming. An array of cut-glass perfume bottles, brushes with mother-of-pearl backs, pots of face-cream and rouge were laid out on the glass top of the dressing table; the polished wooden floor was strewn with exotic shoes, dancing pumps and slippers. A full-length evening dress, blue and green and glittery, like the skin of an exotic snake, was laid across the couch together with a pair of long, black lace evening gloves and an ostrich-feather fan. I didn't have to ask whose things these were.

"He's made a shrine to her," I said bitterly. "A shrine to Mandragora Carfax."

"It's not a shrine. And he didn't make it. But I found these things useful when I came to recreate this house. You should go now. This will be the quickest way." He pulled back a curtain, revealing the full length cheval mirror that I'd first seen in Pyewackets.

"It was you." I stared at him. "*You* bought the mirror from Dorian's shop."

"Indeed I did. I certainly didn't want you to get your hands on it."

"But now I must use this mirror as a portal."

"And if you're a true witch, you will be able to do that. But is your magic the equal of hers, dead as she has been for longer than you have lived?"

"One day, my magic will prove to be far more than equal." I walked up to the mirror. I couldn't see my reflection, Instead, there she was, Mandragora Carfax, looking younger than when I'd seen her last and far more beautiful. She was smiling at me, mocking and superior.

"Aroint thee witch!" I slapped the palm of my hand against the pitted glass. "Go! You're dead. You've been dead for decades. Go! I am the sorceress Morg..."

"Enough! Silence! You forget yourself." Konrad lifted his hand and moved it in an arc across the mirror. "Since I wish you to leave, I will assist you." As the silver of his snake ring, the ouroboros swallowing its tail, glimmered in the gas-light, the glass began to fragment, and then to dissolve, turning into a waterfall of iridescent liquid. "Go now." He propelled me forward with such force that I stumbled. And then I found myself sprawled out face down on the floor in the middle of Pyewacket's, exactly where the mirror used to stand.

"*Oh, my giddy aunt*!" Dorian emerged from the stock room, his face wreathed in astonishment. "Are you all right?"

"I think so." I raised myself up to a sitting position. "Yes, I'm fine. Nothing's broken."

"Well, that's good." He winked at me. "I can't have customers falling over in the shop and suing me for negligence, not that you would, of course. Just one thing, though." He glanced across at the door where the closed sign was facing outwards. "I locked up hours ago. As a matter of curiosity, how did you get in?"

"I came through a time portal," I said. I had some idea that speaking the truth would make such an outrageous impression on him, Dorian would simply laugh and assume I was drunk.

"Oh, that's all right then." He sounded reassured. "I *knew* you couldn't be a professional burglar. So, let me guess, you've been back to 1897 and visited 23 Coleton Street. Fancy some jasmine tea?"

"What did you just say?" I stared at him.

"I asked if you fancied some jasmine tea. But if you don't fancy jasmine tea, there's always camomile or even...."

"No, not the tea," I said. "You know I didn't mean the tea. I can't believe what you just said. You've known all along, haven't you? About Mandragora and Llewellyn and the house in Coleton Street and what happened in 1897."

"Of course I knew. I was there."

"You were...oh! I get it! You're the young actor, aren't you, the one who's mentioned in Llewellyn's book, his *Confession?* You're one of the nine cursed immortals."

"I am." He smiled. "Although perhaps I should correct you and say I am one of the surviving seven."

"I see. I suppose I should be furious with you. But I like you too much for that. So you knew exactly what you were doing when you sold me those things, the cloak, the boots, the key, and the mirror."

"I did," he admitted. "I had an instinctive feeling that you were the next true owner of Mandragora's power the first time you walked in here. And then, when you found the key, that was the clincher."

"Dorian," I said. "It's time you confessed."

We sat at a small rosewood table, drinking fragrant tea out of delicate Minton china cups by the light of a Tiffany lamp. Dorian opened his photograph album, a large tome with marbled covers, interleaved with pages of tissue paper.

"It's all very well to admit you've been around for over a hundred years without ageing," he said. "But I always think it's nice to be able to prove that assertion. So here I am," he turned a page and pointed to a grainy black and white photograph, "in the chorus of a production of *Chu Chin Chow*, 1916, at His Majesty's. And this," he turned the page, "is *Rose-Marie*, on Broadway, 1924. And jumping a few decades, if you look at this picture of the cast line up for *Perchance to Dream*, there I am again. Of course, I didn't always use the same stage name. That would have excited the wrong kind of comment."

"Were you ever a chorus boy at the Alhambra?" I asked.

"Yes, I was. That was where I was working when Mandragora invited me to attend her salon. I adored her."

"You did?"

"Oh, yes. She could be very charming. But she had a temper too. And after that night at Coleton Street she became bitter. It was sad."

"I have reason to believe she seduced a boy of fourteen when she was a woman of forty. That's a crime, isn't it?"

"Not in 1875, it wasn't." He grinned. "The age of consent has varied considerably over the centuries."

"It still doesn't seem right to me. I think she exploited Llewellyn when he was too young to know any better."

"Oh, you can't judge the last century by the standards of today. Not in my view. She was a free spirit. A sorceress. And she helped Arawn Llewellyn become the most powerful adept in London. Hey, look at this." He turned the page of his album. "My one TV performance. Third Dalek from the left in *Dr Who*."

"That's lovely, Dorian," I couldn't help smiling. "But I want to know more about Mandragora Carfax. If she was forty in 1875, then she must have been born in 1835, so when she died in 1901..."

"Oh, but she didn't. Die in 1901, I mean."

"But I found her tomb in the old cemetery and the inscription says..."

"It says that was when she departed 'that life'. Not 'this life'. It's a rather clever clue, reflecting the fact that the reports of her death were faked. What really happened in 1901 was that she left the country, went to America, and had a second life that lasted another twenty six years."

"A second life?"

"Yes. As Carmelia Grande."

"Carmelia Grande? The silent screen actress who used to take her cat with her into the Algonquin Hotel?"

"Indeed. Except," he grinned wickedly, "it wasn't usually her cat she was carrying in that basket. More often than not it was her latest young lover that she'd subjected to a shape-shifting spell. She was something of a Circe."

"Did you know that a prolonged period of transmogrification can kill a man?"

"Oh, she never killed anyone."

She nearly did. I decided not to share this thought. "So," I said. "She isn't in that tomb at all?"

"Oh, but she is. At the very end, she did return to England and she died in a hotel room in Bayswater. And so I was there at her real funeral, in the nineteen twenties. It was a private affair, at dead of night. There were three of us in attendance; myself, Carfax, and an employee of the cemetery who was only too happy to accept a lavish bribe for his assistance. We placed her in the coffin that had been empty since 1901, and put a number of plants on the body, corpse-grass and devil's trefoil, meadow-stink and toad-wort to put her spirit at rest. Of course, it didn't work. Carfax attempted the spell, but he was never more than an amateur. And I'm no adept at all."

"I thought Lord Carfax was killed in the First World War."

"That's what he wanted people to think, 'missing presumed dead'. But the truth of the matter is, he was a deserter and had taken on a false identity. He didn't die until 1960, when he fell under an underground train."

"Fell?"

"The circumstances were mysterious."

"I see." I decided not to pursue this. "So, when you said you found that trunk in old Mr Rogers' stock room, it wasn't true? You had it all the time?"

"No, I *did* find it in old Rogers' stock room. That was true. Where I was rather economical with the truth was when I pretended not to know anything about the contents. It was necessary to keep that back from you." He picked a jasmine flower out of his tea and turned it over in his fingers. "The terms and conditions of her passing meant that only a true witch could inherit her artefacts and that the true witch must discover them for herself. I waited for the right person. And then you appeared, Jeanie Gowdie. And you found the key to her casket. And now, of course, you're entitled to take possession of that too."

"So, are you going to give it to me? The casket?"

"I can't. I don't have it. It was far too full of potent magic to be left in my possession."

"So where is it?"

"It's in her tomb. She won't want you to take it, but you must fight her for it. You'll have to open her coffin. The casket's in there, resting under her feet." He winked at me, playful as ever. "I do hope you're feeling brave."

Forty Seven

There can be no punishment too severe with which to smite a witch-finder. Curse his gonads, rotte his braine, inflict foul-smelling miasmas on his senses, bang kettle drums under his window at night, lette him eate the excrement of newts. But above all, join with others when making a firm stande against him. He is onlie one manne and there is strengthe in numbers.

The words of Grandma Gandy, written downe in the yeare 1696.

Bushy was asleep, snoring loudly on my couch, having neglected, I noted with some dismay, to take off his boots.

"Gowdie?" He turned over drowsily. "Oh, you're back." He sat up, yawning and rubbing his eyes. "Bloody hell, you've been out all night. What have you been doing?"

"I don't want to talk about it."

"Seriously?"

"Not right now, anyway." I switched on the lamp. "Oh, I see, the electricity's back on. That's something."

"Yeh" He nodded. "And it was weird. The lights didn't come back on all at once. First they started flashing on and off, and then I heard scratching at the door. I don't think that was an ordinary blackout. Gowdie, have you still got that book here? You know, the one that Louisa May Alcott *didn't* write? Because I think something or someone's after it. Or worse still, someone or something is after you."

"Yes, I've still got it," I told him. "I've hidden it behind the panelling by the fireplace, and it's protected by a spell."

"And what are you going to do with it?"

"Nothing yet. Just keep it safe from Hopkins."

"Sure it's safe? Like I said, I think someone's after you."

"Someone is. But it's not Hopkins."

"Then who?"

I took a deep breath. Time to confide in him.

"Her name is Mandragora Carfax, and she's been dead for nearly fifty years. But you know about her, don't you? You've read that book, although, in fact, it doesn't tell you everything. But don't ask me too explain all the details just yet. There's something else I have to say. I'm sorry that you've been turned out of the caretaker's room, but you can't stay here. You can see how it is. I haven't got a spare bed, and this flat is really no more than just this one room and..."

"Worried about what the neighbours upstairs might think?" He grinned at me.

"No. And there aren't any people upstairs. I'm the only occupant of this house."

"What? You're joking, empty flats in this part of London? How can that be?"

"The letting agent said something about dodgy plaster in the ceilings up there. So they can't let the whole place out. I wasn't sure whether to believe him, but I didn't care, as the rent for this place was quite cheap."

"Then that's perfect, don't you see? I can sleep upstairs at night, won't take me a minute to pick a few locks, and then I can keep an eye on this place for you in the day time."

"OK." I could see the logic of this. "But whatever you do, don't break anything and don't open the door to anyone."

"Wouldn't dream of it." He yawned again, and stretched. "By the way, what happened to that cat you had with you when you went to Pendle?"

"He's been returned to his rightful home." I felt a lump gathering in my throat.

"That's a relief. The last thing we need right now is some cat prowling around. Hey," he stared at me. "Are you all right, Gowdie? You look a bit pensive."

"I'm just thinking about my favourite book, the one I loved as a child, *The Wizard of Oz*." I said.

"What's that got to do with anything?"

"Oh, nothing....it just that...I've always been disappointed by the part when Dorothy discovers the Wizard is just an ordinary man who's made the people wear green glass spectacles so that they'll think the Emerald City was real. I want her to meet a real wizard, even one who'd done some very bad things. But I can still have my yellow brick road. Who could come with me if I was Dorothy? It has to be three people. So you could be my scarecrow, and Ernest Brunswicker could be my cowardly lion, and as for the Tin Man..." *Konrad. No friend of mine.* "Actually, I'm not sure I want a tin man after all."

"You've lost me, Gowdie." He got up from the couch. "I haven't got a clue what you're on about. Have you got food in the house? I'm ravenous."

"Cornflakes," I said. "In a packet, behind that curtain. No milk though."

"Better than nothing I suppose."

"You could have brought some groceries on your way here." I said this rather more sharply than I intended.

"What? When I had to lug all those books? Anyway, the only shop round here is some posh deli."

"I love Kosminsky's. And they do sell milk. Oh, for goodness sake, there's no need to rip the packet open like that!"

"All right. Keep your hair on! Sorry. What's got into you?"

"Nothing. I'm just very tired."

I couldn't help reflecting on how trying it was going to be, having Bushy stay here, even if he was going to sleep upstairs. I liked my space to myself, and this wasn't a very big space. And Bushy had many annoying habits. Right now, having shaken some cornflakes into a bowl and spilled some on the floor, he was eating them with his fingers, crunching noisily, as he paced around the room. I reminded myself not to be ungrateful; after all, without his help, I'd never have got to Dr Hecate's or retrieved *The Book of Shadows*. On the other hand, this was Bushy, the person whose unwise enthusiasms had led to a dreadful conflagration, to my injury and my incarceration.

"Look, Gowdie," he said. "I want to help, right? So tell me if there's anything else I can do."

It was as if he'd read my thoughts. And there was, of course, something he could do. I needed to be properly equipped if I was going to confront my most bitter adversary.

"This might sound strange," I began. "But tomorrow night, I'm going to have to break into a tomb in the old cemetery at midnight to retrieve a special casket."

"Bloody hell, Gowdie, that's amazing! Can I come?"

"I'm afraid not. But there are certain things I'm going to need and you could help by getting them for me while I'm at work tomorrow."

"Just say the word, Gowdie." He beamed at me. "You can always rely on your True Thomas."

*

"Ah! Miss Gowdie! You have returned!" Hopkins lumbered towards me as I came through the revolving doors into the entrance hall. "And how gratifying to see that you appear to have retrieved the missing books!" He glanced down at the bulging carrier bag in my hand. "Sadly though, I suspect many of them may prove worthless trash. Still...you have done your duty."

"It was my pleasure." I tried to look as innocent as possible.

"I'm sure it was." There was a nasty edge to his voice as he said this. "No, no...Don't hand that bag to me, all those volumes will need fumigating. Think of the bugs and weevils that could be found in some of our subscribers' homes. You must take them to Miss Nantucket, she is an expert in purification."

I'm sure she is!

"Tell me," he continued. "How did you find Dr Trehearne of Penzance? Is he in good health?"

"I'm afraid not," I told him. "He's suffering from early onset dementia and can remember nothing." I felt rather pleased with this hasty improvisation.

"Ah!" Hopkins looked down his nose at me, old goat-style. "Perhaps that explains why the letter I sent him asking him to assure me of your safe arrival has gone unanswered."

"It certainly explains why I was unable to locate all his missing loans," I smiled at him. "Well, I must get on. I need to catch up with my work."

"Indeed." He nodded. "I'm rather afraid that Miss Tank found certain aspects of the clerical tasks challenging. And as for Professor Goldfarb, she has proved a very unsuitable person. Now that you have returned, I shall consider banning her from the reading room altogether."

"But surely you can't do that?

"Oh, but I can. Now, I shall require a full, detailed report of all your movements of the past few days. Have it on my desk by the end of the day. Oh, and Miss Gowdie?"

"Yes?"

"Please don't ever attempt to challenge my decisions, or there will be consequences."

True, I thought, although they might not be the consequences you have in mind. *He whose trousers are too short will soon develop a genital wart.* I waited until Hopkins had lumbered out of sight before breaking into a broad grin.

"Jeanie!" Gerda jumped up from her table, accidentally knocking a heavy volume to the floor. "Thank goodness you are back."

"Hello, Gerda. Where's Cazzie?" I glanced around the empty tables. "And why is it so quiet in here?"

"Oh," she shrugged. "Miss Tank has been commandeered by Miss Plymouth Rock, yet again. And, as you can see, it has been terrible here...such a purge! Both books and scholars gone! But," she lowered her voice. "I have news for you."

"Let's go into the parcels room." I looked over my shoulder. We appeared to be alone, but who knew where an eavesdropper might be lurking. "We can talk more freely in there."

"So," Gerda began. "You remember how I told you about my search for Ernest Brunsvicker?" Vell, I have found him. I returned to his flat and this time, he vas there. We talked. We talked a lot."

"And how is he?"

"Far from happy, as you can imagine. He has been unable to find any other employment, and besides, he does not vant any other employment. This vas the job he loved. In other libraries, they vould make him leave his bicycle outside, and now, at the unemployment office they tell him...but this is not the main thing I vant to tell. He say something very odd to me; a message for you. He was so vorried about you. He said...vat he said sounded a little mad."

"Tell me, Gerda, whatever it is."

"He said 'Tell Jeanie the vitch-finders are coming. Tell Jeanie to be prepared.'"

Forty Eight

One of the sadde taskes you may have to performe, as you grow older, is the laying out of the dead. Flinche not, but have reverence. Stoppe the bodily orifices with linen soaked in cleansing dewe, close the eyes with cold pebbles and secure the jawe. Dress the bodie in cleane cotton. Then saye a prayere, begging the good Lorde that he or she wille be stille forever, and not haunte those who live. Never assume that a spirite is at rest.

The Guidance of Goodwife Gurlie for this daye and every daye

Bats were flying above the dark trees in the old cemetery, an encouraging sign, since for many in the Craft these beloved little flittermice, as Nana and I used to call them, are symbols of good luck. I squeezed through a gap in the railings carrying my shopping bag; it contained a number of practical items, a chisel, a torch, a small garden trowel, some bulbs of garlic, a carton of rock salt, a claw-headed hammer, a jar containing the skeleton of a deformed frog, a black candle, five goat skulls and a pair of gardening gloves. Bushy had been excellent when it came to equipping me for this expedition. Perhaps my high heeled boots, cloak and long red velvet dress weren't particularly suitable for negotiating the overgrown section of the burial ground or for committing a necropolis burglary, but if

I was going to confront Mandragora Carfax, I wanted to do so in style.

As I made my way through the long grasses, ferns, clumps of sticky weed and tangles of brambles, stamping down the undergrowth as best I could, I just hoped I wouldn't be seen from the street by a passing police officer, since the moon was full and unnaturally bright. It seemed I wouldn't need my torch until I was inside the tomb itself.

I stood in front of Abraham Matthewson's mausoleum, gazed at the figures on either side of the copper gates, the beatific marble angel and the grimacing, predatory satyr. A Manichean polarity, what did it suggest about the characters of the dead who lay inside? Nothing comforting, that was for certain and if they'd been placed there as guardians, then I might have to contend with more than the angry spirit of the dead sorceress. I re- read the inscription:

Abraham Matthewson 1793-1888. Alchemist, Inventor Poet
Also daughter of the above, Mary, otherwise
Mandragora Carfax
Departed that life January 10th 1901.
'Judge not, lest ye be judged.'

Judge not...That was a Biblical quotation wasn't it? How odd that it should be here, on such a pagan memorial; perhaps it had been chosen to give an air of respectability, just as 'Inventor and Poet' told so little of the full truth. But there was no time to reflect on this: I wanted to search for another inscription, one that I'd missed the first time I was here.

I put on the gardening gloves and knelt down, pulling the ivy to one side, searching the area at the foot of the steps. Ah! Here it was! A slab of granite embedded in the earth and encrusted with moss. One letter was just visible, an elaborate 'C' in gothic script. I took the trowel and scraped at the slab. At last, the full inscription was revealed:

Carmelia Grande, enchantress of the silver screen.
Interred here August 1927

Enchantress. That was a clever touch. So here it was, three names on a mausoleum that only contained two coffins. And now I must look for the mirror; there was a chance it was still here. I hitched up my dress, searching on my hands and knees, raking through the grass with my gloved hands. There was no sign of it, just a few of the scattered tea lights and the metal dish I'd found before, but then something glinted in the moonlight, something familiar. I picked it up. Yes, it was a gold ring bearing the emblem of a plumed dragon with a ruby for its eye. I had never doubted that Dr Hecate was right, but here was the absolute proof that *he* had been here. I could only hope that sooner or later I'd be able to return his property to him. In the meantime, I slipped the ring on to the ribbon around my neck alongside the key for safekeeping.

I stood up, considering my next move. I supposed I could always take the hammer and use brute force in an attempt to get those copper gates open, but in view of the nature of my mission, magic seemed the more appropriate approach. I took the salt out of my bag and sprinkled it in front of the steps, hoping that this traditional protection against evil would have some effect, then arranged the bulbs of garlic at the feet of the two guardians. Taking a deep breath, I raised my hands:

"*Admit me, in the names of Artemis, Selene, Arianrhod, Hecate and Elatha.*"

I knew that the names of the five lunar goddesses from the Greek and the Celtic traditions have considerable power when spoken by a true witch by moonlight, but I also knew there was a risk of collateral damage if you happen to be in a graveyard where the most undesirable dead things can be raised. I could hear a rustling in the undergrowth behind me; I knew better than to turn and look. I raised my voice:

"Artemis, Selene, Arianrhod, Hecate and Elatha, aid me in the moonlight that you have created. Open the gates to your sister of the Craft."

Had I imagined it, or did that satyr just move? No, it can't have done, although its demeanour, crouching towards me and, I noted, astonishingly priapic, was definitely menacing.

"Are you there, Mandragora Carfax? I've come to take your power. You can call off your guardian." I pointed to the sandstone figure. "He isn't worrying me. In fact, if that's all he's got, I'm not impressed. *Artemis, Selene, Arianrhod, Hecate and Elatha."* I looked up at the moon. "Luna, I call upon you to aid me."

Were these words enough? Perhaps there were others I could use. Last night, in Coleton Street, hadn't *he* been talking about the moon? When I'd assumed he was rambling, mightn't he also have been remembering the fragments of a spell? I held up the gold key:

"I call upon the waters of moon to aid me. *Mare frigoris, mare vaporum, oceanus procellaum, mare vaporum, oceanus procellaum.* I am the last heritant of England and I demand to be admitted!"

To my surprise, the gates clanged open, sending a cloud of dust into the air.

Enter then, you naive girl! You will regret this!

It hardly seemed like a welcome, but I stepped inside all the same.

Skeleton leaves were drifting across the stone floor, old cobwebs floated like sails in the high corners of the ceiling. There were two shelves on either side of the mausoleum, each one bearing a coffin. I could see that the one on the left was the oldest, covered in decaying, faded leather with studs along the edges and with a small, round box in a matching style standing on the top. So Abraham Matthewson must be in the coffin and that box contained his viscera. Not a pleasant thought.

The coffin on the right was of a sleeker design, made from polished oak and with elaborate brass handles in the shape of the eternal snake, Ouroboros, swallowing its tail, just as on Konrad's ring. I shone my torch on the lid; there it was, a silver plate stamped with a monogram matching the one on the tomb, the mirror and the key. I felt more than a little apprehensive, standing there, knowing as I did, what lay underneath. Here was one advantage of that surreptitious interment of 1927. It seemed there'd been no noisy nailing down, nothing that might attract attention, so my claw hammer and chisel wouldn't be needed. It was a heavy piece of wood, however, and I couldn't lift it. The most I could do was slide it across. *The casket's there, resting under her feet.* A thought that was enough to send me into a spin of panic. I had to keep my nerve. *Please,* I thought, as I placed my hands on the coffin lid, *please don't let the shroud have rotted. I don't want to see her face.* But what would I see? I didn't know whether the head would be well-preserved, or mummified or crawling with putrefaction, or just a bleached skull. Since this was the resting place of a sorceress whose spirit was still earth-bound, perhaps the ordinary rules of decay didn't apply.

'Thinks she's so clever...through the fire, through the fire and through the fire again...'

So the whispering had started, had it? Well, I was used to that. But I wouldn't try to move the coffin lid yet; I needed to set up some further protections first.

I knelt down on the stone floor, shook out the rest of the rock salt into the shape of a pentacle and placed a goat skull at each point. "*In the names of Charon and Hades, keep the spirits of the dead confined to your realm and...*"

My invocation was interrupted by a violent crash as the coffin lid slid across of its own volition, then fell against the wall, sending up a cloud of brick dust and dislodging a large spider that must have been dreamily snoozing in its web. The spider scuttled along my arm, causing me no anguish whatsoever, since I'm good with arachnids, but the realisation that Mandragora had awakened was another matter altogether.

Torch in hand, I bent over the open coffin, steeling myself to confront whatever was in there. I couldn't see the remains of anything human, only what looked like a pile of hay. But then I remembered Dorian's account of the interment, all the plants and herbs that had been placed on the body. She, or whatever was left of her, must be under all this dried-out vegetation.

I put on my gardening gloves and reached inside, moving the rustling, dead plants at the foot of the coffin to one side. *Oh!* Here it was! A gold casket with a lid like an elevated roof, inset with red jewels and imprinted with that gothic 'M'. I knew that I mustn't pick it up immediately; there were certain formalities that must be observed.

I held up the little gold key and began my supplication:

"I call upon thee, Mandragora Carfax, born Mary Matthewson, daughter of the adept Abraham Matthewson, to relinquish your power to me, Jeanie Morgana Gowdie, the last English Heritant. With this key, I will open the box.

With my living strength, I will use your tools. With my power, I will lay you to rest and assist you to move on to the summer-lands. Your spirit will no longer haunt this place and..."

"Ha!" The mocking, high-pitched laugh echoed around me, bouncing off the damp walls, shaking the cobwebs and threatening to make my ear drums bleed. "*Ha! Ha! Ha!*" There was a flash of lightning. The dead leaves at my feet began to smoulder.

"I abjure and command thee, Mandragora Carfax..."

I was forced to step back as the leaves caught fire, sending sparks shooting up towards the ceiling.

"Command *me!*" The hoarse voice was like a rusty spring unwinding. "You, who have yet to come of age? *You* should fear me. You know what I can do, but lest you forget ...meet my friends!"

Eeuurgh! This wasn't good at all. The burning leaves had turned into fat, pallid grave-worms, hundreds of them, moving about my feet, gross and questing, their blind heads turning towards me, sniffing me out. I raised my voice:

"Leave this place, accept your death, the summer-lands beckon you." Stepping back, I continued to hold up the key. "*Sinite hoc loco, accipere obitum, uos aestate terra...*"

"You will never take anything of mine!" More grave-worms; they were dropping down from the ceiling now, falling on to my shoulders, into my hair. *Don't flinch, don't brush them away, they're not real...*

"*Da tuis legatum ad vivum.*" How glad I was I'd excelled at Latin at school, despite the fact the other girls had bullied me for it. "Give your legacy to the living!"

"Mine!" There was a clap of thunder, a wild mewing like a colony of diseased feral cats; the rich, sickly smell of putrefaction filled my nostrils. "*Ha! Ha! Ha!*"

"All right." I lowered the key. "I'm impressed, but that's enough. You can cut out the melodrama."

There was a long silence. Then,

"You dare speak to me in that common, vulgar way?"

"Yes, I do dare. Just listen to me, Mandragora Carfax, you need this as much as I do. Why spend eternity in a hell of your own making when you could journey peacefully to the summer-lands? I don't understand it, but our destinies are linked and you can only live through me. There's nothing for you here. You're dead! Dead! Dead! Dead! Now I'm taking your box and I'm taking your power and that's the end of it. Out of my way. *Vicissim!*"

And with this last retort, I leaned over the coffin, grabbed the casket, and cradling it in my arms, ran out of the mausoleum, ignoring her shrieks of abuse and the maggots wriggling through my hair.

I stumbled across the tangle of grass and weeds; brambles caught on the skirt of my dress. At one point, I tripped on the hem of my cloak and almost fell. And then, at last, I arrived at the bench near the grave of Samuel Greatorex, and there, much to my surprise, was Old Nora. She was standing on the path, leaning over the handlebars of her supermarket trolley and the moment she saw me, she broke into a round of applause.

"Yes, that's the way to do it!" she cackled. "You got her all right. You got her. Wages paid in full!" And with a fiendish, gap-toothed grin, she took the necklace of apache tears out of her pocket and flung them unceremoniously at my feet.

I bent down and picked up the necklace, hardly able to believe this turn of fortune. I'd got it back. *His* gift to me, the stones that signified sorrow transformed into eternal beauty. I hadn't lost it after all, even if I had lost him to madness. But Konrad was right; I was the person who'd set that disaster in motion. And somehow I must make amends. In my anxiety to take possession of Mandragora's box, I'd forgotten something. Something that was almost as all-consuming as my quest to come of age.

"Nora?" I stood up, clutching the necklace. "Nora, thank you." I looked around, but she had gone.

Suddenly, I knew what else I had to do. I placed Mandragora's casket under a yew tree and set a protection spell on them. After then, with the apache tears in my hand, I walked back towards the tomb.

Forty Nine

The door of the mausoleum was still open; I must take care to close it before I left. No-one must ever know I'd been here, disturbing the dead. But I still had unfinished business; it mustn't end this way.

"May I enter?" I stood on the threshold. "I want to speak to Mary Matthewson."

*Mary Matthewson is dead...you said so yourself...*The voice was like the creak of a rusty hinge and it was filled with bitterness and contempt.

"Not entirely. I believe it's Mandragora Carfax who's dead, and her power has diminished now that I own all her significant things. The key, the casket, the mirror."

There's no need to gloat.

"Oh, I'm not gloating." I stepped forward. "I'm simply stating a fact. Before you took your true name of Mandragora, before you disguised yourself as Carmelia Grande, before anger and shame entered your life, you were Mary Matthewson, daughter of the alchemist Abraham Matthewson and a novice witch. Like me, you were looking forward to a shining future. And it's Mary I'm addressing."

Get on with it, can't you?

"I will, although you must understand I'm making this up as I go along. I don't have a spell or an invocation for this. I'm just talking from the heart."

Heart! Ha! Ha! H...

"I think I told you to cut the histrionics," I said, in as mild a tone I could muster. "Listen, Mary Matthewson, do you remember the young girl you once were? Perhaps it was the same for both of us. When I was almost thirteen, my Nana told me that one day, I'd be a powerful sorceress. She'd seen me in her scrying vessel, standing with a powerful magus by my side, the two of us crowned with lights. She said it was my destiny."

Why tell me this? Why should I care?

"Because I believe our destinies are linked. I believe your power will live on through me. What life you can still have, you will have through me. And when it comes to love..."

Love? Why mention that?

"Because I believe we share in that too. Because I love him, Arawn Llewellyn. And I can't believe you didn't love him once."

Of course I loved him...my beautiful boy...

"Then please don't hurt him any more. While you cling to jealousy and revenge, you're trapped here, in hell. You need to move on, into the summer-lands where you will find peace."

It was then that I heard something, a very quiet sound I'd often heard in the dormitory at Crowsmuir, in the early hours of the morning. I'd never known then what to do about it and I wasn't sure what to do now, but it seemed to be a hopeful sign, the sound of sobs being stifled and suppressed, the sound of grief.

"So I've taken a lot from you," I said. "And I might even take more. But I want to give you something in return." I placed the necklace in the coffin. "*He* gave me this and now I offer it to you in peace and understanding. I hope it protects and comforts you as you move on to the summer-lands."

I'm making you no promises.

"No, I suppose not," I said. "But thank you all the same."

As I left the tomb, I half-expected to hear that savage, mocking laughter again. But there was nothing but the ghost of a sigh, and the whisper of a dry leaf as it blew across the ground. I retrieved the casket from under the yew tree, and then sat on the bench until dawn, half-hoping that Nora would return and I could go to the Coleton Street of 1897 again but it seemed I was back in the everyday world of the twentieth century with no hope of leaving it again.

The gates must have opened early, either that, or I'd lost track of time. I watched as people began coming in to the cemetery, joggers, a mourner carrying flowers, and people walking dogs. The world seemed benevolent and peaceful in the pale winter morning. There was a domestic atmosphere, a woman filling her watering can from the tap at the edge of the path, another tending a grave as if engaged in their weekend gardening. I saw a young man with a rucksack kneeling by a granite stone; he was holding a string of beads, probably a rosary, and moving his lips rapidly. If I'd seen him at dusk, I'd have feared he was a necromancer, but now, I assumed, he was just expressing his piety and grief. A woman passed me, pushing a pram; a man was trimming the grass. If any of the dead were going to rise, I doubted if they'd do it now, in the clear light of day, with so many people going about their normal business. I could only hope that Mandragora Carfax was at peace at last.

Bushy was waiting for me in my flat when I returned.

"Have you got it, Gowdie?" There was an eager expression on his face.

"Yes." I took the casket out from under my cloak and set it on the table. "I have it."

"Amazing!" He gazed at it with obvious approval. "Have you opened it?"

"No. Not yet. I will...later." I felt deeply weary. "Right now, all I want is a cup of coffee .and some toast. And after that..."

"What?"

"After that, I'm going to tell you the plans for my Coming of Age. I've thought this through carefully and with your help, it should all go smoothly."

"Tell me now!" His eyes lit up. "I can't take the suspense!" He whirled around the room, arms outstretched. "I've been waiting for this for so long!"

"All right, I'll tell you," I said. "Only please sit down. You're making me dizzy."

"OK." He sat cross-legged on the floor. "So shoot."

"These are my plans," I began. "I'm going to hold it in the entrance hall of the library. There will be guests; regular readers and friends. They mustn't know the ceremony is anything to do with magic; that will be for their protection. But they can receive an invitation that says it's my twenty first birthday party."

"You're twenty one in March, aren't you?"

"Yes, but I can't wait until then. We have to move fast; set a date in a week's time. So, among the guests, there must be seven friends who've been especially chosen to take part in the ritual. This is called the Summoning of the Seven. They have to be the embodiment of seven figures drawn from a pack of cards known as the Arcana Magi. I drew the cards when I was with Dr Hecate; the Mystic, the Scholar, the Singer, the Imp, the Saracen, the Helper and the Fool. The Fool is the leader. None of the seven must be a practitioner of magic themselves, and the Fool has to summon the other six, bring them to the ceremony by way of a trick or a ruse. I've decided who they all are, except for the Fool,that is."

"I'd have thought you'd have known that straight away." Bushy grinned. "I'm your Fool, Gowdie. I can't let you choose you anyone else. Consider me your Fool."

"All right." Even as I said it, I had a feeling of unease. Could I really trust Bushy not to make some dreadful error, to get carried away, just as he had done all those years ago at Knox Hill?

"After all," he said. "I love tricks and ruses, they're my speciality. So, what if tell them I'm arranging a *surprise* birthday party for you?"

"That's sounds perfect," I agreed. Ah! Perhaps it would all be fine.

"And who are these six people?"

"I'll write the names down for you. Three of them work at the library, two of them come from round here. One of them might be more difficult to persuade to come along, he's not a party person, but you can ask Gerda Goldfarb to help you."

"Oh, trust me, Gowdie, I'll cope. So what happens once everyone's gathered?"

"I adopt my true name, take possession of Mandragora Carfax's artefacts, and then I perform a spell, smiting Hopkins and preventing him from ever entering the library again. We have to make sure he's not in the building and we don't want Clemency there either. Clemency leaves at eight, but from what you've told me, Hopkins can be found prowling around at any time of the day or night."

"It's risky," Bushy agreed. "We need something fool-proof. I know! What if I forged a letter inviting Hopkins and

Clemency Nantucket to an Awards Ceremony for Senior Archivists and Library Custodians at an exclusive five star hotel in Manchester on that night? They'd be told they'd won a really prestigious award and that a car would be sent to collect them. We arrange the car, and it'll take them somewhere else up in the North, say a disused herring packing factory in Hull, and by the time they realise they've been tricked, it'll be too late. I'm a genius, Gowdie, an absolute genius!" He leapt up, bouncing around the room, clicking his fingers, beaming excitedly. "And what about this smiting spell?" he asked. "Do you want me to help with that? Let me look at the Book of Shadows, there must be something in that."

"No! You mustn't, that would be going against Jabez Corey's wishes. He specifically said..."

"What? What did he say?"

"It doesn't matter. And don't worry about the spell. Some people known as the Elders sent it to me this morning."

Fifty

To make a Salem Salad

A Salem salad is best prepared by a Carib woman of mature years, one skilled in singing and knowledge of the arts of her race. Ask her nicely, and she will helpe you. This anciente spelle will repel all witch-finders, puritans and enemies of the magical arts. It runs thus: take all that is most noxious to hand, asafoetida or the devil's dung, fly alagaric, all types of poison mushrumps, the death's cap toadstool, gathered on a foggie dawne. It should be mixed while cursing he who is to be smitten, heated over a peat fire, and then the fumes being unleashed will repel the enemy.

The receipt of Grandma Gandy, first written down in the year 1695. Stille useful todaye.

Cazzie was waiting for me on the steps of the library.

"Hi!" She greeted me with a grin.

"Hello, Cazzie."

"Poor old you." Cazzie was playing her part well. "Bet you feel pissed off at having to come into work in the evening for a meeting on your day off!"

"Oh well." I shrugged. "Duty calls."

"Shame you missed today. It's been great here without that cow Nantucket or old Jack-Ups. Apparently, they've gone to an award ceremony up North. Can't understand it! Who'd give those two tossers an award?"

"It does sound strange." *Clever Bushy. His ploy had worked!*

"It's been really peaceful all day without the pair of them." Cazzie wrinkled her nose as if about to sniff, and then stopped, apparently remembering she didn't need to indulge in that habit any more. Nana's remedy, complete with the powdered moss from the grave of a drowned sailor, seemed to be working. "Mind you," she added. "It's just as well they haven't been around to complain. There's been a really bad smell in the library all day. It seemed to be coming from Psyche's place."

Ah! The Salem Salad, being prepared according to the recipe of Grandma Gandy. *'Best prepared by a Carib woman of mature years.'* Brilliant!

"Anyway," Cazzie took hold of my arm. "Let's go into the meeting. Mind how you go. There's been a bit of a blackout. Oh, blimey." She held her nose. "That smell!"

The only light in the darkened entrance hall was the flicker of the brazier's flames as they lit up Antioch Corey's death mask. The room was so silent that for a moment, I was afraid we were the only two people here. What if Bushy's invitations had been ignored and....

"*Surprise!*"

An array of coloured disco lights flashed on and off as voices called out in unison and people stepped out from their hiding places behind the pillars. In a moment, I was surrounded by well-wishers. I felt overwhelmed. I hadn't expected so many people. Less than four months ago, I didn't have a single friend in the world but now here were some of the regular readers; Dr Mollison, Maurice Tremlett and Mr Peabody, and here was Dorian, holding a cluster of rainbow-coloured balloons marked twenty one, and there was Ernest, nervously clinging to his bicycle and doing his best to smile.

"Happy Birthday, Jeanie!" Nasir held up a bottle of champagne. "Blimey, fancy you working in a place like this!"

"Happy Birthday, Jeanie." Gerda placed an iced cake with twenty one candles on a table in front of me. "And vat a beautiful dress you are veering."

"Thank you, thank you everyone."

Psyche didn't come forward but she waved from her position near the stairs where she was stirring a large jam-making vat. It was as well she was keeping her distance; Grandma Gandy's recipe was certainly giving off a powerful smell, just as Cazzie said.

"Happy Birthday, Jeanie." Bushy jumped up and down. He looked completely manic. "Come on, everyone! After me!"

"Happy Birthday to you, Happy Birthday to you..."

The singing was cacophonous, especially with Bushy's seal-like barking. Cazzie was definitely off-key. Streamers flew through the air; Nasir whirled a football rattle. I was beginning to feel alarmed as well as touched. It was so kind of so many people to come here, just for me; there was that Japanese gentleman who once held a tea ceremony in the reading room for example. But now it was all getting too noisy, too frenetic; I couldn't think how I was going to switch the mood in order to conduct my solemn ceremony.

"Come and blow out your candles!" Gerda beckoned me.

"Of course." I leaned forward and blew on the flames. Thank you. Thank you everyone. This is wonderful."

"Speech!" Bushy shouted.

"Yes." I said. "There will be a speech. But first, I'm going to have to ask for quiet. I do need to explain something. I hope you'll be patient with me. As some of you may know, this is a special day for me. So I'd like you to indulge me while I carry out a ritual that means a lot to me. Thank you." I snapped my fingers and a glittery, seven-pointed star appeared on the floor in front of the death-mask of Antioch Corey.

"Blimey," Cazzie gasped.

"I'm going to ask seven of you to take up a position," I continued. "One at each point of the star. This has to be done in silence. I crave your indulgence." I held up my hands and waited. Then, trembling slightly, I began:

"I summon my colleague and friend, Ernest Brunswicker to take up his position. Ernest, you have seen the infinite. You are the Mystic. I drew your card."

I was worried about Ernest. I knew he hated parties and I was concerned that the strangeness of this one might appal him. It seemed, however that he was completely unfazed; nodding his head, he wheeled his bicycle forward and took up his position.

"I summon my friend, Gerda Goldfarb, to take up her position. Gerda, you are the Scholar, I drew your card. I summon Psyche, our friend and colleague, to take up her position. Psyche, you are the Singer. I drew your card. I summon my friend Nasir, whose parents were born on the shores of the Sea of Marmara to take up his position. Nasir, you are the Saracen. I drew your card."

"Saracen?" Grinning but bemused, Nasir moved forward. "Ain't that a bit racist?"

"Not at all," I assured him. "The Saracens were brave and noble fighters and gave all those tiresome and interfering Crusaders a run for their money."

"Right." He took up his position.

"I summon my assistant Cazzie Tank, to take up her position," I continued. "Cazzie, you are the Helper. I drew your card."

"Oh, wow!" Cazzie exclaimed as she came forward. "Me? I get to play?" She took up her position with as much solemnity as she could muster.

"I summon Dorian Pyewacket, imp by name, to take up his position. Dorian, I drew your card. And now I summon the seventh, my friend Bushy, known here as Jim the caretaker. Bushy, you are the Fool. I drew your card. Now the seven are summoned."

"The seven are, indeed, summoned," Bushy said solemnly. "And I, the Fool, will unveil the instruments of power." He walked over to a small table and whipped off the black cloth to reveal Mandragora's casket. "Now I, the Fool, will resume my place as I invite the novice to perform her Coming of Age ceremony."

I stood at the table, gazing at the assembled group, pleased to see that everyone was taking this seriously. Then I held up the gold key and began my invocation.

"I, Jeanie Gowdie, the grand-daughter of Maudie Herrick, descendent of the bloodline of Isobel Gowdie, do this day adopt my true name of Morgana. With this key, I will open the box and take possession of these instruments, once the property of the sorceress Mandragora Carfax." I unlocked the box and threw back the lid. "Now I take this ancient scarab brooch, this finger bone of a Barbary ape, this runic blade, this wand, this human skull, this pewter scrying dish and this black mirror of the ancient alchemists, and with them, will perform a spell of deep and lasting power. I am guided by the wisdom of the Elders, the ancestors of the Magus, Jabez Corey, and of Antioch Corey, the founder of this place and..."

"Miss Jeanie Gowdie. You think you're clever, don't you?"

There was a gasp from the assembled company. I looked up at the gallery, the sight of the two figures standing up there made my stomach flip over. It wasn't just the shock of their arrival that made me feel faint with fear; it was the way Hopkins and Clemency were dressed. They were wearing long white robes and pointed hoods similar to the costumes of the Ku Klux Klan, except that their faces were unmasked. There was a coil of rope over Hopkins's arm; Clemency was carrying a set of gleaming, metal instruments. Anyone with a rudimentary knowledge of seventeenth century witch-hunts would have known what those were. I'd seen plenty of old woodcuts depicting those elaborate handles and long, pointed blades ; the weapons of torture known as 'bodkins', used by witch-finders for detecting the devil's mark.

Keep calm, Jeanie. Remember who you are. Remember whose power you are about to adopt. Mandragora Carfax would have turned them both into rats on the spot. You can do the same.

"Stay where you are!" I pointed the finger bone of the Barbary ape at them. "Both of you. You'll regret intruding here."

Hopkins threw back his head and looked down his nose at me in his old-goat style. "Do you think to intimidate *me* with such a piece of silly flim-flammery, Miss Gowdie?" he demanded. "You'll have to do better than this if you wish to outface an experienced witch-finder."

"What's wrong with you, you miserable old fart?" Cazzie yelled up at him. "It's just a surprise party for her birthday."

"Oh, is that what you suppose?" Hopkins began to descend the stairs, his demeanour oozing with deliberation and menace. "But it isn't, you see. Not her birthday. Not until March. And I am the one who has prepared the surprise."

"*The obeah man, he come, he come and take you away...*" Psyche raised her arms and began to sway gently.

"Stop that racket." Clemency's face was a mask of hate. "Stop that unholy row."

"You see him soon, the Obeah man..."

"That's enough!" Hopkins walked over to Psyche and slapped her face. She didn't flinch, but there was a general murmur of disgust around the room. Ernest bounded forward with his bicycle, launching himself at Hopkins.

"Coward!" he cried. "Cowardly to hit a woman."

"On the contrary," Hopkins said. "It takes courage to confront a voodoo queen, for that is what this woman is, hiding here in plain sight with her mop and bucket. I would step back if I were you." He gazed at the gathering, several of whom had already retreated behind the pillars or to the sides of the room in their dismay. I didn't blame them; most of them were shy, scholarly people who'd lived their lives amongst the sanctuary of old books, and who had experienced little physical intimidation.

"Dear me," Hopkins murmured. "So many readers in here after closing time. We can't have this flouting of regulations, can we? Some of you will regret this when you're barred from this place. And there will be fines to pay and not just in money. Well now." He advanced towards me. "I know exactly what's going on here. A coming of age ceremony, complete with the Summoning of the Seven and, I daresay, a carefully arranged spell. Is that cauldron over there bubbling for me? Charming. So medieval."

"You ain't supposed to be here," Cazzie told him. "You weren't invited."

"So it would seem." Hopkins smiled faintly. "But as you see, I have taken it upon myself to view these interesting proceedings. Did you really think, Jim the caretaker, or should I say ex-caretaker, that Miss Nantucket and I would be foolish enough to fall for your little ploy and go to

Manchester? We've never left the building. We've been here all the time, spying on you, listening to every word."

"You can keep out of this." I was quivering with anger now. "Psyche and I have cooked up something special for you. And it's what you deserve."

"Ah, but I don't think your spell is going to work, Miss Gowdie," Hopkins turned to me. "You see, you've made rather a hash of summoning your seven. Now, what do we have?" He began counting them off on his fingers. "The mystic, the scholar, the singer, the Saracen, the helper, the imp and the fool. I don't think any of these people qualify."

"Yes they do! I chose them!"

"But you didn't choose well. I don't think Mr Brunswicker is a mystic; he's just a neurotic who suffers from agoraphobia. I have very little opinion of the scholarship of Professor Goldfarb; did you know she sometimes sits in the library reading the cake recipes in *Woman's Realm*? The woman known as Psyche never sings more than a fragment of song and that badly, a Saracen has to be born in Arabia to qualify for that nomenclature, Miss Tank's attempts to help are feeble to say the least, and just because a man adopts the name of an imp, it does not make him one. But your very worst mistake has been in your choice of Fool."

"Why?" Bushy demanded. "Of course I'm the Fool."

"Ah, Jim. Jim the caretaker." Hopkins pursed his lips. "But you know the rules, don't you? None of the seven who are summoned must be a practitioner of magic. And you *are* a practitioner of magic, aren't you, Mr Findus, or should I say, James Finkelbaum? Miss Gowdie might very well have got away with the summoning the others, but *you* are the one who will ensure her ceremony will fail. Her little coven is one person short. No Fool."

"Of course Bushy's the Fool," I said. "Sorry, Bushy, I have to say this. I know you *think* you once raised a fire demon, but the truth is, you didn't. So I'm telling everyone here, Bushy is not a practitioner of magic."

"Oh, but in his own, raw amateur way, that's exactly what he is," Hopkins drawled.

"Amateur am I?" To my horror, Bushy had jumped up on to a chair and was now standing there, a look of triumph on his face. "Ha! You don't know the half of it, any of you! Ask yourself this, Gowdie, who do you think managed to break up that little *tete a tete* that you were indulging in with Arawn Llewellyn that night at the Red Dragon? Who broke up the spell and pitched you out of the past and back into the London of the present, tell me that!"

"Bushy! No!" In my shock, I forgot that it might be better to keep quiet. "That couldn't have been you! But I never told you about that night, so how could you know, how...unless you really are..." My voice tailed off, as I realised I'd just made the situation a whole lot worse.

"And for your information, Mr Malachi Hopkins," Bushy continued. "I have an object of power here that will outclass you in every way." He reached inside his jacket and brought out a package that was only too familiar to me. "This," he began to unwrap it. "Might look to you like a copy of *Little Women*, but it actually happens to be..."

Put it away, Bushy! I never gave you permission to bring that here.

"Ha!" Clemency exclaimed. "More useless trash! I'll take that! Another book for the pyre."

"It really isn't anything important," I bluffed. "I can't think why Bushy thinks..."

"Enough!" Hopkins seized me from behind. I was astonished by the strength of his grasp, the way his elbow jabbed into my diaphragm, knocking all the breath out of me. There was a murmur of protest; Dr Mollison called out, ‘I say that’s not on,’ then, “Silence, all of you!” Hopkins roared.

“Someone call the fuzz. Where’s the nearest phone?” Nasir spoke quietly and urgently.

“There are no telecommunications in the Antioch Corey Memorial Library.” Hopkins informed him as he pulled me back towards a pillar. “Jabez Corey refused to embrace the twentieth century. Keep still, witch! Don’t think you can kick my shins.”

“Now you’re going to get it, good and dandy.” Clemency spat out the words as she waved a bodkin in my face.

“Vat do you think you are doing, you vicious man?” Gerda strode forward. “And you, Miss Plymouth Rock, you should know better. Vat did Jeanie ever do to you?”

“This!” Clemency turned up her long white sleeves and held out her hands. “She bewitched my gloves and gave me this rash!”

“Bet you done that to yourself, you bitch,” Cazzie sneered. “Stuck your hands in biological washing powder or somefink.”

“Shut your damned mouth!” Clemency yelled. Her soft, New England accent seemed to be undergoing a surprising transition into something more street-wise and Bronx. “And the rest of you better stay put. Sure as hell, I’ll stab anyone who gets in our way with *this*.” She turned slowly in a semi-circle, pointing her bodkin at everyone.

“Or better still,” Hopkins took the bodkin from her, “I will blind the witch.” I saw the point of the instrument out of the corner of my eye and did my best not to flinch. “One quick jab in each eyeball should do it. Which one of you would like to have *that* on your conscience?”

"Cazzie, Dorian, Gerda, all of you," I shouted as Clemency began to wind the rope around my legs. "Get the things from the table, the artefacts of power. Give them to Bushy—I mean Jim—if he's really a practitioner of magic, then he can do something. He can..."

But no, it seemed he couldn't. Bushy, my scarecrow, was now slumped on the ground. "I'm sorry, Gowdie, I'm so sorry," he sobbed.

"This can't be happening," Ernest, my cowardly lion, clung to his bicycle. "This isn't right."

"It's happening all right." Clemency tugged at the rope, binding me to the pillar. "Keep still, all of you. Don't move."

"It would indeed be inadvisable to do so," Hopkins said. "Miss Nantucket, bring the books for the pyre." Hopkins drew back, still pointing the blade at my eyes.

"You vish to burn books?" Gerda stepped forward.

"Naturally." Hopkins assured her. "We intend to cleanse this library thoroughly of its blasphemies and the only way to do that is through fire. But it won't just be books we'll be burning, I can assure you of that."

"May I have permission to speak?" Dorian raised his hand.

"Certainly." Hopkins spoke in a gracious tone. "We do have just a little time to spare while Miss Nantucket arranges the books and lights the kindling."

"For anyone who doesn't know me," Dorian looked round at everyone. "My name is Dorian Pyewacket. I'm not an adept, but I *am* what they call a cursed immortal. I'm proud of that fact. And I'm not afraid to admit it in public."

"Is that so?" Hopkins seemed to be musing on this confession. "What a strange and distasteful boast. Well, what of it?"

"I've had a long and happy life," Dorian said. "Jeanie's only twenty. She hasn't even started her life's work. If you want to kill someone, why not kill me? I'll take Jeanie's place. It's my best offer."

"Dorian, you can't..." I was silenced by Hopkins clapping his hand over my mouth.

"I'm serious," Dorian said.

"Oh, I'm sure you are, Mr Pyewacket," Hopkins drawled, walking slowly towards him. "But don't worry, your turn to be killed is coming very soon. You should know that when I've finished with Miss Gowdie, it is my intention to purge this library of all its adepts and cursed immortals and their sympathisers. Once the witch has been put to death, all will perish in the mass conflagration. You have not been paying attention. Ah, the books. Thank you, Miss Nantucket."

"I, too, vish to speak." Gerda raised her hand.

"Very well."

"I vish to say that I believe Mr Jabez Corey appointed our dear friend Mr Llewellyn to take care of this place. He put all his trust in him. Mr Llewellyn is the rightful Custodian and if he knew vat is happening here now, he vould soon send you packing."

"Yes, but he's not here, is he?" Clemency straightened up and shot her a scornful glance. "It looks as though Arawn Llewellyn has thrown in the sponge."

"Quite so." Hopkins agreed. "My spies inform me that your previous Custodian is now hopelessly addled in his wits, lost in some fantasy of his past, and quite beyond recall. Well, now, we will proceed. Miss Nantucket, will you do the honours and light the pyre?"

"But she ain't got nuffink to light it with," Cazzie jeered.

"Of course I have!" Tearing a page out of *The Book of Shadows* Clemency rolled it into a spill and walked towards the eternal flame.

"There is one more announcement I have to make before the pyre is lit." Hopkins held up his hands. "You may think I have gone to a lot of trouble to dispose of a single witch. But Miss Jeanie Gowdie is no ordinary witch. By her own confession, she is a heritant, almost certainly the last of her kind. It will be a privilege to kill such a one. And now for the cleansing fire!"

I could smell the paraffin; the books must be soaked in it. *Through the fire, through the fire, and through the fire again.* How could something like this be happening? This was far worse than that last night at Knox Hill. They weren't just going to kill me. They were going to kill everyone. And it was my fault. I'd brought my friends here, into this terrible trap.

I looked at the table where I'd laid out Mandragora's artefacts of power. If only someone could put just one of those tools in my hand, I might be able to do something. But then my hands were tied, literally. There must be something else I could do.

I stared at the death mask of Antioch Corey, at the flickering blue flame and those shuttered eyes. Concentrate, Jeanie, think of all those who have gone before you, those whose blood runs in your veins, Isobel Gowdie, and all the others whose names you have yet to learn.

Arawn Llewellyn, you promised me. You said that if I called you, if it was a matter of life and death, if my life was in danger, you would come. Hear me now!

There was no response. Still, there was one more thing I could try. I raised my head and spoke as clearly as I could.

“I, Morgana, humbly request that Antioch Corey should return to this place in this hour of need. *Mortem animam reverti cupiunt*.”

There was a fluttering of wings as the dark plumed pigeon flew down from the blue dome and perched on the ledge of the first floor gallery.

“Get that filthy...” Clemency began, but at that moment, the death mask of Antioch Corey glowed with a bright green light, the stiff eyelids snapped open, and the lips moved.

“I hear the command.” The voice echoed around the entrance hall. “This persecution will cease.”

There was a hush and then Llewellyn appeared, seemingly out of nowhere. He stood in the centre of the seven-pointed star, dressed in a dark blue velvet robe, his face stern and heart-breakingly handsome. As he stretched out his hands, a translucent red dragon, formed of ether and enchantment, appeared in the air and hung there for a moment before swirling back into the mist.

“Mr Corey cannot be here in physical form,” Llewellyn announced. “But I, the newly appointed Magus, have come in his stead.”

“Impressive.” Hopkins observed. “But you have played right into my hands. I knew you would come if I threatened your precious Miss Gowdie. Witness this, ladies and gentlemen. Now I have *both* my main prizes. The Heritant and the Magus. And I shall take great pleasure in killing them both.”

“Do you really believe you have tricked *me*?” Llewellyn looked at him with what appeared to be withering contempt.

“Of course I do,” Hopkins drawled. “You adepts are always making mistakes. Take Miss Gowdie, for example. She has attempted to summon her seven, but she has omitted the Fool. Whatever little spell she's been cooking up in that cauldron, it's not going to work."

"Hopkins your aura is foul," Llewellyn said. "It's like cow dung, slime and bile. And you're wrong. Jeanie does have her Fool. I am the Fool because I haven't fought hard enough for her. I am the Fool because I almost left her, the most beautiful, clever, gifted woman I have ever met and the only woman I can ever love. Yes, Jeanie has her Fool. I am here."

"Very touching." Hopkins sneered. "But a flawed argument. As I said before, the Fool cannot be a practitioner of magic, and, as you have just demonstrated, that is exactly what you are. So neither you nor Miss Gowdie can do anything to me."

"Are you quite sure of that? You won't need that, by the way." Llewellyn snapped his fingers and the bodkin flew out of Hopkins' hand. It landed two feet away where it dissolved into a pool of green slime.

"A neat conjuring trick," Hopkins said. "But I'm not sure we have time to waste on such things."

"Right! Cut the crap!" Clemency screamed. "I'm going to light the pyre!" She thrust her spill towards the eternal flame.

"And you're afraid of fire, aren't you, Arawn Llewellyn?" Hopkins added. "It terrifies and sickens you, doesn't it? Fear of fire is your weakness and I have sniffed out that fact. Ah, well done, Miss Nantucket! That'll soon be a nice blaze."

"Any sensible person would fear fire," Llewellyn spoke calmly. "Normal fire destroys and kills and scars, and the cold fire that turned me into a cursed immortal left me miserable and alone."

I could hear the crackling; I could feel the smoke rising. In a moment, my feet would burn and then...*Don't think about it, don't think about that night at Knox Hill.*

"Fortunately," Llewellyn smiled at him, "I have learned to do this." He stretched out his hands and jets of water spurted from his fingertips, soaking the books at my feet and putting out the smouldering in an instant.

"Very neat," Hopkins nodded. "But fires can soon be relit. And your magic is powerless against ordinary weapons, such as the incendiary device which I plan to throw into this building as Miss Nantucket and I leave. Everyone here will be blasted to hell. What do you say to that, Arawn Llewellyn?"

"I say that you are bluffing and you are outnumbered. We can defeat you."

"Yeh?" Clemency sneered. "You and whose army?"

"This one!" Llewellyn raised his arms. "*Dewch ymlaen ffrindiau!*"

And with these words, spoken in his native tongue, he summoned them, all the adepts and cursed immortals of London. Led by Konrad, they poured down the stairs from the upper galleries, men and women in antique robes and in modern dress, in satin and velvet and tweeds, and, behind them, came a flock of dark-plumed birds. They zoomed towards Hopkins and Clemency, beaks and claws at the ready. The noise was overpowering. The birds were screeching, the adepts were calling out curses in archaic languages, there were screams and cheers, and rising above the mayhem there was the sound of Psyche's singing, if singing is the word to describe such an unearthly noise, so primal and full of dark magic.

"Jeanie, my beautiful Jeanie." Llewellyn was at my side, releasing me from the ropes using nothing more magical than a Swiss army knife but doing so with such swift efficiency that I knew that I'd soon be free. "I'm so sorry."

"I should think you are," I said. "You really took your time."

"There! You're free. Now, run! Go with Konrad. He'll take you somewhere safe and then, when this is over, I'll protect you and..."

"Run?" I stepped down from the soggy pyre. "I don't think so. I am the Sorceress Morgana, and I don't need any man's protection. Oh, look! Who's that amazing person?"

I pointed up to the first floor gallery where Clemency was hurling down heavy volumes of constitutional law. Any one of those books could have killed a person instantly if it had struck them on the head, but now each one simply hung in the air as a tall old man in a black velvet suit threw a levitation spell at them.

"That's Clarence Galsworthy. Jeanie, you must get out of here. The danger's not over and..."

"Arawn Llewellyn," I protested. "Grateful as I am to you for saving my life, you must allow me to cast my spell. One day I'll completely outmatch you in magic and you'll just have to accept it."

"I know that, of course I do. You're the heritant and I'm only the....Careful!" He pulled me out of the way of Ernest's bicycle as it hurtled towards us. We were not, of course, the target; that was Hopkins who'd been running towards the stairs but who was now knocked to the ground. As he attempted to get to his feet, he was promptly felled by a rugby tackle from Nasir.

"Take that, you old tossser!" Cazzie yelled, sitting down on Hopkins' prone body and punching his head.

"*The Book of Shadows*, where is it?" I looked around me wildly. "Has Clemency still got it, or did Bushy....where *is* Bushy? Oh, listen! Psyche's going to sing her song all the way through at last."

I ran to the table, and lifted up the runic knife. I have no idea if anyone heard my voice above the mayhem, but that hardly mattered.

"I, Morgana, in the name of the Elders, in the name of Antioch Corey and in the name of every adept in London, invoke the ancient spell. Smite the witch-finders! Smite the puritans! Psyche, unleash the Salem Salad!"

An appalling stench filled the air, far worse than anything anyone had experienced in the library that day. It was like rotting, fly-blown flesh or a century-old unflushed sewer, it was a foul miasma that prompted people to cover their mouths and noses, choking and even on the verge of vomiting. There was a sound like rushing wind and then everyone was still, looking up at the blue dome as the glass rolled open, exposing the night sky. And then the entity arrived.

I don't believe that any of us saw exactly the same thing that evening and some believed that whatever it was they did see was the result of the hallucinogenic properties of Psyche's punch. I know what I saw; a truly terrifying voodoo spirit, ten feet tall, wearing a belt hung with skulls. Smoke billowed around its naked, paint-streaked body; its open mouth, shark-toothed and red as a wound, gaped like the maw of hell in a medieval mystery play. Slime dripped from the creature's armpits, as if it was some kind of humanoid slug with legs.

"More damn conjuring tricks!" Hopkins struggled to get to his feet.

"Filthy and unhygienic," Clemency agreed. "This place will have to be thoroughly fumigated."

Rolling its bulbous eyes, the entity let out a deep and unearthly roar. Then, effortlessly, it scooped up the two witch-finders, one under each arm and in a flash of sulphurous light, it rose up in the air. And then Clemency and Hopkins were gone.

"Bravo, novice!" A plump woman in a Laura Ashley dress clapped her hands. "That was the best Coming of Age ceremony I've ever seen."

"The Obeah man," Psyche picked up her mop and began to clean up the slime from the tiled floor. "He came and took them away."

Epilogue

It might have been the end of any ordinary birthday party, with many of the guests having left already and the few of us who remained clearing up the debris, the streamers and balloons. Gerda was packaging up small squares of cake; Ernest, leaving his bicycle behind, was sitting on a bench, completing his crossword.

"That was just so cool," Nasir said. "That was the SAS, right? Storming in here and arresting that bloke and his sidekick for attempting a terrorist attack? Can't understand why the newspaper people aren't here. We ought to be on television."

"It won't be on television," I said. "For security reasons. And if I were you, I wouldn't mention what you saw in here to anyone."

"Really?" He frowned. "Why's that then?"

"Because...this is a private party. And also...remember when you were a kid and you slept at your auntie's place in Coleton House, and you heard things? Well..."

"What?"

"It was just as you said," I smiled at him. "Kids imagine things. And adults can as well, when they're under the influence of..."

"Illegal substances," Ernest muttered. "Bad idea to smoke them. Once when I was a student...never again! Nightmares for weeks."

"Vich is not to say the Golem of Yonkers vasn't real," Gerda murmured in my ear as she passed me, a plate of cake in her hand. "I may have seen it tonight."

"Conjurors," Cazzie murmured wistfully, twisting a streamer around her fingers. "I always wanted a conjuror at my party when I was little, but my mum never let me."

"What I used to love was the Demon King," said Dorian. "In a pantomime. He'd come up through the floor, all green smoke, you know, when I was appearing at the Alhambra in 1902."

"So...are they dead then?" Cazzie asked. "Old Jack-ups and Miss Nantucket?"

"No, Cazzie, they're not," I assured her. "They've simply been taken to another place from which they will eventually return and, sadly, will have the opportunity to blight other people's lives if they do choose. But they can never come back to the Antioch Corey Library. They're barred from this place forever."

"Miss Gowdie, a word, if you don't mind." Konrad appeared in front of me, the dark-plumed pigeon perched on his wrist. "May I present to you Mr Clarence Galsworthy, Mr Blavatsky Cummings, and Miss Annie Kensington."

Annie Kensington was the woman in the Laura Ashley dress who'd applauded me earlier, Blavatsky Cummings was a very ordinary looking man in a pin striped suit, Clarence Galsworthy, of course, I could already identify.

"Hello." I shook hands with each of them in turn. "I'm so grateful to you all for coming."

"We don't have much time to talk," Konrad told me. "The four of us are setting off for the United States tonight and our taxi for the airport is waiting. Mr Jabez Corey's will has clearly been subverted and Miss Salutation and

Miss Providence Corey's actions in ignoring his wishes must be challenged without delay. Fortunately, Mr Galsworthy is an experienced lawyer and we will give them a good run for their money."

"And is..." I hesitated. "Is Llewellyn going with you?"

"No. As Magus, he is needed here. And as for you, Miss Gowdie...well, I'm impressed, but I have to say that all the fears I had about you have almost been fulfilled. But not quite, I admit. Now, I have a message for you from the Master. He wishes to take you on a journey to Wales. But perhaps you don't want to go. Perhaps your loyalty now lies in another direction. With Mr Jim Findus, perhaps. I understand that there is some history between you."

"There is, but he's a friend, nothing more."

"Well, it's not my affair. They're both waiting for you. The Master is sitting in his car out in the square and Mr Findus is up on the roof."

"On the roof? I didn't know it was possible to...how do I get up there?"

"Oh, a woman of your ingenious skills will find the way." Konrad shrugged. "As for the rest, make your choice of fools wisely, Miss Gowdie, for any adept who is unfortunate to love one such as you, will not, I fear, be long for this world."

"Bushy? What are you doing up here? You missed the end of my spell, you missed...."

"For God's sake, Gowdie!" Bushy turned to look at me as I stepped on the roof. He was standing so close to the parapet that I was worried he was going to do something stupid, attempt a flying spell, perhaps. "You mustn't do this, Gowdie. You mustn't go with him. Not with Arawn Llewellyn."

"Bushy, I must. I love him."

"He's a spell charmer! He's a cursed immortal! You don't know him at all. You don't know what he might do."

"I know what *you* might do."

"What's that supposed to mean!"

"Bushy, look, I'm sorry. I didn't mean to snap back like that. Everything you did helping me to prepare for tonight was brilliant! You helped me get to Dr Hecate's, you did your best to keep Hopkins and Clemency out of the way and then...."

"Go on, say it. I blew it."

"No. I wasn't going to say that. But...why did you do it? Admit that you were a practitioner of magic, and start waving the *Book of Shadows* about? And what about that night when I was at the Red Dragon? Bushy, how *could* you? What were you thinking?"

"I wanted to save you from him."

"I wasn't in any danger."

"Can you be sure of that?"

"Of course, I can."

"Look, Gowdie, there's something you don't know. And I bet you anything *he* knows and he's been keeping it from you. Here," he took *The Book of Shadows* out from under his jacket. "Take a look! Page 304!"

"You see that's another thing," I said. "You weren't supposed to read that book. Jabez Corey gave it to Llewellyn for safe-keeping and he wanted me to work with him on the translation and..."

"Oh, don't worry, Gowdie, you can have your precious book back." He thrust it into my hands. "But believe me, it'll freak you out. There's a woodcut on page 304, with the title of the Marriage of the Magus and the Heritant, and the figures in the picture look uncannily like you and him, which makes no sense at all since it must date back to the seventeenth century, and underneath it, written in an ancient version of the Basque language, there's a prophecy, telling exactly what will happen if two such people got together. And it's terrible. It's so terrible that..."

"Bushy, stop it," I laughed. "You're not scaring me at all. Listen, thank you for the book." *Into which, I have no doubt, you've inserted one of your clever forgeries.* "But now, I have to go. But you'll be here at the library when I get back, won't you? And we'll still be friends, won't we?"

"Of course. I'm your True Thomas, aren't I? But I just want to ask you one more thing. How can you want to go with a man who's so much older than you?"

"He's only thirty six. He'll always be thirty six."

"You think so, Gowdie?" He gave a short, bitter laugh. "I wouldn't bank on that if I were you."

A storm pursued us as we drove out of London. There were torrents of rain and howling winds, lightning flashes and violent thunder, and then a horned thing with crooked claws landed on the windscreen, seizing the wipers, and almost sending us careering off the Westway to our deaths.

"What was that?" I yelled as Llewellyn, clutching the wheel of the limousine, dispelled it with a stream of ancient Welsh curses.

"A wraith," he said. "Just an after-shock from your spell."

"Is that what it is? I thought perhaps it was because I've brought *The Book of Shadows* with me. There must be so many people who want it."

"I daresay there are. And they're welcome to it. There are some very bad things in that book. When we get to Wales, I propose that we bury it, somewhere deep."

"Why? What things? Why didn't you tell me?"

"Let's not talk about it now. Jeanie, are you all right? This isn't scaring you, is it?"

"Scaring me? Of course not. I'm loving it!"

"I'd have loved it when I was your age." There was a certain tone of regret in his voice but I couldn't understand why. "Now, I suggest we leave the main roads and take the old ways, following the ley-lines. Hold on, Jeanie. I'm going to drive very fast, but we won't get arrested. At this moment, we're completely invisible to the ordinary forces of the law."

We drove through the Cotswolds and across the Wye valley and then approached the dark hills. The storm was subsiding, and the pale light of early dawn was beginning to appear in the sky. As we came into the area of the Black Mountains, he leaned over to me and touched my hand.

"I love you, Jeanie Morgana Gowdie," he said softly. "You've nearly destroyed me, but I'd let you do it all over again."

"I don't know what you mean," I said. "But then I know so little about the minds of men. Oh, look, over there! Those turrets, what is it, ahead, just through the trees?"

"We've arrived," he said. "This is Richard and Ann Llewellyn's ancestral home. My haven in Wales."

We stood together on the mossy hillock, hand in hand; I couldn't understand why I didn't feel exhausted, but I felt as fresh as if I had just woken up.

"When you told me about your little place in Wales, I thought you meant a cottage," I said. "But this is...I'm lost for words"

"It *was* a cottage. But piece by piece, things were added. The turrets, the cellar extension with the underground swimming lake, the book labyrinth...come inside, I'll show you everything. And then...Jeanie, I have to ask this. Are you sure that you want to stay? With me, tonight? Spending a night together for the first time?"

"It won't be the first time." I smiled at him. "Remember that night at Dr Hecate's?"

"No, Jeanie, I'm afraid I don't."

"You don't? But how can that be....oh, of course, you were in a fever. That explains it. Never mind. I'm ready. This is my Coming of Age and I'm ready."

"In that case, if you'll permit me..."

"Yes...oh, yes!"

She became a rose, a rose all in the wood...

Nana's song was running through my mind as I lay there in his arms.

And she gave him her maidenhead that she had kept so long.

"I rather like your little place in the Black Mountains." I said. "It's beautiful. Perfect. And so are you." I kissed his shoulder. "By the way," I added, in a teasing tone. "Did you know you've got some grey hairs?"

"What?" He sat up sharply. "Where?"

"Hold still. I'll just pluck one...here." I held it up for him to see.

"Oh, good grief." He looked horrified.

"Hey!" I laughed. "Don't tell me you're vain. Ageing happens to everyone, and now we'll grow old together. This grey hair means that when I'm ninety, I won't be walking around with a husband who looks like my grandson!"

"Oh, Jeanie, it doesn't mean that at all." He bit his lip. "I'm a cursed immortal, and when a cursed immortal begins to age, it can happen rapidly."

"How rapidly?" I felt the cold fear in the pit of my stomach.

"Very rapidly. In another few weeks I could be...that is... oh, Jeanie, we might not even see the spring together."

I felt sick with despair. Bushy, I thought, Bushy must have done this.

"He's only thirty six. He'll always be thirty six."

"I wouldn't bank on that if I were you."

But then if this was Bushy's doing, and not some natural process, couldn't it be reversed?

"Listen," I said, suddenly resolute. "We can fix this. We can fix anything. You're the Magus, and I'm the Heritant. We can't be defeated. There'll be a spell somewhere, a charm...something to ensure that if you *are* ageing, it will happen at the natural pace."

"Jeanie...Jeanie, darling..." His eyes were brimming with remorse. "I never do anything except let you down."

"That is simply not true," I said firmly. "You came to save me like a hero. You *are* a hero. Years ago, my Nana looked into my future and saw me standing with a powerful magus by my side, the two of us crowned with lights. And my Nana was always right. And no-one can take this night away from us."

The sun was rising over the mountains and a red rose was blooming by the window. I, Morgana, had no idea what I was going to do now, but as I put my arms around the man I loved, consoling him as best I could, I just *knew* this was a beginning, not an ending. I felt no fear at all, as I eagerly anticipated all the sorcery and strangeness that was yet to come.

／
Acknowledgements

Many thanks to everyone who has encouraged me to complete this book including:

My daughter Stephanie, always a source of insightful advice, and a provider of superb cakes and a perfect playlist!

My fellow members of The Dracula Society, with special thanks to Des and Bill, who have done so much to help me launch and promote my work.

The anonymous readers/reviewers on the Romantic Novelists' New Writers Scheme who provided feedback over a period of ten years, and especially to the person who lavished so much praise on the book and even suggested it would make a 'super' film. Reader, I don't know who you are, but you cheered me up no end as all the rejections from literary agents came flooding in!

Thank you, family and friends, for your support. Remembering those, much missed, who gave such valuable advice on writing in the past.

<u>In Memoriam</u>

Norman Hidden

Sharlott Toube

Hilda Birchall

Tony Rath